T
UNI
OF
MAROMSAESC

*A paranormal futuristic
fiction novel*

Wenda S Parsons

*This novel
is dedicated to **GOD**.
It is also dedicated to
my mother Roslis,
my younger sister Wanda
my father William
and everyone who hears
voices or sees visions.*

INTRODUCTION

The Uni of Maromsaesc.
A Paranormal Futuristic Fiction Novel

The year is 2070 and the very first university for the Professional Development of people who hear voices and see visions has opened its doors to 200 first year students. The Uni of Maromsaesc designed by Professor Willemina Zantend with consultations from researchers, psychologists and other academics, has been eagerly anticipated by everyone in the HVSV (Hearing voices and Seeing visions) communities. This novel follows the mysterious dramas and intense controversy surrounding the students, staff, and robots (OBR's = Official British Robots) present at the university from the viewpoints of the two main characters...Perianne Saint (Aridaperianne Dedrick) and Sentira Cagney. It also follows the lives of their close friends at Maromsaesc and other classmates.

Perianne Saint (originally Aridaperianne Dedrick) plots to destroy the Uni of Maromsaesc. She comes from a very corrupt, immoral family that made their billions through criminal Psychiatry practices. Due to a high profile Court case in 2054, which found another top Psychiatry practice guilty of numerous crimes against patients, Psychiatry was abolished causing the Dedrick family to lose all their power and wealth. Perianne seeks revenge for her family and is blindsided to any wrongdoing that has occurred. She is consumed by love and pride at being part of the previously successful Dedrick Psychiatry family. However, Perianne has a secret that she will never talk to her family about. She hears voices too...

Sentira Cagney has different issues. She has heard voices since childhood but cannot always control them. She misses a large part of her formal education due to being frequently distracted by the voices she hears around her. Unqualified and with home schooling that is not accepted by the Education board, Sentira views the Uni of Maromsaesc as her only hope to learn how to utilise her voices to have a successful career and a happy future. She is distant from her father who is often abroad on secret business and although her mother is at home with her, she is raised mostly by her grandmother Nanny Lisha. Sentira is determined to study hard but is distracted by loud voices that she struggles to understand and quieten. Will she learn how to control her voices and have the future career she desires or is she destined to forever be dominated by loud invisible voices that talk freely at random?

Both Perianne and Sentira are tall, athletic, resourceful, brilliant in their own unique ways, beautiful and they both hear voices that no-one around them can hear.

In addition, there are high expectations for the Year 1 voice hearing and visionary students at the Uni of Maromsaesc located in Pelargonium, England. They are the first generation of Maromsaesc students to attend Year 1 professional studies and the eyes of the world's news media are upon them constantly. This, combined with their own social and personal development as young individuals mixing with students who all have similar experiences to each other, increases the pressure upon them. Some of the student's voices soon prove to be more challenging and disturbing to deal with than others...

The Uni of Maromsaesc is set in a future where Hover cars are popular, virtual technology 2060 enables everything virtual to be physically interacted with, human style robots work in most workplaces, virtual mobiles can move and change shape amongst many other exciting inventions.

The Uni of Maromsaesc appears to the outside world as an expensively designed modern university with its eclectic mix of virtual and transparent buildings, nature scenes inspired décor, virtual equipment, student Hover vehicles, indoor park areas, large Games Courts, beautiful lake/gardens and human OBR (robot) staff. Although, to look inside the university...life is not always as lovely as it appears...

"Your visions, your voices, your abilities, your courage, your

perseverance, your love for one another, your intelligence, your failures that you will learn from, your success's and the paths you choose at the end of Year 3 to utilise your gifts will...set a new precedent, a new high standard for HVSV people all over the world. Be your best!"

Professor Wilemina Zantend
Maromsaesc University

I hope you enjoy reading this book as much as I have enjoyed writing it!

Wenda S. Parsons
Author

Disclaimer

This is a paranormal fiction novel. Unless otherwise indicated, all the names, characters, businesses, places, events and incidents in this book are either the product of the author's imagination or written in a fictitious manner. Any resemblance to actual persons, living or dead, or any actual events is purely coincidental. This novel is not a substitute for professional medical advice and should not be relied upon to make decisions of any kind. Any action a person takes upon the fictitious writing contained in this book is strictly at the person's own risk, own responsibility and neither the author nor the publisher shall be held liable or responsible to any person or entity with respect to any loss or damages.

ARIDAPERIANNE

Running as fast as her rain soaked blue and white trainers could carry her, along the muddy, wet, narrow footpath alongside Terrie river, Aridaperianne looked straight ahead. Her eyes blurring intermittently from tears she refused to let fall. Each foot that splashed down into glistening lamplit puddles, on what used to be a smooth cobblestone surface, took her closer to her destination. Her body felt strong with purpose carrying a heavy, dusty brown backpack, as she turned to continue running left by a group of thick tree trunks on either side of her. The tree trunks were the base of very high trees, of which even a 6ft tall 16 yr old like Aridaperianne, would have to crane her neck up towards the skies and still not see the top of their densely populated leaves and branches.

"Wait!" a stern female voice said loudly near Aridaperianne's ear.

Aridaperianne quickly gulped in more air continuing on running. It poured down with rain all around her. The worn cobblestone footpath was empty. There wasn't another person in sight to the left, to the right, behind or in front of her. Turning swiftly again to run in the right direction, following the footpath up hilly grassy ground, Aridaperianne heard a multitude of invisible speakers around her.

"Aridaperianne, there is no other like my pancakes and if you are nice to me, there are pancakes for you too." an older middle-aged female's loud voice said.

"See, I told you she wouldn't listen." a male child's voice replied with gleeful confidence.

"She'll listen." a different male child's voice said sounding full of hope and enthusiasm.

"Be quiet, you're frightening her." the older middle-aged loud voice said.

"I hate you." the first male child's voice who had spoken

said angrily.

"I hate you too." the other young male child's voice said grumpily.

"Why didn't you say wait earlier!" both of the little boys said angrily in unison.

"My pancakes are the best, the absolute best" the older middle-aged woman said in a melodic voice.

"Shut up!" the boys said in unison angrily together.

Aridaperianne ignored them all.

With her usually pale pink cheeks now wet and a little numb from the cold and rain, Aridaperianne ran even faster up the water soaked, grass covered hilly ground, nearly slipping a few times until she finally reached the top. Not skipping a beat, she ran past several buildings to arrive at her Aunty Joan's home on the top floor of a high-rise block of flats.

Just wait, wait and see! Aridaperianne thought to herself brimming with annoyance and embarrassment. *When I get upstairs in my room... I'm... I'm going to deal with these invisible things! I hate them so much!*

Aridaperianne pushed opened the half-broken, crookedly painted black gate with her left olive coloured gloved hand, and tapped in 104 on the intercom telephone, looking sharply to the left and right afterwards. She slowed down her breathing from the run but was not tired.

"Yes, who is it?!" an irritated voice came out from the intercom speaker.

"Aunty Joan, it's me. Open the door I'm getting wet!" said Aridaperianne glancing fast to her left and right again.

"Aridaperianne! Come up quickly!" Dr Joan Dedrick responded with combined love, kindness and enthusiasm in her tone. Her previous irritation having been instantly melted away upon her recognition of the sound of her beloved, brilliant and beautiful niece, Aridaperianne Dedrick. Dr Joan hoped that one day, Aridaperianne would be able to restore the long yearned for Dedrick medical doctor family legacy and bring the expertise of Psychiatry back to dominance and power in the world again.

Dr Joan flashbacked in her mind to the moment she and all her sisters, brothers, mother, father, a few toddler nieces and nephews playing happily on a sensational monarch smoke silk rug,...even her grandparents and great grandparents were sat together on numerous lush, blanche diamond encrusted sofas, in their beautiful, exspansive, very richly decorated modern living room. She had organised her beautiful and highly intelligent family to meet up to watch and discuss the outcome of the R v Caulfield case on a large movie theatre style screen. She had been aged 16 at the time, the same age as Aridaperianne was today...

Dr Joan remembered how she had gently placed her hand resting lightly on her sister Arida's tummy (who was 8 months pregnant) when the verdict was read out by a Judge live on the movie screen in front of them.

Guilty.

The words of the Judge rang instant fear into every person in the room. Even the toddlers seemed to stop smiling after those life altering words were uttered loudly from the movie screen. Mother had stood up swearing and cursing at the screen while father had grabbed onto her in an unsuccessful effort to try and calm her down. There was a lot of noise, shouting and confusion as we all turned to each other in horror frantically speaking about how this decision would affect our family's billion pound psychiatry medical clinics, hospitals and education facilities worldwide...

Dr. Joan's face tightened in a grimace and she felt sweat trickle on her face, down her back and front, exactly the same as she had experienced on that fateful day. The day when it all changed...

Aridaperianne stood by the multi-coloured, grafitti covered lift and pressed the black button to call the lift down so she could get to the top floor. She was drenched with rain but held her head high as if she was just about to gracefully walk into a stunning ballroom where she would be centre of attention. The lift doors opened slowly and with a few sudden pauses finally opened completely. A tall young white man with dark brown hair wearing a brown tracksuit looked up when he saw Aridaperianne, stifled a laugh and deliberately bumped her shoulder on his way out the lift while Aridaperianne walked in. Aridaperianne again didn't miss a beat and pressed her olive gloved finger onto number 24 to get to the top floor. As the lift doors were closing slowly again with the same abrupt pauses, a loud female voice said these words from outside the lift.

"Oti feee skk skk oti feeaaa deak fooo aio aio oti feee.."

With just a small opening left in-between either side of the lift doors, Aridaperianne could see that the brown haired, tall man in the brown tracksuit had slipped on the trail of muddy rainwater from her clothing/trainers and fallen face first on the floor. The lift door shut firmly with a squeaky thud. Aridaperianne ran her gloved fingers through her dripping blonde hair and squeezed out some of the water with both hands turning her head to the side before tapping 24 on the silver lift buttons for a second time.

Inside this lift smells of mould and vomit Aridaperianne thought to herself turning her face upwards and moving further into the opposite corner from where she could no longer see the nausea-inducing mess of creamy, blood stained lumps of yellowish green puke on the floor, a tomato ketchup splattered torn paper bag of half eaten cod and soggy chips present in the adjacent corner.

The lift moved slowly on each floor, with the doors pausing for longer intervals before closing, on each new level.

Why does this lift have to stop on every floor even when there is no-one there?! Aridaperianne thought to herself becoming impatient and nauseous from the sickening stench of vomit in the lift. She held her olive gloved hand over her mouth and nose in disgust and ran out of the lift on the 10th floor as soon as the four sudden pauses with the faulty lift doors would make space enough for her to exit.

Outside the lift on the 10th floor, Aridaperianne turned towards her left, head held proudly high, running past the rows of decrepit flat doors to the emergency stairs. She then began to run up a total of 14 flights of stairs fuelled partly by anger and her strong physical fitness to energise her.

"Aridaperianne." a loud male voice said around Aridaperianne as she continued running up the stairs.

Aridaperianne also heard male and female laughter around her and then voices that sounded neither male or female but kind of animal like laughing to the left, right, above and below her. Aridaperianne's anger intensified until she reached the 18th floor when all of a sudden all the laughing stopped.

"Pancakes, they all need my delicious homemade pancakes." said a woman's voice loudly in a bored tone near to Aridaperianne's left ear.

"Kill them" a young boy's voice said loud and excited by Aridaperianne's right ear.

"No! Kiss them" a different male child's voice said giggling also by Aridaperianne's right ear loudly.

"Kiss me!" both male children said together joyfully close by Aridaperianne's left and right ear.

"Stop!" said a woman's voice booming from all directions.

Sounds of sobbing and crying coming from a mix of children, adults and what could possibly be interpreted as all different sorts of animals noises, surrounded Aridaperianne from every angle. She continued her speed running up the shabby, worn out steps with the sounds and noises gradually growing quieter and quieter upon her arriving at the 24th floor. Aridaperianne took five deep slow breaths and slowed her fast pace to a steady relaxed walk to reach the end of the corridor to get to room 104. A black woman with a mixed race man of white and black origin saw Aridaperianne from a distance (soaked in rainwater with her head held proudly high) and stopped talking, went back into their flat slamming their door behind them. An elderly white woman carrying a baby in her arms with three mixed race boy toddlers of Chinese and white origin, also (by the hurried ushering of the elderly woman) halted whatever it was they had been doing to return back inside their flat slamming their door behind them.

Dr Joan heard the key turn in the lock of her front door and walked from the burgundy leather sofa onto the silk mat wearing a silk kimono containing every colour under the sun and mink fur grey slippers. She watched as Aridaperianne took off her back pack, shaking and squeezing her long blonde hair, before removing her trainers while waving at her from a distance. Then, Aridaperianne went into her room on the right hand side near the front door.

"Aridaperianne, did you get it?" Dr Joan shouted at her niece, her voice full of hope and excitement.

"Yes Aunty, I'm just taking a shower, the bag's in my room. Come and get it!" Aridaperianne shouted back enthusiastically while she threw off her rain drenched black jeans, purple raincoat, and slipped out of her white underwear. She had a gold and silver glitter effects shower attached to her bedroom and got into it with a huge sigh of relief. As the water ran over her hair, face and back, she poured a handful of body wash in her right hand and used her left hand to apply it first around her face and then on her neck, chest, arms until she had covered her whole upper body. She then poured another handful of body wash and applied all over the lower half of her body. Aridaperianne reached for the shampoo and began washing her hair.

Dr. Joan had sat back down on her luxurious burgundy sofa, shook off her mink fur slippers and put both her legs up on one of the silk cushions. She looked around at her stylishly designed living room with its rich artwork, silk mats, immaculate white walls and the latest Applerishin technology TV and Applerishin mobile starting device in front of her. Dr. Joan spoke to a small green square object on her crystal coffee table.

"Applerishin open" Dr Joan said with a yawn. The small green square immediately sprang up into a virtual mobile phone. A light green ray was emitted from the virtual mobile to scan Dr. Joan's face and down the length of her body. Then the light green ray scanned up again to the top of her hair. Virtual Technology 2060 had made it possible that everything created by its company could be physically touched and interacted with despite being computer generated. Therefore, Dr Joan's virtual mobile could be held and operated just like the old-fashioned mobile phones of 2019 for example.

"Good evening Dr. Joan, how can I assist?" said a sexy male voice from the virtual mobile.

"Turn on the World news on Applerishin TV. Thank you." replied Dr Joan. The virtual mobile sent a light green ray out to it's right, directly hitting a pink square box on the white wall, which immediately produced a large virtual TV blasting out a female newsreader's voice.

"Applerishin come closer." Dr Joan shouted at the virtual mobile. The virtual mobile moved up and floated over close to Dr Joan's mouth. Dr Joan moved her head back slightly.

"Volume down by 15" Dr Joan said frowning at the virtual mobile and watching it move away from her mouth and back down onto the crystal coffee table.

"Yes Dr Joan." replied a husky male tone. The virtual mobile sent a light green ray out to the TV and the volume of the female newsreader reduced.

"Can I assist you further?" the sexy male voice came out from the Applerishin mobile.

"No. Applerishin close." Dr Joan said.

"Are you sure I cannot assist you further?" the male voice persisted.

Dr. Joan's eyes narrowed.

"Applerishin close." Dr Joan repeated to the virtual mobile.

"I will close in 60 seconds. But first can I interest you in a list of features that will enhance your Applerishin..." the male voice continued with a hint of desperation in its tone.

Dr Joan reached her hand under the virtual mobile and pressed her left hand palm up underneath it. After 10 seconds the Applerishin virtual mobile turned off. Dr. Joan's eyes narrowed again.

"All the so-called advances in technology, the technology is still not anywhere near perfect." Dr Joan grumbled out loud to herself. "Similar to this rubbish." Dr Joan adjusted her position on her sofa and glared at the news reporter on the virtual TV. The News Reporter was interviewing the head of the new Maromsaesc university, Professor Willemina Zantend, in an English countryside town called Pelargonium. The interview was being held outside expertly designed, multi-faceted (mixed virtual and additional materials) University buildings, with high virtual security fences surrounding the entire campus. This was the new university for the Professional development of people who hear voices and see visions. Dr Joan listened attentively to the interview, as people cheered and sang in the background upon hearing Professor Zantend declare the Maromsaesc University open for applications, for the September 2070 start of Year 1 HVSV studies.

Aridaperianne entered the living room in a silk multi-coloured kimono and mink fur slippers identical to her aunty, with many paper and booklet documents in both hands. She watched the virtual TV for a moment before going over to her aunty and sitting down on the gold silk rug near her. Dr. Joan sat up, bent down to hug her niece and took all the documents from her.

"There's dinner in the microwave Aridaperianne, how are you, are you ok?" Dr. Joan looked her niece in the eyes and smiled. "Don't worry, I am sure you will succeed to bring our family back to prosperity again. You won't have to change into tatty jeans and cheap trainers forever." Dr. Joan said teasingly to Aridaperianne. A voice around Aridaperianne's head laughed loudly. Aridaperianne blushed.

"I am hungry Aunty, I'm going to eat something." Aridaperianne smiled back at Dr. Joan and got up to walk into the kitchen. The kitchen was also expensively decorated and furnished just like every other room in the flat. Their flat was really five flats joined together but as both herself and her aunty always entered into one door, they believed no one would every know. Even with five flats joined together, it still felt small to both Aridaperianne and Dr.Joan. They were used to bigger and better.

Aridaperianne pressed the silver word HIGH on the microwave and said "Microwave heat for 4 minutes.". The microwave glowed silver for a few seconds and began to heat the food. She opened the fridge door and took out a bottle of milk, placing it on the white and grey marble worktop next to a cream coloured kettle. Filling the cream kettle with water from the tap, Aridaperianne said "Kettle boil." and the kettle glowed orange (before returning to its original cream colour) then began to heat the water. Reaching her left hand up to a cupboard on the wall to the left of the microwave, she pressed her thumb on a sensor which opened the long cupboard just enough for the area above her. The remainder of the long cupboard remained closed. She took out the Coffee jar and the sugar jar and put them down on the spotless marble worktop, reaching to press the sensor with her left thumb onto the drawer below the microwave containing cutlery amongst other gold and silver items. Picking up a gold teaspoon, Aridaperianne used her left hand to take out 2 teaspoons of coffee and a teaspoon of sugar. She poured the hot water from the kettle into a white gold mug nearby and removed her plate of King Salmon, Kinmemai rice, asparagus with a topping of curried tomato sauce gravy, from the microwave, placing it gently on a grey and gold marble tray. She lifted the exquisite tray with both hands and walked back into the living room, seating herself on an antique mahogany chair around a beautiful mahogany dining table, to the right of the burgundy leather sofa, and facing the virtual TV.

The news reporter turned away from interviewing Professor Zantend to speak directly to the camera.

"Well, there you have it! A momentous and trailblazing day in history for the Voices and Visions communities and for all of us really, now that we have professional, educational establishments such as the Maromsaesc Universities in five countries so far. There are also future plans to build hundreds more worldwide if the first year of studies at Maromsaesc prove successful. Once again, applications for the September 2070 entry into Year 1 studies at Maromsaesc University in Pelargonium. England can be made online at www.muhvsv.com. Overseas Maromsaesc Universities can be applied for by online form also.

Of course, none of this would have been possible if not for the landmark case back in 2054, R v Caulfied, which led to the immediate decline of, and subsequent abolishment of all Psychiatry practices, clinics and mental hospitals world wide. Since then, there have been many proposals on how to move forward with integrating people from the Voices and Visions communities into society, so that they are treated as mentally healthy individuals entitled to the same dignity, respect, opportunities and human rights as every other person. Anti-psychotic medication, as we are all aware, has been banned from use with people from these communities also since 2054 and in turn, psychologists, professors and academics have all encouraged the need for re-education on how to utilise the skills of HVSV people. These professionals advocate the necessity of a healthy lifestyle including a regular fitness routine, healthy diet, daily meditation, regular access to support networks and private psychologists..."

"Turn it off!" an elderly woman with a high pitched voice said in the air around Aridaperianne. Aridaperianne moved the rice and asparagus about on her plate and took a sip of her hot coffee. She continued to eat and watch the virtual TV at the same time. She glanced over at her Aunty Joan laying back on the sofa.

Is that tears in her eyes? No, it can't be. Aunty Joan is the strongest person I know. Aridaperianne thought to herself with a brief roll of her bright blue eyes.

Dr. Joan suddenly got up from the burgundy sofa without warning and left the room quickly. The sickly sounds of a person throwing up echoed around the spacious living room where Aridaperianne was eating her dinner. Getting up fast from the mahogany chair she had been sitting on, Aridaperianne walked fast through the living room, down the corridor along to one of the bathrooms. Standing outside peering through a gap in the door she watched surprised as her Aunty vomited into the toilet five more times.

Aunty's sick. Aridaperianne frowned to herself.

"Aunty, are you alright? Hold on, I'll get you some water." Aridaperianne turned and ran back into the living room and through to the kitchen where she picked up a glass from the white gold dish rack, quickly filling it with boiled water from the fridge. She hurriedly took the glass back to the bathroom, walked in and handed Dr. Joan the glass of water.

"Thank you Aridperianne." Dr Joan took the glass from her niece and sipped it without looking at her. " Set the timer outside for auto-clean and let's get out of here. I didn't get it on my clothing or slippers." Dr Joan half smiled as she led Aridaperianne out of the bathroom, watching her niece press her left thumb on the sensor on the white wall whereby the doors shut virtually and water began to spray into the now enclosed bathroom, from all directions commencing the auto-clean process.

"Did you set the timer, Aridaperianne?" Dr. Joan said after she noticed her niece had walked away from the bathroom like as if the task was finished.

"Auto-clean 15 minutes!" Aridaperianne shouted down the corridor.

"Aridaperianne, you know the sensor can't hear you from there. You have to be closer than that." Dr Joan grumbled and walked back head held high to return into the living room. Aridaperianne waked closer to the bathroom sensor on the white wall outside of the bathroom, put her mouth close to it and said "Auto-clean 15 minutes.".

The bathroom virtual doors glowed orange and a voice from the sensor said. "Thank you. Auto-clean will complete in 15 minutes." Aridaperianne walked back into the living room, sat down on a mahogany chair and continued to eat her food.

In her mind however, thoughts flitted about anxiously in her head. *Was Aunty Joan sick?*

Aridaperianne had been raised around many different family members to care for her in different locations of the world but only Aunty Joan knew the most interesting stories about her real mum. Aunty Joan told fascinating and heroic stories of what Arida Dedrick was like before she had committed suicide shortly after giving birth to her at the Dedrick mansion. Arida Dedrick was a beautiful, courageous, gifted, academic genius who had started practicing Psychiatry from the age of 10 in clinics and mental hospitals. The patients never knew that they were speaking to a 10 year old newly qualified Psychiatrist as her voice was changed to an adult voice via a feature on the Dedrick Virtual Psychiatrist technology. Patients always saw a virtual adult, usually a virtual adult male with a formal, authoritative voice. Sadly, it was this and many other issues that led to the eventual guilty verdict in the R v Caulfied case.

It wasn't the new Dedrick technology of virtual psychiatrists, it was the fraudulent way in which this technology was being used which quickly exposed hundreds of years of malpractice, abuse of powers, mis-diagnosis, illegal activities and even murders by the largest and most powerful Psychiatry practice in the world 'Caulfied Psychiatry'. Once 'Caulfied Psychiatry' had been found guilty of many different counts, this had spelt 'The End' for Psychiatry practices as a whole internationally. Within a few months of this verdict, Psychiatry had been abolished and it became illegal to practice it anywhere in the world. Aridaperianne received home schooling and being just as gifted as she had been told her mother was, she excelled in her secret, illegal psychiatry training, qualifying for practice at the tender age of 9. But, unfortunately for the Dedrick family, Aridaperianne had nowhere to use her medical training and this intensified their hatred for the HVSV (Hearing voices and seeing visions) communities...

"Applerishin open." Dr. Joan said quietly to the small green square on the table in front of her. The small green square sprang up into a virtual mobile phone as it done earlier pointing a ray of light green onto Dr. Joan's face and scanning her body down and up before greeting her and asking her "How can I assist"

"Turn off Applerishin TV." Dr. Joan instructed the Applerishin mobile. The virtual TV switched off and Dr. Joan picked up some of the documents left on the sofa and began reading through them.

"These are perfect Aridaperianne." Dr. Joan said to herself quietly. She watched her niece finish eating her dinner and carry the grey and gold marble tray into the kitchen. She waited until Aridaperianne came back out to sit down on the burgundy sofa with her before smiling a wide grin at her.

"The Hover car will pick you up tomorrow morning at 4am, Aridaperianne, are you ready?" Dr. Joan said looking at her niece's shining blue eyes that reminded her so much of her dead sister.

"Ready as I'll ever be Aunty! I was born for this!" Aridaperianne laughed and Dr. Joan tried to laugh like her.

"Aridaperianne, you are the hope for this generation of Dedrick's. You must dismantle and discredit the Maromsaesc University from the inside out. I know you hate the HVSV communities as much as the rest of the family." Dr. Joan paused and sat up on the burgundy sofa before continuing. "You have seen what they did to your mother, to our family psychiatry businesses, to our way of life, to Psychiatry worldwide. They... they... they..." Dr. Joan hesitated, feeling vomit rise up in her throat again. She gulped it back down and began speaking again reaching for her niece's left hand and holding it in both her hands. Dr. Joan's voice crackled as she spoke her next words.

"You must succeed Aridaperianne, you will succeed. Remember me, remember your mother, remember our family, remember our Dedrick Psychiatry legacy, how rich and wealthy we once were..." Dr. Joan could feel vomit rising up in her throat again, which she gulped down a second time.

"I will Aunty. I'm ready. I'll never forget what they did to my mother and our family Psychiatry legacy. Never!" Aridaperianne blue eyes flashed with anger and her cheeks grew redder.

"Good." Dr. Joan released her hold of Aridaperianne's left hand, and passed the documents back to her niece. "Here, go and pack these into your suitcase, I have spares if they ever go missing." Dr. Joan pointed at the white wall behind her where an oil painting of the Dedrick family was hanging from the wall. Aridaperianne rose to her feet taking the documents with her and back down through the corridor to her bedroom by the front door of the flat. She entered in and put the documents in the side pocket of the suitcase, sealing it securely with her left thumb print on a hidden sensor.

"Tell her." a male child's voice said in the air around Aridaperianne. Children's laughter followed, loudly heard around Aridaperianne's bedroom. Aridaperianne shut her bedroom door and spoke to the voices.

"I hate you." she said with a mix of irritation and frustration speaking quietly to the air around her and turning her head left and right slowly looking around her room.

"You don't!" more children said in the air around Aridperianne, repeatedly laughing and singing the words near her ears, above and below her. Aridaperianne opened the door and went out into the corridor to rejoin her aunty in the living room, taking three deep slow breaths before she walked calmly back in to sit down on the burgundy sofa.

Dr. Joan was sitting up on the sofa drinking water from a glass, however she promptly put the glass down on the crystal coffee table quickly upon hearing her niece come into the living room. As she had drank down the water too fast, Dr. Joan choked before coughing to clear her airways.

"Aunty, are you ok?" Aridaperianne's previous annoyance was forgotten as she stared at her aunty with love and concern.

"Yes, I'm fine." Dr. Joan cleared her airways by coughing again before speaking. "Are you excited about your plastic surgery tomorrow?"

"Yes, but aunty you know I could have performed the procedures on myself." Aridaperianne said smiling at her Aunty. Dr. Joan who returned a weak smile back at her.

"Well, it will give Robert, Uncle Robert something to work on. He was the most brilliant plastic surgeon in the country until our family businesses were closed down,..." Dr Joan reminisced softly.

Aridaperianne setlled back into the burgundy sofa listening.

"All the other surgeries we had were forced to close too after that horrific case, the Dedrick name was outlawed to run any surgery, clinics or hospitals." Dr.Joan stopped talking, eyeing the anger behind her niece's smile. This was exactly the reaction that she wanted. "Remember Aridaperianne. I want you to remember how much our family has suffered. How much billions we lost. I want you to know how important it is that you sabotage that mad Maromsaesc University so we can reintroduce Psychiatry to the world." Dr. Joan finished speaking and thought in her mind: - Dedrick Psychiatry is the only way to deal with those crazy people.

"I will. I hate the Maromsaesc University and everyone in it already. Dedrick Psychiatry is the only way to deal with those crazy people." Aridaperianne said to her aunty who smiled at her lovingly.

"I know it is." Dr. Joan said amused over how Aridaperianne had said the exact same words that she had been thinking in her head. "Your plastic surgery and training on how to ruin that mad university will last for 8 months. When you finish, you cannot visit me until Maromsaesc Universities are banned everywhere, just like they outlawed Psychiatry. You will have a new face, new body, new identity and you must live, breathe, walk, talk and act like one of them to blend into Maromsaesc, but, always remember your purpose, who you are inside. One day we will all be together again as a family practicing Psychiatry and dosing up the mad people." Dr Joan laughed and Aridaperianne eyes darted to the right waiting a few seconds before laughing along with her.

Aunty will never know I hear voices too. Aridaperianne mused to herself. *I know I'm not like those others. I am normal. I can control my voices. I'm different from the HVSV communities. Their mad and out of control. They're devious liars that hate psychiatry. They made my mother kill herself. I am nothing like them.* Aridaperianne's mind raced full of reasons about how she was different from the HVSV communities.

"So, my training will teach me how to blend in with the mad people." Aridaperianne said out loud to her aunty. "I'd better work extremely fast then. Don't want to be around them too long." said Aridaperianne smugly with a dramatic roll of her eyes which she knew her aunty would understand.

"Don't worry, with the training you will receive, I guarantee that mad Maromsaesc University will be destroyed before there is ever a Year 2, or they can build anymore of those insane schools elsewhere in the country." Dr Joan said with an air of confidence and superiority.

"I can't wait to start." Aridaperianne replied matching her aunty's confident and superior tone, masterfully ignoring the laughing children she heard from all directions in the air around the living room.

SENTIRA

Sentira felt like she was in a dream, laying down on the soft grass with both her dark brown legs bent at the knees, relaxing on a bluish-green park mat under a Pine tree in Chero Coast Park in Chero Coast, England. She held up (with both hands, arms outstretched) her Maromsaesc University acceptance letter. Half squinting her left eye at times which occasionally caught the sun's brilliance through the branches and leaves of the Pine trees around her. She re-read the main body of the acceptance letter.

It could easily be the 20th time so far this morning I've read this. Sentira thought giggling to herself.

Dear Miss Sentira Cagney,

Re: Your application for Year 1 Professional Development for people who hear voices and/or see visions.

It is with great pleasure that we can offer you a place to study at Maromsaesc University for Year 1 Professional development for people who hear voices and/or see visions. We look forward to welcoming you at our Induction Week on the 15th September 2070.

Please find attached further information relating to the University. If you have any questions please use our contact form at www.muhvsv.com.

Yours faithfully

Professor Willemina Zantend.
Maromsaesc University
Pelargonium, England.

Sentira's mind raced with excited anticipation over starting her professional studies at Maromsaesc University.

There will be hundreds of other people just like me. I'll finally find out what I can do professionally with the voices I hear. I can help other people, make new friends. I'll be away from home. Sentira reflected in her thoughts.

"We're happy Sentira!" female elderly voices sang around Sentira's letter and echoed in other places under the Pine trees.

So am i. Sentira communicated back in her mind to the invisible female elderly voices that she could hear but not see.

Sentira didn't recognise these voices speaking around her but felt no fear of them. Sometimes she recognised voices by names she had given them since childhood but as she grew into her teen years, she heard many new voices that she did not know how to name.

I hope the teachers at Maromsaesc can help me find out who you are. Sentira wondered in her mind about how some voices would tell her their names (when questioned) but others met her with silence.

Am I not talking to them properly? Don't they trust me? Do they even have names?

Sentira also wanted the teachers to help her with how to get her voices to listen to her instructions more. At present, if voices continued to talk around her at anytime, she couldn't stop them speaking if they were the unnamed ones. The voices with names would listen to her when she told them to Stop talking, depending on their mood that day. Other unnamed ones kept her awake at night, distracted her to the extent that she had to take days off school, walk out of exams, and leave parties/ events early, if she was able to attend at all.

It had been hard growing up as the only person who heard voices in Chero Coast. She always felt different from as early on as nursery and primary school. She recalled that there were two other children at her primary school who saw people that others around them couldn't see, but they never played with her at break times. Instead, they chose to play games with each other and whatever or whoever they were seeing around them. The teachers at Chero Primary knew that Mitch and Tina saw visions and Sentira could hear voices but decided to treat all the children the same. It soon became obvious however, that

Mitch, Tina and Sentira required special attention.

Sentira's mind flashbacked to a time at Chero Coast Primary when Mitch and Tina were both arguing with the people that only the two of them could see and the teachers stared fascinated by them clueless on what to do to settle them. Eventually their parents had to take them home for the rest of the day. Another time, Sentira had been in hysterical laughter over jokes that Ben and Jason (twin male child voices) had been saying around her desk. The teachers again were unable to settle her to focus in class so resigned to call her grandmother to collect her from school for the day. A significant amount of Sentira's education was missed due to similar occurences. Her grandmother and mother would try to teach her the best they could at home. Even though she was entitled to a free private home tutor, these were often fully booked throughout the academic year and there were long waiting lists regardless of the claims asserted by the HVSV Act 2054.

Under the HVSV Act 2054 every person who heard voices and/or saw visions were entitled to a long list of protections and benefits to help them integrate into society with good well-being free from stigma and discrimination. Every person who heard voices and/or saw visions were entitled to a free private home tutor and/or extra help at school/work if she/he chose to attend school or work. There were weekly payments from the government to pay for those who could not work due to voices or visions that were difficult for the person to control. Each person had free access to private psychologists, sports centres and meditation retreats. People from the HVSV communities had welcomed these changes but had argued the following year that they did not go far enough.

The waiting lists were very lengthy to access any of the benefits stated in the HVSV Act 2054 and many HVSV people were suffering personally and financially as a result. 50 % of HVSV people got in trouble with the Police, as a result of not receiving prompt access to free services that were not available frequently enough to support their needs. There was also no widespread professional training available about how to manage hearing voices and/or seeing visions to allow people to use these skills to benefit themselves and others. So, 95% of HVSV people ended up missing out on vital social development skills and financial income through not being able to attend schools, colleges and universities full time and not being able to work full time. The 'Maromsaesc University for the Professional development of people who hear voices and see visions had been carefully and intelligently designed to change those devastating statistics.

Sentira finally put her Year 1 acceptance letter down, folded it twice and placed it into her fashionably faded red jeans right pocket. She continued to stare up at the branches and leaves of the Pine trees around her, using her right hand to casually block the rays of sunshine that managed to peek through intermittently.

Chero Coast park was fairly busy that summer day and people of all different ages and races walked past her at a distance enjoying the sunshine and the beauty of the park. There were many other people, families of 4 and 3 with young children, solo adult park goers with their dogs, groups of teenagers, etc.. sheltering from the hot sun as well as they could, under the temporary random shade of the magnificent Pine trees. Sentira glanced around at them briefly.

I'm going to miss coming to this park but if I have to go, I have to go! Sentira thought to herself happily.

"Don't worry. We are coming too!" a middle aged female voice said in the air to the right side of Sentira's dark brown skinned face.

"Yes, we are." a middle aged male voice said in the air to the left side of Sentira's beautiful, clear dark skinned complexion.

"All of you must stay here. Only Sentira can go with Rhyle, Louis, Olamide and Gina to help her." an elderly male voice said close to Sentira's right ear that had ruby gold studs covering the full length of her right ear only.

"Noooooo." many children's voices were heard in unison all

around Sentira who remained lounging on her bluish-green park mat, for the most part ignoring the chatter around her. The only part, which sparked her interest vaguely, was that she heard her regular voices names of Rhyle, Louis, Olamide and Gina mentioned by an unrecognisable elderly male voice.

Are they talking about me going away to Maromsaesc Uni. or somewhere else? I don't think Rhyle, Louis, Olamide and Gina will ever leave me anyhow. Sentira thought to herself amused, continuing to half listen, half ignore the voices around her. The voices around her however, soon progressed to louder arguments about who would get to go somewhere with Sentira. Many voices of all different ages, accents and genders argued loudly around Sentira.

"We're going too! You can't stop us!" three male children said over and over.

"Noooooo" two adult women joined in with them.

"There are rules to this. You can't change them. It's too late." a booming elderly male voice said from a distance above Sentira.

"I can do what I want. It's done." more children screamed back.

"I'm coming with her." male voices squealed from all directions.

"Everyone in this park is coming with her. Try and stop us!" male voices said close by Sentira's ears.

At this point, Sentira sat up and mentally tried to tell the voices to stop arguing as it was beginning to annoy her.

Stop fighting, I'm trying to chill. Sentira said impatiently and repeatedly in her thoughts to the voices around her. The voices continued. Sentira said the Lord's prayer in her mind as a teacher at school had suggested that this might help. Unfortunately, It did not work this particular time and the voices persisted. Resignedly, Sentira began to pack away her fruit, sandwiches and sweets into her bag next to her.

Even though, Sentira was used to having to wait until the voices around her were ready to stop talking of their own accord, she felt resentful that this was the reason she had missed out on a normal schooling throughout her life. She hadn't got any formal qualifications, but had passed the exams during home tests with her Nanny Lisha supervising. The exam board did not accept her home taken exam papers and attempts for her to sit exams at school were always interrupted by loud voices that Sentira could not control. Subsequently, Sentira never received any formal recognition of completion of secondary education, which would have made searching for a job difficult, if it hadn't been for her acceptance today into the September 2070 Year 1 Professional Studies at The Maromsaesc University.

Some of her voices that wouldn't stop (even when she told them to in her mind) distracted her from whatever she was doing and blocking them out (suggested by the government HVSV National Advice sheet) only distracted her further from important tasks that required focus and concentration. Only occasionally her mental communication with her voices worked, mostly with the regular voices she was familiar with. These were the voices (at all different ages) of Rhyle, Louis, Olamide and Gina. Sentira hoped that the teachers at Maromsaesc Uni would be able to help her utilise her voices so that she could one day, have a professional career and a bright future but, in which field of work that might be…she didn't yet know. Sentira picked up her bag, stood up, walked past the Pine trees, beautiful daffodils and roses that she also passed by on her way out of Chero Coast Park. She felt her body relax as the arguing voices ceased and she heard birds singing in sync with her regular voice of Gina humming tunefully around both Sentira's ears.

Sentira sat down at the Hover Cab stop, tapped in her I.D. number, destination and password on one of the empty keypads on the wall behind her and went back to sit down on the Hover bench. The Hover bench hovered above the ground adjusting its height to suit the other three people also sitting on it in different places. After 5 minutes, Sentira's Hover Cab arrived and Sentira jumped up off the Hover bench to run towards her Hover cab a short distance to the left. Behind her she could hear the other two people on the Hover bench complaining about how she had nearly toppled them over onto the hard pavement.

"Sh*t! That stupid woman! Were you f**king born yesterday!"

"Oh my God! That silly cow! Are you alright?"

"Help!"

Sentira turned her head and looked back at them. She could see an elderly man on the pavement being helped up by another elderly woman.

I got up too fast, I forgot. Sentira thought guiltily. *I should go back and help them.*

Sentira walked back to the Hover Cab stop and apologised to the elderly man with the bald head and long grey beard who wore a worn faded green and white combat jacket with grey trousers. The elderly man ignored Sentira's apology and continued to vent his disapproval of her disrupting the stability of the Hover bench with a tense lengthy lecture. Sentira tried to be patient and respectful as she had been raised to, when she heard Rhyle's confident, assertive voice speak loudly next to her.

"He's fine. He wants to talk to the woman sitting near to him and didn't know how to start a conversation." Rhyle said loudly near Sentira's right ear.

Sentira trusted the voice as it came from Rhyle and said sorry one last time before walking away quickly to enter the black Hover Cab waiting for her. As she stepped into the Hover Cab, she told the OBR (Official British Robot) driver her reference number and gave it her name. The OBR driver turned its head and a light blue beam came out from it's eyes scanning quickly Sentira's body from top to bottom. The Hover Cab started up and sped off on the highway dodging expertly between other Hover vehicles on the road.

Later on about 30 minutes into her journey, Sentira noticed

the Hover cab had passed a road sign indicating that they had now left Chero Coast. Sentira turned her head sharply to glare at the OBR and spoke quickly.

"Wrong way! Destination repeat: 46 Abbey Lane, Chero Coast, Chero, England." Sentira stared at the OBR driver annoyed.

"Correcting error. The OBR association of drivers offers our sincerest apologies and you will receive a 90 % discount off your fare price. We look forward to driving with you again." a pre-recorded response came out from the OBR driver's mouth.

The OBR driver was of gold and silver appearance full of complex circuitry. There were human versions of OBR Hover cab drivers but they were much more expensive and Sentira couldn't afford them.

Anyhow, I like the original robot driver better than the copy cat human ones. I'm the human and it's the robot. Sentira thought, looking at the road ahead but also keeping a side eye on the OBR driver.

The Hover Cab finally pulled into the gravel driveway on the left side beside the lawn, which had a line of mixed flowers on its borders. Sentira reached down into her jeans pocket, took out a bankcard and scanned it on the OBR driver's hand, who responded by scanning her body again as it had done earlier when she first entered the Hover Cab.

"Thank you for your payment! We look forward to driving with you again. Have a Jelitoonaa day!" said the OBR driver in a happier robotic voice.

"What's your OBR name?" Sentira asked.

"My OBR name is Ken125. Enjoy your Jelitoonaa (Jelitoonaa means awesome or cool in the year 2070) Day, Sentira Cagney!" Ken125 OBR driver replied quickly.

"Same to you." Sentira exited out of the Hover Cab as the door lifted up in the air and she stepped out into the warm sunshine. Walking around the black and grey Hover vehicle and towards Nanny Lisha's front door painted pale yellow with no windows but just a simple white flat square in the middle. The flat white square was the length of Sentira's hand on the door. Sentira touched the white square with her right hand and waited as the white square emitted a ray of light yellow light which not only scanned her, but scanned around the front garden, driveway and about a metre above her too. The door opened and Sentira quickened her pace with excited energy to speak to Nanny Lisha. She found her in the kitchen sitting on a wooden stool talking to her Applerishin mobile.

"…two loaves of … Sentira, I didn't hear you come in." Nanny Lisha looked up at her at her beautiful dark skinned granddaughter with her long, thick afro hair and wide happy smile. "What happened? Did you get in?"

Pulling out the acceptance letter from her pocket, Sentira began to read it to her grandmother dramatically and excitedly.

"'Dear Miss Sentira Cagney, Re: Your application for Year 1 Professional Development for people who hear voices and/or see visions. It is with great pleasure that we can offer you a place to study at Maromsaesc University for Year 1 Professional development for people who hear voices and/or see visions'! See you soon at Induction Week on the 15th September 2070! Nanny! I'm in!" Sentira ran over to Nanny Lisha and hugged and squeezed her gently.

"Oh, I'm so happy for you Sentira!" Nanny Lisha held onto Sentira's hug with her eyes brimming with water. As Sentira released from the hug, she could see that Nanny Lisha wanted to cry.

"This is it Nanny, everything is Jelitoonaa." Sentira said softly in a confident tone into Nanny Lisha's right ear, moving to the side a long grey thick braid of afro hair to the back of her grandmother's back. Sentira understood why her grandmother looked a mix between elation and sorrow. Growing up, she had heard all the horror stories about how people like her and her grandmother were treated throughout history. Tales her grandmother had told her about her encounters with

32

psychiatrists, psychologists and police. The pills, injections, Nanny was forced to take and the mental hospitals she was in and out of. Sentira's face momentarily expressed disgust as she remembered.

The 2054, R v Caulfied case changed everything, changed my destiny. Jelitoonaa! Snapping back into the present, Sentira smiled again and laughed out loud. Her laughter became even more excitable as she could hear Rhyle, Olamide, Gina and Louis laughing along with her from different parts of the kitchen. Nanny Lisha soon picked up on her granddaughter's joyful laughter and started to laugh too as tears came down her face. Her hands shaking a little, she took the acceptance letter from Sentira's hand and read it for herself, her eyes widening with interest and wonder.

"Come on Nanny, let's go and watch the trailer for the Maromsaesc Uni. again! That will make it even more real" Sentira moved away from her grandmother and looked around her at the Applerishin mobile on top of the kitchen counter.

"Applerishin, this is Sentira." A ray of pale yellow light scanned Sentira's entire body up and down.

"Hey, Sentira, welcome back! Hope you are having a Jelitoonaa day! How can I assist you ?" the Applerishin mobile replied matching Sentira's enthusiasm.

"Applerishin play The Maromsaesc Uni. trailer on Applerishin TV." Sentira pulled another wooden stool from under the kitchen counter, and sat down next to her grandmother swinging her legs back and forth between the wooden side legs of the dark beech kitchen stool.

The trailer for the Maromsaesc University began and Sentira watched the full 10 minutes. After she had finished watching, she turned her face away from the small screen in the kitchen to see her grandmother's expression. Nanny Lisha wasn't there.

"Nanny Lisha! You're missing it!' Sentira sang happily getting up from her stool and looking through the window of the kitchen door to the lush vegetable and flower garden outside.

Nanny Lisha wasn't there either. Sentira searched around the bungalow. She went into the sitting room and each of the 3 small bedrooms.

"Nanny Lisha! Come watch the trailer with me!" Sentira said out loud again outside the bathroom door.

"Sentira, I'm on the toilet!" Nanny Lisha's bemused voice echoed out from the spacious bathroom.

"Oh, sorry Nanny. When you're finished." Sentira shouted back to her. Rhyle mumbled something quietly in Sentira's left ear. 'What?' Sentira spoke back to Rhyle in her mind.

"She's crying." Rhyle said gently in Sentira's right ear. A sudden sadness passed over Sentira's face and she felt ashamed that she had been so caught up with her animated exhilaration regarding her acceptance to Maromsaesc, that she hadn't even asked Nanny Lisha how she was feeling that day. Sentira walked back down the narrow cream coloured corridor which was lined with artwork that Nanny Lisha had created herself over the years. Upon reaching the neat, half modern, half antique kitchen, Sentira opened the fridge door taking out a carton of orange juice placing it on the wooden kitchen counter. Next, Sentira opened the freezer door took out two beef burgers, placing them on the grill of the electric enamel-coated oven. Sentira could see her acceptance letter on the other side of the counter near the Applerishin TV so she moved quickly to retrieve it and folded it neatly, ending up safely in her faded red jeans pocket again.

"Sentira, you're going to need an Applerishin mobile before you go. I'll get one for you." Nanny Lisha said walking back into the kitchen with a slight limp on her right leg. "This can be your gift from me to celebrate your place at Maromsaesc." Nanny Lisha sat back down on the dark beech stool she had sat on previously and began to scroll down on her Applerishin phone.

Sentira remained quiet for a while, thinking.

"What did Terri say and your dad?" Nanny Lisha asked.

"Haven't told them yet. Mum went to work early and

Dad's still ... away somewhere." Sentira shrugged. Nanny Lisha glanced up for a moment at her granddaughter. Sentira was chopping onions on a wooden chopping board with a calm expression on her face. Nanny Lisha paused before continuing.

"Terri will be happy for you too." Nanny Lisha said. "Ooooh that smells nice, can you put on two burgers for me aswell?"

"She'll be happy I'm gone for 3 years." Sentira said stifling a laugh while returning back to the freezer in order to put two more beef burgers on the grill.

Nanny Lisha smiled. "Chop some onions, tomatoes and lettuce for me too." There was another silent period between the both of them. This time lasted longer as Nanny Lisha and Sentira got lost in their own thoughts. Outside the sun shone brightly and the birds sang in the air as they dipped and dived gracefully landing in Nanny Lisha's garden, the neighbouring gardens and on the rooftops of houses.

Today seems too good to be real... Sentira thought to herself. *It's all Jelitoonaa*

"I'm going to sit in the garden Nanny." Sentira said walking past her grandmother's slim frame bent over her Applerishin mobile, her two long grey afro braids hanging delicately over both shoulders. Nanny Lisha wore a long yellow dress with white streaks in different places which also had a low neck line, low back line and three narrow oval shape holes down each side. In contrast, Sentira had on faded red jeans which had splits at both sides from the middle of her thighs downwards. She also wore a white crop top, black trainers and her hair unlike Nanny Lisha's was in its original natural afro shape, big and free.

Sentira took out a spray bottle from her bag and sprayed a mixture of Black castor oil and water all around her hair to keep it soft. Standing in the middle of the garden, Sentira took 3 slow deep breaths, noticing the song of the birds, the beauty of the flowers, the natural movement of the grass (from the gentle summer breeze) and feeling the warmth of the sun on her face. She loved nature.

This planet is a gift and a blessing. Sentira thought to herself.

"Sentira, don't forget the beef burgers!" Nanny Lisha's voice came ringing out from behind the kitchen door. Sentira awoke from her daydream and turned back to go inside the kitchen. She checked on the burgers, they were dark brown on both sides.

"They're ok, Nanny." Sentira decided and made sandwiches using wholemeal rolls for herself and her grandmother, remembering to include the tomatoes and lettuce with Nanny Lisha's. Sentira's burgers just had onions as a topping. Together both grandmother and granddaughter went outside and sat near the back of the garden on a round wooden garden picnic table with four separate benches and a yellow parasol sun shade. Sentira carried both sandwiches on a tray with glasses. After putting the tray down on the picnic table, Sentira went back inside to get a carton of orange juice from the fridge. When Sentira came back, Nanny Lisha was still on her Applerishin mobile and seemed very engrossed by it.

"Nanny, it's just a phone." Sentira laughed at the deep concentration etched on Nanny Lisha's face as she stared and scrolled on her Applerishin mobile. Nanny Lisha continued to look intensely at the Applerishin screen.

"One day I'll get you the Upgraded phone where you don't have to scroll, it just scans your brainwaves." Sentira said before biting into her Beef and onions sandwich. Eventually, Nanny Lisha looked up at her granddaughter, frowning before opening her mouth to comment back.

"There will never be a day I let that kind of spy technology into my house." Nanny Lisha declared and picked up her sandwich taking a big bite out of it. In between mouthfuls of her sandwich, Sentira continued on.

"What's the difference? Everything online can be spyed on. They are putting up more of the new OJW all over the shopping centres now so we might as well get used to it." Sentira concluded sounding bored. She wasn't bothered by the latest OJW Technology which could sense changes in a person's brainwaves which guided the OJW viewer (the person who read the OJW) to know a wide range of information. This was initially invented to help speed up the shopping experience. The idea was that people could enter a bank or a clothes shop and immediately upon entering, the staff would be ready with the item, statement, cash or whatever required, due to information gained with 60% % accuracy, of what the customer's banking or buying requests were. OKW tech. also helped to lessen crime by getting an idea of people's true intentions, therefore making the world a safer place or so the developers claimed.

"Oh Sentira you are still young. One day you will see that if you can't have privacy in your own thoughts, then you just may as well be an OBR and not human." Nanny Lisha chewed the last part of her sandwich in her mouth, before taking a few large gulps of her orange juice. She resumed scrolling on her Applerishin mobile. Sentira didn't say anything. She didn't feel like a debate. It was too beautiful a day. She wanted to celebrate.

"Ok, Nanny Lisha, let's talk about something else... I'm going to Maromsaesc University in 4 weeks time!" Sentira's elation returned and a huge grin returned to her face. Nanny Lisha half grinned back at Sentira before speaking to her.

"Ok, done." Nanny Lisha said firmly to her Applerishin mobile, then looking up at her granddaughter she continued on "Sentira, I've applied for your Student HVSV Grant, sent... a copy... to your email. Have you thought about which of the halls you want to stay in? What about the Robin Hall next to the lake?"

"Any one you choose I'll stay in. I don't mind." Sentira replied drinking more orange juice from her glass.

Nanny Lisha scrolled down on her phone for a few minutes before speaking again.

"You can stay at Jay Hall near the Recreation Ground." Nanny Lisha confirmed.

"Ok...no...it's be too noisy there, I won't be able to study. What were the other choices again?" Sentira responded back.

"Robin Hall next to a lake, Goldfinch Hall located at the back of Robin Hall, Chaffinch and Starling Halls located behind Jay Hall." explained Nanny Lisha. Sentira got up from her bench and sat closer to her grandmother peering along with her at the map of Maromsaesc University buildings, including the halls of residence and the grounds.

"Actually, there's a long pathway before getting to the park area near Jay Hall." Sentira observed out loud. "Can you see Nanny?...So I will stay at Jay Hall. Thanks for booking it for me."

"It's my gift to you Sentira." Nanny Lisha said proudly. "For the first year I will pay all your rent, food and any books you need for your Applerishin Workbook. The College will supply those and you have your mobile with you? I didn't see you use it since you got here... you haven't lost it again, Sentira!" Nanny Lisha rolled her eyes scrolling more firmly down the page on her Applerishin mobile.

"Sorry Nanny. I flushed the opening device down the toilet by accident last week." Sentira admitted apologetically. The Applerishin opening device that Sentira was referring to, described the small box shape that upon voice command of it's owner, proceeded to scan with a beam of light to check the identity of the user. Next the opening device would (upon successful identification) spring up into the virtual Applerishin mobile ready for usage. Sometimes the opening device would spring up into an Applerishin mobile before scanning the person and then scan for user identity. Other times it would scan while still in a small coloured square box shape. It all depended on which version Applerishin mobile a person had.

Nanny Lisha stared at her granddaughter in her eyes and told her to be more careful with her mobile as this was the only way she would be able to contact her or her parents if there were any problems at Maromsaesc. Sentira listened quietly to her grandmother's warnings. Whenever her grandmother used that serious stare at her, she always got the feeling that some kind of drama was about to happen, so she nodded and promised Nanny Lisha that she would remember the conversation.

"Listen!" unknown voices male and female said from different areas of the garden at varying volumes. Sentira did not turn her head but listened to her grandmother who was still staring at her somewhat like in a day-dream and lecturing her about keeping her mobile with her at all times. After what seemed like to Sentira, a strange part of her happy (Jelitoonaa!) day, Nanny Lisha finished her serious lecture and got distracted with her Applerishin mobile again.

"I'll look after my new phone, Nanny." Sentira got up from her bench and said "Thanks. Just going to get some water." As she walked back through the garden to get a bottle of water, Sentira's face changed to worry as she heard Gina's voice sob out loud.

"There's danger ahead." Gina said in a cry loudly by Sentira'a right ear.

Sentira entered the kitchen and drank down half the bottle of water, busying herself by cleaning the kitchen. She waited a long while for Rhyle, Gina, Olamide or Louis, to say some words around her, to reassure her, to tell her not to worry. This time, none of them did. Sentira paused her hurried cleaning movements and took out the Maromsaesc acceptance letter from her faded red jeans pocket again. A smile came to her face as she re-read it to herself. Glancing up and seeing through the kitchen window, her grandmother sitting on the bench at the back of the garden, Sentira began to reassure herself

I'll keep my mobile with me. What could go wrong? Everyone will be like me. Sentira thought.

Suddenly, the sounds of children laughing loudly behind her made Sentira turn quickly. The laughing stopped as soon as she turned around. Re-placing her acceptance letter safely back into her jeans pocket, taking a slow deep breath in and out, Sentira sighed and went back to the kitchen sink to finish the washing up.

WELCOME TO MAROMSAESC

Aridaperianne Dedrick sat still on the wooden chair in the Main Hall of the Maromsaesc University, rigid with pent-up anger. Her new undercover student name was Perianne Saint. She took a few slow, quiet breaths through her newly made nose and remembered her purpose for being there.

This uni won't know what's hit them very soon. Perianne plotted in her mind while smiling at the man sitting next to her who smiled back.

I'm the perfect actress. Perianne thought to herself, turning her head back to look at Professor Wilemina Zantend who was giving a welcome speech to 200 students, 50 tutors, 50 support OBR (Official British Robot) staff and a TV camera crew of 5.

"...here at the very first Maromsaesc University for the Professional development of people who hear voices and see visions, we welcome each and everyone of you with all our heart, acceptance, ambition and friendship." Professor Zantend paused as everyone erupted into thunderous applause and squeals of happiness.

"Alright, alright, quiet down." Professor Zantend affectionately reprimanded the people in the Hall. There was some laughter and Professor Zantend continued on. "You are the future teachers...lawyers...artists...healers...psychics...spiritual leaders...entrepreneurs...businesswomen...businessmen...and...any career path you choose after you have completed your degree will benefit from your HVSV abilities!"

The audience again responded with loud applause and cheers. Sentira jumped up from her seat like many others and clapped her hands above her head in the air and forward towards Professsor Zantend. She couldn't wait for Nanny Lisha to watch the Opening speech of Year 1 Professional Studies on the news tonight.

I wonder if the camera got me. Sentira thought happily to herself.

As the volume of cheers and clapping reduced down, Sentira returned back to her chair and waited for a piece of paper (displaying her team number and classes timetable) which had been circulating in the hall to reach to her. When her timetable was passed to her, she quickly read over the list of classes excitedly. She was in Team 3. Classes started at 10am from Monday to Friday and finished at 4pm. There were a wide variety of classes including Meditation, Sports, Voice Communication, Complex Voices, Shaman Studies, Spiritual Voices, Business & Marketing and Psychic Development classes amongst many others. Although, some of these classes would not be held until Term 2 or Term 3 of her Year 1 Degree course.

Perianne read through her timetable imitating the excitement of the other students around her but it was all part of her act. Inwardly, Perianne believed this was the worst day so far in her life.

All these people need to be hospitalised. Perianne bemoaned to herself scanning through the list of subjects again on her Team 3 timetable.

They are so ill. Perianne reminded herself in her mind, outwardly faking a smile to the man sitting next to her as he pointed out that they were in the same Team. To her hidden annoyance he carried on talking to her.

"I'm Noah, what's your name?" a young man aged around 19 years spoke to her in a deep voice. He had blond hair, sky blue eyes and a slim physique with freckles all over his arms, which were visible next to his white vest top and pale blue jeans.

This mad boy has no chance with me. Perianne thought proudly. She smiled sweetly back at him. Even though the Dedrick family had lost their billion pound Psychiatry business, and she was not raised in the luxury mansion of her ancestors, Perianne was still used to the best behind closed doors of the high-rise block of flats she had grown up in. Uncles, aunts, distant relatives, had gifted her and Aunty Joan highly expensive presents whenever possible. It did not concern Perianne where the money came from. It just meant that she was only outwardly poor, but used to a very rich lifestyle through all the gifts she received.

I know who I am, I know what I deserve. Perianne reminded herself in her thoughts.

"What's your name?" Noah repeated expectantly.

"Perianne Saint... I just heard a voice say, this is taking forever!" Perianne joked with Noah, keeping up her undercover character as a student at Maromsaesc University and pushing to the side her thoughts as Aridaperianne Dedrick.

Noah laughed. "I wish it would last forever. This day is going to go down in history. We're part of the historical Maromsaesc University that is going to give so many opportunities for us all!" Noah said with enthusiasm. "All I'm hearing are women singing around my ears quietly." he sat back and relaxed in his chair.

What are they singing? Give me pills, give me injections! Perianne sarcastically thought in her mind.

"That's so beautiful!" Perianne leaned closer to him, looking him in his eyes smiling. She wondered what her Aunty Joan would diagnose him as.

Schizophrenia. Perianne pondered to herself. *He seems naive. Maybe he can be used in my purpose.* Perianne thought, happily chatting to Noah about some of the classes on both their timetables.

Sentira felt like she was dreaming. She re-read over her timetable.

The first term is like an introductory living well with voices programme. I think... the Spring and Summer term will be the real self-discovery terms for me where... I will find out how I can best utilise the voices I hear to find a career I love. Sentira thought to herself full of hope.

"So, what do you make of all this?" a petite woman with ginger and black dyed long hair next to Sentira asked.

"It's a very well-thought out, structured and clever timetable. I'm sure I will know which career path to choose at the end of the 3 years. What about you?" Sentira asked.

"It's alright." the petite woman said looking at the paper in Sentira's hand. "You're Sentira."

"Yes. And you're…" Sentira leaned over to read the piece of paper in the woman's hand. "…Michaela. Good to meet someone else like me finally!" Sentira said excitedly.

"You mean you don't know anyone else who hears voices? Everyone back home heard voices. Where are you from?" Michaela said.

"Chero Coast. Where are you from?" Sentira asked.

"Petersfield village." Michaela replied.

"Is that up North?" Sentira enquired further.

"No, it's in the middle of England." Michaela replied back.

"So, everyone in your school heard voices too?" Sentira asked in amazement. She knew that some people were lucky enough to be around others like them but had not met anyone who actually had grown up in this way before. "What was that like?"

Suddenly a ringing bell sound resonated loudly around the Main Hall. It was the test fire drill, which they had been informed about earlier during Professor Zantend's welcome speech.

"I'll tell you later." Michaela said to Sentira with a wink, getting up from her wooden chair and pulling a shoulder bag over her right arm onto her shoulder. Sentira got up also and followed the lines of people outside of the Main Hall, through the fire exit door nearby and out past a few more modern virtual university buildings, towards the virtual entrance gates of Maromsaesc University.

At the front of the University, all the students and staff names were called out by one of their Team tutors. A tall dark-skinned man with a bald head shouted out for Team 3 to come over to where he was standing. The Team 3 students gradually made their way through the crowds of people and formed a line in front of their tutor. All the other students had done the same in front of their Team tutors facing the entrance of Maromsaesc University. The Team 3 tutor began to call the name of 25 students in his team. When he had finished he introduced himself.

"My name is Mr. Andrew Juniper. I teach Cooking, Complex Voices and Voices for Healing classes. We..." Andrew paused talking while other tutors (three women and two men) joined him to face the Team 3 students, then he continued on. "We will be checking to make sure that everyone in Team 3 is safely evacuated from the University in the event of a real emergency, a real fire. Let me introduce Miss. Jane Garrison who teaches Meditation class. Mr. Simon Winchester who teaches Voice Communication. Mrs Michelle Lear who teaches Health & Well-being. Mr Ben Kroon who teaches Confidence & Self-esteem and finally Miss Relinda Gower who will be teaching the Living with voices discussion group. Welcome to Maromsaesc!" Andrew exclaimed exuberantly. The Team 3 students clapped and cheered for a while. Mr Juniper calmly waited until the clapping had stopped before beginning to speak again.

"And we look forward to seeing you Monday at your first class, Meditation class starting at 10, over in the Team 3 study building. To make it very simple, we have named all the doors of the classes by the name of the class so very, very easy to find. After the Applerishin Entrance Security has scanned each of you, you can enter the classroom and there should be no reason for anyone to get lost." Mr Juniper finished off his last sentence with a smile and there was some laughing heard from the back of the Team 3 line.

I'm really here! I can't believe this! Sentira thought to herself.

I'm really in this mad place. I can't believe this! Perianne thought to herself. She watched the other students around her. *They all look so happy and excitable.* She observed. *Good. It's easier to fool people when they're like that.* Perianne plotted deviously in her mind, with her fixed yet natural appearing smile blending in with those around her.

Students separated from their formal lines and wandered around the University buildings. Some in groups of two or more and others wandered around by themselves, checking out the cafeteria, the classroom buildings, the gyms, the recreation grounds, the lake area, the halls of residence, libraries, etc... Some had their Applerishin mobiles and were filming everything they could see. Others queued outside the Maromsaesc gyms waiting for the Applerishin Virtual Security to scan them so they could take a look inside. Others waited outside the Student Cafeteria waiting to be scanned before they were allowed to go inside and eat. It was a very lively atmosphere all over Maromsaesc University for the first Induction Day ever, for a university of it's kind. The sun shone warmly outside, teachers mingled with the students, birds sang in the air, it all seemed perfect.

"Be careful." Rhyle, Olamide, Gina and Louis had been repeatedly saying around Sentira's ear at random times since she had been on the long Hover Cab journey from Chero Coast to Pelargonium. When Sentira tried to communicate back to question what she should be careful about, she was met with silence. This was unusual and Sentira was concerned but not overly worried.

I'm at Maromsaesc. They will teach me how to interpret my voices properly rather than me just guessing their meaning. Sentira thought confidently to herself as she queued in line to be scanned to go into the Student Cafeteria.

Inside the Maromsaesc student cafeteria, Sentira noticed that all of the staff were OBR's. Some were in their original robot form and others were the human style OBR's. All were helping to manage the Cafeteria in some way. Some were dishing out food, others were cleaning tables and there were OBR chefs that could be seen behind a transparent screen behind the self-service counter preparing food. Sentira said thank you to the female human OBR who handed her a tray and introduced herself as Ann OBR.

"Would you like me to advise you on the healthy options we have prepared for you today?" said Ann OBR.

"No thanks. I can choose myself." Sentira replied back. She walked to the first self-service counter and chose two beef burgers straight away. She loved beef burgers and no amount of healthy food advice was going to change that. Sentira did however, compensate for the beef burgers and added wholemeal bread, lots of lettuce, tomatoes, onions, garlic along with 2 bananas, a pear and apple. The beef burgers reminded her of back home in Chero Coast where Nanny Lisha shared her taste for her favourite choice of sandwich.

If only Nanny Lisha had got to come to Maromsaesc when she was a teenager like me. Sentira mused as she looked around the Cafeteria to find a place to sit down and eat her sandwich and fruit. She found a chair alongside a long table seated in the middle of the Cafeteria. It was very noisy, so Sentira ate her lunch and chose to call Nanny Lisha when she got back to Jay Hall (one of the Halls of Residence next to the Maromsaesc Recreation Ground).

Perianne was also in the Maromsaesc student cafeteria. She took the tray off the human OBR with a polite thank you, as she had noticed mostly everyone else was doing. One of her ideas to fit in was simply to imitate, imitate and imitate again how everyone else behaved. This way, no-one would suspect her of anything bad that just happened to mysteriously occur at the University.

Saint. Perianne Saint. Perianne (originally Aridaperianne Dedrick) thought to herself. *It's a good fake name. I'm a saint who couldn't possibly do any wrong.* Perianne smiled, but her smile soon dropped when she saw the student selection of food for lunch.

What's all this? Perianne said in her mind in shock. *I can't eat this!* Just as Perianne was going to ask to speak to the Head OBR Chef, she caught herself and remembered that this was what most of the other students were eating and she was here to blend in, to be unnoticed.

If I start to complain that there's no King Salmon, Kinmemai rice, Wagyu beef, Kobe beef, Gold leaf bread, Pink Radicchio lettuce, Heirloom tomatoes, Yubari King Melons... my cover will definitely be blown before I've even started. Perianne quickly decided in her thoughts, as she chose the beef burgers (which appeared more brown than the rest) and added extra lettuce, onions, garlic and tomatoes. She picked up a banana and 2 apples and poured herself a glass of apple juice. She touched her Student card on the OBR at the end of the self-service line and looked around to see where she could sit down and eat her food. Perianne wondered if her Aunty Joan could send her some of the food she was used to. She hoped that she wouldn't be sick eating all the cheap food on her tray.

Perianne began to walk towards an empty area of the Cafeteria and again stopped herself.

No. I'm here to blend in. Perianne mused while changing direction to sit with a group of students near the middle of the Student Cafeteria. The lively sounds of students talking loudly and enthusiastically to each other and their voices distracted Perianne but she focused on trying to eat something and tried to appear to be just like everyone else. Perianne had taken only three bites out of her beef burger when she suddenly felt nauseous like something was coming up from the back of her throat. She tried in vain to swallow it back down again but it was too late, and Perianne let out a stream of brown and yellow vomit from her mouth.

"Ewww!" a female student with short blond hair exclaimed next to Perianne, jumping up away from the table and quickly grabbing hold of her tray at the same time.

"Are you alright?" a female brown haired student asked on the other side of Perianne.

Within minutes two human OBR's had run over to their table, one started to clear up the vomit mess and the other wiped around Perianne's mouth with a damp sterile cloth.

"How are you feeling? Would you like to come with me to get medical assistance? Are you able to walk or do you need transportation?" the human OBR said with less empathy than a real life human. This was one of the ways you could catch out a very realistic human OBR from a real life person. The human OBR's were not very good at showing the appropriate emotion in various situations. They were more suited to business or working environments even though they were used mostly everywhere.

Perianne frowned up at the human OBR's robotic words of pre-programmed concern.

"I'll take her to the medical room." the woman with short blond hair said kindly to Perianne whilst turning to narrow her eyes at the human OBR. She put down her half empty tray and watched Perianne closely as she walked with her to one of the Medical centres located close to the Cafeteria. There were toilets in the Medical centre and the blonde haired woman waited patiently for Perianne to finish throwing up some more in one of the toilet unisex cubicles, before sitting down next to her outside the door to see one of the Maromsaesc nurses.

"My daughter needs your help!" an elderly woman's voice said near to Perianne's ear. Perianne felt instant anger. Not only was she sick off the disgusting cheap food at Maromsaesc but she was already hearing new unfamiliar voices.

"You must help us! You can hear me!" said two elderly women simultaneously near the front of Perianne's face.

"Why isn't she helping us mummy?" a child's voice said around Perianne's left ear. Perianne silently sent thoughts to the voices around her.

Stop talking to me! Perianne said in her thoughts to the voices.

"Mummy, she's angry! You made her angry!" a little girl's voice wailed loudly before gradually getting quieter and fading away altogether. The woman with the blond hair tried to break the silence.

"I'm Lisa. What's your name?" Lisa said to Perianne.

48

"Perianne Saint." replied Perianne quietly. Perianne felt drained. She wanted to just get to her room at the Jay Halls of Residence and talk privately to Aunty Joan. However, she was alert enough to know that entering the student Medical room would be a good opportunity to try and see what medications they had in case she needed to use them for her purpose.

"Hope you feel better, Perianne. Was it the food? Do you think you are allergic to something in the beef burger?" Lisa asked sensitively to Perianne. Perianne heard the genuine concern in Lisa's voice.

I can use her. Perianne thought deviously.

"I'm not sure. It's never happened to me before today, before I ate at the Maromsaesc Cafeteria I've never vomited in my entire life!" Perianne explained to Lisa.

"Really? Did your voices warn you?" Lisa enquired inquisitively. "I heard a voice say "The Ginger beautiful girl near, stay at the other side, my dear." an old man's voice, immediately before you were sick."

"I heard a man's voice say "the beef burger is foul, go the other way round." Perianne responded hoping that Lisa wouldn't sense any sarcasm in her voice.

About three adult male voices laughed heartily around Perianne's face and ears.

"A psychic voice! I bet you wished you had listened to it right?" Lisa responded gently.

"It's hard to know when they're speaking the truth so most of the time I don't." Perianne replied feeling better now that she was already fooling another dumb voice-hearer.

This Uni will be closed sooner than I think. Perianne mused to herself as she stood up to be scanned by the Medical room Human OBR nurse before entering.

Perianne's surgically created bright, green eyes took in quickly everything that was in the student medical room. She had an excellent visual memory and knew she wouldn't forget any of the details. As the Human OBR nurse gave her two bottles of water for her to drink if she needed, the OBR asked her questions about her health and informed her how she could prevent getting sick in the future. Perianne's mind was elsewhere. She already knew that she couldn't eat the cheap meat in the student cafeteria anymore, it was easy to work out.

Drink plenty of water. Perianne repeated the Human OBR's medical advice in her mind. *This is below beginner level common sense.* Perianne thought amused. She observed her surroundings. The medical room was standard. There was a sink in the far right hand corner with soap, paper towels, disinfecting hand sanitizer and surface wipes nearby. There was a virtual examination/medical couch which she was sitting on, a virtual chair, a virtual record book, drinking water machine with disposable cups, a life saving defibrillator on the opposite side of the sink, first aid kits, fire safety supplies, evacuation virtual chairs for people with mobility impairments and a medical supplies cabinet.

That's it. Perianne thought as her eyes passed over the medical supplies cabinet. *Here's where they keep the real drugs that may be of use to my purpose.* She had considered asking her Aunty Joan to send her some of the old style banned anti-psychotic tranquilisers in a parcel to her at Maromsaesc but the OBR, Human OBR's and Applerishin security were far too advanced to allow a parcel containing those illegal drugs through into the University. Perianne wondered if the OBR medical staff had some of the banned tranquilisers in the medical supplies cabinet in case of an emergency with any of the students.

Surely, they've thought of an emergency plan if the crazy students get out of control? Perianne thought to herself while the Human OBR nurse led her and Lisa towards the door. The Human OBR nurse had checked Perianne's blood pressure, temperature, peered into her mouth and had subsequently given Perianne the all clear.

"Remember to drink plenty of fluids and you can first try eating bananas, dry crackers or toast when you feel hungry again. Please call us if you have any further symptoms. I have noted your complaint about the beef burgers cooked in the Student Cafeteria and…" the Human OBR nurse was abruptly interrupted by Perianne.

"No,.." Perianne said suddenly. "I don't want to make a complaint. The OBR Chefs can't cater for everyone's tastes and… the beef burgers were not ok… for me."

The Human OBR nurse looked at Perianne with faint emotion in her eyes.

"I'm sure the beef burgers are delicious for the rest of the students. I don't want any changes whatsoever made to the Maromsaesc Cafeteria menu." Perianne stated with what she hoped was a brave, self-less and kind voice.

"Are you sure?" said the human OBR nurse with the same small glimpse of emotion in her eyes.

Perianne glanced at Lisa and raised her chin slightly higher.

"Yes. I'll be all right. Thanks!" Perianne said mustering up another fake smile. Lisa smiled at her.

It's working! Perianne thought triumphantly. Lisa was impressed by her already and believing every word that came out of her mouth. She gently took hold of Lisa's arm and tugged on it hinting (with a quick look to the left and back), at running off from the Human OBR nurse, which is what they did. Lisa ran out of the Medical Centre giggling and laughing with Perianne to get away from the Human OBR nurse, when the Human OBR nurse had turned her back to write Perianne's notes in the virtual Record book.

Sentira had heard the commotion in the Student Cafeteria as she was getting up from her chair. She saw the human OBR's and the OBR's rush over to the other side of the Cafeteria to assist with whatever had happened. Then she had watched with curiosity as five of them had returned back to their workstations soon after.

It couldn't have been that serious. Sentira reassured herself. *Maybe someone had an allergic reaction to the food.* she pondered. Sentira continued to wander around the Maromsaesc buildings by herself, occasionally bumping into other students who she joined in quick happy conversations (about the University) with. A few hours later, Sentira was in Jay Hall, sitting on her bed folding clothes from her suitcase to put into her wardrobe. Her student roommate hadn't come back from touring the University yet and Sentira chose the grey double bed next to a window overlooking the Maromsaesc Recreation Ground pathway. She wanted to be able to see outside at the view of the long pathway leading up to the Maromsaesc recreation ground. She wanted to see the green grass that encompassed the cobbled pathway and the beautiful flowers amongst the grass that also peeked out at times through the cobbled path. After she had finished packing away all her clothes, Sentira called Nanny Lisha.

"Nanny Lisha! I'm here!" Sentira said excitedly as she heard her grandmother say hello.

"I know! I got all your messages and video clips. How is it? How are you feeling?" Nanny Lisha replied lovingly.

"It's just everything I've ever wanted Nanny Lisha. It's... it's like I'm in a dream, a beautiful dream." Sentira replied wistfully.

"I wish the miracle of Maromsaesc had happened in my day...So, have you made your first voice hearing friends?" Nanny Lisha asked enthusiastically.

"Yes, I've been speaking to so soooo many people just like me!" Sentira exclaimed.

Nanny Lisha laughed along with her granddaughter's excitement.

"Good. Good. I knew you would love it there." Nanny Lisha replied. "Maromsaesc is the future. It's miraculous! You feel like you've found a place you belong, where you're valued and nurtured, where you can learn and grow, where you can be yourself, am I right?" Nanny Lisha said gently.

"Yes." Sentira said more quietly this time. "I hope I don't sound like I'm showing off Nanny. I'm just happy that's all." Sentira said softly. She guessed her grandmother felt many different emotions about today. It was a victory for the HVSV community, but it could never erase the millions of past lives that had been wasted, lost and cut short due to the damage done by some Psychiatrists, some Mental hospitals and the devastating discrimination and stigma inflicted on HVSV people throughout history. At certain times in history, people had even been burnt as witches for talking about the voices or visions they experienced. However, that was all in the past and today was a day that signified permanent change and Sentira was overjoyed to be part of it.

It seemed as if Nanny Lisha had read Sentira's mind because she next said the following...

"It's ok Sentira. Yes, in the past people like us and all the other students you see at Maromsaesc University haven't been treated right...but this...this is a new day in our history, a day of change and you and I are part of it, even though I'm not there." Nanny Lisha laughed softly to cut through the seriousness of what she had just said. She didn't want Sentira to think too much about the past or the sadness related to it. She wanted Sentira to be happy at Maromsaesc studying with a view to choosing a career, which best suited her as a voice-hearer.

"So..." Nanny Lisha said from the comfort of her sitting room laying down on her natural fabric sofa, her legs propped up and crossed at her ankles on the opposite sofa arm. "So... Will I see you on the Welcome to Maromsaesc video on the News later this evening?" Nanny Lisha asked, changing the subject back to present day and Maromsaesc University.

"Nanny, I stood up and clapped with my hands over my head to make sure of it!" Sentira said laughing. Nanny Lisha couldn't help but laugh at the child-like behaviour of her granddaughter at times.

"Sentira, that's Jelitoona! As all you teenagers say. Now listen to me." Nanny Lisha said with a seriousness in her tone. "I want you to try and relax before classes on Monday so you can take it all in and learn as much as you can."

Sentira took a deep breath in and out. *Ok, I am very excited Nanny but I'm not unable to relax enough to pay attention in all my classes.* Sentira considered in her mind before responding back.

"I will Nanny. How's mum and the rest of the family?" Sentira changed the subject. She didn't want to be reminded of the responsibility that every student had by being the first teenagers ever to attend Maromsaesc University in Pelargonium, England. Professor Zantend had spoke of how they (the first generation of Year 1 Maromsaesc University students) would have the whole world watching their progress, their behaviour, their ability to learn and succeed whilst there. To quote Professor Zantend who had said the following words (during her 'Welcome to Maromsaesc University' speech.): -

> "Your visions, your voices, your abilities, your courage, your perseverance, your love for one another, your intelligence, your failures that you will learn from, your success's and the paths you choose at the end of Year 3 to utilise your gifts will… set a new precedent, a new high standard for HVSV people all over the world. Be your best!"

"Have you called your mum yet?" asked Nanny Lisha sounding surprised. Sentira sighed quietly.

"Mum was sleeping. She got home early hours this morning from her flight back from seeing Dad. I didn't want to wake her." replied Sentira. "I sent her all the same messages and video's that I sent you."

"Ok…and your friends back home in Chero Coast?" Nanny Lisha enquired.

"I don't' have that many friends Nanny, just a few people."

"It's good to keep in contact Sentira."

"Yes, I have texted them too." Sentira replied. "Nanny, I'm going to have to go, I can see someone about to be let in my room by Applerishin security, it's… a mixed woman with curly hair…yes I will send messages to Dad too… if mum gives me his new number…yes…ok…I will… Talk to you again Nanny! Bye!" Sentira heard Nanny Lisha say bye back before she pressed off on her Applerishin mobile. She looked again at the Applerishin security virtual screen on the wall next to her wardrobe. It clearly showed an image of the person about to be given access to her shared room number 10 Jay Hall. It was a mixed race shapely woman with freckles and shoulder length curly thick black hair. All of a sudden, Sentira heard crying sounds all around her ears loudly from the voices of people of all ages.

Stop! Sentira said firmly in her mind to the voices and luckily for her this time they did. Before the last sob was heard however, Gina's familiar voice, which had been saying "Be careful" on and off throughout the day returned again and said

"Watch her."

ROOM 25 JAY HALLS

Perianne waited impatiently for the Applerishin Security to scan her in order to identify her as Perianne Saint before allowing her access to her room number 25 at Jay Halls. As soon as she had put one step forward into the open archway after the virtual door had been removed by the Applerishin Security, she smelt cannabis.

Drug use! Perianne thought happily. *More discredit to Maromsaesc.* Perianne walked further into the room and could see a mixed race Chinese and white woman kneeling on her bed smoking a cannabis cigarette next to an open window. She had mid-length black hair in a bob hairstyle and didn't even turn as Perianne walked in the room. Perianne easily found her large mauve suitcase laying flat on the dark green bedroom rug next to her grey double bed near a plain cream wall. There was a photo of the Maromsaesc University in a silver and gold frame above her misty grey headboard. There was also a framed picture above the misty grey headboard on the other side of student room number 25, belonging to her new roommate. Perianne started to open her large mauve suitcase and unpack. After around 10 minutes, the woman on the misty grey double bed on the other side of the room finally glanced over in Perianne's direction.

"Hey, I'm Annchi." Annchi said, finishing her cannabis cigarette and moving her legs from under her to stretch them out over the side of her misty grey double bed.

"I'm Perianne. How's it going?" Perianne said whilst still unpacking her clothes from her suitcase into her wardrobe.

Please don't try and offer me your cancer inducing drugs. Perianne thought sarcastically so herself. Next, as if somehow Annchi had heard the thoughts coming from Perianne's mind, Annchi said calmly.

"I've got a medical certificate which means I can use Medical cannabis at anytime. I hope you don't mind." Annchi explained before Perianne had a chance to question her.

"Of course not." Perianne said hiding her disappointment. She had forgotten that Medical cannabis was legal for all who had a medical condition that required it.

I wonder what medical condition she has. Perianne wondered.

"I'm Perianne. Isn't this all soooo Jelitoonaa being at Maromsaesc for the first year of Professional development for people who hear voices and see visions!" Perianne exclaimed imitating the enthusiasm she had heard most of the other students express around her. Annchi was quiet for a while before answering.

"It's good." Annchi finally said getting up to go into the shared toilet on the opposite end of the beds. Perianne carried on unpacking and drinking from a bottle of water on her bedside table.

She's not as talkative as the rest. Perianne observed bored. She looked at her Applerishin virtual mobile attached to her right wrist. It was a small purple square shape and would transform into a virtual mobile upon a voice command and correct identification of the user. Most Applerishin virtual mobile starting devices were either a flat square design or small square design and had a virtual attachment to the user so it was near impossible for the user to lose their starting device. The starting device would alarm loudly if it were 2 metres away from it's user and some versions could hover around the user attaching itself to the user's clothing or wrist at times to stay within the 2 metre rule. Once the starting device was in the Applerishin virtual mobile form however, it could be lost or stolen unless a user had a more updated version of the virtual mobile, which Perianne had. If a virtual mobile was lost or stolen, it still could not be used by anyone but the registered owner.

"Applerishin open." Perianne said quietly to the small purple square attached to her right wrist. A virtual Applerishin mobile sprang up from the starting device and a light purple ray scanned Perianne from her head to her feet and back up again.

"Welcome Perianne Saint! How may I assist you?" the Applerishin virtual mobile said.

"Call Mama Lucy." Perianne said to the virtual mobile next to her.

"Calling Mama Lucy, mother." Perianne's virtual mobile said in a robotic voice.

Perianne had insisted that she brought with her one of the latest OBR Applerishin virtual mobiles even though she was supposed to blend in with the other students. The newest OBR Applerishin virtual mobiles cost around £200,000. They appeared similar to other Applerishin virtual mobile designs but the technology far exceeded the older Applerishin virtual mobiles. For example, the OBR Applerishin virtual mobiles could transform into or create a human OBR or OBR temporarily upon the user's request. The user could easily pre-program and control the OBR's behaviour and actions. This was one of the unique features of OBR Applerishin virtual mobiles.

"Tell anyone who asks it's a gift from a rich ex-boyfriend." Aunty Dr Joan Dedrick had warned her before she came to Maromsaesc. Perianne suddenly felt a cold chill and a wave of intense seriousness crossed her newly made features. She couldn't leave her virtual OBR phone, (it reminded her that she was not like the other students) so she had agreed that if anyone found out she had an OBR mobile, she would concoct a believable story.

As long as I don't use the main features, no-one will know how much my mobile is worth. Perianne reassured herself in her thoughts. *I, Aridaperianne Dedrick have a very wealthy ancestral line. Soon to be restored.* Perianne concluded in her mind.

"Mama Lucy, is that you? It's Perianne." Perianne said lovingly to Mama Lucy aka Aunty Dr Joan Dedrick.

"Perianne! How's everything at the Maromsaesc University?" said Mama Lucy genuiniely happy to hear from Perianne. Mama Lucy's response was heard by Applerishin virtual sound devices whereby the Applerishin user could talk in privacy to a person or robot and it would only be heard in the user's ears, a bit like the old-fashioned ear phones. When the Applerishin sound devices were in use, the person's ear would glow light purple or a light version of whatever colour the Applerishin virtual mobile starting device had begun as.

"Oh, you know Mama, all's Jelitoonaa!" Perianne faked a small laugh. She had heard a lot of the other students use this word in the context of something being very good, amazing or brilliant. She thought the word sounded pathetic but if it would help her to blend in at Maromsaesc then she was prepared to use it. Mama Lucy (Aunty Dr. Joan Dedrick) paused for a while then spoke again.

"I see you're fitting in very well!" Mama Lucy exclaimed back at her niece remembering that this is what must happen if Aridaperianne was to sabotage the Maromsaesc and leave there unnoticed and innocent of any wrongdoings.

Mama Lucy was happy that Aridaperianne (Perianne Saint) was already beginning to speak like the other students and couldn't recall any previous conversation that she had heard her beautiful and highly intelligent niece use the word "Jelitoonaa" Mama Lucy continued to listen with light amusement.

"I've sent you videos, and messages about Maromsaesc Mama and you can see the Welcome speech by Professor Wilemina Zantend on the News this evening. How have you been Mama, I miss you...I really miss you." Perianne said genuinely.

Perianne missed Aunty Dr Joan Dedrick, she missed her old face, hair, the delicious rich food and comfort of living in Aunty Joan's home. Perianne did not miss the high-rise flat she had to return home to every time she went out somewhere. Inside Aunty Joan's home however, she could almost forget the outside world.

One ok thing about Maromsaesc is they actually have virtual lifts in their halls of residence and university buildings. Perianne mused. *And they work, unlike back at the Terrie flats.*

"I received them Perianne and I've been very well, thank you. It's still hot here. It's like the summer is never ending." Mama Lucy responded changing the subject to the weather in Terrie Valley.

"That's good Mama." Perianne said. Suddenly a voice spoke over her left shoulder.

"Countdown to the race starting. All together now... 10... 9...8...7...6...5...4...3...2...1" said a stern female voice. Perianne couldn't tell the age range and frowned at the uninvited interruption to her trail of thoughts. The voice continued.

"And they're off!" shouted a teenage boy's deep voice next to Perianne's right shoulder. Perianne let out a loud sigh, and then immediately regretted doing so.

"Everything alright?" Mama Lucy asked hearing the change in her beloved niece's tone. Perianne pretended to be moving things around on her bedside table noisily as she listened to the voices speak around her.

"Slow rider in the lead, with ... no... with...no... catch me if you can in first place. Catch me if you can is in the lead. Slow rider is now in second place!" the stern female voice said over Perianne's right shoulder in a serious tone.

Then a teenage boy started crying loudly by Perianne's right ear. Perianne rolled her eyes. She could deal with these voices but no one, definitely not her family... must ever know that she heard them.

My voices are different from the mentally ill ones that sick people hear. Perianne reminded herself confidently.

"I'm ok Mama," Perianne finally replied back to Mama Lucy. "Just trying to organise my items on my beside table, it's a little small." Perianne let out a short laugh which had a hint of bitterness.

"If you need anything, let me know, anything at all." said Mama Lucy inquisitively. Perianne felt like laughing another bitter laugh but knew it would make her Aunty realise that something was wrong. Instead, Perianne lied just like all the other times her voices had interrupted, when she was with

Aunty Joan Dedrick aka Mama Lucy.

"I'm fine Mama Lucy." replied Perianne sweetly. Just at that moment Perianne's voices stopped talking as Annchi came out of the bathroom.

"Mama, my roommate is here and I want to talk with her... Yes, I will... I have those...Ok...Ok...Talk tomorrow. Bye!" Perianne watched her Applerishin mobile reduce back into a small purple shape and attach itself on her right wrist. When she looked back up again, Annchi was looking down at her grinning.

What is she smiling at? Perianne wondered in her thoughts.

"Did you hear them?" Annchi asked Perianne, her dark brown eyes open wide. Perianne held back another bitter laugh or loud sigh, she wasn't sure which.

"Hear what?" Perianne asked.

Surely this mad girl doesn't think that her voices are the same as mine. Perianne thought to herself in amazement.

"I heard teenage girls, about 7 of them I think, crying and whispering...it was out here and I couldn't make out what they were saying exactly. Thought that you might be able to hear them too." Annchi said hopefully.

"No I didn't hear anyone crying. I was on the phone to my Mama Lucy." Perianne replied back to Annchi.

Mine are different to yours. Perianne silently warned Annchi in her mind.

"Oh." Annchi's hopeful expression became a calm stare. "Oh sorry." Annchi's face grew light red and she turned to walk over to her side of the room where she duly flopped face down on her double bed and fell asleep. Perianne got to work, busying herself by rearranging furniture in the shared room and cleaning everything, especially in the bathroom. She found cleaning equipment, sprays, rags and plastic gloves in a silver storage cupboard in a corner of room 25.

Perianne swept the already clear, spotless floors and the dark green bedroom rugs. She dusted the corners of the room though there was no dust to be seen. Perianne was pleased to see that her room had an Applerishin virtual health-safe border sensor that could be activated whenever a student had an infectious illness like the flu for example. Perianne didn't like to share her space mainly because of the risk of germs being more easily spread to her. Cleaning was a boring task to Perianne but she had to have her entire student shared room sterilised thoroughly before she could fall asleep in it.

I don't want to spend the entire 3 years being sick all the time. Perianne thought to herself then stood still. *3 years, why did I think that…I can be out of here in a year if I act quickly.* Perianne concluded. Her mind-racing full of ideas of what she could do to ensure that Maromsaesc and any other HVSV schools planned for the future would be forever discredited, banned, abolished, cancelled, just like they had cancelled Psychiatry and the Dedrick family businesses.

I have a purpose. Perianne thought. Her new surgically created features wrinkled into a grimace as she went on with cleaning the bathroom. She lifted her head up from bending down to rinse out the bath and saw a reflection of herself in the freshly wiped clear virtual mirrors, which covered that side of the bathroom. Perianne turned her face left, to centre to right, to centre to left and looked up and down at her new face.

Uncle Robert promised me he would get my old features back after I ruin Maromsaesc. Perianne remembered. Suddenly, she heard teenage girls whispering words in another language around her shoulders.

I need to work fast. Perianne thought, taking 5 slow deep breaths in and out, she mouthed the words "Leave me!" to the air around her left shoulder and the air around her right shoulder where the voices had been heard. The voices stopped. Perianne smiled. The majority of times she could stop the voices speaking and other times she had to wait until they finished, but on those rare occasions she had enough sense to ignore them. This is what separated her, from the average unstable voice-hearer, Perianne strongly believed.

I need to work fast! Perianne repeated in her mind, looking around the spotless pale green bathroom. *I need to be out of this place before I'm put in Year 2 of this nut house.* Perianne took off the plastic gloves, pressed her left red sandal on the black lever at the base of the silver bin to put the used gloves and now dirty rags inside of it.

Next, Perianne stepped out of the bathroom and saw that Annchi was still sleeping. Feeling a bit tired herself, Perianne returned back into the bathroom and had a shower. When she had finished, she sat on her misty grey double bed, moisturised her skin, wrapped her long, wavy ginger hair in a red silk towel, put on a t-shirt and leggings then fell fast asleep.

ROOM 10 JAY HALLS

Some way below Perianne's room number 25, was room number 10 Jay Halls. In Room 10, Sentira was talking with her new roommate a mixed race freckled black and white woman called Brandi. Brandi had a curvy figure and wore a fitted rose and tulip's patterned flowery crop top, matching miniskirt and white leather slider sandals. Sentira had asked her where she had got her outfit from and found out that Brandi designed her own clothes and made them. Brandi had spoke in detail about her dreams of becoming a world famous fashion designer and bringing her own personal signature style to the world. She proudly showed Sentira some of her drawings of other designs she intended to make when she could fit it in with her studies. Sentira had innocently asked her why she didn't attend a fashion university instead of Maromsaesc.

Brandi had replied that she didn't need to learn anything else in a Fashion college. Her dad was going to buy her, her very own Fashion store to manage when she completed the three years at Maromsaesc, as a gift for her achieving her Certificate of Professional Development for people who hear voices and see visions. Brandi was to focus on controlling her complex voices more, finding out what benefits they can be to her in her upcoming fashion business. This was Brandi's reason for being at Maromsaesc.

Sentira listened to Brandi talk more about her father and how close they were, how he supported all her dreams and worked long hours as a train driver to save to fund his daughter's education and ambitions. Sentira thought of her own father, who she hadn't seen for around 4 years due to him being abroad on confidential government business.

Why couldn't my Dad be…no…this woman's story sounds too good to be true. Sentira thought to herself but just smiled along with Brandi's stories of her Dad back home in London and feigned interest in the images of Mr Ropen that Brandi showed her proudly on her Applerishin virtual mobile.

"So how complex do your voices get?" Sentira asked Brandi curiously. Brandi (who had been sitting down next to Sentira chatting on her misty grey double bed) suddenly stood up and pulled her bright pink suitcase over to her side of the shared room.

"I don't want to talk about it." Brandi mumbled to herself while walking across the room.

"What did you say?" Sentira further enquired still full of curiosity about this new person she would be spending the next 3 years with. "I'm sorry, I didn't hear you." Brandi sat down on her bed and propped her suitcase up so it was standing up next to her legs. She began opening her suitcase from the top and pulled the zip down both sides before speaking.

"I hear voices that talk about serious illness and deaths that are to happen within 24 hours. I fall asleep wherever I am and have dreams of who the person is only after that person is either dead or has been diagnosed. Before then, I don't have any clue who the person is that the voices are warning me about. It's sad…it's just so sad." Brandi said sadly and tears rolled out of her eyes onto her youthful pale brown freckled cheeks. Sentira immediately rushed over to her and put her left arm around her and squeezed Brandi's right arm gently.

"It's ok, don't cry… I didn't know. I shouldn't have asked you." Sentira said to Brandi with empathy and concern. "I'm sure the teachers at Maromsaesc will have plenty of ideas to help you." Sentira concluded to Brandi confidently. "You don't have to talk about it to me, just wait till the Complex Voices class, ok?"

"O..Ok." Brandi replied in between sniffles of tears, which leaked through her nose and onto a white tissue Brandi had produced from her colourful skirt pocket when she had first started to cry. "Sorry, I was trying not to cry." Brandi said to Sentira with what looked like a sulking child expression to Sentira.

I've met so many other voice-hearers today and each one is different. Sentira observed to herself. Sentira knew that she could hear random voices at anytime but so far none of them had been prophetic enough to predict death or disease accurately or strong enough to put her in a sleep like trance at anytime. She felt a compassionate love and empathy for Brandi.

"We can help each other while we learn. We're friends now, right?" Sentira said to Brandi.

"Friends." Brandi said giving Sentira a tight hug.

Afterwards, Sentira went back over to her side of the room giving her new friend time to unpack and call her family. Sentira opened her virtual journal app on her Applerishin mobile and out sprang a virtual journal and virtual pen to write with. Sentira wrote down about the crying she had heard and the words "Be careful" and "watch her" just before her new friend Brandi had walked into room 10 Jay Halls.

I think she's ok. Sentira thought to herself readjusting her long twist out afro hairstyle into a messy ponytail on the top of her head, (some curly strands left out dangling around the sides), with a red satin scrunchie. She remembered that sometimes the voices she heard were referring to persons not present or even just a worried voice which worried for no reason. Sentira wrote some of her experiences down in her virtual journal, so she as to remind her to ask the teacher's at Maromsaesc if they had any new ideas to the possible meaning and purpose of each individual voice.

Sentira hoped she would be able to find meaning and use out of every single voice she heard. She further dreamed of finding a career that she could enjoy and bring money into her life to help herself and payback Nanny Lisha (and her parents) for all their support and money they had given her over the years. Nanny Lisha took out loans and used credit cards to help fund her education and Sentira's parents worked so hard she hardly ever saw them. Sentira couldn't feel the same closeness for her parents as she did for Nanny Lisha because of them not being around her when she needed them.

The Applerishin Security alarm went off and both Brandi and Sentira looked over at their separate virtual security screens next to their individual wooden shimmering brown wardrobes. The energy of all the Applerishin technology in a room would oftentimes make some of the furniture shimmer for a reason only the virtual mobile designers could explain, which they refused to do, stating it would breach their confidentiality code of conduct.

Two young men aged around 18 or 19 stood outside Applerishin security doors waiting to be allowed in. The Applerishin security OBR voice started to describe the men.

"Mr. Noah Matthew and Mr. Craig Dearnan Year 1 registered students of the Maromsaesc University request permission to enter Room 10 Jay Halls. Would you like to speak to them through Virtual intercom." said Applerishin security.

"I'll come out!" Brandi said excitedly.

"Yes, open virtual intercom." Sentira said at exactly the same time as Brandi.

"I didn't understand your response. Would you like to speak to Mr Noah Matthey and Mr Craig Dearnan through Applerishin Virtual intercom?" repeated Applerishin security. However, Brandi was already at the virtual security door talking to it. She stated that she was Brandi Ropon and to open the virtual security doors. The Applerishin security responded to her request.

"Miss Sentira Cagney is also present in Room 10. Security requires both occupants to grant access to this room." Applerishin security asserted. Brandi looked over at Sentira hopefully and even smiling again after the sadness she had expressed earlier. Sentira felt good to see her new friend Brandi happy again so she nodded her head, walked over to Applerishin Security and waited for it to scan her to confirm that she had also consented to allow access to room 10 for Noah and Craig.

The Applerishin virtual security door disappeared temporarily and Noah who was a blond haired, blue eyed 19 year old white man was standing with a black haired, brown eyed mixed race black and white man.

"Wow! So much security in this place!" Noah exclaimed when he saw Sentira and Brandi. "We've had to be scanned by Applerishin tech. at least a hundred times already!"

"Yeah, it's like they don't trust us." Craig laughed looking at Noah.

"What are you all up to? We've been going round to everyone's rooms getting them to meet up at Maromsaesc lake tonight or tomorrow night so we can have a fresher's night." Noah handed Brandi and Sentira leaflets detailing the following: -

> Team 3 Marom rave! Tonight or tomorrow! Or both!
> Music, barbecue, dancing, games and more… at the Maromsaesc lake 9 till late, FREE ENTRY.

"What's your names?" Craig said looking up at the women and then down again at his Applerishin mobile.

"Brandi and she's Sentira. And your Craig and Noah?" Brandi replied. "I think tomorrow night I'll go. What do you think Sentira?" Brandi turned away from staring at Noah to look at Sentira.

"Yeah, tomorrow night would be Jelitoonaa!" Sentira replied enthusiastically.

"Let's do it!" Brandi said grinning at Sentira.

Noah grinned back at Brandi and winked at Sentira. Craig was busy tapping information into his Applerishin virtual mobile, which was an older version of the mobile. As the men turned to walk away from room 10 Jay Halls, Craig shouted back.

"See you tomorrow, Sentira, Brandi!"

The Applerishin virtual security doors resumed.

"He's right. There's too much security all over this university. Why do we have to be scanned so many times?" Brandi said to Sentira.

"I think it's just because we're the first in the country

to ever attend a Maromsaesc university for voice-hearers and they want to keep us all safe." Sentira replied. The Applerishin security and OBR's everywhere didn't bother her.

"Don't you feel like we're constantly being watched?" Brandi persisted.

"I'm used to it!" Sentira laughed. "I've felt things watching me since I was born!" she exclaimed.

"Really? I haven't. Not like this." Brandi insisted. "Anyway it doesn't matter." Brandi finished sounding bored. Brandi went back on her Applerishin mobile and Sentira went back to writing in her virtual journal.

Craig and Noah were standing outside Perianne's room number 25. Noah began to hear voices around him singing. His facial expression changed from one of amusement to a calm serenity. Noah heard singing of all ages, male and female and to him it sounded beautiful, it was a Jelitoonaa feeling. Craig noticed that Noah's face had changed.

"You look spaced out Noah." Craig said amused to Noah. "Are you still thinking of that girl you sat next too during the Welcome speech? What was her name again?... Peri... Periaid... Peri..."

"Perianne. Nah, just hearing the most Jelitoonaa singing everywhere around me." Noah replied and his face flushed red.

"Singing? Ok." Craig replied sounding bored. They both waited for the Applerishin virtual security doors to disappear so they could invite more students to the Marom rave. The Applerishin virtual security doors disappeared and there stood Perianne wearing a t-shirt and leggings. Annchi stood there also wearing the same original light blue trousers and white v-neck vest top she had worn all day. Perianne's expression beheld a mixture of impatience and curiosity but Annchi's eyes were gleaming with laughter.

"I knew you were coming." Annchi said to Craig and Noah. "I saw you both in my dream." she smiled confidently at the two men who smiled back. Perianne looked down at her new roommate in disbelief.

Before or after you smoked an ounce of weed. Perianne thought to herself sarcastically but instead she said to the group.

"Wow! Annchi!" Perianne exclaimed, then to the men she said jokingly "I've got a psychic in my room." To her surprise, Craig and Noah didn't laugh. Perianne was about to make the joke again when she stopped herself and suddenly realized that they all believed that it was true.

They really believe that some of their hallucinations are of psychic origin. Perianne mused to herself.

"So, what's going on?" Perianne said diverting her gaze to Noah who was still blushing red. Noah looked down and then back up again, his face clearing slowly back to his normal pale-skinned colour.

"We're having a rave tomorrow night at the Maromsaesc Lake at 9. Do you think you can make it?" Noah said quickly, handing leaflets to first Annchi and then Perianne. Annchi and Perianne took the leaflets and read over them.

A rave! Perianne thought fast. *How can I mess this up?*

"All right, we'll see if we can make it and let you know." Annchi answered Noah. "But who are you? Are you ... Craig....and Joseph?"Annchi asked glancing back at the brightly coloured leaflet in her hand.

"I'm Craig and he's Noah." Craig replied. "And you are?"

"Annchi and this is ... what's your name again?" Annchi said to Perianne.

"I'm Perianne Saint. It looks fun. I'll be there." Perianne said decisively. She didn't need to wait for Annchi to make her decision. It was another chance to psyche out the students and find out more ways to bring this university down into the scrap heap as fast as possible.

"And how about you?" Craig asked Annchi.

"I don't know. I'll see how it goes tomorrow." Annchi replied.

"Jelitoonaa" Noah said, his face growing steadily red again. "Come on Craig, we've still got the other halls to get to before we can eat." Noah said to Craig who waved at Annchi before walking off with Noah. The Applerishin security doors re-appeared at room 25.

Noah and Craig walked together in silence for a few minutes along the spotless cream corridors which had framed photos of inspirational voice-hearers along the cream walls and fire exit virtual doors at either end. They got in the virtual lift together. Just before they reached to the ground floor Noah turned to Craig and said quietly, "I heard singing that got louder around those two women."

"So, what does that mean to you?" Craig replied uninterested, his mind elsewhere shuffling his leaflets around with his hands.

Noah bent down to retie one of his black trainer laces, which had been undone since they left room number 2 a few hours ago. Retying his laces quickly, he looked up at Craig with wide blue eyes.

"I don't know." he replied imitating Craig's uninterested tone.

MAROM RAVE

The Marom rave was in full swing. Craig and Noah played loud Jelitoonaa (cool, awesome) music from Applerishin virtual speakers that echoed around the glistening Maromsaesc lake and the lush green grass areas around it. There were over 100 students in attendance at the Marom rave. Some were talking to their voices or other students, some were dancing, others eating while sitting and students standing and drinking. Jelitoonaa music is a form of music developed in the 2060's which was an addictive mixture of beats and rhythms from every culture in the world intertwined in each song and euphonious singing lyrics by popular Jelitoonaa artists. The atmosphere was joyful and of course very, very Jelitoonaa!

Perianne made sure that she went around talking to everyone. It was a very warm night and she had chosen to wear a long red summer dress with splits by each side of her legs. Subsequently, this made her long slender light pink coloured legs, visible whenever she moved or when she sat down. She had on cream sandals and didn't wear any jewellery, except for a black choker with an eagle design in white gold hanging on it. She had her Applerishin starting device attached to her Applerishin virtual watch on her right wrist.

Perianne observed the other students very carefully as she made friends with many of them. Some were openly talking to the air around them or even the air above them or to the ground.

They all look crazy. Perianne thought to herself. She casually (in a friendly way) asked one of the students (a man called Jake) about why he was talking to the air around his shoulders during their conversation, he had replied that he was talking to one of his voices.

And they have no shame. Perianne thought fast while Jake went back to talking to his voices that Perianne could not hear. *He definitely should be on some sort of medication.* Perianne looked around her with her fake smile stuck to her face. *They all should be.* Outwardly, Perianne danced and laughed with the other students who were completely unaware of her intense hatred for them.

"Perianne!" Noah shouted over at Perianne, who was dancing with a group of three men and two women. Perianne ignored him and continued dancing. She was beginning to relax and enjoy the fact that she was fooling everybody. Besides, the Jelitoonaa music was very loud so Noah's shouting was barely heard. Noah shouted a few more times and began waving his arm also. Then, when Noah realised this wasn't getting Perianne's attention, he came over from where he was standing by the edge of the Maromsaesc lake, moving determinedly in and out of the crowds of students, only stopping to dance with a few women along the way. Soon Noah reached Perianne and lazily slumped his right arm over her shoulders.

"Perianne! Having a good time!" Noah spoke loudly into Perianne's right ear. Perianne slowed her dancing down to a halt. At any other time, anyone who approached her like this would have had his/her arm pushed away from her. She disliked men who thought they could invade her personal space without even knowing who she was. This time however, was an entirely different set of circumstances; therefore Perianne listened while Noah continued talking with his arm around her.

I can use him. Perianne thought while pretending to join in with a dance that Noah was now doing in front of her to the Jelitoonaa music. Other students joined them and soon there was a group of nearly 30 Maromsaesc students dancing a newly made up dance that had just been created by Noah. It was a mix of body shaking, bending down low, swaying, stepping forward and back again, leaning to one side, then the next and repeated. When that Jelitoonaa song had ended the students all shouted for the song to be replayed. After it was replayed about three times, Perianne left the dancing group with

Noah following behind her.

Perianne felt thirsty and hungry. She headed over to one of the four OBR barbecues (barbecues operated by OBR's) at the opposite end of the Applerishin virtual music speakers. Noah walked briskly to keep up with Perianne's quick walking pace.

"Heart attack, they say it was." a female voice spoke around Perianne's ears.

"No, it was indigestion." a male voice replied loudly in front of Perianne.

"How can someone die from indigestion?" the female voice argued back.

"How can someone die from indigestion?" the male voice replied in a teasing manner.

"Leave me alone." the female voice said.

Perianne felt familiar anger welling up inside of her. She didn't have time to go back to her room and deal with the voices the way she usually would so she decided to try something she had watched most of the other students doing.

I can copy the way the other students talk openly with their voices. Aunty Joan isn't here. Perianne reassured herself.

"Leave me alone!" Perianne said to the air around her in a way that she had seen so many other voice hearers do on TV and at Maromsaesc University. The voices stopped. Perianne felt relieved. This again, confirmed to her that she was different from other voice-hearers. She knew that she had more control, her voices didn't command her to hurt others or herself and she wasn't insane. Still, in her heart she understood why no one in the Dedrick family could ever accept that she heard voices. Her family (Perianne included) were at war with the HVSV communities. To choose to tell any member of the Dedrick family that she experienced similar voices to the people they all despised, would have consequences that were unimaginable.

I have control of mine. I am different. I am a Dedrick. Perianne reminded herself confidently.

As she had guessed, Noah didn't even question why she had

just spoken to the air around her.

He thinks this is all ok. Perianne mused to herself while choosing a chicken burger to eat instead of the beef that had made her ill at the Maromsaesc Cafeteria yesterday.

A wide variety of barbecued food was laid out on the circular wooden tables, near to the OBR (Official British Robot) barbecue area. There were chicken burgers, beef burgers, veggie burgers, fish burgers, fish fingers, cheese sandwiches, ham sandwiches, toppings such as onions, garlic, cucumbers, tomatoes, lettuce, kale, and so on. The drinks were wine, beers, rum, brandy, orange juice, coca-cola, fizzy water, water, apple juice and pineapple juice. Perianne poured herself some red wine in a plastic wine glass and took a bottle of water from the table. Noah poured a large plastic cup of a mix of all the alcoholic drinks on top of the table. Perianne felt like laughing at him.

He'll make himself sick. She thought amused.

"Got to try everything before it goes Noah!" Perianne said enthusiastically to Noah as he stood next to her again, while she leaned her back on a tree munching into a chicken burger with lettuce and kale.

"That's right." Noah said gulping half of it down in one mouthful. "Life is for the living."

"Yeah, ok." Perianne mumbled her reply finding a chair to sit on as some other students had moved on from sitting down and eating, to getting up and dancing instead. Noah sat down on another empty chair next to her.

"Did you organise all this?" Perianne asked Noah in-between drinking and eating.

"Ah…no, it was organised by the university. They just wanted me and Craig to promote it." said Noah with a burp at the end of his sentence.

The Professor and the teachers allowed this 'Mad Hatters Tea Party. Perianne thought to herself. What if something was to go wrong? Then it would be the university to blame. Perianne schemed in her mind.

Noah swallowed the last mouthful of drink left in his large

plastic cup. He wasn't hearing singing anymore around Perianne like yesterday, now he heard animals. Animals such as dogs barking, horses, donkey, snakes, birds, cats, monkeys and lions. He didn't tell the animal sounds to stop like he knew some other voice-hearers did. He liked to listen to most of the voices he heard. Noah missed the beautiful singing he had heard yesterday and hoped that the more time he spent with Perianne he would hear it again. There were so many other attractive women at this Marom rave, Noah wasn't sure how he felt about Perianne now. He felt confused but she was so friendly that he wanted to hang around her to see what could happen.

Noah's drunk. I'm not. Perianne thought as she stood up to place her paper plate and plastic wine glass into the nearby virtual bin. Noah got up and started his new dance again, first in front of Perianne (who returned to sitting down looking at her Applerishin mobile) and then with a group of students nearby. The new dance style, which had appeared fun when it was first introduced, now looked uncoordinated and out of step as some students tried to drunkenly dance the moves. The effects of all the alcohol that was being consumed by everyone was now starting to show.

Chaos, total chaos. Perianne observed to herself as she watched most of the first year Maromsaesc students dance wildly, erratically and wobbly with each other to the Jelitoonaa music from the Applerishin virtual speakers. The Applerishin virtual speakers glowed a visually stunning mix of colours and radiated colourful rays out onto the natural dance floor of lush green grass and pretty flowers. Nearby the dance floor, beheld the beautiful Maromsaesc lake and another barbecue food area.

Perianne noticed that a few of the students she had talked with earlier were walking towards where she was sitting from a distance. Perianne quickly told her Applerishin mobile to call Mama Lucy (aka Aunty Dr. Joan Dedrick).

"Mama Lucy, how are you?" Perianne said loudly as the two

women and one man stood near her. She waved at them with her left hand and pointed at her Applerishin mobile. Then she showed them four fingers with her left palm facing the students. The students (one with a bottle of rum in his hand and at least 10 empty plastic cups in his other hand) smiled happily at Perianne and wandered off back onto the glowing natural dancefloor.

"Ari...Perianne! What's going on?" Mama Lucy said in a tired sleepy voice.

"Nothing, I just wanted to hear you." Perianne said feeling a rush of loving emotions upon hearing the voice of her Aunty who had raised her since birth.

"I was asleep Perianne." Mama Lucy replied a bit louder than before.

"Oh sorry Mama Lucy." Perianne replied.

"It's ok." Mama Lucy said with a sigh. "Can you call me in the morning?" Mama Lucy said.

"Yes Mama. Goodnight." Perianne finished the call and her virtual sound device stopped causing her ears to glow light purple as the call ended. Perianne had forgotten that the time was 1am Monday morning and other people were sleeping. She decided to head up to Jay Halls soon. She had made new friends and showed everyone she was just like them. This was so that no one would suspect her when bad things and destructive events started to occur at Maromsaesc.

Perianne got up from her chair and half walked, half danced through the students. Then all of a sudden she heard a loud scream and stopped in her tracks. There was a no-one around who looked like they had screamed like that It was a long piercing shrill scream. However, Perianne's eyes were drawn to a young woman with a large afro sitting on the grass near the lake with a group of 12 Maromsaesc students. Perianne sat down at the back of the group to listen to what was going on.

"... Rhyle said around the front of my face in a deep gruff voice, "get plastic surgery very quickly! I can do it for her.

The surgeon is here!'" Sentira grinned as some of the students laughed seeing the funny side of what had been said. Sentira was enjoying herself more than she had ever done in her life. Here she was, a year 1 Maromsaesc student, talking about funny stories of Rhyle, Louis, Gina and Olamide to the other voice-hearers. The other voice hearer students clearly understood that her regular voices were very funny at times just like she did.

Everyone in the group began to swap stories of funny voices they had heard and interesting scenarios where their voices had said words that made them laugh out loud. After five other students had finished telling their humorous stories, most of the students sitting around Sentira had tears in their eyes and droplets of water rolling down their faces because they were laughing so much. Others were holding onto their tummy and bending forward while laughing hysterically.

They're all drunk. Perianne thought resentfully. Her voices didn't make her laugh. She continued to listen in.

"...and Gina began to imitate the school teacher's voice beside my ear and I couldn't stop laughing! The teacher had to take me out of the class and call my Nan to come and take me home for the rest of the day. Then, the next day, the same thing happened again, and the next day and the next day!" Sentira said to the other students jokingly. The other students burst out into fits of giggles and laughter.

What's so funny about missing your school education? Is that why you and these others act so retarded? Perianne thought angrily to herself.

Sentira's eyes met Perianne's for a while and when they did, both women had a sense of time standing still. In that instant, Sentira felt a cold chill wash through her body, while in exactly the same instant, Perianne felt herself growing hot through hidden anger. Sentira blinked a few times and spoke directly to Perianne.

"How about you? What's your name?" Sentira said cheerfully.

"Perianne. Perianne Saint." answered Perianne, then she added quickly. "Year 1 Maromsaesc Uni! Jelitoonaa!" waving her arms above her head in a friendly wave at the other students sitting by the lake. They waved back at her. Perianne planted a new enthusiastic and happy smile back of her facial expression.

"Tell us some of your funny stories Perianne!" a man with a shaven head said turning his head around to face Perianne sitting behind him.

"Yeah, tell us something funny, make us laugh." another man with a blond afro hairstyle said, turning his body around to see Perianne.

"I don't have any funny stories." Perianne said truthfully.

"Yes you do." a woman with ginger braids in her hair said knowingly.

"You must have at least one?" Sentira said in disbelief at Perianne. Perianne grew angrier.

"Ok, yes, I remember just one." Perianne said deciding to creatively invent one to keep up her popularity.

"Say it! I want to laugh!" exclaimed a woman wearing a short denim skirt and a blue off the shoulders fitted top.

Perianne's mind raced very fast.

"I've had the same as her." Perianne finally said. The students looked back at Sentira and then returned to look at Perianne. "I've been in school and a little boy's voice in front of my face began to imitate the teacher's voice and I …I was laughing so loudly, the school teacher sent me home for the rest of.. of the week!" Perianne ended her invented tale with laughter, which she hoped would sound genuine to the other students listening. There were a few giggles heard but nothing like the laughter expressed at Sentira's original story a few minutes prior.

"Anyone else?" Sentira said to the students sitting around her. The students faced back towards Sentira. Sentira stood in front of the group confidently wearing a leather look fitted black trousers with a loose white top that hung fashionably off one shoulder. She wore green canvas shoes and her long afro hair was styled in a well-defined twist out hairstyle, which reached down to her waist.

Some of the students shook their head meaning "no" or shrugged their shoulders. All the funny stories for that night had been told or at least the stories that the students wanted to share had been told. Sentira knew there had to be many other funny stories about voices but she didn't press the students to keep reliving their memories.

"Ok, just any funny stories now…doesn't have to be about voices…can be about anything you like." Sentira said curiously.

"Anything?" the light-skinned man with the blond afro hair asked. "Ok, I've got one. Have you heard the joke about the voice-hearer and the psychiatrist?" the man paused. The other students looked around at each other and some shook their heads "no".

"Neither have I because Psychiatrists don't exist!" the man with the blond afro laughed loudly at his own joke. The other students laughed along with him.

Perianne kept her happy smile fixed in place and hoped the other students were too drunk to notice her laughter was not as real as theirs. Inside she was boiling up with hidden rage steadily.

Who do these mad people think they are? Perianne thought feeling hurt and upset. She had to get away from them. She knew her purpose and she knew her training to be the perfect actress at Maromsaesc (so that no one would suspect her when things started to go wrong) but, this scene…the insulting way they had laughed about Psychiatrists, the loud music, the red wine, that Noah man, the way everyone appeared so overly happy… was pushing her to break out of her character. She could feel it. Perianne got up, unnoticed by all the other students sitting on the grass, unnoticed by all except Sentira.

Sentira's dark brown eyes followed Perianne's movement to stand up and watched her walk away.

Did someone upset her? Sentira thought to herself. *What did we say?* Sentira looked back down at the other students sitting around her, and observed that they were unbothered by the woman with the long wavy ginger hair wearing a red long summer dress, leaving the group.

They're probably too happy and drunk to care. Sentira concluded in her mind but she privately couldn't help feeling an instinctive knowingness within, that there was something strange about Perianne. She didn't understand what it could be though. Sentira looked back again at the other students who were now sitting or laying casually on the grass talking with each other or their voices. Some were still drinking, a few were kissing and cuddling each other and others were expectantly waiting to see if Sentira would start up another group chat. Sentira addressed those few students who were waiting to see if she had any more funny stories to tell.

"I'm just going to get a drink." Sentira said to them. "Do you want me to get you anything?"

"No, we're all right." a man with blond hair replied.

"Ok, I'll be back." Sentira said before walking away to go over to the other barbecue area. She wondered if they had any of her favourite beef burgers left. She reached into the pocket of her black leather look trousers and pulled out her previously started up Applerishin virtual mobile.

The time was 1:40am Monday morning. The first day of Maromsaesc classes. Some of the students had left early because of this reason. Sentira was having so much fun, she didn't want the Marom rave to end.

This is a voice-hearer's heaven. Sentira thought excitedly. She bit into the final beef burger she had found by itself on the wooden table in the barbecue area. She also drank down a beer she found in an oval shaped purple ice-bucket under the table. Sentira felt like all her dreams had come true. It didn't matter that she still had to attend classes for three years and successfully pass them to gain her degree certificate in Professional Development for people who hear voices. Sentira wasn't worried about which career path she would choose after 3 years anymore, she was living in the moment. She was young, carefree, a talented voice-hearer, happily enjoying life amongst other young, carefree talented voice-hearers and students who saw visions.

Oh yeah. Sentira realised to herself. *I nearly forgot about the students here that see visions aswell.* Sentira casually sat down on the clean wooden table. The OBR's had been busy cleaning up after the students and the barbecue area was spotless. A human OBR smiled at Sentira sitting down on the wooden table and Sentira giggled.

"It's ok. I won't break it!" Sentira shouted over to the human OBR. The human OBR stopped smiling and walked away from Sentira towards the Applerishin virtual speakers. Sentira leaned back on her hands and began swinging her legs back and forth in the air. She felt a little giddy but she wasn't drunk.

The visions students are similar to the voice hearers. Sentira observed. *They talk to the air around them like us, some hear words and conversations like us.* Sentira mused. *I guess the main difference is that they can see who they're talking with, and...if they don't like what they see they have to find ways to make that person or visual image go away.* Sentira thoughtfully wondered in her mind about the students who see visions.

They Maromsaesc students were separated into classes pertaining to their main ability. There were many students that heard voices and saw visions too but it was the skill that they needed education and guidance with the most, that determined which classes they were put in. For example, if a person heard voices and saw visions at the same rate, then the Maromsaesc application form questioned which ability would the student gain the most benefit from, if this ability were to be focused on and developed. It was also encouraged for students who complete their 3-year training Degree course for the Professional development of people who hear voices, to study for the Degree course in the Professional development of people who see visions afterwards. Those who successfully studied both degrees, would be eligible to study for a higher Masters degree which was currently an emerging idea by Professor Wilemina Zantend.

"Eaten them all!" Rhyle's voice sighed near Sentira's left ear. Sentira continued swinging her legs back and forth. She could hear Rhyle talking around her and soon slowed her pace a little, moving her face a little to the left to attentively listen.

"Has her mobile started up?" an elderly Gina asked.

"Beef burgers, look!" a young Rhyle exclaimed.

"Where?" a young Olamide responded.

"Fooled you. Fool." an elderly Rhyle replied.

"Mobile to Sentira." an elderly Gina said.

"Jelitoonaa." Olamide said calmly.

"Didn't leave me any." a child's voice belonging to Rhyle said.

"Beat you." an elderly Louis said.

"Sentira…Sentira…" a teenage Louis said.

Sentira listened to them talk, happy to hear their familiar voices around her. She automatically assessed in her mind that her regular voices were just talking randomly. She didn't sense intuitively any reason for concern hearing their words, unlike the foreboding "Be careful." voice she had heard during her Hover Cab journey to Maromsaesc on Saturday and at other times recently. So far nothing bad had happened to her since she had been at Maromsaesc therefore, what that voice could potentially have been warning her about, Sentira didn't have a clue. The words "Be careful." were repeated randomly (not only by her regular voices) in different accents but also by male and female voices of all different age ranges. Sentira stopped swinging her legs remembering the different voices that had said "Be careful." Rhyle, Olamide, Gina and Louis continued to talk around her left side and at a short distance from Sentira.

"You're bothering her." an elderly Olamide said.

"You are bothering her!" a child's voice of Olamide replied.

"Beat you, today, tomorrow, the next day, the next day and on Friday." a teenage voice belonging to Louis teased.

"Friday is not for me and Thursday is not for me." an elderly voice belonging to Gina said.

Sentira decided to tell her regular voices to quiet down, she was starting to get a headache. She was sure that it wasn't her regular voices that had caused the headache. It was remembering her worry about the intimidating "Be careful" voices and the image of that girl with the wavy ginger red hair and long red dress kept appearing in her mind's eye intermittently.

What was in that beer? Sentira thought to herself as she stepped down from the wooden table. Then, she confidently spoke to the air around her left side.

"Speak more quietly Gina, Olamide, Louis and Rhyle. I've got a headache." Her regular voices fell silent. However, Gina's voice soon interrupted the silence.

"She's forgotten this." the elderly voice of Gina squealed. Sentira turned around to see what Gina was referring to and saw her Applerishin virtual mobile laying on the wooden table behind her. Sentira picked up her virtual mobile and placed it in the back pocket of her black leather look trousers.

"Thankfully we tell her things cause she never remembers." Olamide's child voice said softly near Sentira's right ear.

Sentira took out her virtual mobile again to see what time it was. It was 2am. She returned her virtual mobile securely into her back pocket and began to walk towards the Jelitoonaa virtual speakers. Sentira walked past the Maromsaesc lake on the left hand side and past many students casually dancing, talking or embracing each other. Close to one side of the Jelitoonaa speakers, Sentira again saw the woman with the long wavy ginger red hair.

She's come back down again. Sentira thought to herself and slowed her pace to watch Perianne from a distance.

Perianne felt a raging, furious anger bubbling up inside of her. She had replayed the cruel joke about psychiatrists over and over again in her mind. Her family had suffered badly from the abolishment of Psychiatry worldwide and she was sure that her mother's suicide was somehow related to what had happened to the Dedrick family businesses. So, Perianne had gotten changed into a cream vest top and white leggings with brown canvas shoes to find the man who had said the joke about psychiatrists. Her plan was to befriend him and use him later for her purpose to bring down Maromsaesc University. Psychiatry was the most effective way to manage these crazy voice hearers and those that claimed to see visions. Perianne could not rest until Psychiatry was re-established, in particular Dedrick Psychiatry, the very best of all the Psychiatry practices throughout history.

Out of the corner of her eye, she could see the woman with the long afro twist out hairstyle, the leather look black jeans, and the off the shoulder white top. Perianne stopped and looked at Sentira. Sentira looked back curiously. Before both could decide what to do next, the man who had said the Psychiatry joke walked past Perianne with two female Maromsaesc students towards the barbecue area. Perianne broke her gaze with Sentira and followed them over to the barbecue area. She started to chat and joke with them using the charm she had learned during her training for Maromsaesc by Uncle Dr.Robert.

"Blend in." Uncle Dr.Robert had told Perianne during her training for how to behave at Maromsaesc. "If they believe you are one of them, you can find out ways to sabotage the credibility of the entire university very easily."

Perianne had listened very carefully.

"Be like them, laugh like them, dance like them, even help them at times…I know…it…you can do this Perianne! The whole Dedrick family have confidence in you. You are the brightest and the best of the new generation of Dedrick's." Uncle Dr Robert finished with a flourish of his arms. He had dramatically gestured with his arms towards Perianne to indicate that she stood out in the family due to her genius in her Psychiatry home schooling. This is why she had been chosen to destroy Maromsaesc undercover from the inside. Perianne promised her Uncle that the next time she saw him, the Dedrick Psychiatry family businesses would be up and running worldwide and their billionaire riches would return. Everything would be exactly the same as before the R v Caulfied case, and...before... her mother had killed herself. Except, Perianne knew in her heart that her mother would not return.

Perianne expertly planted another happy grin on her face as she chatted with the light skinned man with the blond afro hair, dark red t-shirt and dark blue jeans. The other two women were joining in also. Perianne talked about the new Jelitoonaa dance and asked the man with the blond afro hair whose name was Kaden to show her the moves again. Kaden did some of the moves and stopped.

"No, it went more like this." Perianne danced next to Kaden who resumed dancing also.

"Ook se ak is hee ac dlo fo slli soc doe si." a squealing female voice said loudly just above Perianne's head.

Suddenly, an image of fire burning appeared within Perianne's newly created green eyes from her plastic surgery earlier that year, which went unseen to others. She felt so intensely angry, hurt, upset...

Kaden stumbled and fell sideways onto one of the large barbecues, he screamed out in pain but managed to get up from the barbecue shaking his left arm beside him.

"Arrrghh!" Kaden screamed out again. "Water, throw water on it!" Kaden said to Perianne.

Perianne thought fast.

"Blend in...even help at times..." Uncle Robert had said.

Perianne looked around the barbecue for any bottles of water and quickly discovered a half empty ice bucket, which contained only cool water in it. All the ice in the ice-bucket had melted away earlier. She lifted the ice bucket and moved it closer to Kaden.

"Kaden put your arm in here, quick!" Perianne shouted over to Kaden who was still waving his now blistered and burnt left arm in a vain attempt to cool it down.

Kaden fell down on the grass and put his left arm into the ice bucket of cool water still yelling in pain. One of the human

OBR's came over to them at this point, made a quick assessment of Kaden's injuries and called for a Hover ambulance to come to Maromsaesc University. Perianne and the other two women were trying to speak words of comfort to Kaden as the blistered burnt redness of his arm appeared to be spreading to his shoulders aswell.

Sentira watched in horror some distance away from the barbecue area which now had extra human OBR's running towards the group of students with medical staff from a nearby Hover ambulance just behind them. She hadn't seen when Kaden got burned. After watching Perianne chatting for a long time she had become bored and headed back towards the Jelitoonaa speakers intending to go to her room at Jay Halls. When she was nearly at the virtual speakers however, she had heard Kaden scream out. Before she could reach him, she could see that a human OBR was ordering students to "stand back" while the barbecue area was bordered off by a virtual security fence.

Sentira could see Kaden's face twisted in agony with his left arm in an ice bucket of cool water and Perianne covering the other half of his body with someone's pink cardigan. Kaden's body was shivering, even though it was still warm outside.

Perianne tried to keep Kaden warm with a pink cardigan that one of the female students had given her to cover Kaden with. Inwardly, Perianne felt ecstatically happy.

Trouble already! And, classes at this doomed uni. haven't even started yet. Perianne happily mused to herself, her face a decisively crafted look of empathy, concern, kindness and compassion.

LESSON TRANQUILITY

Sentira sat next to Brandi at one of the long student tables in the spacious, open plan Maromsaesc Cafeteria, answering her questions about what had happened to Kaden earlier that morning at the Marom rave. Brandi had left the Marom rave early telling her friends that she felt tired and wanted to get some rest before the first week of classes commenced. This meant that she had missed the drama that had occurred later on. Brandi moved her fried egg to the side of her plate and placed two slices of cheese on her white buttered toast instead.

"How did the barbecue switch on by itself? Something doesn't sound right." Brandi observed, biting into her cheese and toast sandwich. Then, leaning in closer to Sentira and whispering into her left ear, Brandi said. "The human OBR's probably had something to do with it."

Sentira made a quick grimace expression.

"Don't tell me you're one of those people who believe all the old movies about robots taking over humanity?" Sentira replied her face returning to a calm expression.

She took a sip of her warm English tea. So many people had been brainwashed by movies of robots taking over the world, that it had taken 50 years from mass production of OBR's and Human OBR's for them to be introduced into mainstream society, which had happened only in recent years.

"I know some of the OBR technology needs improvement though, like the Hover Cab OBR's." Sentira said remembering how sometimes her OBR Hover Cab driver would get lost after she had instructed it of her desired destination. She preferred the OBR's to the Human OBR's but this was due to a cosmetic preference. Sentira just liked to remember that it was a robot she was interacting with and not a human however she wasn't scared or intimidated by the Human OBR's. Neither did she believe in any of the robot-takeover conspiracy theories that came about due to people's fears exasperated by the media oftentimes.

"Ok...think what you like." Brandi replied dismissively using a knife and fork to cut the fried egg on her plate into smaller pieces. Another female student to the left of Brandi had overheard their conversation and joined in.

"The barbecues were turned off by midnight." said the female student. "That's the OBR's job."

"See!" Brandi exclaimed turning to Sentira and back again to the woman on her left. "The OBR left it on!"

Before Sentira could respond back, there was a loud announcement over virtual speakers coming from all four corners of the Maromsaesc Cafeteria's high ceiling. The high ceiling in the Cafeteria was visually impressive to look at. It had been imaginatively decorated with illustrative artworks created by famous voice hearers and people who have seen visions, throughout modern history.

"The Maromsaesc Cafeteria will be closing in 10 minutes." said an OBR voice clearly from the virtual speakers. Most of the students who had been sitting down or standing around in the Cafeteria started to gradually leave to go to their first year one classes.

Sentira and Brandi left their trays on the table and exited the Cafeteria together to find their way to another block of buildings at the university where the first Meditation class was to be taught.

Upon arrival outside the virtual security door (clearly marked in virtual writing Meditation. Team 3), Sentira and Brandi waited for the Applerishin security to scan them from top to bottom before allowing entry to the classroom. Inside the Meditation classroom at a distance were transparent Yoga mats separated from each other on a soft light purple carpet. There was a student changing room area immediately to the right where Sentira, Brandi and other students could remove their footwear to be barefoot or wear some other comfortable footwear. Sentira and Brandi found places on the transparent mats. Both had opted to be barefoot.

The Meditation tutor, Miss Jane Garrison, was a 5'8 young Indian woman in her 20's with long black hair in a ponytail on top of her head. She wore an all grey leotard and was barefoot like some of her students. Her face was calm and expectant.

"All right, everyone settle down." Miss Garrison said loudly. The students quietened. "My name is Miss Jane Garrison. I will be your Meditation teacher for the Autumn Term of Year 1 studies towards your Professional Development degree for people who hear voices and see visions. I am a qualified Meditation teacher. I graduated with the highest honours from Chero Coast University with a Masters in Meditation." Miss Garrison paused as if waiting for applause from the Team 3 students. None came, so Miss Garrison continued.

"Ok. I'll just remind you all that there are fire exit virtual doors at either end of this Meditation class. If the fire alarm goes off you are to leave your mats and any personal items in the changing rooms and exit the class straight away. Is that clear to everyone?" Miss Garrison firmly reminded the students.

Some of the students replied "yes" or "yeah" in response to her question.

"Good. Now, roll call time!" Miss Garrison said smiling for the first time at the students. "I want you one at a time to introduce yourselves to everyone by saying your name and what you think meditation is, in your own words. Starting with you." Miss Garrison pointed at Perianne sitting in the front row wearing a cream leotard and showing perfectly manicured feet.

"Hey everyone, my name is Perianne Saint. Meditation is a vitally essential mental exercise, which focuses on a person's breathing while sometimes repeating a mantra. Meditation is for purposes of relaxation, recuperation and/or to achieve heightened spiritual awareness." Perianne explained.

"My name is Annchi Kang. Meditation is…to chill, to rest, to breathe slow and deep in a meditative state of being." Annchi said.

"Meditation is… Oh…Hi Team 3, my name is Bataar Dabrai. Meditation is the art of being one with oneself in peace and harmony." Bataar, a strong, well built Indian and Chinese man said.

"I'm Cahya Anthri, hi. Meditation is a where time stands still but… voices can interrupt whenever they feel like it." replied Cahya, a plump, curvy white woman with short natural ginger-red hair. Some of the other Team 3 students laughed while others didn't.

"One of the meditations I will teach you in the upcoming weeks," Miss Garrison interrupted the students laughter. "…will allow you to enter a deeper level of your subconscious mind where I am hopeful, you will be able to gain more control over when the voices speak around you. "Ok, you may continue." Miss Garrison looked at a slim Indian man on a transparent mat close by Cahya's mat.

"Advik Chandran. Hello, hello." Advik paused as if trying to remember what he was supposed to say next. "Oh, Meditation is being silent to clear your mind fully." Advik finally answered. He spoke to the air around him and said firmly. "Be quiet I'm in class!"

Miss Garrison moved on to the next student sitting nearby Advik, and the students answered her by saying their name and what they thought meditation was. Other students spoke to the air around them at various times during their introductions. When it was Sentira's turn to speak, Sentira adjusted her posture and spoke clearly and confidently.

"Hi everyone! My name is Sentira Cagney, Team 3 Maromsaesc Student. I believe that Meditation enables the person to remember the peace they hold within and this can be done anywhere, anytime and anyplace. You just need to quiet your mind." Sentira said.

Miss Garrison moved onto the next person sitting nearby

Sentira, who was Sentira's roommate Brandi.

"Hey all, I'm Brandi Ropen. Team 3!" Brandi said waving her arms in the air. "I think meditation is a way to quiet down the voices you hear even if only for a short period of time." Brandi said.

After all the students had finished introducing themselves and giving their opinion of what they thought meditation was, a virtual screen appeared behind Miss Garrison displaying the words.

"Meditation is sensing or being aware of the tranquillity within us at all times."

Miss Jane Garrison.

"Meditation is sensing or being aware of the tranquillity within us at all times." Miss Garrison repeated the words written in a refreshing, glowing green colour on the virtual screen. There were images of trees, mountains, lakes, rivers and flowers behind the words creating a stunning visual display in the dimly lit, Meditation class.

"Now, there are many books, videos, online information, manuals etc. about how to meditate, the correct way to meditate and beginning meditation. Some of you may have already read or watched these but I want you all to start afresh." Miss Garrison said calmly. "This is Meditation class for your Professional degree for people who hear voices and/or see visions. Therefore, the meditation I teach for this course, will be slightly different from any meditation techniques you may have learned before."

Miss Garrison walked over to her Hover mat, which was colourfully decorated in beautiful scenes of nature similar to those on the virtual screen. It was in the front centre of the class and Miss Garrison sat gently down on it with her light brown legs bent underneath her in a relaxed, upright, kneeling position.

"Why don't we have Hover mats?" a blonde haired male student from the back of the classroom said, loud enough for Miss Garrison to hear.

A few other students giggled.

"The Hover mat is for me to be able to manoeuvre around all of you to help you individually." answered Miss Garrison calmly. Then she sped quickly through the lines of transparent mats with students on, to get to be beside the man who had spoken up from the back of the class. "Just like this." Miss Garrison smiled gently at the man with blond hair who looked unimpressed back at her. Miss Garrison sped back off to the front centre of the class again and resumed her teaching.

"Sit in any position that you feel comfortable in. I choose to sit in a kneeling position but this is just my personal choice. You can meditate walking, running, dancing, standing and even talking or singing. It's all about accessing the tranquil mind within." Miss Garrison spoke encouragingly to the students.

The room was not completely silent, often a student would speak to the air around them quietly so as not to disturb the class. Everyone was used to this so when it happened it was mostly overlooked.

"Ok, now you are all in your relaxed position, we can begin. Close your eyes and take a long, slow, deep breath in…and…a long, slow, deep breath out…a long, slow, deep breath in…and…a long, slow, deep breath out…a long, slow deep breath in…and…a long, slow, deep breath out…a long, slow, deep breath in…and…a long, slow, deep breath out. Your breath connects with your tranquillity within. You may hear voices around you…respond with your tranquil mind…I'm not going to tell you how to respond…let your tranquil mind observe without judgement or attachment." said Miss Garrison to the students who were sitting, laying down on their fronts or backs in all different types of positions on their transparent mats.

After a while, Miss Garrison saw that a few students were talking openly to their voices and shook her head. Moving deftly on her Hover mat, Miss Garrison got up close to those students and said to each one "Respond with your tranquil mind, no words." The students opened their eyes at hearing the tutor's voice and nodded in reply before shutting their eyes again to continue the meditation.

Miss Garrison circled around the group of students in the Meditation room a few times observing them all with a serene expression on her face. A complete silence descended on the class for twenty minutes until a student's voice cried out breaking the silence.

"I can't do it. They want to know why I'm not speaking back to them." a muscular brown haired man with a short frame exclaimed loudly and stood up on his mat defiantly.

Miss Garrison was next to him within a few seconds on her Hover mat.

"Return to the breath, close your eyes again one more time…" Miss Garrison reassured the student who still appeared ready to walk out. "Here, sit with me on my mat and I will guide you."

The muscular man looked around anxiously at the virtual security door and back again at Miss Garrison's Hover mat. He decided against leaving the class early and sat down on the opposite end of the Hover mat which extended a bit more to allow more space for him to lay on his back, just as he had been positioned previously on his transparent mat.

"Ok, I want you to close your eyes. Take a long, slow, deep breath in…and…a long, slow, deep breath out…a long, slow, deep breath in…and…a long, slow deep breath out." Miss Garrison said calmly. "You are in control. This is about you and your well-being. This is your life. Nothing can dominate you. You talk to the voices when you say so, when you're ready, when you're free." she paused looking at his reaction before proceeding. "For now, just observe and listen. Your tranquil mind will speak for you. Your relaxed breathing will connect to your tranquil mind. Trust your tranquil mind to speak for you. Breathe long, deep and slow, breathe…long, deep and slow… you're doing good."

Once again, the whole Team 3 class fell completely silent

for a further 20 minutes. The only noise heard being the shuffling noises of some students changing their position on the transparent mats occasionally to get more comfortable.

Perianne adjusted her position for a third time on her transparent mat beneath her. She was very bored. The only thing that sparked her interest had been the man who stood up frustrated that he wasn't supposed to talk back to his voices during meditation. Her heartbeat had raced excitedly wondering if she wouldn't have to do much to ruin Maromsaesc after all.

This university could just die a natural death. Perianne thought to herself opening one of her eyes and turning her face around to see the anxiety-ridden, muscular, short framed man a few rows behind her. *I might not have to do anything.*

Perianne's excitement had fallen however, when the Meditation teacher quickly managed to return the distressed student back to his meditation practice. Perianne frowned inwardly but kept her relaxed expression outwardly.

Sounds of waves rising and falling onto a beach gradually started to grow in volume around the Meditation class. Beginning very quietly at first, then slowly rising in volume to become gradually louder yet gentle. The wave sounds came from the virtual speakers, which were attached to the four corners of the ceiling above the students.

"Keep breathing deeply…a long, slow, deep breath in…and…a long, slow, deep breath out…and…a long, slow, deep breath in…and…a long, slow, deep breath out." Miss Garrison instructed the students in a voice just loud enough to be heard over the sea waves sounds. "You may open your eyes when ready, remember your tranquil mind…remember you can access it at anytime." Miss Garrison said.

The muscular, brown haired man with the short frame opened his eyes and Miss Garrison gracefully moved her arm to the right indicating that he should step down from the Hover mat as the meditation was now complete. The brown haired man whose name was Tom did so, his face now with a more relaxed look than 20 minutes earlier. Tom sat back down on his student transparent mat continuing to take long, slow, deep breaths in and out. Miss Garrison sped her Hover mat back to the front centre of the Meditation class.

"You've all done very well." Miss Garrison said with a soft smile. "The tranquil mind is with you at all times. Now, would anyone like to talk about how they experienced hearing voices while meditating? You can speak freely, this is a non-judgemental university and we respect each other."

There was near silence for a few minutes, only broken by the occasional quiet voice of a student talking to voices in the air around them.

"It was lovely. I saw this dreamy scene of white clouds floating towards me and an image of myself wrapped in a kind of white, thick duvet with lots of nature illustrated pillows, like... like on the virtual screen, and they...were all flying slowly around in different directions. It was Jelitoonaa." Brandi answered the teacher's question in detail.

"I saw the same thing!" Noah said from the back of the class.

"Did you?" Brandi responded turning to look at Noah.

"Yeah!" Noah replied in amazement.

"Wow!" Brandi said back to him with a wink.

Perianne listened to this revelatory discourse with hidden disbelief.

Noah. Don't believe him! He flirts with every student in this university. Perianne thought to herself remembering how Noah had danced with her at the Marom rave, showed interest in her, and then wandered off to dance and flirt with other students both male and female.

"This is your tranquil mind showing you images. There is no need to label them, define them, understand them or do anything with them. Let them be as they are." Miss Garrison kindly explained to Brandi and Noah. "Anymore experiences during meditation that anyone would like to share?" Miss Garrison repeated, her eyes looking keenly from left to right at each individual student. Again, there was a short silence before anyone spoke up in reply to the Meditation tutor.

"The voices of two elderly men that I hear most of the time shouting around me got quieter, the longer I meditated." Cahya explained. "I usually shout back at them." Cahya laughed. "When I'm on my own and won't p*... I mean annoy my family." she finished grinning.

A handful of students laughed along with her.

Perianne didn't believe a word Cahya said about the meditation making the voices she heard quieter; she didn't trust what was said by any person in this mad institution.

Perianne had continued to hear conversations in the air around her during the 40 or so minutes she had been meditating. Her voices didn't get quieter. They stopped for a while before another one started. Perianne knew this could happen for a while until she spoke back to them firmly either in her mind or quietly to the air around her. She allowed them to talk only to prove to herself that the teacher's theories at Maromsaesc were all useless.

The voices I hear are different. Perianne quickly reassured herself. *I have more control and I'm not mentally ill or dangerous.* She thought dismissing the tiny speck of worry that was attempting to take seed in her mind.

She further replaced her tiny fear by remembering stories about her mother Arida, Aunty Dr. Joan Dedrick, Uncle Dr. Robert and the rest of the Dedrick family. She remembered all the happy stories of the rich lifestyles and powerful Psychiatry practices her family had previously owned worldwide, before the R v Caulfied 2054 case had destroyed it all...and...caused her mother to kill herself. Perianne felt rising anger bubbling inside her again like an easily ignited fireplace that took only a split second to rage red flames of burning hot heat. She took a deep breath in and out to quench the fire within which threatened to reveal who she really was. She was Aridaperianne Dedrick, daughter of the gifted, highly intelligent Psychiatrist, Dr.Arida Dedrick. She belonged to one of the most successful, powerful and talented billionaire line of Psychiatrists in medical history and…one day…those billions would return. Perianne lifted her chin higher and sat up taller on her transparent mat in the lotus position. Then she relaxed into a casual knees bent to the side look.

I have to keep undercover. Blend in. Perianne took another slow, long, deep breath in and a slow, long, deep breath out as she had just learned from the Meditation teacher, Miss Garrison.

"The voices around you can become quieter, they can speak louder, perhaps speak at the same time." Miss Garrison explained to the students. "You can hear animal sounds, sounds of nature, crashing, thunder, screams, yells, laughter, crying." she paused gathering the students reactions to her words.

The Team 3 students were listening quietly and patiently. Miss Garrison continued.

"What I'm trying to teach you is that whatever you hear, you can access your tranquil mind to be at peace with it. The voices are expressing their experience for their purpose, you can choose whether or not you want to be involved in it or not." Miss Garrison said wisely.

"It's not that easy!" Tom shouted, some distance away from Miss Garrison, his expression defiant.

"Things that are worthwhile are not often easy at the beginning." Miss Garrison answered Tom. "I assure all of you that if you keep up and maintain your practice of meditation… of accessing your tranquil mind and being aware that it is within you every second of your life. Soon you will find you can be tranquil, not only with the voices and sounds that you hear but with your emotions too. Meditation will benefit your overall well-being."

"When is it our break Jane?" Tom replied to Miss Garrison assertively.

"Yes, ok, break for 15 minutes then come back at 11:20am." Miss Garrison said quickly stepping off her Hover mat and walking to her brown leather shoulder bag in the front right hand corner of the room. She took out a clear bottle of white liquid and took a gulp of it.

The Team 3 students began to talk to each other and their voices. Some students chose to remain sitting on their transparent mats. Some students went towards the changing room so as to replace their footwear before going outside.

Perianne chose to go outside with Annchi and Cahya in tow. They walked together through the long student corridor passing by many other virtual security doors with the names of each class printed in virtual writing on the outside. Sometimes students would look up and talk about the famous voice hearer or another influential person who saw visions, highlighted in gold virtual frames on the cream coloured walls.

"I'm inspired. Are you inspired?" Cahya said to Perianne who was staring at the writing under the photo of a woman called Kannika Hanna. Kannika Hanna, (according to the written description) was the first voice hearer to be employed as a teacher at the Maromsaesc University.

"I'm inspired to smoke" Annchi replied watchfully searching the corridor for a virtual smokers-extraction fan, so she could activate it with her fingerprint and smoke her cannabis cigarette. Annchi's eyes soon found one nearby and hurriedly activated it before lighting a joint.

In 2070 Britain, smoking any type of cigarette is permitted everywhere, dependant upon the requirement that the smoker had to activate a virtual smokers extraction fan and smoke next to it. If the owner of the establishment did not however install any virtual smokers-extraction fans, then the person could not smoke on their premises. There were protests throughout Summer 2060 about the virtual smokers-extraction fans. Many people blamed the new invention as the main cause of the high rise in Cancer patients in 2051 to present day. At the same time, there were protests about large organisations choosing not to install the controversial fans, as severely limiting and hindering those who needed to smoke cannabis for serious medical conditions. Many people could not work due to their workplace not having virtual smokers-extraction fans, even though they were capable of doing the job. The debate about the virtual smokers-extraction fans. Still remained unresolved today.

Annchi puffed away on her joint leaning with her back against the wall casually and her right leg bent at the knee. The virtual smokers-extraction fan emitted a ray of grey light continuously on Annchi's joint. Any excess smoke nearby was being pulled into the grey coloured ray and up through the grey ray all the way into the virtual smokers-extraction fan.

"Oh look! Here's a copy of the Judgement from the R v Caulfied 2054 case that abolished that medical practice...what was it called...?" Cahya exclaimed scanning the small print on the gold and silver virtual framed sheet of written information.

"Psychiatray, psychiatrick,...psyc...I can't read it, it's so small." Cahya squinted her eyes and peered more closely at the writing in the virtual gold and silver frame.

"Psychiatry." Perianne said before she could stop herself.

"Yeah, psychia...psychiatry...." Cahya replied. "They have that word written so small compared to the other words, I can just about see it."

Perianne felt an instant dislike of Cahya.

"It's going on too deep now, I don't want to remember the horror that was done to people like us before the R v Caulfied 2054 case was won. It makes me sick." Cahya said to Perianne with a worried expression.

Annchi kept smoking a short distance away next to the virtual smokers-extraction fan.

Perianne didn't reply straightaway and pretended to be reading over the R v Caulfied 2054 judgement information on the virtual gold and silver frame with phoney interest. She was tempted to say what she really felt about the R v Caulfied 2054 case, to say how it wasn't fair that all psychiatry had to be abolished worldwide because of the actions of the Caulfied worldwide Psychiatry practices. She wanted to tell Cahya that she didn't know anything about Psychiatry and how it had helped people like her in the past live longer, more productive lives with their voices and visions. Psychiatry wasn't all bad like the R v Caulfied 2054 case had claimed it to be.

Why do people forget that there are two sides to every story? Psychiatry has done more good than the alleged damage. Perianne thought passionately to herself.

"Don't read it then." Perianne eventually answered Cahya, quickly adding. "It's too disturbing to read." in an after attempt to soften her first response.

Cahya appeared not to notice the tension in Perianne's voice and continued on.

"Yeah it is." Cahya replied. "So what do you think of the meditation class so far?" Cahya said changing the subject. A hopeful gentle smile returning to her rounded cheeks.

Perianne didn't feel like talking about the meditation class anymore. She was starting to feel embarrassed that she was even at Maromsaesc and irritated at having to act friendly towards the mad people that had destroyed her family's billion pound psychiatry practices worldwide.

Pick up the keys to the truck, arrive at 10:30am, destination Pelargonium. a loud elderly woman's voice said next to Perianne's right ear.

"Shut up!" Perianne mouthed silently to the air on her right hand side.

Cahya noticed Perianne doing this and smiled at her.

Perianne faked a smile back.

She thinks I'm like her. Perianne thought in disgust. She walked away to a Maromsaesc student food & drink virtual vending machine and placed her hand on the sensor to confirm her identification before ordering a coffee by speaking her request to it. A large coffee was dispensed and Perianne sipped it slowly while half listening to Cahya talking about voice hearing and the classes she was looking forward to that week. The large coffee soothed Perianne.

Sentira was still in the Meditation class laying on her back with her knees bent on one of the student transparent mats.

She had the familiar feeling of being in a dream.

I'm really here...at Maromsaesc University. Dreams do come true. Sentira thought passionately to herself. *If I have kids they will study here, and my grandkid's and great grandkid's probably too.*

"Be careful!" a teenage boy's voice whispered into Sentira's left ear.

Sentira frowned. She didn't recognise this voice. She preferred when she heard the regular, familiar voices of Rhyle, Gina, Louis and Olamide.

"Be careful of who?" Sentira said quietly to the air on her left hand side.

There was no answer.

"Gina, are you there?" Sentira quietly called the name of Gina.

Gina did not answer.

At that point, other students began to re-enter the Meditation class and Miss Garrison took her place again on her Hover mat in the front centre of the room.

"Ok. Virtual security says you're all present." Miss Garrison spoke quietly to herself. Then, looking up at the Team 3 students, she took a long, slow, deep breath in and out. "Meditation class is now in session. Quiet please!" Miss Garrison ordered the class firmly but gently.

The students gradually stopped talking with only a few quietly still speaking, to communicate to the voices they heard around them.

"Now that you know how to access your tranquil mind, I would like you to try talking to your voices with tranquil communication. You don't always have to respond verbally you can also respond mentally, which I know some of you do already." Miss Garrison explained.

"I can do that." Sentira said out loud enthusiastically. "I mean, I can talk verbally and mentally to my voices. Sometimes they listen, sometimes they don't." Sentira finished.

"Good. Can anyone else speak to their voices through mental communication?" Miss Garrison questioned the students. Half of the students put their hands up and the other half didn't.

"How can I speak in my mind to voices, they won't be able to hear me?" Tom asked from the second from back row.

"How do you know they can't hear you when you use mental communication?" Miss Garrison inquired.

"They get angry and want to know why I'm not speaking back to them." Tom replied sounding irritated.

"Ok. The more you practice communication with your tranquil mind… very soon they will hear you and be as calm as you are." Miss Garrison answered self-assuredly.

Tom looked like he wanted to say something else but instead he stood up and started walking grouchily towards the changing area, grabbing his sports bag and out through the virtual security door.

"Do you want me to go after him?" Perianne offered, trying not to sound too excited at this sudden turn of events in her favour.

Miss Garrison nodded with a relieved smile at Perianne.

"Some students may need more time to find their tranquil mind." Miss Garrison said returning to address the remaining students.

Perianne walked towards the changing room to quickly collect her bag and put on her trainers. Then she stood gleefully waiting for the virtual security door to scan her allowing her to exit the Meditation room.

Sentira watched the expression on Perianne's face curiously, as she saw her jump up fast to go and find Tom.

She looks happy to get out of class. Sentira observed intuitively.

FIRE BURNS

Two minutes…eight minutes…ten minutes, then twenty eight minutes had passed since Tom had stormed outside of the first Meditation class for Team 3 and Miss Garrison was becoming more concerned. Her usual smooth, serene face had at least two visible worry lines now showing on her forehead. She did not try to go after Tom, choosing instead against the option of leaving the remainder of her class alone during their very first session. So, she did what she considered a good teacher would do in this situation. She tried to keep calm and carry on teaching.

"…and the tranquil mind will ensure you hear your voices clearly and know that your response can be directed from this place of pure, peace and tranquillity. The…" Miss Garrison continued to teach her class.

Most of the Team 3 students appeared unbothered by what had happened earlier and were watching and listening to Miss Garrison. All except Sentira.

Sentira could see the faint lines of worry appear on and off on Miss Garrison's forehead while she was speaking to the class and felt empathy for her. Perianne and Tom had been away from the class for a total of 30 minutes. Sentira felt uncomfortable like as if something bad was going to happen but she didn't know when, where or what it was.

"Go, Sent..ira, Sen…ira." an unfamiliar toddler's voice gurgled next to Sentira's right ear.

"Sen…ira, Sen…ira, Go." another strange new toddler's voice gurgled next to Sentira's left ear.

"Jane." Sentira waved her right arm and hand in the air to get Miss Garrison's attention.

Miss Garrison stopped speaking and gently nodded her head slightly in Sentira's direction.

"Jane, sorry to interrupt your teaching, can I go and see

where Tom and Perianne are? They've been gone for 32 minutes. I think they might have got lost." Sentira asked Miss Garrison.

Miss Garrison hesitated and looked like she was deep in thought. Sentira instantly regretted saying that she thought Tom and Perianne were lost, as now Miss Garrison would probably worry that she too would get lost in the large university grounds. Sentira waited patiently for Miss Garrison to give her permission to leave the Meditation room. It seemed as if Miss Garrison was meditating on what to do next with her eyes open.

2 minutes passed by.

Sentira heard a few of the students behind her whispering that Miss Garrison had fallen into a wide-awake trance. Other students seemed bored and began to start conversations with their voices in the air around them.

"Jane?" Sentira called Miss Garrison's first name again.

This time, a light seemed to go on behind Miss Garrison's brown eyes and she opened her mouth to reply to Sentira.

"Yes, thank you. Please inform Tom that I will be contacting him after class to discuss his views and I am very sorry but...I cannot leave my students alone in class on their first day." Miss Garrison kindly explained to Sentira, regaining her earlier momentum. Miss Garrison looked around the Team 3 students, her worry lines fading into her usual clear, calm and serene look. "Ok, does anyone have any questions about accessing the tranquil mind before class finishes soon?" she continued.

Sentira stood up, waved at Brandi, collected her cream and red shoulder bag from the Student changing room and replaced her white with orange lines canvas shoes to her feet. Sentira stood by the Applerishin virtual security door waiting for it to scan her up and down so she could exit the Meditation room.

Once outside, Sentira looked up and down both directions of the long corridor. The Meditation class was situated close to the centre of the corridor. The corridor was full of virtual security doors, virtual gold frames of famous voice hearers and people who see visions (including written articles about them) and some students, OBR's and human OBR's walking about. Sentira couldn't see anyone that looked like Tom or Perianne.

Where are they? Sentira thought to herself. She walked down one end of the corridor and back down again in the same direction from which she had came.

Still nothing.

More students began to come out of the virtual security doors. It was midday, student lunch break. Sentira quickly walked along the corridor and pressed down on the virtual lift sensor to call a lift so she could get to the ground floor. The virtual lift arrived and Sentira stepped in, spoke her destination and waited patiently for the virtual doors to open again indicating that she was on the ground floor.

On the ground floor, there was a virtual student reception desk equipped to deal with all queries from students, staff or visitors situated close by the virtual lifts. Sentira made her way towards it, manoeuvring through a group of students who were standing around talking to each other and the air around them. The virtual reception desk was managed by OBR's and human OBR's. A human OBR was ready to help as soon as Sentira reached the edge of the virtual nature scene inspired, semi circle shaped reception desk.

"Welcome to Maromsaesc Student study block. How can I assist you today?" a human OBR said with a monotone voice.

"Did you see students Tom Puffint and Perianne Saint in the student building and where they went to? Sentira questioned the Human OBR.

"I am not authorized to inform you Miss Sentira Cagney, of the precise location of Tom Puffint and Perianne Saint. Please return again with the correct authorisation. Thank you. Enjoy your day!" the Human OBR smiled an emotion lacking smile and stared at Sentira as if waiting for her to walk off.

"Ok." Sentira replied disappointed. She turned around to

explore the student ground floor. There were transparent virtual walls, statues of famous voice hearers and people who saw visions in history. There were the usual virtual smokers-extraction fans, virtual vending machines, toilets, virtual fire exits and also a very large indoor park area.

The indoor park in this Student Learning Block contained real trees, a variety of flowers, green grass, a small lake with ducks on it, and a small waterfall powered by Applerishin technology. Sentira walked around in awe looking at the wonder of indoor nature as many other students did the same.

After twenty minutes of searching around the Maromsaesc indoor park area, Sentira forgot about looking for Tom and Perianne. Sentira sat on a hilly part of the grass nearby the waterfall, watching the water fall and hit the lake below with bubbling splashes descending outward in spreading ripples of circular motion.

Jelitoonaa. Sentira thought in a dream like state.

"Go." a male toddler's voice gurgled next to Sentira's right ear.

"Sen...ira...Go." a female toddler's voice gurgled next to Sentira's left ear.

Sentira sighed and reluctantly stood up.

Go where? Sentira tried to mentally communicate with the toddler's voices around her ears, which continued to repeat the same words all around her.

The babies voices did not answer her.

Sentira remembered what Miss Garrison had said about accessing her tranquil mind and took a few slow, long deep breaths in and out while walking towards the virtual security main exit doors.

Outside of the student learning block, Sentira made her way through virtual pathways between various student buildings, passing many other students and teachers along the way. The Maromsaesc University buildings were created from a mix of virtual and other building materials with some transparent or nature scenes inspired designs that were beautifully crafted. Small student Hover vehicles carried disabled students or those who for any reason chose not to walk along the transparent and nature inspiring virtual footpaths.

Sentira stepped quickly to the right as she saw one of these compact student hover vehicles approaching at speed in her direction. She knew they were programmed to re-direct or stop if they came within a metre of any human being, but it made good sense to her to step out of the way anyway, just in case.

With only 10 minutes left of the student lunch break, Sentira entered the Maromsaesc Cafeteria and peered around the large student dining area. There was still no sign of Tom and Perianne. Sentira took a tray from a Human OBR waiting to serve the students and picked up a ham with lettuce sandwich, a banana and a bottle of freshly squeezed orange juice. As she went to pay the Human OBR (at the end of the self-service food section) she saw the familiar red-ginger, wavy hair of Perianne and the natural smooth, straight brown hair of Tom. Both were exiting the Cafeteria through temporarily opened virtual security doors.

Oh well. Sentira thought to herself while taking a food bag from the Human OBR containing her purchases, and placing it in her shoulder bag.

She quickly jogged over to the virtual security exit of the Student Cafeteria to get to her next class. The next class was Sports class. Realising that she was running a little late to get over to the Gym block for Team 3 (located on the opposite side of the University from where she was), Sentira stepped into a waiting Student Hover Vehicle in the corridor outside the Cafeteria.

"Team 3, Gym block." Sentira instructed the Hover vehicle.

Upon sensing her voice command, the Student Hover vehicle emitted a ray of blue light which scanned Sentira to confirm her identity. Her identity confirmed, the Hover vehicle next swiftly transported Sentira on a 5 minute journey to the Gym block where Team 3 were to meet for their first Sports class.

Arriving at the Gym block, Sentira stepped out of the Hover vehicle and the transparent door closed automatically behind her. She was halfway towards the Gym block entrance when she realised she had forgotten her cream and red shoulder bag with her food and virtual mobile. So, Sentira switched direction and turned back to the Student Hover vehicle to retrieve her bag. The Student Hover vehicle opened its transparent door again and Sentira took her bag from the floor where she had left it.

It didn't scan me this time and... why didn't the sensor let me know my bag was still in there? Sentira wondered to herself as she jogged towards the Gym block past two large Game courts.

Inside the virtual reception area of the Gym block, Sentira made her way to the student changing area. In the student changing area, she got dressed into a grey with black stripes at the sides, fitted sleeveless crop top and matching gym shorts. There was no one else in the changing room. Sentira took out her virtual mobile from her bag. The time was 1:05pm.

Am I the only one who's a little bit late? Sentira worried to herself.

Then, Sentira remembered that all the students were supposed to get to their Sports classes ten minutes early. This was for the students to be allocated to their chosen Sport beforehand so as to gain the full 1 hour benefit of an exercise of their choice. After the Sports hour finished, there would be precisely 15 minutes for the students to shower, get changed and make their way to the next class. Luckily, the next class was conveniently situated nearby the Gym block.

Sentira slipped back on her white with orange lines canvas shoes and reduced her virtual mobile back into a flat, small, orange square shape by voice command. She watched it attach to the side of her sports shorts before moving on.

Sentira entered the Team 3 gym full of energy. Some of the 25 Team 3 students were using the virtual exercise machines and others were leaving the gym through another virtual door to use the Games courts outside. Sentira could see Brandi walking briskly on a colourful nature inspired virtual treadmill. Brandi waved over at Sentira who waved back. Sentira could see Noah too and Craig (who had invited them to the Marom rave last night) lifting weights in another corner of the large student gym.

Sentira checked the virtual Sports list board behind her as a Human OBR watched her. There were Human OBR's all over the gym helping the students and supervising. Sentira re-read the list of Sports on the virtual Sports board. There were many different options. Sentira chose to go outside in the Games Court and walked to one of the virtual exits to go outside again. Sentira hoped she would see Tom and find out how he was doing.

Outside in one of the Games Courts, Perianne jumped in the air to receive the basketball that had just been thrown to her. She dribbled the ball easily dodging other students, getting the ball through the hoop scoring a three pointer. Perianne felt ecstatic as she ran back down the basketball court to try to get the ball back from the opposition. Earlier, she had a very long talk with Tom, which lasted throughout lunch break. Keeping up the role of Perianne Saint, she had empathised with him and encouraged him to keep trying to find his tranquil mind, reassuring him that he would be able to have more control over his voices soon. She had told him to "be patient and trust the teachers." Yet, inside Perianne's mind, she was overjoyed that there were already two failures at Maromsaesc by day one of classes.

The two clear failures that Perianne observed were the health and safety issues with the Human OBR operated barbecues and the second was that the Meditation class was not helping the students handle their voices. Kaden was in hospital with serious burn injuries to his arm and Tom had a fiery temper and stubbornness that Perianne knew would help her purpose in the future. Even when she was explaining to him the ways in which meditation could help him, he persisted in responding sarcastically. Tom only seemed to calm down after he had eaten 4 sausages, chips with beans (from the Student Cafeteria) and drank a chocolate milkshake.

Maybe he has low blood sugar as well as psychosis. Perianne mused to herself.

When Tom had stopped his sarcasm about the Meditation class, he had told Perianne that he never wanted to attend Maromsaesc. He explained that he had always found hearing voices to be f***ing sh**. He relayed a story about how he had got in a fight, which wasn't his fault with one of the teachers at his former school. The female teacher had been making jokes about the voices he heard which was illegal for her to do so Tom had punched her in the face. Unfortunately, the dispute ended up in a courtroom. The judge had ruled that either he would go to a youth detention centre for voice hearers and people who see visions for 3 years, or he could attend Maromsaesc University to study and learn to control his anger under supervision. Tom's parents had been very relieved that their son was given a choice and credited the judge's leniency with the work of a brilliant lawyer who had spoke up in defence of their son's behaviour in Court. They had insisted to Tom that Maromsaesc University would be his best option and Tom had reluctantly agreed.

Perianne listened to all the information that Tom was telling her and noted in her mind that there were criminals attending Maromsaesc. She wondered how many more students had criminal backgrounds and because of a delusional judge got offered a place at Maromsaesc, thinking this would change them. Perianne decided to do a background search on all the Team 3 students using her advanced virtual mobile features later that evening...

Perianne jumped in the air and caught the basketball again for a second time. She dribbled it expertly down the court, just the same as before and scored a two-pointer goal by getting the ball through the hoop on her first attempt. Perianne smiled at her teammates while running to get the ball back again.

They can't play basketball. If I wasn't here... Perianne

thought to herself.

"Five loaves of bread, thank you." a female voice of a middle aged woman shouted loudly in the air behind Perianne.

Perianne stopped dribbling the basketball she had just got from an opposing player. Then she frowned in dismay as the same opposing player regained control of the basketball from her.

No! Perianne thought and ran alongside the opposing player looking for an opportunity to steal the ball back from him. The opposing player was Bataar who grinned while dribbling the ball cleverly past Perianne's teammates where he scored a three pointer by getting the ball through the hoop. Perianne ignored the voices and concentrated on the basketball game. The voices continued to chatter around her, however, with no signs of stopping.

"Five pennies for you." a young male voice said around Perianne's left ear.

"For five loaves of bread!" a middle aged female voice replied.

"Five loaves is more than enough for one lady." a young male voice answered back near Perianne's right ear.

"Five loaves…Do you know I have eight little ones to feed." a middle aged female voice said.

"Do you know there's a war going on? You're selfish." a young male voice retorted back beside Perianne's left ear.

Perianne ignored the voices around her and caught the ball passed from another team player. She bounced the ball confidently down the court and got the ball through the hoop a third time.

Yes! she thought. *No voices can stop me doing anything I want.* Perianne carried on chasing after the opposing player with the ball.

"Perianne." a man's voice said loudly next to Perianne's right ear.

"Perianne." a woman's voice said loudly next to Perianne's left ear.

Perianne missed a chance to catch the basketball, which was mistakenly thrown within her reach by the opposing side.

Maybe I'll take a break. Perianne thought and said to the rest of her teammates.

"I'm taking a break!"

Perianne saw Sentira sitting nearby on a seat watching the basketball game on the court and shouted over at her.

"You can take my place, I'm getting a drink of water." Perianne shouted at Sentira. She wanted someone to replace her on the court so they didn't stop the game and come over to talk with her.

"Ok." Sentira said and stood up to run and take her place on the basketball court.

Perianne sat down on a wooden bench, a short distance from the sidelines of the basketball court. She mouthed the words "Stop" in three different directions around her.

The voices she had been hearing stopped.

Perianne took a swig of water from a small water bottle, which had been attached to a sports bag around her waist. She waited for her breathing to get back to normal again. While cooling down from playing basketball, she watched the dark brown-skinned black woman with the long, black curly afro hair (styled in a messy ponytail like hers at the back of her head) join in the game. She ran her fingers through her own long, wavy, messy ginger red ponytail. She watched Sentira jump high in the air, catch the ball and bounce it skilfully down the court scoring a three-pointer goal by getting the ball ably through the hoop. Perianne lifted her small water bottle to her mouth again to take another swig, but it was empty.

"Applerishin mobile open." Perianne said to the small square shape attached to the right side of her white leggings. The Applerishin starting device sprang up into a virtual mobile and a ray of pale yellow light scanned Perianne from top to bottom.

"Good afternoon Miss Perianne Saint, how can I assist you?" said Perianne's virtual mobile.

"Search all UK news for reports of Kaden Sallow and Maromsaesc University for voice hearers and people who see visions." Perianne said quietly, still watching how Sentira played basketball.

Her basketball team was still in the lead. Perianne activated her virtual sound device by pressing her finger on an app on her mobile. The virtual sound device caused a yellow coloured glow around Perianne's ears and the sound from her virtual mobile could now be heard inside her ears.

"There are news reports about Mr Kaden Sallow student at Maromsaesc University dated present day on all news channels. Which News channel's report would you like to hear Perianne?" asked a pre-programmed male voice from Perianne's virtual mobile.

"Play News report from BN 2070 channel." Perianne said to her virtual mobile.

"Playing news report from BN 2070 dated Monday, 29th September 2070 9:00am...Second degree deep burns scald Maromsaesc student at illegal student rave! Maromsaesc student Kaden Sallow 19, suffered serious, agonising second degree burns to his left arm at an illegal party held by students of the newly opened Maromsaesc University. The Maromsaesc University is a Professional university designed specifically for the Professional development of voice hearers and people who see visions.
The terrifying accident occurred at around 2:30am this morning when over 100 students attended the Marom rave in the Maromsaesc university grounds by the Maromsaesc lake. Professor Willemina Zantend (Head of the Maromsaesc University) has yet to give a formal statement about the depth of Kaden Sallow's arm injuries and there has been no reply to our request for more details about the alleged illegal Marom rave."

Perianne listened to the news report intently, her ears still glowing yellow from the virtual sound device being in use.

"The Pelargonium main hospital has also refused to comment." the male reporter's voice carried on speaking through the virtual sound device. "However, an anonymous insider who was present at the Marom Rave said that he heard screams of excruciating pain and agony coming from Kaden Sallow when he moved away from a Human OBR (operated) barbecue. Our anonymous insider said that Kaden's left arm was visibly red, swollen and blistered. We contacted the Human OBR Pelargonium company about the safety of their Human OBR barbecues but have not received a response so far. The family of Kaden Sallow have not yet replied to our request for updates on this story. The BN 2070 channel would like to wish Mr Kaden Sallow a quick recovery and hope that he is well enough to return to his studies at Maromsaesc University as soon as possible."

"In the meantime, there are many questions that must be answered for the safety of all… How did a Human OBR barbecue cause so much pain to a living person? Should all Human OBR barbecues be retracted amid these new valid safety concerns? What does this tell us about our reliance on Human OBR's to do the jobs that previously were done overall by living persons? And why… were students at the controversial Maromsaesc University in attendance at an illegal rave without supervision by staff at Maromsaesc? All these questions and more, we at BN 2070 channel hope to answer within the next few days as this new unfolding story develops and we are permitted access to obtain more vitally important information."

"Our next major news headlines involves the over-protective OBR zoo keeper who…"

Perianne touched her virtual mobile screen to end the BN 2070 channel broadcast and the yellow glow also disappeared from around both her ears. Her face remained calm as she processed what she had just heard. She had learned that Kaden was at the Pelargonium hospital. Professor Willemina Zantend had refused to comment on what happened at the Marom rave,

Human OBR (operated) barbecues maybe retracted…

*Illegal rave…*Perianne mused to herself, thinking that even though this was a good start towards her purpose of sabotaging Maromsaesc, it was nowhere near enough controversy.

Off to a good start! Perianne reassured herself satisfactorily. *And it's only the first day here.* She further reflected. *More must go very wrong at this mad uni.*

Just like many of the news reports of 2070, there were errors in the reporting of events. The Marom rave was not illegal. In fact, the teachers at Maromsaesc had helped organise it so it would be held safely to ensure a good time for all. It was carefully designed as a Welcome to Maromsaesc 2070! party for all the students to socialise and enjoy the evening before their studies commenced. Students, Craig and Noah had written on their application forms of their passion for the "Jelitoonaa" music (the most popular music of 2070) so they were the natural choice to advise and help out with the Marom rave. It was all done with the consent of not only the staff at Maromsaesc but approved by Professor Willemina Zantend.

Perianne continue to watch the basketball teams play and refused to join back in when Sentira asked if she wanted to. She didn't want to play any more Basketball with the "freaks". Her mind raced with hundreds of ideas on how to end the Maromsaesc university forever. Perianne had so many ways to sabotage the university spinning around in her head; she was surprised that outwardly she appeared so calm and collected. She peered into her virtual mobile mirror and undid her messy ginger-red ponytail, shaking her long waves from left to right. She missed her real blonde, straight hair, hair that was like her mother Arida's hair. Perianne felt the all too familiar heat rising within and around her as she gathered her loose ginger red strands together again in a messy bun at the back of her head.

"Sports session will finish in 10 minutes for Team 3 Maromsaesc students. Our Games Courts are open at all times with Human OBR's and OBR's supervising. Please come again." a Human OBR said in a voice much louder than the average human voice could every possibly attain.

The single Human OBR voice boomed around all the Games Courts in the student Sports area and was as effective as a virtual speaker. Inside the student Gym, the same message was spoken by another Human OBR at exactly the same time as the Human OBR on the Games Court that Sentira and Perianne were playing on. All the Human OBR's and the OBR's had a connection with each other.

Perianne waited for Sentira to walk nearby her so she could talk with her.

"Hey, we won!" Perianne said with as much enthusiasm as she could muster.

"Yes, your team did. I joined at the last minute." Sentira replied downplaying her part in the basketball's team's success. Sentira felt an instant wariness around Perianne so she changed the subject. "How is Tom doing?" she asked.

"You're really good! Are you going to join the Maromsaesc Basketball team? With your athletic frame and height, you'd be Jelitoonaa." Perianne replied ignoring Sentira's question about Tom.

Sentira glanced quizzically at Perianne while they both continued to walk together towards the student Gym and changing room area.

"It's just my first game. I don't know yet." Sentira answered.

"Have you played before? What do you think about Maromsaesc so far? Isn't it Jelitoonaa!" Perianne continued with added emphasis on the word "Jelitoonaa". She had heard this word used by every student she had been around at Maromsaesc and wanted to show Sentira that she was cool like everyone else. This would help her purpose and she would never be discovered as a fraud.

"How is Tom doing after you left the Meditation class to speak to him?" Sentira repeated her earlier question in a kind voice.

Maybe if I ask more gently she will hear me. Sentira thought as she and Perianne reached the student changing room and began to take off their respective sports gear.

She sounds like she's fishing for information about what I said to Tom. Perianne thought.

"Oh, he's fine. I told him that Maromsaesc is a new experience for all us voice hearers and people who see visions so we have to be patient and trust the teachers." Perianne said pulling down her leggings at the same time.

There were virtual borders around each of the students that appeared after a student retrieved his/her items from the high 7 foot tall lockers/changing bays. This way, every student could get changed in privacy but still be able to talk to each other if they wished and were close enough to hear. Applerishin security prevented anyone from entering another person's locker/changing bay and all the virtual borders were dark enough so that a person could not see who was inside.

Sentira didn't answer Perianne.

Is that all? Tom was angry and upset and this girl calmed him down by telling him to be patient and trust the teachers? Sentira thought to herself with a quizzical expression on her face. She continued to get changed.

Perianne exited her locker/changing bay wearing a light orange dress with black sandals.

Sentira exited her locker/changing bay at the same time wearing a light purple dress with black sandals. Both women had taken down their long hair from the ponytail hairstyle, so that it now cascaded around their backs and shoulders, reaching down to their waists.

"What's the next class, Sentira?" Perianne tried again to get Sentira to open up and talk with her.

Sentira felt puzzled. There was something not genuine about this woman and she insisted on talking with her. Luckily for Sentira, Noah walked past and answered Perianne's question before Sentira could think of how to respond.

"Voice communication." Noah said in passing as he walked with Craig to the virtual security doors.

Sentira quickly followed behind them. She wanted to get

away from Perianne and the uneasiness she felt around her. Here she was at Maromsaesc University, the University of her dreams and what could only have been imagined by her grandmother Nanny Lisha. No-one was going to interfere with her studies. She was going to complete Year 1, Year 2 and Year 3 of her Degree for the Professional Development of people who hear voices and see visions and go onto becoming successful in any career she chose after that. She didn't have to like everyone and her instinct told her not to like Perianne.

I'll try to sit near Tom in one of the classes and see if he needs any help. Sentira thought to herself.

Perianne walked alongside Sentira to the Voice Communication class in the Student learning block next door to the Gym. Neither of them spoke. The men in front of them also did not speak and as they got in the student virtual lift together. Eventually, Noah commented on the silence between all of them.

"Are we all mentally talking to our voices?" Noah said jokingly.

Craig grinned and Sentira giggled.

Perianne smiled.

The Voice Communication class was situated on the first floor but due to an indoor park area (located in every student learning block) the first floor was quite some way higher than the ground floor so the virtual lift was the quickest way to get there.

Virtual technology 2060 had come a long way since its first original idea in 1968. V.T. 2060 tech. enabled everything to be made virtually with the added value of people being able to interact with virtual objects, virtual buildings etc…just the same as they would with the old-fashioned buildings, objects and so on. Sentira, Perianne, Noah and Craig could stand in a virtual lift in 2070, whereas in the year 2000 for example, this was not possible.

Virtual technology 2060 was occasionally intertwined with some of the previous ways of constructing buildings, objects, usually when the designer or manufacturer wanted to save costs. Unless, you had the money to finance it or knew someone who could design virtual equipment, or construct virtual buildings, it was cheaper to pay for the materials used previously in 2018 like wood, brick, stone, etc…Some wealthy people chose to live in the old-style houses to deter thief's from knowing how much money they had. A virtual tech 2060 designed home was often a sign that the owners had huge wealth.

The Maromsaesc University appeared to the outside world as a very rich university with its eclectic mix of virtual and transparent buildings, nature scenes inspired décor, virtual equipment, student hover vehicles, indoor park areas, large Games Courts, beautiful lake, outdoor park areas, Applerishin virtual security and Human OBR/OBR staff. There also still remained an extended area of land left available for further developments and expansion of the University.

Perianne waited for Applerishin Virtual security to scan her before she gained entry to the Voice Communication class. She stood still as her eyes took in the layout of the Voice Communication study room. There were individual virtual nature scenes inspired tables with matching virtual sofas that had changing images of nature scenes. Beautiful images of sandy beaches, forests, flowers, plants, ocean waves, mountains and waterfalls appeared on and off. Even the flooring design was virtual and inspired by scenes of nature. All the students stood around in awe before finding their places to sit down.

All except Perianne.

Is this where all the money stolen from Psychiatry went? Perianne grumbled to herself, before sitting down at a virtual table with her name on it, feeling sick to her stomach.

UNASKED CONTACT

The Voice Communication teacher, Mr Simon Winchester was running late. The Human OBR's reassured the students every 5 minutes that the tutor was delayed and would be with them shortly. In the meantime, the Team 3 students chatted to each other, their voices and occasionally to the Human OBR's standing in the four corners of the room supervising. Perianne talked with Annchi sitting close by her virtual table. She was just about to suggest that they should go to main reception to find out what happened to the Voice Communication teacher, when a slim build, 5'8 white man with low cut dyed blonde hair and a trimmed brown beard and moustache entered the room. Mr Winchester, dressed in dark blue jeans and a crisp white shirt, walked briskly into the classroom. He appeared as if he had been running and was slightly out of breath. He called one of the Human OBR's over to him and talked to her for a while. The Team 3 students waited.

"My apologies everyone! I am sorry that I am late for your very first Voice Communication class here at Maromsaesc University. Unfortunately, I had to attend a staff meeting which ran over time." Mr Winchester explained. "Right, we will begin straight away. Human OBR's say that everyone is present except for Kaden...right, ok...let's begin."

There was a short pause as Mr Winchester spoke to one of the Human OBR's again for a second time. Soon, a large virtual screen appeared (seemingly out of nowhere) from a few metres behind Mr Winchester. On the virtual screen the following virtual words were displayed in front of a moving ocean waves and sandy beach image.

What is Voice Communication?

"What is voice communication?" Mr Winchester asked Team 3 in an inquisitive deep male voice.

All the Team 3 students were quiet for a short while and

then Bataar raised his hand tentatively in the air, along with a few other students. Mr Winchester nodded in Bataar's direction indicating that he could speak.

"Is it when we talk to voices around us that only we can see." Bataar said.

Mr Winchester did not reply but instead nodded at another student to answer the question. The next student to try and answer the original question was Annchi.

"Voice communication is talking back to voices. Communicating with them." Annchi said.

Mr Winchester nodded at yet another student to answer his original question. This time Noah had a try at answering the question.

"Is it when you hear a voice and you speak your own view so you're in charge and not the other way round." Noah said confidently.

Mr Winchester nodded at another Team 3 student to speak. It was Brandi.

"Voice communication is talking with voices." Brandi said sounding bored. She felt sleepy and wasn't sure how long she would be able to stay awake in this class for. She hoped Mr Winchester would finish the class early.

Mr Winchester listened to a few more student responses and then spoke again.

"Those are all very good answers. However, the correct answer is..." Mr Winchester turned to face the virtual screen behind him. Appearing clearly in blue letters in front of images of ever-changing scenes of nature, were written the following words.

Voice Communication (in Voice-hearer studies) is the clear transmission of our thoughts, words and actions to express our truest intentions, so as to be understood accurately by the unknown.

Mr Simon Winchester

Mr Winchester turned back to face the Team 3 students with a triumphant look on his face.

"Voice Communication (in Voice-hearer studies) is the clear transmission of our thoughts, words and actions to express our truest intentions, so as to be understood accurately by the unknown." he repeated enthusiastically.

"Thoughts, actions, words." Noah said out loud to Mr Winchester. "I do that already."

"Me too." Sentira joined in.

"So do I." Brandi said sounding tired.

"Yes, I am aware that most of you have found ways to communicate with your voices already and this is brilliant! But, for the purposes of this degree level course, we are going to learn much more aspects involving Voice communication." Mr Winchester paused for dramatic effect. "With your thoughts, words and actions, do you always get the response you would like from your voices?"

The Team 3 students were silent. Mr Winchester let the silence fill the room for thirty long drawn out seconds before speaking again.

"Ok. Well, the good news is that this class will teach you steps to help you learn how to truly communicate with your voices. I will sometimes also refer to them as the "unknown"… is this ok with everybody?" Mr Winchester raised one eyebrow and turned his head to the side as if listening out for a challenge to his ideas.

None of the students said anything.

"Good." Mr Winchester continued. "At the start of each class I will set a task for you to practice during the lesson and for homework too, along with a written assignment once a week."

Some of the students groaned out loud.

"Don't worry, it's not going to be difficult. You already have everything you need to pass this course. We at Maromsaesc are going to be teaching you valuable self-management skills to a professional level, that's all." Mr Winchester grinned at the group encouragingly. "And you all have my direct contact number to call me if there are any questions." Mr Winchester ended his final sentence with a distinct air of satisfaction.

The Team 3 student's faces were a mix of scepticism, engagement and passivity. Oblivious to this, Mr Winchester proceeded on with the lesson and the remainder of the class went by fairly smoothly with each student practicing one of the three ways of communicating with voices. Using thoughts, words and actions. This was selected by a virtual task board springing up out of the virtual table, guiding the student on what the task would entail.

Perianne reluctantly figured it would be useful to concentrate in this class as she could find out something, which could help her utilise her voices for the purpose of sabotaging Maromsaesc. Sentira seriously tried to focus on her task as best she could; her future career depended on it. Even Tom appeared more calm and focused in this class, happily free to talk to his voices when he wanted to, unlike in the Meditation class.

The alarm rang around the Voice Communication classroom signalling the end of the lesson. The Team 3 students duly got up with their bags to leave when suddenly Bataar exclaimed out loud.

"Brandi's asleep. Mr…Simon." Bataar said to Mr Winchester who was standing near his virtual table.

Mr Winchester's face flushed red. All the staff at Maromsaesc were aware of students who required extra help. Brandi Ropen was one of those students. She had a voice hearing ability that was difficult to handle and she was highly sensitive with it. No known medical cause had been found, for why Brandi could fall asleep at anytime and have dreams of people who had died or were about to die. Mr Winchester knew that Brandi's voices consistently had the reoccurring theme of "serious illness and death" and that this upset Brandi frequently.

Mr Winchester frowned and waved at a Human OBR to come over to Brandi's virtual table. The Human OBR came over and assessed Brandi by checking her pulse and observing her. Then the Human OBR was quickly joined by two medical OBR's, who entered the room within minutes. A medical OBR gently lifted Brandi onto a Hover stretcher where she was then escorted fully asleep out of the Voice Communication classroom.

Perianne watched closely the event being played out in front of her and furrowed her eyebrows.

Brandi needs a qualified psychiatrist. Perianne thought decisively. *She should be in hospital under constant observation.* Perianne firmly believed with strong conviction as she headed outside the Voice Communication classroom with Annchi.

Later that afternoon, dinner in the Maromsaesc Cafeteria for the Year 1 students went by uneventful. The students were mostly excited, hungry, and tired after the first day of their Professional studies so after eating their meals, most quickly exited the Cafeteria to return back to their respective rooms in the halls of residences.

Back at Jay Halls, Perianne and Sentira relaxed separately in different rooms. Sentira, (in room 10) wrote in her virtual journal about ideas she had learned from today's voice hearing classes. Perianne, (in room 25) waited and watched as a Human OBR installed a virtual smokers-extraction fan in a corner of the room (near Annchi's bed) upon her request for them to do so.

*****

The next day, Sentira rubbed her eyes and stretched both her arms above her head. As her eyes slowly got used to the natural light peering through her colourful nature scene inspired curtains, she turned over in her bed lazily. She nearly jumped up in surprise as she saw a Human OBR (with the appearance of a slim, long brown haired, tall white woman) standing in front of her bed glaring down at her. Sentira's eyes instantly opened wide-awake. She glared back at the Human OBR. Robots didn't intimidate her.

"What is it?" Sentira asked frowning at the Human OBR.

"Brandi is awake. She slept for 7 hours, woke up and was given a plate of white rice, tomato gravy, barbecued flavoured chicken drumsticks and cauliflowers. She had a cup of tea with a teaspoon of sugar." the Human OBR said to Sentira.

Sentira's dark brown eyes darted left and right, her initial surprise turning into amusement.

"Er…thanks for letting me know." she replied holding confident eye contact with the robot that had a human guise.

"Contact student medical emergency services whenever you notice Brandi Ropen sleeping for longer than 10 hours at night or during the daytime for longer than 30 minutes. Thank you Sentira Cagney." said the Human OBR before leaving Room 10 through virtual security doors.

Sentira felt relieved that Brandi was ok and could hear her roommate taking a shower in the bathroom. After they had both got dressed and were on their way to the student Cafeteria, Sentira opted to speak about Kaden and the Marom rave, which was on most of the UK news channels.

"Maybe Kaden fell asleep like me and fell onto the Human OBR barbecue which woke him up in severe burning agony." Brandi suggested to Sentira after finding a place in the Cafeteria where both of them could sit down together.

"Could be." Sentira replied biting into her cheese sandwich with lettuce and tomatoes which she had selected from the self-service buffet. There was a short silence between the two women as they ate breakfast then Brandi spoke up.

"So much pain, screaming…fires all over." Brandi said. "I dreamt of fires, lots of them and children screaming…I saw their charred faces, charred bodies." Brandi's expression changed into one of grief and sadness.

Sentira flinched and considered changing the subject back to Kaden again, but she was also in part curious as to the visions and voices that Brandi witnessed.

"Have you ever tried to find out who the people are who die in your dreams or are about to die soon, in real life? You could be a psychic or help grieving families find out how their loved ones died." Sentira said optimistically, hoping for a friendly reply back from Brandi.

Brandi turned her back on Sentira and said, "I want…be happy, I can…be happy…I love fashion …I…design." Brandi's voice shook with nervous tension. "Do you think I want to be crying for the rest of my life every day dealing with relatives of the dying or deceased?" Brandi shook her head disbelievingly, her eyes brimming with tears.

Sentira didn't know what to say. So, she said nothing. For the remainder of the breakfast period, they sat together eating without speaking. Brandi was still too upset to talk about her visions and voices and Sentira decided that she would try not to talk about it again unless Brandi wanted her to.

Outside the Health and Well-being classroom (on day 2 of Year 1 Maromsaesc studies), Perianne waited for the Applerishin virtual security door to disappear to allow her access. Inside the room, she could see that some of the other students were already sitting together in groups of four, at light brown wooden tables and similarly coloured chairs. Perianne's bright green eyes searched the room for Kaden Sallow, Tom Puffint or Brandi Ropen to sit near to. It was only day 2 of the Degree course for the Professional development for people who heard voices or saw visions, but Perianne had already identified three people that could further her purpose. Kaden, however, was nowhere to be seen. Tom was seated at the back of the room with Craig and Noah. There was one empty seat left at their table so Perianne headed in that direction, but then she passed another table with one empty seat. Brandi Ropen was at this table with Sentira and Annchi. Annchi called out to Perianne happily.

"Perianne, I've saved you a seat." Annchi said as Perianne walked by her table.

Perianne grinned widely.

"Annchi, I thought I lost you. You've saved me a seat. Thanks beauty. Jelitoonaa! How's everyone doing?" Perianne asked the other Team 3 students sitting at the wooden table.

"This room isn't as nice as the one yesterday." Brandi said grumpily, ignoring Perianne.

"I think its because they have different budgets for each class. They probably couldn't afford virtual technology in this class." Sentira replied to Brandi.

"I don't like it." Brandi said. "It's plain! Where's the colour and design?"

"They should have got you to decorate it." Sentira said.

"I know." Brandi answered. Brandi wore one of her own fashion designs. It was a light pink jumpsuit made from a mix of cotton, chiffon and silk with bright silver spots indented around her waist area where a belt could have been. From her waist up there were more silver spots outlining her bra area covered with a layer of light pink coloured chiffon material. She wore open toed silver sandals, with her feet manicured in a half pink and half silver pattern. Her loose curly hair dyed half pink on one side hanging just above her left shoulder and her natural brown loose curls in thick braids hanging down touching her right shoulder.

Sentira heard Rhyle and Gina (two of her regular voices) calling her name next to her ears. In her mind, she talked back to them, using mental communication.

"Has anyone tried that "tranquil mind" with voices idea from Jane?" Sentira asked the group at the table, simultaneously trying to use her tranquil mind to respond to Rhyle and Gina who were still calling her name by her ears.

"Sentira." Rhyle said near Sentira's left ear.

"Sentira." Gina said near Sentira's right ear.

"I tried that. It can work." Annchi offered her opinion of using her meditative tranquil mind to communicate with voices.

Perianne grimaced inwardly.

If you're always high, every idea is a good one. Perianne thought to herself. She wanted so badly to tell everyone that they were all mentally ill and that there wasn't a single class at this insane University that could save them. Instead, Perianne's friendly warm (expertly trained) smile remained pleasantly on her face.

"Have you tried it?" Sentira asked Perianne.

Perianne appeared thoughtful for a while, as if pondering

how to answer. She didn't want to sound too over-enthusiastic for any of the ideas that the crazy staff at Maromsaesc taught their students. Yet, she knew, if only to blend in with everyone else that she had to show some interest.

"It worked when I was in class as I noticed I had more control. After class it was more…well…" Perianne said and sighed before continuing on. "I'm trying to use my tranquil mind right now." Perianne dramatically outstretched both her arms on the wooden table, breathing in and out slow, deep, long breaths.

The rest of the group watched her in silence.

Next, Perianne began to mouth the words "Stop" to the air around her, first to the left, to the middle and finally to the right side of her. "Stop talking, I'm in class!" Perianne said dramatically to the air in front of her, nearly appearing as if she was talking to Sentira who sat on the opposite side.

Annchi began laughing loudly and Brandi grinned at Perianne.

"Hates you." an elderly Rhyle said loudly in the air around Sentira's left ear.

"Be careful." a young Gina said loudly in the air around Sentira'a right ear.

Sentira froze in her seat. She felt shocked. She took a few long, slow, deep breaths to calm herself. If it were another voice saying the words "hate you" around her, she probably would have not thought much of it.

Gina, Rhyle, is it Perianne? Sentira communicated mentally with her voices. She hoped that the words were not related to any student in Team 3. Here she was, day 2 of her ecstatically, happily anticipated "Jelitoonaa" Maromsaesc studies, and two of the voices she had grown up with sounded like they were warning her of something.

Was it Perianne Saint that her voices were warning her to "be careful" around?
Sentira mused and waited for one of her regular voices to respond back to her while continuing to breathe in and out

slowly.

Annchi and Brandi were now chatting casually with Perianne, exchanging jokes about the Meditation teacher and "finding your tranquil mind."

Perianne Saint Sentira thought in her mind. She had an uneasy feeling about her since the Marom rave. The quick, unusual, cold sense of foreboding, which persisted since the first time Sentira had seen her, to present day, whenever Sentira was near her. The woman, that she felt in her heart she should not be friends with.

"You will know soon enough. Be patient." Olamide's young and old voice said from behind and in front of Sentira at the same time.

"Hates you." an elderly Rhyle said again.

"Be careful' a young Gina repeated.

"Team 3! Good morning!" a light skinned black woman suddenly announced clearly and assertively from the front of the Health and well-being classroom. "My name is Mrs. Michelle Lear and I'm your Health and well-being teacher for Term 1. I could also be your tutor for other class's in Term 2 and Term 3 but those timetables haven't been written yet."

The Team 3 students quietened down, with only a few still continuing to talk to their voices around them in lowered tones.

"Applerishin security has confirmed that everyone is in attendance except Kaden Sallow. Has anyone had any contact with Kaden to find out how he is?" Mrs Lear inquired.

Perianne waited a while for someone else to speak up before she raised her hand in the air.

"I read in the news that he's at Pelargonium Hospital with second degree burns but I don't know how he's doing today." Perianne said with a concerned expression.

"Ok, thank you. I am aware of the reports on the News Channels. Are any of Kaden's friends in this Team?" Mrs Leah asked the class. The class remained silent, then Perianne spoke again.

"I think he's friends with a woman with short blonde hair and a woman with black curly hair from Team 5. I don't know their names." Perianne answered with a shrug of her shoulders.

"Ok thank you. What's your name?" Mrs Lear asked.

"Perianne Saint." Perianne replied.

"Perianne Saint..." Mrs Lear looked down at her virtual notebook in her hand and touched the screen a few times. "Peri...Oh yes! You're the woman whose quick thinking saved Kaden's burning arm from further injury. Well done!"

Perianne nodded and smiled a gentle smile, which she hoped looked like to everyone as a genuine humble, modest and brave smile.

"For those of you who haven't heard already, Perianne Saint, helped prevent further burn injury to Kaden's arm after he had accidently fell onto the OBR barbecue at the Marom rave. Perianne cleverly guided Kaden to quickly immerse his arm, in cool water for a period of time until the Human OBR medical staff and the Hover ambulance arrived. I think Perianne deserves a round of applause!" Mrs Lear said enthusiastically.

The room burst out into clapping, whistling and cheering. Perianne stood up and took a bow in three different directions and grinned at the students. Sentira clapped quietly, only smiling because of the fact that Perianne's actions did save Kaden's arm, not because she liked Perianne as a person. Annchi and Brandi were cheering loudly and Annchi rose from her seat giving Perianne a big hug. Sentira noticed how Perianne's face winced as Annchi put her arms around her, although the wince was replaced fast with that familiar wide smile Perianne often flashed on and off around herself, other Maromsaesc students and Maromsaesc staff.

Please start the class, Mrs Lear. Sentira thought to herself as the clapping faded down and Mrs Lear spoke again.

"Professor Willemina is in contact with Kaden's family and she will be updating us all on his recovery by the end of this week. So, please do not worry. Human OBR barbecues and OBR barbecues have been retracted from use at Maromsaesc University, in other parts of the country and the world pending an investigation into the safety of these products. I just want to reassure you all that we at Maromsasc University maintain the highest standards of Health and safety. Any accidents that occur are extremely rare. Please read your Health and safety virtual manuals in your rooms at Jay Halls whereby you will also find a list of contact numbers. Now, any questions before I begin today's lesson."

The Team 3 students were quiet again with the exception of a few who were talking to their voices.

"Good. We'll begin. Open your virtual textbooks to page 1 of your Health and well-being Maromsaesc Year 1 course.

Sentira opened her textbook and decided to stop thinking of Perianne and concentrate on learning as much as she could towards her Degree qualification for the Professional Development for people who hear voices and see visions.

Perianne could hear male and female voices around her ears calling her name. She pressed her fingerprint on the virtual pad in front of her on the wooden table to open her virtual textbook and pretended to be focused on the wording on the page. Inside her mind, her thoughts raced with ideas on what to do next.

Brandi is weak, I can see it. Tom hates this university nearly as much as I do, Annchi is weak, Sentira is... Perianne's face winced again as she thought of Sentira's name. *Sentira doesn't like me really; it's obvious, well not yet... I still will find some use out of her.* Perianne plotted in her mind.

The Health and well-being class went by smoothly with no negative occurrences, as did the Sports class and the Confidence & self-esteem class. By dinnertime (early evening at Maromsaesc) Perianne was livid inside but outside she appeared just like any other Team 3 student. She sat with Brandi, Annchi and Sentira and pretended to be busy eating and chewing so she didn't have to talk so much. It had taken a lot of energy today to pretend to be friendly with the "mad" voice hearers and especially to be friendly to Sentira. Brandi Ropen seemed to like to be around her and she had listened to Perianne's jokes throughout the day, sometimes sharing jokes of her own and laughing with her and Annchi. Now and again, Sentira would interrupt the conversation with her tales of what her regular voices had said in the past, but overall Perianne considered that she had been the centre of the small group's attention. She blended in, more than Sentira and this gave Perianne some sense of satisfaction. After dinner, the group of four Team 3 students went back to their separate jointly shared rooms.

At 2:10am Wednesday morning on Day 3, Brandi Ropen turned swiftly left and right, then left again on her misty-grey coloured double bed in Room 10 Jay Halls. Her misty grey duvet laid half on her bed and half hanging down on the floor. With her eyes still tightly closed shut, she sat up abruptly on her bed shaking her head with both freckled hands over her mouth. Her curly, half-dyed pink and half brown hair that had been hidden away in a multi-coloured silk wrap, now soon about to break free.

Brandi's curvy frame was sweating profusely in a loose red nightshirt (the initial B in silver stars at the front and back) and her tired body dropped back down again softly landing on her misty grey bed sheet. Her head landed back in the same place as before on her grey pillow.

Twenty minutes passed and there was a relative calm in the room during that time. Light, gentle snores could be faintly heard coming from Sentira's side of the room and Brandi turned only one more time whilst still in a deep sleep.

"No...no...please God...No." Brandi muttered these words from her mouth still fast asleep. She began turning swiftly left and right, then left and right again, still with both her eyes tightly closed shut. The silver starred letter B at the front and back of her dress stuck to her skin along with other parts of the red cotton material wet with sweat.

"I don't want to see it. Get me out of here!" Brandi shrieked loudly sitting up fast on her messy misty grey double bed.

Sentira heard Brandi's voice during her sleep, and opened both her eyes widely, turning her face to Brandi's side of the room in a jolting manner.

Brandi had gotten up off her bed and wandered around Room 10 with her eyelids tightly closed. She bumped into wardrobes, into walls and the side of Sentira's double bed a few times, but none of this awoke her from her sleep-walk.

"Are you alright, Brandi?" Sentira said out loud.

Brandi continued to sleep walk and bump into things. Sentira tiredly tried to get up from bed but she was still sleepy and fell back down again. She reached over to a bottle of water near her double bed and took a few sips of it, rubbing her eyes using the back of her thumb on her right hand.

Is this real? Or am I still asleep? Sentira mused to herself sleepily.

Brandi was now standing upright on her misty grey double bed shaking her head and muttering the words "No" repeatedly. Then, Brandi's dark green eyes opened and she let out a pained sob, tears streaming down her freckled face. Sobbing, she moved towards the window next to her double bed and opened it. The window next to Brandi's bed would only open a small way and Brandi began to push her well-built body against the window in an attempt to force it open.

Sentira panicked. She realised that if she didn't try to stop Brandi, the window (made of one of the old-fashioned glass materials) would shatter and severely injure her roommate and friend. Sentira sprang up from her bed, full of adrenaline, ran across to Brandi's bed, stepped up on it and placed both her arms around Brandi's arms from the back pinning them down to her sides. It was a struggle for Sentira to keep Brandi's arms still at first and the two of them fought for a few minutes longer before Brandi's body went limp in Sentira's arms and her dark green eyes closed shut.

Sentira laid Brandi back down on her double bed, tidying

the bed sheets around her on the bed and replacing the duvet, which had fallen on the floor. She could see that Brandi was still breathing as her chest rose and fell but she was breathing fast. Sentira had learned about anxiety and panic attacks from Nanny Lisha. It could be that Brandi was hyperventilating in her sleep, having a panic attack. Sentira's face filled with worry and concern. She felt drained after the energy she expended restraining Brandi from smashing the window to jump outside. Quietly closing the window by Brandi's bed and locking it securely, she sat at one edge of Brandi's bed watching her sleeping. Soon, Sentira's eyes too began to close again.

Thirty minutes passed by...

Sentira couldn't stay awake much longer, so she sleepily got up from Brandi's double bed and made her way in the dimly lit room to her own misty grey double bed. She slumped face down on her bed with no energy left to pull the duvet over her and fell fast asleep.

"No...No...Please...I don't want to see it..." Brandi's voice shrieked into the night air again.

Sentira's eyes flew wide open. Her sleep hadn't been as deep as before and she jumped up off her bed in one movement to help her roommate Brandi.

Brandi continued to scream the words "No." in her sleep and kept moving about left, then right and then left again.

She's having another nightmare. Sentira thought full of concern for her friend. She wondered if she should call the Medical Human OBR as she was instructed to if Brandi had slept for too long, but this was different. It wasn't about Brandi sleeping during the day, or about Brandi sleeping too long. Her friend was sleepwalking and having what seemed like very real, vivid nightmares. Sentira also worried about why Brandi had wanted to jump out of their bedroom window after her eyes had opened from the sleepwalking. Brandi could have seriously hurt herself if Sentira didn't hold her back in time.

Has she tried to jump out of windows before? Sentira wondered sadly.

TOO MUCH TO HANDLE

Room 10 Jay Halls was located on the second floor of the tall, student block of flats near to the Maromsaesc recreation ground. If Brandi had managed to break the window, she would not only have been cut by the shattered glass but also would have suffered further injuries due to the distance of the drop and the angle in which she would have landed. Sentira worriedly listened to Brandi screaming out in her sleep and wondered if she should call the Medical Human OBR. She hoped Brandi would fall asleep peacefully instead as she didn't think what was happening to Brandi had a medical cause.

Brandi needs someone with a lot of wisdom and knowledge of this type of voice-hearing experience to help her to handle it better. Sentira thought squeezing her friend's hand gently as her screams quietened down. Sentira's mind recalled a scene during the Health and well-being class where Brandi had been laughing and joking along with Annchi and Perianne.

She's not sick. Sentira reassured herself.

Brandi's eyes blinked a few times, then she opened them fully. She looked sadly at Sentira sitting next to her on her double bed and her breathing started to slow down.

"Is it over?" Brandi got up slowly and reached over to a bottle of water nearby on the bedroom floor.

Sentira didn't answer. She wasn't sure if Brandi would try and smash open the window again.

Brandi took a large gulp of water as her breathing returned back to normal.

"Was I talking in my sleep-walk?" Brandi asked Sentira curiously trying to work out why Sentira was sitting on her bed with a face full of concern. "Sorry, I do this sometimes. You can ask the Human OBR's for added soundproof borders for this room, you know?" Brandi suggested feeling defensive. It wasn't her fault that the staff at Maromsaesc didn't inform Sentira that she sleepwalked and sleep-talked.

"No, it was a good thing there were no soundproof borders as I wouldn't have heard you screaming or been able to help." Sentira answered truthfully.

Brandi glared at Sentira mistrustfully.

"Help me... how can you help me?" Brandi responded sarcastically.

Sentira felt like she had been slapped in the face. Here she was, staying up to ensure that Brandi was ok, missing her own sleep, worrying about her, stopping her from smashing the glass window to jump out and...Brandi wasn't even grateful.

She's tired and upset. Sentira mused.

Brandi suddenly pulled the misty grey duvet, which Sentira was sitting on, causing Sentira to lose her balance and nearly fall of the double bed.

"Careful!" Sentira exclaimed.

"Why are you sitting there? Do you enjoy watching me?" Brandi replied angrily.

"I was trying to help you. I had to stop you smashing through the glass window and jumping out after you sleep walked around the room for half an hour!" Sentira responded indignantly.

"And why did you stop me? Why do you care?" Brandi angrily retorted back. She found her virtual mobile, which was already activated under one of the grey bed sheets and pressed on the screen.

"Perianne, are you awake? It's Brandi, I had..." Brandi's voice cracked as she spoke. "I..I had a dream about the four children and...and... two women being burned, burned slowly in one of the old-fashioned brick houses. Yes...I heard their voices...I heard everything." Brandi started to sob loudly. "Yes, come down...ok...bye."

"Are you calling Perianne to come to our room?" Sentira asked Brandi incredulously.

"Yes...is...is...is that a problem?" Brandi said in between gasping sobs. "She's really nice and said she would help me to handle my dreams better." Brandi explained, her voice gaining a small measure of hope.

Sentira shook her head.

Brandi didn't even notice as she was wiping her face with tissues and staring at the virtual security screen waiting to see when Perianne arrived.

How did Perianne and Brandi get so close so fast? Sentira wondered to herself tiredly and got up off Brandi's double bed to make her way back to her own. She felt very tired and there were new classes today that she wanted to focus and learn from. She pulled her duvet over her and pretended to be asleep.

Soon the virtual security screen showed two people outside Room 10 Jay Halls. It was Perianne and Annchi. Perianne had on silk red pyjamas top and cream slippers. Annchi had on a short yellow nightdress and fluffy pink slippers. Brandi gave permission for them both to enter the room.

When the virtual security doors disappeared, Perianne rushed over to comfort Brandi, embracing her in a long hug. Brandi started crying again, more softly this time.

Sentira opened her eyes halfway to watch what was going on.

"Don't worry, you're going to be good, I promise you. We're here now. It's ok." Perianne said reassuringly to Brandi. Annchi joined in, sitting next to Brandi also on the double bed.

"Yeah, we can help you." Annchi lit a joint and passed it to Brandi. "It helps me calm down after I have one of my attacks."

"Annchi! Not now." Perianne laughed. "I told her not to bring any joints, down with her. It's her answer to everything!" Perianne giggled.

Brandi's expression changed into a mischievous smile, although she didn't laugh.

"Yeah, let me try it." Brandi said to Annchi.

Sentira's eyes opened wider as she watched Annchi show Brandi how to smoke a joint, remembering to turn on the virtual smokers-extraction fan near the double bed headboard. Sentira's room (she shared with Brandi) happened to have one of these fans fitted after they had been randomly selected to occupy it. This was unlike Perianne's and Annchi's room number 25 where Perianne had to request one from a Human OBR. Sentira rolled her eyes. She believed that smoking contributed to damaging the lungs and caused diseases such as cancer. She didn't think they offered any long-term solution to anything, just a temporary high, which a person would eventually have to come down from. Sentira shut her eyes again and pretended to be asleep. She hoped that they wouldn't try to offer her any.

Perianne laughed loudly and Sentira's eyes flew open instantaneously. She saw Annchi on the floor, sitting in the lotus position with her eyes shut taking exaggerated deep breaths in and out. Brandi took a long puff of her cannabis cigarette and another smile formed on her tear stained, freckled face. Annchi imitated the Meditation tutor, Miss Garrison and started to speak like her.

"Find your tranquil mind, take a long, slow, deep breath in and a long, slow, deep breath out. Allow your tranquil mind to guide you and everything will be all right." Annchi said in a very good impersonation of Miss Garrison's speaking voice.

Perianne laughed genuinely again.

Brandi smiled weakly.

"Why aren't you smoking Perianne?" Sentira interrupted the group, rubbing her eyes and pushing down her duvet away from partly covering her face. She couldn't listen to Perianne's gloating laughter anymore and not say anything. Her laughter sounded disturbing to Sentira. It sounded cruel and overbearing. There was no way she could sleep around Perianne.

Perianne's face froze for a few seconds with a fixed grin on her face looking straight at Sentira's slim frame moving to sit up on her misty grey double bed.

"We thought you were sleeping?" Perianne said sweetly, quickly composing herself.

"I tried." Sentira replied just as sweetly.

"Join us! Do you smoke?" Perianne asked Sentira in a friendly tone.

"No. Do you?" Sentira retorted back.

"I have allergies and smoking is one of them." Perianne replied with the same friendly tone as before.

This Sentira woman will not bring me out of my character or stop my purpose. Perianne thought to herself. She smiled resignedly indicating that if she were able she definitely would be smoking with Annchi and Brandi.

"Me too." Sentira said kindly.

I can like you to look after my friends but, Perianne...you don't fool me. Sentira thought in her mind.

Annchi continued to do her funny impression of Miss Garrison. Brandi sat up on her messy double bed smoking, next to the virtual smokers-extraction fan. Eventually, Annchi grew bored of acting like Miss Garrison and Brandi finished her joint. Perianne and Sentira sat on opposite sides of the room in silence. Both of them not looking at each other. Annchi sat back up on Brandi's bed and acknowledged Sentira for the first time.

"Did we wake you up Sentira? Sorry about that." Annchi said happily to Sentira.

"No, I was awake, just trying to sleep when you both came in." Sentira replied. "I tried to help Brandi too. She was very upset."

"She would be." Annchi said putting her arm around Brandi's shoulders. "Weed to the rescue!" Annchi exclaimed exuberantly causing Brandi to giggle.

Perianne giggled too, happy to find an opening to laugh again. She felt ecstatic. In Perianne's mind, Maromsaesc University had already failed in many ways. Soon her purpose would be complete. The Dedrick Psychiatry family business would be in the perfect position to make a highly successful comeback into society.

The four women sat around for a little while longer. Then, Perianne told Brandi that Annchi and her were going to get a few hours sleep before class that morning. Perianne and Annchi hugged Brandi and waved "bye" to Sentira sitting opposite them. When they were gone, Brandi laid back down on her misty grey double bed and fell asleep, snoring loudly.

Sentira drank some more water from the water bottle by her bed and soon fell asleep. Before she fell asleep however, she heard a child version of Olamide's voice speak pleadingly around her ears saying clearly the words: -

"Watch her…Power…Be careful… Not a saint."

THE FIRST FEW MONTHS

The Living with voices discussion class tutor, Miss Relinda Gower (a petite, blonde haired white woman) was already present in one of the old-style classrooms with hardly any virtual equipment in it. Some of the Team 3 students groaned as the virtual doors disappeared and they could see that this classroom was not as modern as some of the others. Miss Gower guessed correctly what they were thinking.

"It's ok." Miss Gower said knowingly loud enough for the students walking in to hear her. "The Living with voices discussion class will be held in a virtual room in Year 2, after more funding comes through." She smiled at the Team 3 students, most of which were now seated down on wooden stools behind wooden tables, two students at each.

"Applerishin virtual security says everyone is present except Kaden Sallow…" Miss Gower started to speak but was interrupted by one of her students.

"Is Kaden coming back?" a brunette woman asked from the back row.

"Yes." replied Miss Gower. "Kaden Sallow will be returning to first year studies, here at Maromsaesc University in 3 weeks time. He is to be discharged sometime this week and will be recovering at home with his family until he is well enough to rerturn." Miss Gower informed the class kindly. "Right, can you open your Living with voices textbooks to page 5, please."

Perianne opened her old-style paper textbook and read the words on the page.

Living with Voices Discussion Class

In the above course we will be utilizing our skills of debate and discussion, to advocate for and critique the many ways that a person can live successfully and happily with hearing voices. This will greatly help your understanding of yourself and of other people who are non-voice hearers. The course Living with Voices Discussion is separated into two...

Perianne's smile dropped a little. She realised that to pass this course, she would have to act like the teaching at Maromsaesc was accurate, even though she disagreed with it. The critique part, Perianne knew she could excel at, however that would not be enough for her to get through to Year 2.

I have to still be a student at Maromsaesc in Year 2, just… just in case I can't sabatoge this "mad house" in my first year. Perianne's mind raced. She thought about Brandi, Tom, Annchi, Kaden, the Marom rave accident,…these were all hopeful options to ruin the University but would they be enough? As a back up plan, Uncle Robert and Aunty Joan had warned her that she should excel in all her Maromsaesc Studies so if the worst were to occur (Maromsaesc remained open for Year 2 and Year 3) she would still be a student who could continue her work for the destruction of voice-hearing schools once and for all.

Perianne flicked through the pages of the textbook, scan-reading a few pages and memorising them with her brilliant mind.

Sentira sat next to Brandi and was flicking through the pages of her paper textbook also, memorising new information with her brilliant mind. She decided to put her concerns about Perianne and worries about Brandi to one side and concentrate on her studies. She was here at Maromsaesc to succeed and gain her Degree certificate in the Professional Development of people who hear voices. To achieve this, she needed to focus more, as at any time she could hear too many loud voices which would make her lose time from her learning, just like at other schools in the past. Sentira hoped that the new ideas she learned at Maromsaesc would make it easier for her to somehow control the volume or the time when her voices spoke to her. These first few days, she had been lucky, with not too many loud voices making it impossible to concentrate, but

Sentira knew it wouldn't last.

I can hear loud voices at anytime. Sometimes they don't stop for hours. Sentira recalled with a frown. *I must make use of the times when they're quiet or can be controlled.* Sentira lowered her head and peered even more closely at the words of page 5 of her textbook.

Both, Perianne and Sentira focused on learning as much as they could for the next few months at Maromsaesc. Meanwhile, Kaden returned healthy and healed to his Maromsaesc studies in November 2070 and Tom had one more angry outburst in the Cooking class. Brandi had three more sleep walking "death" dreams and Annchi made other students laugh with her jokes about the tutors while she smoked everyday, oftentimes with Brandi.

The newspapers soon grew bored of the story of the illegal Marom rave because they could not obtain any factual evidence to prove their claims, especially since Professor Willemina refused to speak with them. Kaden Sallow had given an interview about what happened at the Marom rave. However, because it contradicted the newspapers initial reports, Kaden's version of events never made it to print. The newspapers claimed that the story was no longer in the public interest but they would be following the story of the Human OBR barbecues and their safety issues.

The sun set in the frosty, autumn skies above Maromsaesc University and the Year 1 students slept soundly in their rooms. On this particular night, even Brandi was in a deep, untroubled sleep. Everything gave the impression of a peaceful, "normal" night at Maromsaesc in Pelargonium. None of the students or staff could have foreseen what was about to happen next.

None, except Perianne.

MADDENING

The warlike sounds of heavy, strong human and metallic footsteps rang out around the usually quiet Jay Halls in the early hours of Friday morning. Perianne awoke with glee. It was happening! Earlier in the week, she had told Aunty Dr Joan by coded message (that only the Dedrick family could decipher) about the drug use at Maromsaesc. Aunty Joan had coded back to her that she would anonymously get the Pelargonium Police onto it and to be ready for whatever could happen next. That was on Monday. Perianne had waited four whole days in inward, eager anticipation of what could potentially occur anytime soon at Maromsaesc University.

A Drug Bust! Perianne thought excitedly. She feigned a frowned expression when the virtual security screen pre-warned her and her roommate (Annchi) that there was an OBR Policewoman and a real human Policewoman outside their virtual door.

Annchi too had woken up with all the noise and was staring in horror at the virtual security screen which had lit up in red as a pre-warning that there were authoritative persons outside that would be gaining entry very soon (with or without her own or Perianne's consent.).

"Shit!" Annchi said visibly alarmed. "I was sleeping. What are Pelargonium Police doing outside our room?" she looked at Perianne accusatorily.

Perianne shrugged her shoulders and tried not to look at Annchi while hurriedly putting on her dressing gown and slippers. It was cold outside and she didn't know if this "Drug raid" could lead to them all being led outside and searched. In addition, Perianne didn't want Annchi to see the grin that kept trying to raise itself to the surface of Perianne's light pink cheeks. Annchi copied Perianne and rushed to put on a jumper and pull up her loose pyjamas. A robotic voice spoke from the virtual security screens in Room 10.

"Pelargonium Police will have access to Room 10 Jay Halls in 60 seconds and counting."

"Shit!" Annchi repeated again. "Where is my Medical Cannabis card? Perianne have you seen it?!" Annchi asked Perianne desperately.

Perianne eyed Annchi curiously while looking up at the virtual security screen to see where the countdown was.

Now I'm seeing how paranoid Annchi gets under pressure. Perianne observed in her mind. She shrugged her shoulders and rubbed her eyes acting like she was still sleepy. Perianne, in fact, felt wide awake with excitement and could picture the headlines later on this morning on all the news channels.

Suddenly, the virtual door disappeared and a human Policewoman with short cropped brown hair and pale skin came in with full body armour and two laser guns on each side of her. An OBR Policewoman followed behind her.

"Pelargonium Police! Stand up and put your hands on your head now!" the human Policewoman shouted at the two students in Room 10.

Perianne did as she was instructed. Annchi stood up and let out a scream as an OBR Policewoman ran directly to her bag on the floor next to her double bed, emptying out the contents on the floor. Annchi was visibly very nervous and the OBR Police were fitted with technology that could sense this type of anxiety. The OBR Policewoman picked up the bag of cannabis and stood directly in front of Annchi, looking down at her from it's 7 foot tall, intimidating robot height.

"Does this belong to you, Annchi Kang?" the OBR Policewoman (who was also wearing the same full body armour as the human Policewoman) said menacingly.

Annchi looked like she wanted to cry. She didn't speak.

Perianne wanted to smile but she used all her adrenaline-fuelled excitement to hold herself back from laughing loudly.

These voice hearers are pathetic. Perianne mused to herself, her hands still on her head.

Somewhere within her, Annchi finally gathered up the courage to speak.

"Yes...I...I have a medical condition and sm...smoke medical cannabis." Annchi looked over at her jacket thrown carelessly the night before on the floor, by the base of her misty grey double bed.

"I..I have a...Medical Cannabis card." Annchi glanced over at her dark blue jacket on the floor. "It's in my coat pocket."

"Do you have anymore bags of cannabis?" the OBR Policewoman persisted to question Annchi loudly.

The human Policewoman appeared to feel some empathy for Annchi and interrupted her colleague's questioning.

"OBR, check her blue jacket and see if she has indeed got a Medical Cannabis Card." the human Policewoman said in a commanding tone.

The OBR Policewoman immediately left Annchi and searched through the left and right pockets of Annchi's dark blue jacket. Then she searched inside the dark blue jacket in the inner pockets and found a small card and another bag of cannabis. The OBR glared at Annchi and spoke to the human Policewoman from a distance.

"I have one Medical Cannabis card registered to Miss Annchi Kang and another bag of medical cannabis." the OBR confirmed.

"Ok." answered the human Policewoman, and without any apology to Annchi, she quickly moved on to talk to Perianne. "Do you Perianne Saint have any bags of illegal cannabis in your possession or anywhere else in this room?"

"No." Perianne replied. She figured the less she said the better. She didn't want to have to go through the frightening OBR Policewoman mini-interrogation that Annchi had just endured.

"I will be conducting a search of Room 10 Jay Halls and you are both to go wait in the reception area until I am finished on behalf of the Pelargonium Police Force. Do you both understand?" said the human Policewoman.

Perianne and Annchi mumbled "yes".

Then as if in afterthought, the human Policewoman added. "We received very clear information that there are illegal drug users at Jay Halls, Maromsaesc University and this is our standard procedure of investigation of this particular form of crime. Thank you both for your co-operation."

"I need to smoke now." Annchi said meekly to the human Policewoman.

"OBR, check the validity of the Medical Cannabis card and if it is valid, return the bags of medical cannabis to Miss Annchi Kang." said the human Policewoman.

The OBR Policewoman scanned the Medical Cannabis card against the back of her robotic hand and it glowed green indicating that it was a valid card. The OBR returned the card to Annchi and the two bags of medical cannabis.

"Thank..." Annchi began to speak. "Can I smoke now?" Annchi asked pleadingly.

The human Policewoman nodded.

Annchi lit a joint as she and Perianne were led outside Room 10 by the OBR Policewoman. Other students along the same corridor were also being led out of their rooms by OBR Police to walk towards the virtual lifts to be taken down to reception.

On the ground floor, in the reception area, the students were ordered to sit down in rows of chairs already laid out for them. Most of the students looked bewildered and sleepy, others were trying not to smile, some were crying and distressed. Perianne thought this was the best day so far since she arrived at "mad" Maromsaesc.

Sentira and Brandi sat down on the chairs, two rows in front of Perianne and Annchi. Bataar and Kaden sat near them. Perianne could also see Tom and Advik sitting in row 2. Behind her, she recognised Lisa (the woman who had helped her when she vomited up the food from the Maromsaesc Cafeteria) and Cahya Anthri (another Team 3 student, a plump curvy, white woman with short natural ginger hair.)

Cahya looked amused and a few giggles were heard from Lisa, which were quickly replaced by a more appropriate serious expression on her face. Perianne knew enough about "hearing voices" to realise that it could be their voices talking around them making them laugh at what was a very serious, dramatic incident at Maromsaesc. She brimmed with excitement imagining the headlines later that morning on all the News channels.

Pelargonium Police raid First Voice Hearing University in surprise Drug Bust! Perianne imagined the News channels would say, *or Maromsaesc Illegal Student Drug Den uncovered by OBR Police.* A smile escaped onto the surface of Perianne's face and she mouthed a few words in the air to the front and right of her. This was to make it appear, to the OBR Police watching everyone, that she was talking to one of her voices.

The OBR Police allowed the Team 3 students to talk to each other and their voices, but they had formed a circle around the students (seated in 5 rows). This circle of OBR Police, each at 7 foot tall wearing full Police body armour with two laser guns at each side of their waists, presented a dominating and alarming environment. Most of the students were quietly speaking or whispering.

A few Maromsaesc staff, Human OBR's and OBR's were walking around offering water, hot chocolate, biscuits and sandwiches to any of the Team 3 students who wanted to eat or drink. Sentira observed how even the Maromsaesc Human OBR's and the Maromsaesc OBR's showed small signs of what seemed like fear when around the Pelargonium OBR Police. The way the hands of the Maromsaesc robotic staff would shake more and the way their usually monotone robotic voices sounded more high-pitched now that robot Police were around. Sentira wondered if this was due to their programming, that some robots were designed to show fear towards authority for whatever reason, she didn't know. It was "Jelitoonaa" to watch the robot staff at Maromsaesc show some kind of human emotion albeit during these unnerving circumstances.

After 30 minutes, 25 human Policewomen and men entered the circle of watchful OBR Police, who duly spread out to the sides to form a line at the back of the students. The human Police stood in front of the Team 3 students. The Policewoman who had entered Perianne's room earlier spoke out in a loud, powerful voice.

"Thank you all for your co-operation. We have conducted a thorough search of Jay Halls and are happy to inform you that there were no illegal drugs or illegal drug usage found at your Halls of Residence here at Maromsaesc University." the human Policewoman paused placing her left hand briefly on her laser gun, then as in an afterthought retracting her hand back down to her side again.

"We will be conducting regular unscheduled searches at Maromsaesc University which is for your own protection." the Policewoman continued on.

Some of the students groaned audibly.

"Listen, we want you to succeed here at Maromsaesc." the human Policewoman changed tact and softened her voice, but still with enough power and energy to be heard clearly. "Perlargonium is proud to be the first town in Britain to have a Maromsaesc University and we don't want anything to disrupt the chances of more universities for voice-hearers and people who see visions, being built elsewhere in Britain and around the world."

The students remained quiet.

Sentira could see some of the Team 3 tutors waiting by reception. An OBR Policeman walked over to the tutors and spoke to them. The Team 3 tutors walked towards the students. The Human Police and the OBR Police began to exit the ground floor reception area, leaving the tutors to further explain the night events.

Mr Juniper and Mrs Lear addressed two rows each while Miss Garrison addressed one row of students. The tutors apologised to the students and said that classes would start one hour later than normal due to what had occurred. They further suggested that if any student wanted to miss their Health & Well-being class due to feeling overtired they had permission to do so.

"You are safe at Jay Halls and you are safe at Maromsaesc University. The Pelargonium Police have informed me that as part of your protection and to uphold the integrity of the University, that they will be conducting regular unscheduled searches. I know you are all very tired and if any of you have any further questions, the Pelargonium Police have sent you all messages containing links as to the work they do." Mr Juniper explained confidently to the students.

More students groaned audibly. They got up from their seats talking amongst each other more loudly and expressively this time before following the tutors back to their individual rooms at Jay Halls. Some students talking to their voices, as well as each other, and some talking to the tutor along the way. The students described what had happened when the Pelargonium Police entered their bedrooms in detail to the tutors who listened with concern.

Sentira felt happy that there was a good reason why the Pelargonium Police had searched their bedrooms that night at Jay Halls. She wanted Maromsaesc to grow as a worldwide University and anything that would help protect them (the students) from harm was a good thing.

Perianne felt happy that everyone had been woken up for a drugs raid but wondered why there wasn't any cannabis found in Brandi's room?

*****

Later that morning, at the Health and Well-being class, the Team 3 students noisily filled in the tutor, Mrs Michelle Lear, about more stories from the early hours of that morning. Mostly relaying stories about when the Pelargonium Police had raided their bedrooms.

Sentira was interested to hear how some of the students were treated differently from others, according to what her friends and other classmates had said. Annchi insisted that she had been terrorized by an OBR Policewoman, while Bataar, Kaden, Noah and Craig had opposing stories. These men spoke of how the Pelargonium Police waited 15 minutes before entering their rooms, bringing with them, hot chocolate, biscuits and sandwiches. They joked and chatted with them about voice-hearing and the future of Maromsaesc as a world-class University. Then, they had kindly asked permission from the men before searching anywhere.

Bataar, Kaden, Noah, Craig, Sentira and most of the students believed the reasons the Police gave for the "drug raid". Brandi, Annchi and Tom were among some of those who thought that what the Police did was wrong and they continued to speak negatively about what happened for the rest of the day whenever they could.

Over the weekend, the students at Maromsaesc received many emails and messages from the News Media around the world, requesting first-hand details of the "drug raid" and the "Illegal drug use at Maromsaesc University". No-one knew how the students emails had been leaked to the press. All the Team 3 students had been given clear orders by the tutors not to communicate with the News Media. They were told that Professor Willemina Zantend herself would be participating in a News conference alongside the Pelargonium Police. This was so that a true account of the early hours of Friday morning could be clarified. The News Conference was held on Saturday morning, the News channels adapted their stories of the incident for the Sunday morning News reports. On Sunday evening, the emails for the students kept coming through. It was as if, the newspapers had conceded to adapt their story but didn't truly believe there was no spark without fire.

"I've received 52 emails from all over the world at the weekend." Bataar exclaimed to Kaden who sat next to him in on his transparent Meditation mat on Monday morning.

"68." Kaden replied back. "They're desperate."

"68." Bataar repeated shaking his head.

"I don't get why they would keep sending them if the newspapers changed their stories on Sunday morning. I mean, what else more is there to say. They know the truth." Bataar sighed changing his sitting position to the lotus position ready for the day's Meditation class.

Kaden was talking with his voices and didn't reply.

"Don't let Jane catch you talking to voices in her class." Bataar warned humorously.

Miss Garrison was running 15 minutes late to the Meditation class and some of the students were talking openly with their voices, whilst others were meditating or speaking with their classmates.

"My tranquil mind told me to raise my voice." Kaden grinned at Bataar.

"Use your tranquil mind Team 3, why is it so noisy in here!!" Tom shouted loudly from the back of the classroom jokingly.

Most of the Team 3 students laughed.

Sentira didn't laugh and opened one of her eyes inquisitively. She had been using her tranquil mind and had managed to block out all the student chatter except Tom's loud voice just now. Gradually, she had been getting used to accessing her tranquil mind to communicate with her voices. Sentira felt happily optimistic, because (as of present day) she hadn't experienced any loud voices during class times that would force her to leave the classroom. However, she believed that she didn't understand the "tranquil mind" as well as Miss Garrison. So far, to her, the "tranquil mind" was a meditative place in her head, which made her feel at peace with whatever volume her voices spoke around her. Her unexpected voices seemed to listen more to her calm (almost meditative response) to them. Often within 5 minutes they had been quietening down.

So far, so good. Sentira thought to herself. She had already noticed many improvements in her understanding of herself and her voices, than before she had attended Maromnsaesc University. The combination of the Meditation class, Voices communication class and the Living with voices discussion class were her favourite classes (in Term 1) that all benefited her immensely.

In Term 2, there will be more new ideas for me to practice. Sentira thought excitedly to herself as Miss Garrison walked into the classroom and commenced teaching the Team 3 students.

The two hours of Meditation class flew by quickly. Miss Garrison handed out virtual papers titled "End of Term 1 Meditation Test" while manoeuvring expertly around the Team 3 students on her Hover Mat. The only student who groaned at this was Tom.

"I know I've failed!' blurted out Tom's loud voice from the back of the classroom.

Miss Garrison turned her Hover Mat around in the opposite direction to face Tom.

"You've been doing "Jelitoonaa" Tom. I am very impressed by your progress and the progress of all my Team 3 students. The Term 1 Meditation Test is very straightforward and the pass rate is 50% so none of you have anything to be concerned about." Miss Garrison said reassuringly.

Tom's face went red with anger but he didn't say anything to Miss Garrison.

Soon, the Meditation class came to an end and the Team 3 students collected their bags and put on their shoes, ready to go for lunch before Sports class.

Sentira noticed how red with anger Tom's face got and how Perianne was now walking fast to catch up with Tom, who was nearly running to get out of the Student learning block. Sentira saw that Tom had left his virtual paper on the floor by his transparent mat and picked it up, quickening her pace to catch up with Tom also.

"Tom, wait up!" Perianne said loud enough for Tom to hear. She hadn't been speaking to Tom as much as she had in the first few weeks of Term1, instead focusing on other things that would further her purpose to ruin Maromsaesc University.

"Tom, you forgot your virtual paper." Sentira yelled from close behind Perianne, who was now running to catch up with

Tom who had broke into a run seemingly to get away from both of the women.

Gradually, Tom's run slowed down into a jog, then a walk. He turned around and saw Perianne followed closely by Sentira walking in his direction.

"Are you following me?" Tom smiled at Perianne and then smiled at Sentira.

Perianne returned back to him a wide grin and Sentira smiled genuinely at Tom.

Sentira felt relieved that Tom was in a good mood. She worried throughout the time that she had first saw him running, about the possibility of him doing something bad to himself like Brandi had tried to do. She wanted to help him and reassure him that he just needed time to adjust to the teaching at Maromsaesc. Sentira outstretched her arm and showed Tom the virtual paper for the Meditation End of Term test. Before Tom could respond, Perianne interrupted.

"Tom, I'll email you the paper. All those virtual papers must be overflowing in your room!" Perianne expressed a dramatic groan that made Tom laugh.

Sentira withdrew her outstretched arm with slight embarrassment.

"Why were you running?" Sentira asked Tom.

"If there is one thing here at Maromsaesc that's useful, it's the Sports class." Tom replied looking up at Sentira who stood much taller than him. "and I like to run and lift weights." he added.

"Are you on your way to get some lunch?" Perianne asked Tom as he began to walk away from them. "I'll join you."

"Yeah, I am." Tom said to Perianne sounding unbothered.

"I'm on my way to the Cafeteria too." Sentira chimed in happily.

Together, the three Maromsaesc students strolled to the Student Cafeteria without speaking until they had chosen their food and drink items. Then, each found a place to sit down. Sentira waited and then luckily managed to sit in a seat next to Tom, after Perianne had quickly sat down at the only vacant seat (at that time) opposite Tom minutes earlier.

"Wow! I've got another 40 emails today again from the News channels?" exclaimed Perianne, before taking a sip of her warm English tea.

"Delete them." Sentira replied, in between chewing her bacon and toast from her sandwich.

"I can't! There's too many!" Perianne giggled.

Tom bit down into one of his sausages and held a few chips ready to eat next in his left hand.

"Tom, are you still getting emails from the News people?" Perianne inquired.

"Just a few." Tom replied disinterested. He paused from eating his chips and spoke to the air around his left side. He was talking to his voices and distracted from the women talking around him. Everyone else close by at the table ignored Tom as it was a regular, everyday sight for all the students at Maromsaesc to use various ways of communicating with their voices or visions at any time.

Perianne and Sentira were not ignoring Tom. Both women wanted to get his attention for different reasons. Perianne wanted to see how far she could push Tom's weaknesses to ruin Maromsaesc. Sentira wanted to help Tom see the value of his Maromsaesc studies. Both women eagerly waited for Tom to visibly stop talking to the air around him. Tom however, did not stop talking to his voices until the Human OBR spoke to inform the students that the Student Cafeteria would be closing in 10 minutes.

Perianne and Sentira followed behind Tom as he made his way through the student crowds and exited the Cafeteria.

"Let's run to the Sports class!" Tom said enthusiastically smiling at Perianne and Sentira. "The winner gets to choose the sport we play." Tom added before sprinting off in the direction of the Gym block.

The trio ran a very close race, with all three of them jointly in the lead for much of the journey over to the Gym block. They raced past the two large Games Courts and Tom just managed to touch the virtual entry door for the Gym block first. Perianne and Sentira touched it a few seconds after at the same time.

The Applerishin virtual security confirmed that it was Tom who had reached the virtual door first by scanning Tom from head to toe with a ray of light green light. Tom confidently walked through the door, which allowed only Tom to enter. This was due to the latest Applerishin virtual technology that made it seem the virtual door had disappeared completely. In actual fact, the virtual door only appeared to have disappeared entirely. If Sentira or Perianne had tried to walk through at the same time as Tom, they would have hit an invisible rubber type of wall that they could feel but not see with their eyes or enter through.

"We're running." Tom said with a grin nearly as wide as the one fixed on Perianne's face most of the day. "Meet you all at the Athletics stadium behind the Gym block."

At the Athletics Stadium, Tom arrived before Perianne and Sentira. He started to perform various stretches to warm up. The Athletics stadium had 10 other Team 3 students there, some talking to their voices, some performing various stretches like Tom and others were doing push ups. There were 8 Human OBR's and 4 OBR's in different parts of the Athletics stadium ready to assist the Team 3 students as required.

Sentira got to the Athletics stadium at the same time as Perianne, although they did not walk together. Sentira walked with Cahya and Bataar while Perianne found company with Noah and Craig. They all warmed up before starting to jog around the Athletics stadium. After one lap had been completed by all, each of the Team 3 students eventually finished in their own time at their own pace. Next, Tom challenged Perianne, Sentira, Noah, Craig, Bataar and Cahya to a 100m Sprint race.

"What's the prize?" Cahya asked Tom.

"Me." Tom replied and winked at Cahya.

Cahya blushed momentarily and then spoke.

"I want a real prize if I'm going to run again. That drained my energy." Cahya said, with a frustrated expression at something that only she could see on her right hand side.

"Go rest then." Tom said to Cahya with a puzzled expression.

Cahya didn't look tired at all.

"I will." Cahya walked off to sit on one of the spectator's seats.

Tom's face grew red again and he turned to face away from the other Team 3 students to hide it.

Perianne saw a glimpse of his anger and went up to him.

"Tom, are you ok?" Perianne asked softly.

"Yes!" Tom said angrily.

"Come on, let's start running!" Sentira said, quickly sensing an argumentative Tom was about to come out.

Tom got into his starting position along with Perianne and Sentira on either side of him. He mouthed a few words to the voices he heard on either side of him. Bataar, Cahya and Noah also did the same.

"On your marks...get set...Go!" a Human OBR shouted loudly with no emotion in his voice.

Tom sprinted off very fast and maintained a good lead for a while. Then, Perianne overtook him while hearing a boy toddler's voice gurgle words in an unknown language: -

"Ooka ssss ei ei gou uu dd ahhh" a boy toddler's voice said beside Perianne's ears loudly.

Suddenly, Tom tripped just as he passed the finish line, half a second behind Perianne. He fell onto his side and then onto his back, slamming his fists against the ground in irritation.

Perianne slowed down her pace and turned around to see that Tom had fallen.

"I hate this place!" Tom whined in pain.

Perianne observed him from a distance as Sentira and Noah helped him sit up. A Medical human OBR came running over to administer first aid as Tom's leg was bruised and he clutched his ankle as if he had possibly sprained it.

I hate it here too. Perianne angrily thought in her mind, but she would never blow her cover and show her real emotions to the "mad" people.

A Medical human OBR commenced to wrap a bandage around Tom's ankle very tightly. Tom flinched and withdrew his left foot quickly away from the Medical human OBR's reach.

"I'll do it!" Perianne sang out happily from a gap in between the crowd around Tom.

"Do you want Perianne Saint to assist you?" the Medical human OBR said to Tom without feeling.

"Yeah, just get it done." Tom complained exasperatedly to the Medical human OBR.

Perianne took the bandage off the Medical human OBR and proceeded to bandage snugly Tom's left ankle. Tom did not flinch once under Perianne's care and he began to look more relaxed.

"Thanks Perianne." said Tom grinning.

It's just a sprain, you could have bandaged it yourself. Perianne thought, but instead she smiled kindly back at him.

"Anytime." Perianne replied happily. "Why don't you sit down and watch. I can get us some drinks." Perianne continued, leading Tom by the arm while he limped over to the spectator seats and sat down.

Sentira still didn't trust Perianne but she decided not to go over to Tom as she was enjoying running around the track with Bataar, Noah and Craig. They had made her laugh during the warm up lap and the sprint race by dodging in and out of the track lanes, causing the OBR's supervising to display red error messages on their chests frequently. The OBR's did not intervene in the race. They would only disqualify those runners that made errors at the end of the race. It was a Sports class, not a formal competition, so the Team 3 students were free to train at the Athletics stadium anyway they chose within safety limits.

Tom sat one seat away from Cahya, who was talking openly

with her voices that she heard on each side of her. Tom took the bottle of water from Perianne and drank most of it down in one go. Perianne sat down next to him, also drinking water from a water bottle but more slowly.

"Applerishin mobile open." said Tom to the flat square blue shape attached to his wrist.

Tom's virtual mobile sprang up and a light grey ray scanned Tom from top to bottom.

"Welcome back, Tom Puffint! Wishing you a speedy recovery! How can I assist you?" said the virtual mobile in a female voice.

"What new emails do I have?" Tom asked his virtual mobile.

"You have 25 new emails from Pelargonium News, Bournemouth News, London News, Durham News, Chero Coast News..." the virtual mobile replied.

"Stop." Tom said. He picked up his virtual mobile and began to press down on it quickly using his right thumb alone.

Perianne pretended to be watching the runners on the track, but in reality she could see clearly over Tom's shoulder what he was typing. Tom either didn't notice Perianne or didn't care as he kept on pressing quickly (typing away) on his virtual mobile.

Perianne felt her heart leap with joy as she sneakily read Tom's message to the Pelargonium News. Tom expressed (anonymously, using an undisclosed email) his deep disappointment and upset about being a student at Maromsaesc University. He listed many different reasons including the dangerous Human OBR barbecues, the ineffectiveness of the teacher's ideas and the "Drug raids". His final sentence contained the following words: -

"...in my opinion, the Maromsaesc University for voice hearers and people who see visions isn't going to work...it has already failed."

STUDENT TROUBLE

Sentira's eyes flew open as she heard Tom noisily get up during the first half of the Meditation End of Term Test, dramatically lifting up his transparent mat and slamming it back down on the floor. The OBR's in each four corners of the room moved towards Tom and Miss Garrison swiftly reached Tom on her Hover mat.

"Tom, what's wrong?" Miss Garrison asked gently.

"I can't do this! My voices want to know why I'm not talking back to them." Tom shouted in frustration. "I've told you this before!"

"I've tried to help you as much as I can Tom. I'm afraid you have left me with no other option but to issue a warning on your record of behaviour. You will not be able to attend Meditation classes for the remainder of this term." Miss Garrison said quietly but firmly.

Tom didn't say anything as an OBR stood at both sides of him. He looked left at the OBR and right at the other OBR warily.

"What are they for?" Tom asked.

"The OBR's will take you to see Professor Willemina Zantend. She will conduct a fair review about your future at Maromsaesc." replied Miss Garrison. "I cannot have my class disturbed anymore, especially not during an End of Term test which will contribute to their Year 1 final grade." Miss Garrison concluded.

Everyone in the Meditation room watched Tom being taken away by the OBR's. Sentira intuitively read Tom's facial expression.

Tom doesn't care if he gets kicked out. Sentira mused to herself.

"I am very sorry Team 3, the Meditation Test will have to be restarted at our next session. Or…if the whole class agrees we can restart after a 30 minute break." Miss Garrison suggested.

Miss Garrison sat in the lotus position on her Hover mat, located now at the front of the class. Then, she moved her Hover mat a short distance, to reach a bottle of clear liquid on the floor behind her. She took a few big gulps of this clear liquid before replacing the bottle back on the floor. Next, she returned her Hover mat back to the front of the Meditation class viewing her students anticipatorily.

"Ok! Let's take a vote!" Miss Garrison said. "All those who wish to delay the End of Term Meditation Test till the next session on Monday, raise your hands." Miss Garrison inquired of the Team 3 students.

No-one raised their hand.

"Break for 30 minutes. Test will resume at 11am." said Miss Garrison.

Some of the Team 3 students stayed in the Meditation room and others went outside the classroom. Sentira ate a sandwich on her transparent mat. Perianne sat on her transparent mat and did some Yoga stretches.

After 30 minutes passed by, the Team 3 students (who were outside) returned and resumed their positions on their individual transparent mats.

"Virtual security has confirmed to me that everyone is present, except Tom, of course. End of Term Part 1 Meditation Test – Observation of students use of "tranquil mind" will commence now!" Miss Garrison announced happily.

Miss Garrison felt relieved that Tom was gone from her Meditation class and now hoped that the Team 3 students would do well in their tests thus proving her theories to be highly effective. It wasn't just her job that depended on the student's success at Maromsaesc, it was also about the future of Universities for voice hearers and people who saw visions. The future of which, would be greatly influenced by the achievements of the first year Maromsaesc students. Miss Garrison strongly desired that her Meditation classes be a brilliant success or, as the students would say, a "Jelitoonaa" success.

The End of Term Meditation test involved Tutor observation of the students meditating for 20 minutes. This was to demonstrate that they were using their tranquil mind with their voices and not speaking audibly or making physical movements to communicate. That was part 1 of the test. Part 2 of the End of Term Meditation Test involved a written element whereby the Team 3 students had to write in their own words about the "tranquil mind and voices" including the benefits and disadvantages of using this form of communication with voices.

Miss Garrison hoped that there would be more advantages written by the students than disadvantages. From earlier conversations with the students, all she had heard was positive feedback. Except from Tom Puffint. She wondered if he would return for her Term 2 Psychic Development class and if so... would he still have similar outbursts. Miss Garrison dismissed thoughts of Tom from her mind and carried on with observing the student's test meditation session.

*****

There was no End of Term test for the Sports class.

The Voice Communication class End of Term test, was a written test divided into 3 questions, time allowed: 30 mins per question.

End of Term 1 Voice Communication class Virtual Test Paper.

Question 1: Describe as many ways as possible of communicating effectively and safely with voices. Give examples of the usage of each form of communication. Rate the methods of communication by numbers. Number 1 being the most valued method of communication.

Question 2: How would you explain your top three most effective ways of communicating with voices to a 10 year old child?

Question 3: Name 3 circumstances in which your top 3 ways of communicating with voices may face challenges. For each circumstance, list solutions for those challenges.

The Team 3 students could take up to 3, five minute breaks during the test if they needed to use the toilet or get a drink. There were two OBR's and two Human OBR's in all four corners of the Voice Communication class that were supervising.

Sentira chose the use of her "tranquil mind" as her most effective form of voice communication, followed closely by mental communication and vocal communication.

Perianne chose vocal communication as the most effective form of voice communication, with facial expressions and body movements coming in second and using the "tranquil mind" as her third choice. Perianne believed her answers to be true.

Perianne knew that the big difference between her and the other voice-hearers was that she was able to control her voices more often and they did not affect her sanity or behaviour. In Perianne's mind it was voice-hearers like Brandi, Tom and Annchi that clearly required medication and psychiatric intervention. Overall, Perianne concluded privately that only very rarely a few voice-hearers (like her) were able to remain sane while hearing voices. Perianne remained fixed on the idea that the majority desperately needed help from a Psychiatrist.

Preferably, a Dedrick family psychiatrist. Perianne mused. She further thought that even if some of the students appeared able to control their behaviour now, eventually their mental illness would rise to the surface. However, by then it would be too late. Perianne put down her virtual pen and looked up at the back of Sentira. Sentira had her head lowered, busily writing down on her virtual answer paper.

Sentira's mental illness will show up one day. She's not as perfect as she makes out she is. Perianne thought, picking up her virtual pen again and writing down opposite opinions from the ones that she had just expressed in her mind.

That evening, in Sentira's room (number 10 Jay Halls) Brandi was feeling restless. She wanted to go and get a cannabis cigarette from Annchi but felt nervous. She worried about the Pelargonium Police's surprise "Student Protection visits" as they had now been renamed as. Brandi complained about the "Student Protection visits" to Sentira.

"Why can't we be told when they're going to f***ing visit!" Brandi whined to Sentira clearly sounding tense and frustrated.

"I don't know." Sentira replied truthfully. "I guess that's their rules." she said with a small shrug of her shoulders.

Brandi flopped down backwards on her misty grey double bed dramatically with her arms spread wide open.

"If I didn't have to pass this Degree course to get my fashion design business, I wouldn't even be here." Brandi spoke softly to herself.

Sentira wasn't sure what to say to Brandi. She didn't want to see Brandi try to break open the window and jump out again. She thought that Brandi had been doing better. There had been no sleepwalking or nightmares for a few weeks but today she appeared visibly anxious.

"You're Jelitoonaa in all the classes! I know you'll pass all the tests Brandi. Don't worry." Sentira said reassuredly. "Christmas break is coming up and you can visit your family. Take a break from studying."

"And then after Christmas is done, what then? More studying, no weed!" Brandi whined much louder this time, then hesitated before speaking again. "Do you think the virtual security technology records us talking in our rooms?" Brandi said quickly, as if noticing all the virtual security tech around her for the very first time.

"I don't think so. Otherwise, all the times you've smoked weed in here with Annchi and Perianne…the Pelargonium Police would have seen it when they checked our rooms." Sentira said smiling at Brandi.

"They're so dumb." Brandi said, a smile returning to her face. "Well, that means I can get Annchi to bring me some more quickly."

"I wouldn't risk it Brandi. It's not worth it." Sentira dismissed Brandi's idea and shook her head causing her long, twist out styled black afro hair to sway gently on each side of her. "Annchi told me that she still has nightmares about the 7 foot OBR who stood in front of her, questioning her. If she didn't have her medical certificate...she would have been taken to a cell with Police OBR's in it watching her and... who knows what else they do." Sentira shuddered remembering how Annchi had described the Police OBR's intimidating presence in Room 25, Jay Halls.

Brandi suddenly flung her bright green silk pyjama-covered legs around, off her misty grey double bed in one swift movement. She had on fitted green silk pyjamas with the initial B embroidered in a transparent material on her back, and a smaller B in the middle of her chest (also transparent). Brandi faced Sentira squarely.

"I'll just have to get a medical certificate like Annchi." Brandi said to Sentira decisively.

Sentira heard laughter from some of her regular voices consisting of Rhyle, Gina and Olamide, all around her. Sentira ignored the laughter. This was serious. Brandi was acting weird. It wasn't Jelitoonaa. The laughter from Sentira's regular voices were heard in front, above, at her sides, behind and below her. Sentira took a deep, slow breath in and a deep, slow breath out.

Brandi waited for Sentira's response, but all Sentira was doing was taking deep breaths in and out. Brandi smiled knowingly at Sentira.

"Your voices are talking around you, right?" Brandi said. "You don't have to take deep breaths in and out to access your "tranquil mind", you're supposed to just be able to "find it"." Brandi informed Sentira confidently.

"See. You're a smarter student that I am!" Sentira exclaimed and the two women laughed together.

With the tension in the room easing, Brandi laid back down on her double bed and put on a movie to watch on the virtual screen in front of her. The loud sounds coming from the movie distracted Sentira from listening to her regular voices. The voices of Rhyle and Gina were still around her but they were not speaking loud enough for her to make out the words they were saying.

I don't want to tell Brandi to turn the volume down, she's alright for now. Sentira observed, pressing her hand on a sensor on the wall near her double bed.

The sensor activated the virtual sound-border. The "virtual sound-border" was located in the middle of the room which once activated, ensured that no sounds would come from Brandi's side of the room into Sentira's side of the room. Sentira hadn't used this virtual sound-border much. She felt she had a responsibility to listen out for Brandi's sleepwalking and nightmares during the day and nighttimes. Not, because the Medical OBR had told her to, but because she cared about Brandi. Sentira therefore planned to turn off the virtual sound border, after she had finished studying.

Sentira opened her virtual textbook for the Living with voices discussion class and began reading. Her regular voices, Rhyle, Gina, Olamide and Louis talking around her as she did so.

After a few hours, at around 11pm, Sentira unwittingly fell asleep face down on her virtual textbook. The virtual textbook was faulty and spread out due to the weight of her face, until she moved her head to the left side of her face. Then, the virtual textbook partly bulged out into a small ball shape where it was not weighed down by Sentira's head.

Applerishin virtual security started to announce that Perianne Saint and Annchi Kang were requesting entry to Room 10 Jay Halls. The security message only got as far as announcing the first syllable of Perianne's name, when Brandi interrupted speaking quickly and excitedly to her virtual security screen.

"Access approved." Brandi said hurriedly. She looked over at Sentira's sleeping face and noticed that Sentira had forgotten to turn off the virtual sound border. "Jelitoonaa." Brandi said to herself softly.

Brandi smiled as the virtual security door disappeared and

Perianne and Annchi walked into Brandi's side of Room 10 Jay Halls. They sat down on Brandi's misty grey double bed and Annchi immediately lit a cannabis cigarette next to the virtual smokers extraction fan.

"Brandi! It's us. How's it going?" Perianne said excitedly.

"I'm here too!" Annchi said giggling passing the joint to Brandi.

Brandi took a long inhale of the cannabis cigarette. She felt calmer straight away.

"Where's Sentira?" Perianne asked curiously before looking around and seeing that Sentira was asleep with a virtual sound border in-between the two sides of the room.

"You put up a virtual sound border! Jelitoonaa!" Perianne exclaimed.

"I didn't. Sentira must have forgotten it on." Brandi replied, puffing away on her cigarette.

Perianne grinned at Sentira's head on top of the virtual textbook, which was obviously faulty and had an unusual half squashed appearance. Perianne's mind raced fast with ideas of what trouble she could cause for Maromsaesc, especially now that Sentira was asleep and the virtual sound border was up.

"It's Jelitoonaa that Sentira's asleep and that she left the virtual sound border on, I think she can be a bit too serious sometimes." Perianne said with a sigh.

"Yeah." Annchi agreed.

"Yeah," Brandi said after a few more puffs of her joint. "She told me that I shouldn't risk getting caught by the PP and to stop smoking." Brandi said.

Annchi and Perianne burst out into fits of giggles. Brandi didn't laugh and continued on smoking.

"If PP bust in right now, I'd just say that the weed is Annchi's who has a legal right to smoke." Brandi said confidently smiling; taking more drags of her joint.

Annchi grinned and lit a joint for herself.

Perianne had got up and was standing by the virtual sound border in the centre of the room. She stared at Sentira sleeping with an inquisitive expression on her face. She briefly wondered what Aunty Dr Joan Dedrick would diagnose Sentira as. Regaining her undercover character as Perianne Saint, Perianne turned around to face the other two students.

"Let's call Noah, Craig, Tom and Advik to join us!" Perianne suggested to Brandi and Annchi, her bright green eyes twinkling with amusement.

"Jelitoonaa" Annchi replied winking at Perianne.

Brandi kept on smoking, staring at the smoke being taken up by the ray of blue light that emitted from the virtual smokers extraction fan. She acted as if she didn't hear a word that Perianne had said.

"That's a yes, then." Perianne said and sent a few text messages to Noah, Craig, Tom and Advik via her virtual mobile.

Twenty minutes passed before Noah, Craig and Advik presented themselves to the Applerishin virtual security at Room 10 Jay Halls.

Brandi listened to the announcement with surprise on her face.

"Give access Brandi, we don't want Sentira to wake up!" Annchi said hurriedly.

"Access approved." Brandi said sounding unsure.

The virtual security doors disappeared.

Noah entered Room 10 with 3 bottles of brandy and a few glasses in his hand. Craig came in with 2 bottles of rum and Advik brought in a few bags of popcorn. Noah sat next to Perianne and put his arm around her shoulders, whispering in her ear. Perianne resisted the temptation to elbow him in the chest and throw him on the floor, which she was physically strong enough to do.

He hasn't got a clue. No one does. They're not smart enough... Perianne deviously thought to herself.

The truth that remained hidden was the fact that she was Aridaperianne Dedrick, part of the genius Dedrick Psychiatry family legacy. How could this "mad" voice hearer think he stood a real chance with her? Perianne smiled sleepily at Noah.

I'm the perfect actress. Perianne thought.

Advik and Craig stood up looking around the room and at the three women sitting on the misty grey double bed.

"So, what are we gonna do now." Advik, a dark-skinned, slim Indian man (Team 3 student) wearing a grey tracksuit asked sounding bored. He spoke inaudible words to the air around his left shoulder to communicate with something that only he could hear.

"I've got drinks!" Craig replied smiling at Brandi.

Brandi laughed, feeling much better now that she had a joint to smoke. Craig sat down next to her on her double bed and offered her a drink of brandy which Brandi accepted smiling at him. Annchi got up and stood by Advik and placed her arms around his waist, resting her head on his chest. Each pair began to talk to each other. Some were getting high off the joints being passed around and others starting to drink mixes of rum and brandy. Perianne didn't consume either, because of her "allergies".

Thirty minutes later (the air reeking of alcohol) Annchi and Advik began to make out on the floor. Craig and Brandi also were kissing and touching on Brandi's double bed. Perianne allowed Noah to kiss her but kept brushing off his hand when he tried to feel any part of her body. Brandi and Craig were moving faster than the other two couples (who were still fully dressed in their pyjamas kissing), while Brandi and Craig had started to undress each other passionately.

Annchi and Perianne glanced at Brandi, exchanged knowing looks and winked at each other, giggling. They hid laughter with their hands, as they left room 10 Jay Halls with Noah and Advik, leaving Brandi and Craig alone together.

*****

The next morning, Brandi woke up naked with Craig's naked body lying next to her fast asleep. Craig had a blissful expression on his face. Her misty grey bed sheets and duvet were dishevelled on her double bed. She pulled one of the bed sheets over her body covering herself, staring in surprise across at

Craig. She could see an empty wine glass and two empty bottles of rum and brandy on the floor. She heard voices around her speak loudly but couldn't make out what they were saying. She screamed out loud, fell sideways back down on her messy bed and fell asleep.

Craig woke up startled by the scream he heard in his sleep, just in time to see Brandi fall sideways onto the bed next to him. He blinked a few times. His memory of what had happened last night wasn't clear. He rubbed both of his eyes with his left hand. Where were his clothes? What happened last night? Did he get naked with Brandi? No, surely he would have remembered. Then it all came rushing back to him, the brandy, the rum, the smoking, the laughter, Brandi's naked body on top of his...

Craig slowly moved off the misty grey double bed so as not to wake Brandi. He put his hand on his head momentarily in disbelief before picking up all the remaining empty bottles and wine glasses. Quietly, he placed them in the virtual suction-bin on the wall near the centre of the room. The virtual suction-bin opened as he attempted to put the bottles and glasses through. It then pulled the items from his hands (via a grey beam of light) and moved them down into the suction-bin before closing again.

He rushed to put on his black pyjamas and grey socks which were scattered around the double bed in various places. He was extra careful not to wake Brandi as he gently put back in place the misty grey bed sheets as best as he could. Craig replaced the matching grey duvet on the double bed also. Once fully dressed, Craig left Room 10 Jay Halls swiftly through the open virtual security exit. As he walked along the corridor to get to the lift to return to room 2 Jay Halls, Craig lowered his head in shame.

Sentira turned around in her own misty grey double bed, rubbing her eyes sleepily. She stretched both her arms over her head and let out a long yawn. She noticed the virtual textbook beside her on her bed.

I fell asleep reading. Sentira thought tiredly, bringing both her arms back down to her sides. She turned again to face Brandi's side of the room and saw that the virtual sound-border was still up. Lazily pressing her hand on the sensor near her bed head, Sentira deactivated the virtual sound-border. She looked up at the time on her virtual screen above her bed head. It was 8am. Classes started at 10am. The Health and well-being class would be the first class today.

Sentira whispered "Good morning Rhyle" to the air on her right hand side.

"Good morning Sentira." Rhyle whispered back near Sentira's right ear.

Sentira got up from her misty grey double bed and went in the bathroom.

Forty minutes later, Sentira was dressed and ready to go downstairs to get breakfast. Even though, she had the morning News on, Brandi was still not awake seemingly oblivious to all the noise in the room.

"Watch her." Olamide's adult voice said softly by Sentira's left ear.

"She must be at her classes today, Olamide. Give it a break" Rhyle said loudly by Sentira's right ear.

"Rhyle, keep your voice down, you'll frighten her." Olamide's teenage voice retorted grumpily.

"Both of you must stop telling her what to do." an elderly voice belonging to Gina firmly said in front of Sentira's face.

"Watch everyone please!" Olamide's toddler voice said from behind Sentira.

Sentira didn't vocally communicate back to her regular voices but instead tried to use her "tranquil mind" as taught by Miss Garrison. She did this by remembering how she felt during meditation and remembering the point where her voices were responding without her thinking thoughts to communicate with them. It was like part of her mind was crystal clear but her voices still understood what she was trying to say without her thinking it or saying it. Sentira knew she had found her tranquil mind at these times. However, this morning it wasn't that easy. Rhyle, Gina, Olamide and Louis were arguing around her and her instinct was to be firm and speak out loud to them.

"Lower your voices!" Sentira said loudly.

Her regular voices continued to chatter around her from various directions and gave no indication of stopping. She took a few long, slow, deep breaths in and out while hearing her regular voices fighting each other at varying volumes near her. Sentira grew distracted and packed the wrong virtual textbooks into her shoulder bag. She glanced over at Brandi. Brandi was still sleeping. Sentira walked over to her, still hearing Rhyle, Gina, Olamide, and Lous talking around her all the way.

Sentira crouched down beside Brandi's misty grey double bed and could see that Brandi was in a deep sleep. The alarm on Brandi's virtual mobile had been playing "Jelitoonaa" music for 10 minutes (which often woke Brandi up straight away) but this time it appeared Brandi was in one of her long, voice-hearing dream sleeps.

A wave of worry passed over Sentira's face and she ignored her regular voices around her. Anxiously she spoke to the virtual screen above Brandi's bed.

"Call Medical Human OBR for Brandi Ropen." Sentira instructed the voice sensor on the large virtual screen above Brandi's bed head.

The Medical human OBR entered Room 10 Jay Halls within minutes and Sentira informed it that Brandi had been sleeping all night and was not waking up. The Medical human OBR sat on Brandi's misty grey double bed and a ray of light orange light came out of both it's eyes which scanned the full length of Brandi's body, three times.

"Brandi Ropen's vital signs are very good. I will observe her until she wakes her up. You must attend your classes here at Maromsaesc University. Thank you for calling Medical human OBR to assist you today. Have a Jelitoonaa day!" the Medical Human OBR said assertively, staring at Sentira as if waiting for her to leave the room so it could get on with it's job.

"Thank you Medical OBR." Sentira replied, unsure if she should leave her friend alone with this programmed, female human lookalike robot.

"Have a Jelitoonaa day!" the Medical human OBR said louder this time with increased firmness in her voice.

Sentira pulled her shoulder bag over her shoulder reluctantly and left room 10 Jay Halls to go to the Student Cafeteria for breakfast. Rhyle, Gina, Olamide and Louis talking around her all the while.

In Room 10 Jay Halls, the Medical human OBR bent down to the level of the grey double bed, turned it's head and peered curiously at Brandi's face very closely. It's human OBR face just inches away from Brandi's nose. Then, it moved the grey duvet down exposing the top half of Brandi's naked body but she was still covered from her waist downwards. Again, the human Medical OBR turned it's head sideways and peered very closely at Brandi's tummy area. It then stood up and a light orange ray came out of the Medical human OBR's eyes scanning Brandi's tummy area. The scan was repeated a total of 10 times. The Medical human OBR replaced the grey duvet and stood watching over Brandi protectively.

After a few hours, Brandi rolled over twice on her double bed to lay on her right side. The Medical human OBR stood still in observation of her. Brandi rolled over onto her left side and nearly fell off her misty grey double bed. The Medical human OBR lay down on the floor with its arms outstretched ready to catch her if she fell. Then, Brandi started to speak words in her sleep.

"Don't want to see it! I don't care!" Brandi shouted with her eyes firmly closed shut, sweat showing on her freckled face and bare shoulders.

The Medical Human OBR returned to standing. It watched Brandi very closely, it's face expressionless.

"I'm going to be sick. I can't see this again." Brandi muttered to herself still fast asleep, but luckily she didn't fall off the edge of her bed.

"No!" Brandi screamed out, her hands reaching up onto her face and covering her eyes, which were still tightly closed shut. Sweat dripped along her arms, hands, face and neck. Just as quick as Brandi had spoken in her sleep, a sudden silence descended upon Room 10 Jay Halls and Brandi appeared peaceful. Her breathing slowing down to normal.

Meanwhile, in the Health and Well-being class, Sentira was having trouble getting her regular voices to calm down. She had tried every idea known to her since childhood and had also tried the more recent teachings taught here at Maromsaesc. She felt an unfamiliar anxiety within herself as she attempted again to use her "tranquil mind". She needed to tell Rhyle, Gina, Olamide and Louis that she was in class and it was important for her to hear what Mrs Lear (the Health and Well-being tutor) had to say.

Sentira was just about to give up and tell Mrs Lear that she needed to take a 10minute break, when her regular voices stopped talking loudly around her. She was about to breathe out a sigh of relief, when new voices started to shout at her from a distance, calling her name and Brandi's name. Sentira took a long, slow deep breath in and out and tried to find her "tranquil mind" again. She felt embarrassed that after months of good attendance in all her classes, today she lacked control of her voices. Reluctantly, Sentira stood up and went to inform Mrs Lear that she wanted to take a 10 minute break. Mrs Lear reassured Sentira that it was ok to take breaks and she didn't have to ask.

I know it is. Sentira mused to herself exiting the Health and well-being classroom. She began to recall all the memories she had of missing lessons at school due to loud voices that wouldn't stop talking. Tears welled up in Sentira's eyes as she leaned against the wall outside the Health and well-being classroom.

Other students were outside in the corridor too, talking openly with their voices or just learning against the walls using their virtual mobiles. Sentira moved off from the wall and walked along the corridor in the Student learning block. She read and looked at some of the framed stories and photos of inspirational voice-hearers. Sentira rubbed tears away from both her eyes before they had a chance to fall.

New voices of various age ranges, both male and female, were still shouting at a distance from Sentira (around a few metres away). They were calling her name and Brandi's name from all directions. She turned sharply behind her after hearing a loud female child's voice shout "Sentira" close to the back of her. She decided to address this particular voice and said: -

"I'm in Health and well-being class, I can't talk right now. Please keep the noise down." Sentira requested of the loud female child's voice, she could hear but not see. The new voices ignored Sentira's instruction and continued on. Sentira ignored them back and kept reading the inspirational voice-hearer stories on the wall in the corridor.

A tall, dark-skinned man with a shaven head in his mid-40's walked by and stood near Sentira reading the framed story of Professor Wilemina Zantend. It was Mr Andrew Juniper, one of the tutors at Maromsaesc University.

"Awesome, how one woman can change the course of history for the future of voice-hearing and people who see visions in society." Mr Juniper said proudly. He looked down at Sentira, who although she stood at 6 foot herself felt short around Mr Juniper who was 7 foot tall.

"Jelitoonaa." Sentira replied, smiling up at Mr Juniper.

They both continued reading for a while before Sentira moved away to return to her Health and well-being class. The stories she had read encouraged her, inspired her and made her even more determined to succeed.

This is only the first term of my 3 year Degree. By the end of the 3 years, I will be more in control. Sentira thought confidently to herself smiling and ignoring the shouting voices all around her. She would check in on Brandi after class during her lunch break, maybe the voices would quieten down then.

Resuming her seat in the Health and well-being classroom, Sentira smiled at Mrs Lear and opened her Maromsaesc virtual notebook.

CHANGES

Sentira waited for Applerishin virtual security to scan her before she could gain entry to Room 10 Jay Halls. When she entered into the room, she could hear the sounds of water running fast in the bathroom. The Medical human OBR was nowhere to be seen.

"Brandi! Are you awake?" Sentira said loud enough for Brandi to hear her over the noise of the shower water running.

"Yeah, I am!" Brandi shouted back.

"You slept long!" Sentira exclaimed. "It's half 12."

Sentira sat down on her misty grey double bed and took out a ham and lettuce sandwich, which she had quickly purchased at the Student Cafeteria before going to check up on Brandi. To her surprise, the loud voices calling her name and Brandi's name had stopped completely after she had entered the reception area of Jay Halls, so Sentira felt more at ease again.

"Are you coming to Sports class? I've got you a ham and cheese sandwich, and a drink if you don't want to go to the Cafeteria." Sentira said happily.

Brandi didn't reply. Sentira continued eating and drinking her hot chocolate until Brandi came out of the bathroom.

Eventually, Brandi exited the bathroom wearing a bright pink tracksuit with the initial B in black appearing repeatedly at the sides of her tracksuit top and bottoms. She also had on bright pink trainers and her curly half red and half black hair pulled into a messy bun at the top of her head. Brandi took the ham and cheese sandwich off Sentira's bed and took a few sips of the Hot Chocolate that Sentira had bought for her.

"How much do I owe you?" Brandi asked in between sips of her drink.

"It's alright, you would do the same for me." Sentira said to Brandi smiling at her.

"Jelitoonaa." Brandi smiled back. "What did I miss this

morning?" Brandi asked, not looking at Sentira.

"Oh, nothing much." Sentira replied taking the last bite from her sandwich and picking up her hot chocolate from her bedside table. "Mrs Lear talked about the Omega 3 content in different types of fish and the benefits of eating fish for good brain health."

"Oh ok." Brandi said in response.

"I know about healthy eating. It's just putting it into practice." Sentira laughed.

"Are you ready?" Brandi said changing the subject. She had finished her sandwich and had her sports bag in her right hand and her cup of hot chocolate in her left hand.

"Yeah, let's go." Sentira said, picking up her own shoulder bag and taking her hot chocolate with her.

The two women left Room 10 Jay Halls to go to the Sports class, talking to each other along the way. No more loud voices were heard by either of them throughout the day.

A few days later, in the beautifully designed "Voice Communication" classroom, Perianne sat at one of the virtual nature scene inspired tables on a virtual sofa which changed intermittently images of scenes of nature. She did not glance down at the lovely images of sandy beaches, forests, flowers, ocean waves, mountains or waterfalls but waited patiently for the tutor, Mr Simon Winchester to give the virtual envelopes with the End of Term 1 test results to human OBR's. This was so that the human OBR's could distribute the test results to the Team 3 students.

Today was the last day of classes and this was the final lesson before the Team 3 students went on winter break for the Christmas season. Perianne felt extremely angry that Maromsaesc was still here and that she would have to pass all the "insane" tests to remain a student to continue her purpose. She smiled a wide, over-happy smile at Annchi who turned around excitedly to grin at her from her virtual sofa, a few metres in front of Perianne's own virtual sofa.

The human OBR's neared to Perianne's virtual table and

placed a nature scene inspired virtual envelope in the centre of it. Perianne opened her virtual envelope quickly. In the background, she could already hear some of the Team 3 students around her talking animatedly about their End of Term 1 test results.

I must have passed. These tests are nothing compared to my medical and psychiatry exams. Perianne reassured herself smugly. She pulled out the virtual nature scenes inspired card inside and saw a line of A grade results for each Term 1 class. Perianne momentarily felt disgusted with herself. She didn't believe most of the answers she had given in the tests. She just wanted to pass. Her hidden disgust faded as she remembered that without her passing the Maromsaesc degree course syllabus, she wouldn't be able to continue being a student to one day finally sabotage Maromsaesc forever. Voices began to talk around Perianne's right and left ears.

"Speaking of fires and houses, please remember to check the smoke alarms." a middle aged woman's voice said around Perianne's left ear.

"Everything is very safe and secure, I can assure you." replied a female child's voice.

"Please check again, I cannot have my customers or staff in any type of danger. Do you understand?" a middle aged man's voice said.

"Danger. Why would they be in danger and the house is fireproof. You misunderstand me." an elderly man's voice said.

"Fire can spread very quickly. Prepare better." a female child's voice said.

Perianne listened to the invisible voices chatter around both her ears. She spoke to them confidently and said: -

"I'm in Voice Communication class, stop distracting me." Perianne said to the left side of her. "Stop talking." Perianne turned to her right side and said.

Just then, Mr Winchester walked near her virtual table, smiled and nodded at her.

Perianne returned back to the Voice Communication tutor,

one of her winning wide smiles back, but inside she was raging.

My voices are different; I'm not like these mad people. Perianne firmly reminded herself in her thoughts. *I'm a Dedrick, part of the Dedrick family of psychiatry and we will return to power, it's just going to take a little longer than I expected.*

Perianne got up from her virtual, scenes of nature sofa to talk to Annchi, Brandi and Sentira who were showing each other their virtual card results. Noah, Craig, Advik and Tom stood nearby talking about their results also. Bataar, Kaden and Cahya joined them.

"We all passed." Tom said answering Cahya's curious, expectant look at him and the other men.

"So did we." Cahya replied. "Ready for Term 2." she said to Tom with a smile.

Tom didn't smile back but instead turned to speak to Kaden and Bataar.

"Are you all staying on to Term 2 then?" Tom asked.

"Yeah, are you?" Bataar replied while Kaden and Cahya nodded.

Tom frowned in response as the other Team 3 students waited for his answer to his own question. Tom looked to the right and left side of him before staring back at the other students.

"There's no Meditation next term is there?" Tom finally said in response.

Bataar laughed.

"You don't like Miss Garrison?" Bataar said, his thick black eyebrows raised questioningly at Tom.

Tom stared at Bataar and a tense silence ensued for around a minute.

Kaden and Cahya looked at each other, then at Bataar and Tom anticipatorily. They both marvelled about if Tom was going to get angry again, like they had seen him do so many times before in other classes. They couldn't understand his angry outbursts and wanted to see if something dramatic was about to be ignited.

After a few minutes of silence with Tom and Bataar staring confrontationally at each other, Tom walked away. Bataar shrugged his shoulders and turned to talk with Kaden and Cahya who looked relieved that Tom had decided to walk away. Noah, Craig and Advik were engaged in conversations with Annchi, Brandi, Perianne and Sentira about their plans for the Christmas holidays.

"I'm staying with Nanny Lisha for a few weeks before coming back to Maromsaesc for Term 2." Sentira said happily.

"She sounds lovely your Nan." Brandi replied. "Didn't she go through that prehistoric mental health system before the fall of Psychiatry after the R-v-Caulfied case in 2054?" Brandi asked innocently.

"She did." Sentira said and a shadow of sadness passed over her usually happy face so she changed the subject quickly. "She's going to be so happy to hear that I've passed my first term at Maromsaesc with all A's!"

Perianne's ears had perked up at the mention of her beloved Psychiatry. Previously, she was only half listening to the excited chatter around her about the results students had received from their End of Term 1 tests. Perianne held her true thoughts within herself, yet it was getting much harder as the days turned into weeks and the weeks had turned into months at Maromsaesc. She wished so badly, on many, many different occasions, that she could defend Psychiatry with all her heart, intelligence and passion, but she couldn't risk it anything that would jeopardize her undercover mission at Maromsaesc. Consequently, Perianne's fake smile remained on her facial expression, appearing as real as she could muster. This, and other acting techniques Perianne used, seemed to be working. She was popular, had made friends at Maromsaesc and now she had confirmation of being one of the most talented students in Team 3 due to her consistent A grade results for Term 1. Perianne showed genuine concern with her green eyes, as she had been taught to by Uncle Dr. Robert Dedrick, during her acting sessions training with him in preparation for attending Maromsaesc.

Term 2 will be my final term at Maromsaesc. Perianne thought to herself. She pretended to be interested in Sentira's tales of the injustice done to her grandmother and millions of other voice hearers who were mis-diagnosed unfairly as having a medical condition.

Suddenly, Perianne's voices started to talk around her loudly.

"The ants have higher activity in the summer. The summer months are the hottest in the UK, did you know?" a teenage male voice said around Perianne's left ear.

"Ants. Er...no, never considered the behaviour of ants before." a middle aged female voice said around Perianne's right ear.

"Quiet" Perianne said clearly to the left and right sides of her. The loud voices stopped speaking. Perianne smiled a true smile. She was nothing like these "mad" voice-hearers or people who saw visions.

I'm in control. Perianne mused gleefully to herself.

The Christmas holidays soon arrived at Maromsasec and there was a triumphant, "Jelitoonaa" vibe of happiness and jubilation everywhere, amongst both students and staff. Even the human OBR's and the OBR's seemed more pleasant in their communication of emotions. These were the very first students at Maromsaesc and the majority had succeeded in passing successfully their first term. The newspapers, somehow, picked up on the stories of the successful Term 1 students A grades and these positive stories made the front page headlines of News broadcasts around the world, to the inner, hidden distress and dismay of Perianne.

Perianne met up with Aunty Dr Joan Dedrick in a secret location and worked on how to implement new ways to destroy Maromsaesc faster and permanently. They only laughed at times when they discussed these new ways. Yet, there was still love and admiration between Aridaperianne and the Aunty who had helped raise her after her mum had died. They ate expensive food and had expensive luxury items around them. However, these were all gifts from family members who refused to disclose where they acquired the money. It couldn't be from Psychiatry, as they were no longer permitted to practice. So, where was the money coming from? Perianne was so happy that they received these expensive items that she didn't bother to ask too many questions.

Sentira met up with Nanny Lisha in Nanny Lisha's old-fashioned brick house, and had a wonderful Christmas season full of hope, love and laughter. Nanny Lisha loved hearing all the stories about Maromsaesc University. Sentira spoke about the other voice hearers in Team 3, the Maromsaesc University buildings, the classes, the tutors, the OBR's…She watched every video clip Sentira had filmed around the University with her eyes lighting up with excitement at each clip.

The three-week holidays went by quickly and soon it was time for Perianne and Sentira to travel back from their different locations to Pelargonium. They were to rejoin the other students at Maromsaesc University for the "Welcome to Term 2" speech by Professor Willemnina Zantend. This speech was due to be held the next day after students returned on Thursday. Thereafter, there would be one weekend before the new Term 2 classes started on Monday, 12th January 2071. The Hover cabs into Pelargonium were subject to long delays and instead of the anticipated 7pm arrival time, Perianne and Sentira's separate Hover cabs arrived late on Thursday evening.

Perianne met Annchi in Room 25 and they stayed up talking till past 1am the following day. Sentira found Brandi fast asleep in her misty grey double bed and went to bed early after phoning Nanny Lisha to tell her that she had arrived for Term 2 of her Maromsaesc Studies.

Friday morning at 10am, the Year 1 students sat in the newly part refurbished, Main Hall on virtual nature scene inspired chairs in the Main Hall. Some were speaking to their voices openly, others talking to other students and some sitting in silence possibly using their "tranquil mind" as taught by Miss Garrison. Soon, the students quietened down as Professor Willemina Zantend entered the Main Hall and took her place at the front centre of the Hall facing 200 students, 50 tutors, 100 support staff and a TV camera crew of 5.

Professor Willemina had light makeup on which accentuated her vibrant, young looking features and wore a black and cream patterned business suit, dark brown low-heels on her small feet. Her mid-length curly black hair styled back in a neat bun at the back of her head with a single curly black strand hanging free at both sides of her face. A strong, athletic mixed race black and white woman in her early 70's, she smiled happily at the Year 1 students. Her powerful, confident aura caused Perianne to stare apprehensively at her uncertain, hoping that the brilliant albeit "crazy" voice-hearing visionary Professor would not somehow be able to see through her facade.

Perianne had researched about the Professor, as had all the other members of the Dedrick family. They were shocked to discover that Professor Willemina Zantend had 5 years training in Medicine, Psychology, Science, Mathematics, Languages, and numerous other fields of learning. The Professor's academic brilliance could not be undermined. It still puzzled and frustrated the Dedrick family (and other previously top Psychiatry families) as to why the Professor had chosen to support the education of people who heard voices and saw visions, by creating the Maromsaesc Universities.

"Year 1 Maromsaesc Students!! Welcome back for Term 2!!" Professor Zantend exclaimed, her voice booming around the Main Hall due to virtual speakers amplifying her voice.

There was loud applause and cheering with some students standing up clapping with their arms outstretched over their heads. Professor Zantend looked around at all the exuberant students and nodded her head at them grinning. As the thunderous applause faded down, the Professor continued to describe the changes that had been made to the University buildings (including virtual screens added to most classrooms and new virtual seating in some rooms). She further commented on how proud she was about the successful reviews about Term 1 at Maromsaesc in the News press worldwide.

There was no mention of the troublesome articles about the Marom rave, Drug bust or any negative aspect that had been reported by the media during Term 1. The Professor kept her "Welcome to Term 2" speech positive, inspiring and hopeful, which is what most of the Year 1 students needed to hear. She reminded the students that they had a responsibility to set an excellent and exemplary precedent for future students at Maromsaesc Universities, by trying their best to learn as much as they could.

"Learning will guarantee each and everyone of you succeed at Maromsaesc." Professor Zantend said assuredly. "By the end of the 3 years, you will all be very much in control and confident in how you can use your abilities for yourself and others in service to your chosen field of work and throughout your life."

Sentira listened carefully to the words of Professor Zantend with awe, love and pride flowing within her. She couldn't believe how lucky she was to be born at such a time in history, as to be able to attend the very first University for people who had similar abilities as her. In her grandmother's generation, the notion that there would be specialized Universities for the Professional development of people who hear voices and see visions, would most definitely have been laughed at, scorned and disregarded as nonsense by the world at large. Sentira smiled at the Professor with genuine admiration and respect.

A virtual screen turned on behind Professor Willemina as she talked to the Year 1 students, staff and camera crew, displaying the words that the Professor had said during the "Welcome to Maromsaesc" speech at the start of Term 1. In virtual, dark blue writing the words said: -

"Your visions, your voices, your abilities, your courage, your perseverance, your love for one another, your intelligence,

your failures that you will learn from, your successes and the paths you choose at the end of Year 3 to utilise your gifts will... set a new precedent, a new high standard for HVSV people all over the world. Be your best!"
Professor Wilemina Zantend.

Each word temporarily grew larger changing into a virtual tree, flower, butterfly, bird, wave or beach image that burst like a bubble (after the word was spoken by Professor Wilemina Zantend) then returned to being a dark blue, virtual word on the virtual screen. This created a stunning, dramatic and colourful visual effect on the large virtual screen at the front of the Main Hall.

More clapping, cheering and applause erupted from the Year 1, Term 2 students, as Professor Zantend finished the last sentence. All the virtual, dark blue words changed into beautiful scenes of nature, appearing on and off with sounds of nature gently coming from the virtual speakers, at each corner of the Main Hall. The camera crew filmed everything and there were camera flashes from students after the Professor finished her speech. She left the Main Hall with two human OBR's (one male and one female) following behind her.

Human OBR's and OBR's entered the Main Hall to help give out the Term 2 timetables using the old-fashioned, paper version to the Year 1 students. The mix of virtual documents and the old-fashioned paper documents was widespread during the 2070's, as society slowly adjusted to the new, more expensive virtual substitutes for traditional materials such as paper, brick, stone, etc...Many people still chose to use the old-fashioned materials because they were more affordable. This delayed the complete worldwide rollout of the new virtual technology.

Perianne received her new Term 2 timetable for the spring Term at Maromsaesc, from an OBR who handed out the paper timetables to all the students in her row, before moving onto the row of virtual chairs behind her. She looked down with brief scepticism passing over her face. It was like a flash of truth that could have given away her real feelings towards her Maromsaesc studies, if anyone had been paying attention to her. Luckily, for Perianne, it was a very fast display of her true emotions and the Year 1 students around her didn't appear to have noticed anything.

The Year 1 students were excitedly talking about their new Term 2 timetables and communicating with their voices around them. Perianne's wide grin had returned and she pretended to be just as excited as the students all around her. She held up her paper timetable using both hands and brought it up to eye level. She began to read the timetable of new classes that she would very soon have so many opportunities to sabotage. Thinking these deceitful thoughts brought a more genuine wide smile to Perianne's face and she relaxed more.

Psychic development...Self-defence...Complex voices...Voices for healing... Perianne mused to herself unimpressed. She turned to Annchi, sitting next to her, smiled at her and said: -

"We've got so much to choose from this Term! What do you think?" Perianne said feigning excited interest in the new Term 2 timetable.

Annchi looked at her with tired eyes but a very happy expression.

"Jelitoonaa!" Annchi replied confidently. "Don't worry we'll both pass." Annchi said as if sensing some level of discomfort in Perianne but reading it completely wrong.

"Oh, I'm not worried. How hard can it be, right?" Perianne replied back assuredly.

"Not hard at all...well for us maybe." Annchi responded cheerfully.

Perianne winked knowingly at Annchi who smiled back.

Annchi really thinks I like her. Perianne thought smugly, continuing to grin at her friend while she talked about all the new classes she was looking forward to. Perianne knew that this was all due to her perfect and skilful acting, which she had implemented since the first day she had set foot on the University grounds of Maromsaesc.

Perianne recalled in her memory back during Term 1, when she had gone out with Annchi at 11pm one cold, winter evening. They had met some of the men from Team 3 in the park area near the Maromsaesc lake. The men were Noah, Craig, Advik and Tom. The men were standing by the edge of the lake throwing stones in it, to see if they could get the stone to skim over the surface of the water. They were also talking to each other and their voices openly. Noah had challenged Perianne to a simple game of "stone skimming" and the two of them stayed together talking and arguing about who was the best at this challenge. Craig, Tom and Advik moved away as soon as Perianne joined Noah, as it was obvious to them how much Noah liked to be around Perianne.

Perianne remembered too, how Advik and Annchi had got on really well and she could hear them laughing together at a distance from her and Noah. Annchi was smoking a joint and sharing it with Advik. Tom and Craig went for a walk around the lake, talking to their voices now and again in a casual and relaxed way. After a few failed attempts to kiss Perianne, Noah had told Perianne that Craig was infatuated with Brandi. Perianne had (as innocently as she could) agreed that one night they would try and get Craig and Brandi together...

Perianne moved her happy smile away from Annchi's direction when Annchi turned to talk with one of her voices, on the opposite side from where Perianne was seated. Perianne smiled over at Brandi who was seated next to Sentira in the row behind her. Brandi smiled back and leaned forward on her virtual chair to talk to Perianne.

"Perianne! How are you doing?" Brandi exclaimed, happy to finally talk to her friend who she had not seen throughout the Christmas holidays.

"I'm Jelitoonaa Brandi! And yourself?" Perianne said excitedly. "Wow! Term 2 here we come!"

"I know! I think the creativity class will be Jelitoonaa! We get to choose from creative topics, like art, fashion design, photography,...I've chose the fashion design option already."

Brandi replied enthusiastically. Brandi wore one of her own designs as usual, a nature-scene inspired jumpsuit and a cropped, fitted, white cardigan, which accentuated her curvy figure.

Perianne and Annchi had not spoken to Brandi about the night they had invited Noah, Craig and Adivk to Room 10 Jay Halls because of Craig's distressed plea to everyone (except Brandi) that was present that night. Craig had regretfully described to them (while drunk on Rum, outside by the Maromsaesc lake) how Brandi had woken up briefly and then fell into one of her "voice-hearing deep sleeps". He said that he had tried many times to talk to her after classes, but she acted like that night with him never happened. Craig confessed to the group that he was scared to tell her what they did together. He said that he believed her "voice-hearing deep sleep" had given her some sort of amnesia. Craig drunkenly continued on (slurring his words) saying that he didn't understand why Brandi showed no recollection of how she had "got naked" with him. Noah had tried to reassure Craig that they would set him up with Brandi again during the day this time, but Craig was too drunk and upset to listen. Craig kept on drinking while sitting by the Maromsaesc lake, staring into the night sky with tears in his eyes. Noah had stayed with him until eventually Craig fell asleep by the Maromsaesc lake, and a human OBR carried him back to Jay Halls.

"Sentira, what do you think of the new classes?" Brandi asked Sentira, as most of the Year 1 students started to get up from their virtual chairs to exit the Main Hall.

"I love it!" Sentira replied with a wide genuine grin similar to Perianne's cleverly masked one. "Are you going to the Cafeteria? All this excitement is making me hungry!"

Brandi laughed with Sentira and they exited the Main Hall together to walk along the virtual pathways to reach to the Student Cafeteria. Perianne and Annchi walked behind the two women but did not try to join in their conversation. They were listening to Brandi speak to Sentira, both curious as to when Brandi would finally remember what she did that night with

Craig in Room 10 Jay Halls.

At the student Cafeteria, all the students queuing to be allowed entry were scanned by Applerishin Virtual security one by one. Once inside, the students were greeted by human OBR's and directed to take seats along the long wooden tables. The student buffet was gone and there was now an open area with much shorter tables in its place. Each wooden table now had a single small virtual screen in-between every two chairs, which the students could order their food and drink from. Payment was also taken via sensors on the virtual screens.

"Jelitoonaa!" Sentira said, tapping her finger on the start icon in the centre of the virtual screen that she shared with Brandi who was sitting next to her.

"Jelitoonaa!" Brandi agreed. "Order quick so I can have a go. I'm hungry too." Brandi teased good-naturedly.

Sentira took a few minutes to decide what she wanted to order and cancelled her selection twice before settling on a dish she was happy with.

"Why didn't they make these voice activated though?" Sentira mumbled to herself.

Brandi heard her and replied.

"Probably because it's too noisy in here most of the time and the VS (virtual screen) wouldn't be able to process the sounds into words." Brandi replied thoughtfully

"True." Sentira said. She took out her virtual mobile from her pocket (which had been started up since she woke up this morning) and selected her payment card options. Then, she placed her virtual mobile in front of the virtual screen so the payment could be taken for her order. Her order consisted of a Chicken burrito bowl with rice and beans, a warm real spinach water drink and two small bananas.

"Mmmm, that sounds nice. I'm going to order that chicken…" Brandi started to speak then paused as the many different varieties of food and drink options were presented to her in realistic virtual format on the screen.

"So much to choose from!" Brandi continued.

"Now, you know why I took my time." Sentira said kindly.

"I'm not searching through all these options." Brandi decided. She searched under selected food options for chicken and quickly found the same Chicken Burrito bowl with rice and beans as Sentira had chosen.

"Done." Brandi said satisfactorily.

"Did you order a drink?" Sentira reminded her friend.

"Oh yeah!" Brandi said. " Let me see…drinks lists…I want… oh, I'll just get orange." Brandi concluded using her virtual phone in her right hand to scan one of her payment cards.

Both women waited just over 5 minutes before they were served their food and drink by one of the human OBR Cafeteria staff. Brandi ate fast as if she hadn't eaten all morning, finishing her Chicken Burrito bowl with rice and beans long before Sentira. She touched "start" on the virtual screen and ordered another Chicken bowl with rice, beans and extra chicken.

Sentira sipped her warm spinach water and re-read all the new classes for Term 2 at Maromsaesc on her paper timetable. She continued eating from her chicken bowl at the same time.

"Psychic development…" Sentira said in-between chews of mouthfuls of rice and chicken. "You could find out if you have some psychic or spiritual meaning to your voice hearing dream abilities." Sentira suggested innocently.

Brandi dropped her arm down and replaced her fork back in her Chicken Burrito bowl. Thin, worry lines appearing on her forehead showing up clearly through her previously perfect natural makeup.

"Why do you have to spoil it Sentira?" Brandi said accusatorily staring into the space ahead of her.

Sentira immediately regretted her innocent comment about Brandi's voice-hearing dreams. However, she also felt a defensiveness and pride about their studies at Maromsaesc. Sentira knew that she shouldn't feel guilty for being optimistic about her friend's voice-hearing dreams, albeit consistently "death related voice-hearing dreams".

"Brandi." Sentira said as softly as the noise in the student

Cafeteria would allow her to be heard. " This is what we're here for. To find out how we can use our abilities to benefit ourselves, our families and society."

"That's what you're here for Sentira." Brandi replied her brown eyes blazing with anger betraying her fairly calm facial expression. " I'm here to pass these classes so my parents can buy me my own fashion store when I complete my Degree."

Sentira was stunned at the sudden change of mood in Brandi. She hoped that one of the Term 2 classes would be able to reveal something useful about Brandi's "voice-hearing death dreams" that could make her more at ease with experiencing them.

VT 2060

The Team 3 students waited separately for the Applerishin virtual security to scan them before they could enter the Psychic Development classroom in the Student Learning Block. There were some sighs of dissatisfaction from the students when they saw that the classroom was one of the old fashioned designed rooms with little virtual equipment. There were individual desks made out of wood and wooden chairs. The walls were painted a pale cream even though some virtual material peered through from the outside mix of virtual and brick designed walls. There was a virtual screen at the front centre of the room, which was one of the few signs that indicated that this was the year 2071.

"What's all this!" Sentira joked to Brandi, hoping to make her laugh and relax a little.

Brandi giggled, covering her hand over her mouth in an exaggerated gasp.

Kaden and Bataar started to lift the lid of their desks and shutting it back down again humorously, behaving as if they were seeing this strange construction for the very first time.

"Look, no virtual screen!" Bataar exclaimed

"I've found an ancient paper bundle in mine!" laughed Cahya, joining in with Bataar and Kaden.

The tutor Mrs Lear walked into the Psychic Development class quietly and overheard some of the Team 3 students making fun of the room.

"Ok, settle down, class in session!" Mrs Lear's assertive voice said clearly.

The Team 3 students quietened down, apart from a few students who continued to talk quietly to their voices around them.

"I assume you all remember me from Term 1's Health and Well-being class. Well, you're all very fortunate as I get to teach you for Term 2's Psychic Development class also." Mrs Lear (a light-skinned black woman with long, black straight hair) said enthusiastically.

"Please do not discriminate as to which surroundings your classes happen to be in at Maromsaesc University. Each class is specifically designed for you to learn as much knowledge as you can. Insofar as the learning materials are available, your education will not be affected by what kind of desk you are sitting at." Mrs Lear explained with a gentle smile.

"We don't need to do any introductions." Mrs Lear continued on, now looking down at an old-fashioned clipboard in her right hand. "Applerishin virtual security confirms that everyone is present. OBR's please enter room." Mrs Lear said the last sentence directly to her virtual mobile resting on her teacher's desk at the front left of the room where she was standing.

Five OBR's entered the Psychic Development classroom, each carrying five paper version textbooks. Bataar, Kaden, Cahya and another Team 3 student called Lisa (a peitite woman with short, blonde hair) exchanged knowing looks at each other. Lisa couldn't hold back a small burst of laughter and everyone in the previously quiet room turned to look at her.

"Sorry, one of my voices said something very funny." Lisa said out loud.

Mrs Lear looked disapprovingly at Lisa before her facial expression returned back to it's relaxed, friendly demeanour. The five OBR's finished handing out the paper textbooks for the Psychic Development class and exited the room to go onto their next tasks to be done as Maromsaesc staff robots.

"Has everyone got a textbook?" Mrs Lear (now seated on a wooden chair behind her wooden teacher's desk) asked the Team 3 students confidently. "Good. Let's begin."

The first Psychic Development class involved reading through the introductory chapter of the textbook. The introductory chapter explained that the textbook would cover the topic of Psychic ability and how it related to hearing voices.

There was not much time for the students to talk to each other, however some still quietly talked to their voices. Mrs Lear used the remaining hour and ¾ of the time left, to read from the textbook and give her own opinions on the content she read. Every opinion was lengthened by long, detailed example stories of every point she made.

After the first Psychic Development class, the Team 3 students ate lunch and played sports. By 2:15pm, the Team 3 students were waiting outside the Voices for healing classroom. When the students entered this classroom there were squeals of delight and shouts of "Jelitoonaa!" which Perianne could hear whenever the virtual security door disappeared temporarily to allow a student to walk through. She didn't need a psychic tutor to foretell her that the Voices for healing classroom was probably one of the modern, virtual classrooms.

The "mad" Maromsaesc students are going wild in there. Perianne grumbled in her mind.

Perianne waited for Applerishin virtual security to scan her from head to toe before allowing her access to the Voices for healing classroom. She had guessed right. The Voices for healing classroom was a modern, virtually furbished classroom with all the latest virtual equipment that a classroom required. It was similar to the Voice communication classroom from Term 1 studies at Maromsaesc. This time however, there were virtual textbooks, virtual notebooks and pens and virtual earpieces, already neatly laid out on the virtual tables attached to virtual sofas. In addition, the virtual sofas were more personalised, whereby the student could control the images that were shown on their virtual seating/table, insofar as they did not choose anything illegal or images that the tutor objected to. This rule was stated clearly by a virtual content warning label at the side of each virtual table

Perianne felt a familiar wave of anger wash through her, although she did not show it outwardly in anyway that was noticeable by the people around her.

Is this where all the money taken from Psychiatry went? Perianne thought angrily to herself. She tried to ignore the beauty, ingenuity and creativity of the room and instead focused on the many new ways she had discussed with Aunty Dr Joan Dedrick about how to finish Maromasesc University in Term 2 forever. She pretended to be reading her virtual textbook while decisively choosing to block out the excited, happy conversation all around her from the other Team 3 students. Nevertheless, Perianne's studious appearance didn't prevent Annchi and Advik coming over to her virtual two-seater sofa. Annchi sat down next to Perianne and bounced up and down on her part of the sofa which now had images of volcanoes, mountains and the blue sky appearing at regular intervals.

You "mad" little kid. Perianne wanted to snap at Annchi but she kept her thoughts to herself. Perianne bounced up and down once on her part of the sofa and grinned widely at Annchi.

Annchi began to enthusiastically describe how she thought that some of her voices had a psychic element to them. Perianne listened disbelievingly but did not show it.

"Jelitoonaa!" Perianne exclaimed back at Annchi matching her energy.

"Maromsaesc is going to help me become a Psychic Medium." Annchi continued on.

"So you keep telling me!" Advik said with a teasing sigh, smiling at Annchi who smiled back at him.

Perianne observed that Annchi and Advik had gotten even closer during the Christmas holidays; it was obvious by the way they smiled and looked at each other. Perianne wondered how she could use their relationship for her purpose of destroying Maromsaesc for good.

Maybe Annchi could get pregnant and drop out of Maromsaesc. Perianne devised cunningly to herself. *The News headlines would read...Teenage pregnancy at Maromsaesc University forces student to quit her studies!...no, that isn't devastating enough. The press might only blame the student, not the University... But, if something were to happen to her while pregnant on the Univer-*

sity grounds…

"Perianne, are you listening to me?" Annchi questioned, noticing that her friend's smiling gaze was looking at the mountain image on her virtual sofa and no longer making eye contact with her.

Perianne laughed loudly to deter Annchi from searching for any other meaning to why she wasn't paying attention. Luckily for Perianne, Annchi laughed with her.

"It's these virtual sofas." Annchi said, defending her friend before she could reply.

Perianne nodded in response grinning back at her.

Just then, a tall, dark-skinned black man wearing a lavender shirt with a grey tie, dark navy trousers and brown shoes entered the classroom. It was the Voices for healing tutor Mr Andrew Juniper.

"Everyone settle down, Voices for healing class is about to begin!" Mr Juniper stated loudly, so that the Team 3 students would stop talking and return to their virtual sofas, if they were not already seated.

"I'm Mr Juniper as you already know and I will be teaching Voices for healing during your Term 2 Maromsaesc Studies. Are there any questions?" inquired Mr Juniper. He exaggeratedly (when speaking the last sentence) looked at the air to his left side, then right, then above his head, to the floor and finally behind him.

Most of the Team 3 students laughed, knowing that Mr Juniper was a voice-hearer himself and did not mean any malice with his joke.

"This illustrates the first point that I would like to make to you all…it's not…that …serious." Mr Juniper said calmly yet assertively. "My second point is that laughter is one of the most effective healing gifts we have been given as human beings. Your voices that you are able to hear are also gifts. In this class, we will explore creative ways that your voices can be used for healing, either for yourself or other people."

Mr Juniper paused momentarily before proceeding. "Some

of you may not think there are any ways that the words/sentences/sounds/music, etc…could be used for healing, however, please be patient and keep a sense of optimism as the weeks go by. By the End of Term 2, every student in this room will be able to identify some healing benefit of a word, sentence, poem, song, animal sound, car engine noise, pen drop, hand clap, shout, whisper, argument, …". Mr Juniper humorously added.

The Team 3 students interrupted Mr Juniper's varied examples of what they could hear with more light-hearted laughter.

"It's not funny!" Tom shouted from the back of the class.

The Team 3 students stopped laughing and everyone stared at Tom anticipating one of his angry outbursts.

"Maybe it's not funny right now Tom." Mr Juniper said kindly. "If you need any extra tuition I am free after class till 5pm for you and anyone else who needs it."

Tom relaxed back down in his virtual sofa seemingly satisfied with the tutor's response or just happy that he had stopped the other students from laughing. No one really knew what had halted Tom's fiery anger for now but all were quietly relieved that it had been quenched.

It was the Maromsaesc (Year 1) students first day back at classes. There were new classes and a huge amount of new information to learn, therefore most of the students didn't want any unnecessary drama that they had experienced in Term 1 to re-occur. The classes were more complex for Term 2, there were advanced tests and continued excellent high standards were expected of the students. The world was watching. The majority of the students felt intense pressure to "be the best" as Professor Willemina Zantend had told them they should strive to be. For some of the students, their voices created enough interest, drama or excitement and this increased their desire not to be involved in any extra dramatic happenings anywhere at Maromsaesc during their degree studies.

Sentira wondered what Professor Willemina Zantend had said to Tom after he got kicked out of the Meditation class in

Term 1. She recalled how Tom had been escorted out of the classroom by OBR's. Sentira noticed small changes in Tom's management of his anger issues, but did not think that Tom's temper had ceased altogether.

"Be careful." Rhyle's teenage voice said around Sentira's left ear suddenly.

Sentira raised both her black eyebrows upon hearing Rhyle's familiar voice speak around her. She half listened to Mr Juniper's lecture about finding the healing purpose of whatever sounds a voice-hearer may hear, and half listened to her voices chatter around her.

"Only half of students will be Maromsaesc graduates." Rhyle's middle-aged voice said around Sentira's right ear.

"Leave it out!" an unfamiliar female voice shouted a distance away from Sentira's face.

"It's not wise to tell her more than she needs to know, you will frighten her." Gina's elderly voice said angrily in the air behind Sentira.

"I will tell everything if I choose to. None of you can stop me doing anything I want. There are no rules." Rhyle's child voice whined in the air around Sentira's left ear.

"Sen..ir...ra. Not trueeee." an unfamiliar voice babbled in a toddler's voice next to Sentira's right ear.

"It is true! Be careful!" Olamide's teenage voice shouted a distance away from Sentira's face.

"We're fooling her." three or four female child voices laughingly said from behind Sentira.

Sentira tried to focus on listening to the words being spoken by Mr Juniper at the front of the Voices for healing classroom. She used the "tranquil mind" method that Miss Garrison had taught in Term 1. This worked for 30 minutes before loud voices consisting of not only her regular voices, but new unfamiliar voices began to speak around her. These included animal sounds of dogs barking and cats howling. Using her "tranquil mind" became increasingly difficult with the noisy barking of dogs and the hissing of cats adding to the constant chatter of the voices she heard. Sentira stared at the tutor, Mr Andrew Juniper and felt a new type of anxiety creep into her spirit, which slightly embarrassed her. Here she was on her very first day back for Term 2 of her Maromsaesc Studies and already she felt forced to miss some of the lesson due to too many uncontrollable, loud sounds around her.

Sentira continued to try and listen to Mr Juniper's words, anxiously hoping that he would not be able to see that she was struggling already. Her mind flashbacked to her school days, when Nanny Lisha would come and collect her whenever she was too distracted by her voices to pay attention in class. Maromsaesc was Sentira's dream. It was also Nanny Lisha's dream.

I refuse to allow anything to prevent me from achieving my degree. Sentira thought determinedly. She abruptly stopped trying to use her "tranquil mind" in frustration at it not working fast enough, and reluctantly decided to take a break from the Voices for healing class. This break would give her time to try and communicate vocally with the voices and animal sounds around her. There was an unspoken rule at Maromsaesc, that when a tutor was in the classroom, the students should be respectful and speak quietly to their voices around them. If a student wanted to raise their voice, or speak louder to their voices they should take a break or ask the tutor's permission. Oftentimes this unwritten rule was adhered to by most of the Team 3 students, the majority of the time out of respect for the academic staff and their degree studies.

Full of shame and embarrassment, Sentira waited until Mr Juniper was busy helping another Team 3 student (with controlling the virtual images on his virtual sofa) before sneaking out of the classroom quickly. She felt very upset and didn't want to face Mr Juniper, unsure if she would cry or worse have an angry outburst like Tom. This would be very unlike her but she was breathing faster than normal and could feel her hands shaking nervously. Sentira had never experienced such bad anxiety before when hearing voices or sounds, and she was confused and embarrassed.

Perianne watched amused as Sentira got up quickly from her virtual sofa (which had the images of blue butterflies all over it) grab her orange shoulder bag from the virtual floor and race out of the classroom with her head lowered.

Ha, ha. Perianne intuitively guessed correctly to herself. *Trouble in Maromsaesc Land. Day 1, not yet 5pm.*

Some of the other Team 3 students saw Sentira run out, but unwittingly none of her close friends did. Sentira's close friends including Brandi and Annchi were (along with most of the Team 3 students) listening to Mr Juniper explain other "Jelitoonaa" features about their virtual sofas. These features included music features, how to "call an OBR" for a student request feature, amongst other interesting attractions at the side of each virtual sofa. As Mr Juniper described in detail about the how to "call an OBR" feature for a student request, OBR's entered the Voices for healing classroom holding virtual textbooks in both hands.

"And here are your Voices for healing class textbooks, virtual textbooks of course." Mr Juniper smiled. "Only the best for my students."

The OBR Maromsaesc staff began to place a virtual (predominantly orange coloured) textbook on each individual virtual table. When an OBR placed a virtual textbook on Sentira's virtual table, it paused and observed the empty virtual sofa where Sentira had been seated a few minutes prior. The OBR swivelled its head slowly in a full circle looking carefully around the entire Voices for healing class area. Then, the OBR ran to the class tutor and informed him that Team 3 student Miss. Sentira Cagney, was not present to receive her virtual textbook.

"Are you aware of her absence from this classroom, Mr Juniper?" the OBR asked in a monotone voice.

Mr Juniper shook his head frowning. He was about to start teaching from the first chapter of the Voices for healing virtual textbook and didn't have time to search for a missing student.

He was just about to send the OBR out to look for her, when a Team 3 student with long wavy red hair cascading down her back, raised her hand in the air. The student began waving her hand from left to right to gain his attention. It was Perianne Saint.

"I'll look for her." Perianne shouted over the chatter of the Team 3 students around her.

Mr Juniper looked at her quizzically. There was no way Perianne could have heard the quiet conversation between him and the OBR from close to the back of the Voices for healing classroom.

"I've just noticed her virtual sofa is empty." Perianne answered Mr Juniper's curious look, before the teacher could question how she knew what the OBR had just told him. "I guessed that's what the OBR could be speaking to you about." Perianne added convincingly.

Mr Juniper quickly nodded at Perianne indicating he had given permission for her to look for Sentira. He was keen to get started with the work from the virtual textbook and regretted taking so long with his introductory lecture. With his tutor copy of the Voices for healing virtual textbook, Mr Juniper positioned himself in the front centre of the classroom and commenced reading from Chapter 1.

Perianne jumped up from her virtual sofa, swiftly picked up her black & gold shoulder bag from the virtual floor and ran to exit the classroom. Once outside, she looked up and down the student corridor to see if she could catch a glimpse of Sentira. She looked for Sentira's distinctive long curly twist-out style, black hair and the equally distinctive bright red tracksuit Sentira had been wearing. Interestingly, there were many students outside in the long student corridor from all different Teams of Year 1. Some were talking to their voices loudly, others were eating, drinking or smoking near virtual smokers-extraction fans.

This is supposed to be class time. Perianne mused happily to herself. *Why then are so many students on break? Could it be the classes are not working?* Perianne concluded sarcastically in her mind. She headed towards the virtual lift to go down to the Ground floor of the Student Learning Block.

Once on the ground floor, Perianne looked around everywhere for Sentira. She walked past the statues of famous voice hearers and people who saw visions in history. She passed by the virtual vending machines, toilets with virtual security doors, fire exits…until she reached to the large indoor park area.

The Maromsaesc indoor park area of the Student Learning Block contained real trees, a variety of flowers, green grass, a small lake with ducks on it, and a small waterfall powered by Applerishin technology. Perianne seemed oblivious to its beauty as she accidently brushed past other Year 1 students on her mission to find Sentira. She plotted to stir up some kind of trouble to help her with her purpose of dismantling Maromsaesc. Perianne felt a rush of excited malice when she finally spotted Sentira sitting on a hilly part of the grass nearby the waterfall. Her excitement grew as she could hear Sentira engaged in a very serious sounding passionate discussion, with some of the voices around her.

Am I sensing anger coming from Miss. Perfect Maromsaesc Student? Perianne thought happily to herself as she stood behind Sentira waiting for her to stop talking to the voices around her. Perianne continued to listen to Sentira while standing behind her.

Sentira was so engrossed in her communication with the voices around her, she did not realise that anyone was standing at the back of her.

"I'm here to study. You cannot talk to me during class." Sentira said in a loud firm voice to the air around her left side. "This means, no words, no sentences, no animal noises, no singing, no crying or yelling or screaming…Nothing at all! This goes for you too. Rhyle, Gina, Olamide and Louis. I'm sorry. My degree is too important to me. It's too important for Nanny Lisha. It's too important for the future of voice-hearers." Sentira's voice broke a bit at the end of the last sentence.

Perianne stood still listening, being very careful not to break out of character and push Sentira off the hilly part of the grass into the bright blue-green lake below the scenic foamy waterfall. She listened eagerly for a further five minutes. Occasionally glancing around her to make sure none of the other Team 3 students or the tutor Mr Juniper were also in the Maromsaesc Indoor park area. The more she listened to Sentira talk to her voices, the more she could potentially learn about how best to use Sentira to destroy Maromsaesc. Perianne recalled the words of Aunty Dr Joan Dedrick on Christmas Day.

"Don't waste any opportunity. Every person, every human OBR, every OBR, can be used in some way to destroy Maromsaesc." Aunty Dr Joan Dedrick had warned Perianne repeatedly over the few weeks they had spent together during the winter holidays.

Suddenly feeling a renewed sense of urgency for the real reason she was attending Maromsaesc, Perianne interrupted Sentira's conversation and spoke up from behind her.

"Sentira!" Perianne exclaimed. "I've been looking for you everywhere! Mr Juniper asked me to find out what happened to you."

Sentira turned sharply around, noticing Perianne for the first time standing tall and confidently behind her wearing cream & black jeans with a fitted white body top. Sentira stood up to face her with a disapproving expression on her face. Perianne returned Sentira's look with a questioning stare into Sentira's eyes. The two beautiful women looked at each other with an unspoken combativeness that both could feel but each held back from expressing at this time. Sentira chose to break away from the unnerving staring contest first.

"Oh, yes. I forgot to tell Mr Juniper." Sentira said to Perianne, moving past her and walking away towards the exit of the Indoor Park area.

Perianne followed behind her and caught up easily with Sentira's fast walking pace.

"Are your voices being too loud? Mine too. I'm just taking a break for a few minutes." Perianne lied to Sentira, assuming accurately that this could be why Sentira had left the Voices for healing class without telling anyone.

"Nothing I can't handle." Sentira replied, turning her face to look at Perianne walking quickly beside her. She imitated one of Perianne's wide grins and Perianne grinned back at her. Sentira had spoken to Nanny Lisha about the warnings her regular voices had given her, which Sentira believed related to Perianne. Nanny Lisha had told her a phrase that she had heard back when she was in her twenties.

"Never let her see you sweat." Nanny Lisha had said light-heartedly.

Sentira's grandmother had then continued on by telling her not to worry about any warning voices, and to simply thank the voices for their concern over her safety. She also added that it was important for her to carry her virtual mobile with her everywhere. Sentira had laughed at how "Jelitoonaa" Nanny Lisha had been about her concerns over Perianne. Although, she wasn't sure why Nanny Lisha insisted her virtual mobile had to be with her at all times.

Sentira and Perianne reached the virtual lift and both women stepped inside the colourful interior, which continued to change colours at the same time as the outward virtual appearance. When the virtual doors closed, a pale yellow ray scanned both Perianne and Sentira simultaneously from the top of their hair to the shoes on their feet. A pre-recorded voice asked their destination and Sentira replied.

"Level 5, Voices for healing classroom." Sentira said, facing in the direction where the pale yellow ray had come from, at the left side of the virtual lift.

The virtual lift began to move upwards for a few seconds, then all of a sudden the virtual flooring of the lift disappeared causing Sentira and Perianne to fall a metre and a half onto the soft emergency virtual flooring below. Sentira let out a short scream as she bent her legs and held her arms out instinctively to protect herself. Perianne landed, bent her knees and somehow managed to stop herself from tumbling over further. Sentira lost her balance and fell on top of Perianne, who in turn toppled over on the soft emergency virtual flooring, trying to push Sentira's body off from her with shouts of "Get off me! Sentira!"

OBR's, human OBR's, some Year 1 students and visitors to the university all came running over to where the two women were on the floor pushing and yelling at each other.

"Why did you fall on top of me?" Perianne exclaimed loudly.

"How could I control where I fell! It's the virtual lift. It malfunctioned!" Sentira responded loudly back.

"Did I fall onto you Sentira?" Perianne replied angrily holding her right arm which was red from where Sentira had fell on her with a small bleeding scratch on it.

Just then, Perianne noticed the crowd of people gathering around the virtual lift entrance and changed her tactic immediately.

"Sentira, it's ok, don't worry about it." Periaane reassured Sentira. "Are you hurt?"

Sentira felt relieved that Perianne had stopped shouting at her but very confused over why the virtual lift had malfunctioned so dangerously. Two medical human OBR's checked Perianne and Sentira's vital signs by scanning them with light green rays over the entire length of their bodies. Both women were declared fit and well.

"No injuries have been sustained. OBR engineers will conduct an investigation into why this virtual lift has stopped in mid-use." a human OBR reported, speaking to the watching crowd and also to Sentira and Perianne.

"Until then this virtual lift will remain closed. There are other virtual lifts located to the left of the reception area which will remain available for transportation to other levels of the Student Learning Block here at Maromsaesc." continued another human OBR with long brown hair wearing dark jeans and light blue blouse.

The crowd did not disperse immediately however, as there were a multitude of questions aimed at the human OBR's, the OBR's, Sentira and Perianne. Questions including: -

"What happened in the lift?" a Year 1 Maromsaesc student with black afro hair wearing blue jeans and a red shirt shouted over at Sentira.

"Why did the virtual flooring suddenly give way?" another Year 1 Maromsaesc student with long blonde hair wearing a grey tracksuit shouted in Perianne's direction.

A few flashes from virtual mobiles were seen by Sentira and Perianne who were now sitting outside the virtual lift entrance (on virtual chairs) drinking water and answering questions from the security OBR's.

The human OBR took charge of the crowd again and repeated her earlier statement with added firmness in it's voice and a significantly louder tone.

"No injuries have been sustained. OBR engineers will conduct an investigation into why this virtual lift has stopped in mid-use. Until then this virtual lift will remain closed. There are other virtual lifts located to the left of the reception area which will remain available for transportation to other levels of the Student Learning Block, here at Maromsaesc." reiterated a Human OBR for the second time to the crowd of worried curious and shocked people.

"Thank you for your patience and we apologise for all inconvenience incurred by this afternoon's occurrence." another OBR added after the Human OBR had finished repeating it's earlier statement.

"A full report of the outcome of our investigation into this virtual lift will be ready to view on the Maromsaesc student website in a few hours." a different OBR announced to the anxious crowd.

The Year 1 students and the visitors to the Maromsaesc University were naturally very interested in the accident at the virtual lift. The safety of VT (virtual technology) 2060 was scrutinised and doubted by nearly all the general public at some point (according to information in yearly public opinion polls). Most people did not understand how virtual inventions could now be physically touched, held, stood on, interacted with, used to build houses and schools, etc... just as if it was made of the old-fashioned traditional materials, e.g. paper, wood, brick or stone. It was widely accepted that only highly intelligent, VT 2060 trained persons understood the concept of how VT 2060 could be designed to these exceptionally high standards. VT 2060 products (built by qualified trained persons) were designed to be extremely safe and had passed hundreds of thousands safety trials before being distributed worldwide. So, if VT 2060 was feasible and extremely safe, why did these rare accidents or errors still occur?

Human OBR's and OBR's began to gently usher the crowds back away from the broken virtual lift and then they installed a virtual security border a few metres around it. This was so that no-one but authorised Maromsaesc OBR, human OBR personnel could enter into it.

OBR's escorted Perianne and Sentira away to a different virtual lift, remaining protectively with both of them until they reached their original destination of Level 5, Voices for healing classroom.

MEDIA FRENZY

In the student Cafeteria, there also could be seen two large virtual screens on opposite sides of the cream old-fashioned brick walls. Most of the Year 1 students watched as "Breaking News" flashed across the screens with a photographic image of the front view of Maromsaesc University. Next, followed images and video recordings of Perianne and Sentira in a heap on the emergency flooring inside the virtual lift, OBR's helping them, along with a crowd of people demanding explanations as to how the virtual lift malfunctioned. Some of the Year 1 students were looking at their virtual mobiles instead, choosing to read about the latest about Maromsaesc on their phones. The "Breaking News" articles viewed on the virtual mobiles began with dramatic headlines such as: -

Maromsaesc virtual lift disaster! Two students seriously injured! a news channel in France reported online.

Board of Virtual Tech. safety threaten to sue Maromsaesc for not following strict safety protocols. a Scottish news channel headed their online article.

Two students injured in dangerous Maromsaesc cover up! an Irish news channel reported online.

"We thought we were going to die!" Year 1 Maromsaesc student informs reporter following virtual lift catastrophe. a Chero Coast online News channel stated.

Should Universities contain any VT 2060 equipment? Read below about the most recent Maromsaesc virtual lift chaos! a Pelargonium news channel headlined with a lengthy article including photos of Perianne, Sentira, the Ground floor of the Student Learning block and the front view of Maromsaesc University included below.

Every news broadcast and news report online contained falsehoods of various kinds. Then, without warning, the virtual screen turned off and the loud monotone voice of an OBR speaking could be heard echoing around the student Cafeteria.

"Can I have your attention please, Year 1 students?" the OBR announced loudly.

The Year 1 students listened while still eating and drinking.

"Miss Sentira Cagney and Miss Perianne Saint, you are requested to attend Professor Willemina Zantend's office immediately. There are two student hover vehicles waiting for you outside the Student Cafeteria. You both may take your food and drink with you if necessary." another human OBR announced at exactly the same volume as the first OBR that spoke.

An OBR stood behind Sentira and Perianne to ensure that the two women complied with the order from Professor Willemina Zantend. Both students were followed outside the Student Cafeteria and watched closely while they boarded their individual student hover vehicles.

The destination of each hover vehicle had already been pre-set to:-

Professor Willemina Zantend's office, Maromsaesc University.

PROFESSOR ZANTEND'S OFFICE

The student hover vehicles (transporting Sentira Cagney and Perianne Saint) hovered their way through virtual pathways between various student buildings, moving swiftly along the transparent and nature inspired virtual flooring. The student hover vehicles could seat two persons in each, but still had the appearance of a neat compact vehicle. They appeared similar to the old-fashioned cars, but without the area at the front to contain a car engine called a bonnet. Student hover vehicles did not require an engine to work. They contained what was referred to as H.V. tech 2060 (hover vehicle technology 2060) underneath each vehicle, which was so flat and small in size that it could not be seen without unique H.V. tech 2060 viewing equipment.

The student hover vehicles parked outside the large virtual door of the virtual building entrance to the Maromsaesc staff offices. As Sentira stepped out of her student hover vehicle, she heard a few of her regular voices talking around her left ear.

"This will be good!" Rhyle's child voice exclaimed happily.

"We like her!" Gina's adult voice said excitedly.

"Ooooo I'm excited!" Olamide's elderly voice said around Sentira's left ear.

Sentira smiled to herself. Her regular voices were, in this instance, seemingly expressing her own happy anticipation at being called to speak to the Head of Maromsaesc University. Rhyle, Gina and Olamide apparently shared her excitement about hearing what the brilliant Professor Zantend had to say. Sentira knew she hadn't done anything wrong to be reprimanded about, so was certain that it must be something to do with the virtual lift accident.

Perianne stepped out of her student hover vehicle at the

same time as Sentira but felt much less enthusiasm about having been summoned to speak to Professor Zantend. She knew she would have to remember to be extra careful how she acted in front of the Head of Maromsaesc. Even her own family members in the Dedrick family were somewhat dubious yet privately in awe of the gifted genius of Professor Wilemina Zantend. To this present day, it continued to bemuse Perianne as to why such an academically gifted woman would turn her back on psychiatry, in favour of creating these Universities for "mad" people. Her family (Dedrick family), other previously famed top psychiatry families could not understand it. According to all of them it didn't make any sense at all and the talents of the Professor should have been put to better use in the field of Psychiatry.

Both women waited for Applerishin virtual security to scan them to confirm their identity before entering into the Maromsaesc staff offices building. It was an all virtual building and glowed magnificently from the outside, and within the virtual walls from the inside. There was a ground floor reception area, indoor park area, virtual statues of famous voice-hearers and people who saw visions in various places. It had been designed nearly exactly the same as the Ground floor of the Student Learning Block, but the main difference was that there were no Year 1 students anywhere. When Sentira and Perianne entered, they were the only students in the Maromsaesc staff offices virtual building.

A security OBR escorted the two women from the front entrance of the Ground floor to a virtual lift. They all entered and waited while the OBR made the selection of Level 10 (the Level floor where Professor Zantend's office was located.) Another short walk from the virtual lift for around 5 minutes ensued. Sentira, Perianne and the security OBR walked along a long virtual corridor with images of famous voice hearers and people who see visions appearing to come out of the virtual walls intermittently to speak a pre-recorded version of their story if requested. Sentira had seen these on the Maromsaesc

University short films online. She mentally reminded herself to ask one of the famous voice-hearer virtual images to tell their story to her, after the meeting with Professor Zantend had completed.

Professor Willemina Zantend's office was the last virtual door near the other end of the virtual corridor, away from where Perianne and Sentira had originally exited the virtual lift. The two women waited for Applerishin virtual security to scan them to allow entry after accurate confirmation of their identity. The security OBR left them alone in an expansive, open plan virtual room. It had a few similarities to the virtual corridor, which they had both just walked through. There were virtual images of famous voice hearers and people who saw visions throughout history appearing on and off in random areas of the virtual cream-coloured walls. There was a main cream coloured large, virtual executive desk in the centre of the room with a single virtual dark red sofa chair behind it. The backs of two separate cream virtual sofas faced Perianne and Sentira.

There were also virtual-smoker extraction fans, virtual food and drink machines, virtual large screens, virtual flooring, virtual doors leading to toilets and a virtual boardroom type set up with a transparent virtual security border around it. In fact, there was so much virtual technology and equipment in the office, it had to be one of the most expensively furbished rooms in the entire University. The Professor herself, however, was nowhere to be seen.

"Jelitoonaa!" Sentira exclaimed looking around the modern, visually stunning room in amazement. She temporarily forgot that she didn't like Perianne (she only acted friendly with her because Brandi and Annchi liked her) and turned to speak to her, eager to share her joy.

"Perianne, can you believe how beautiful this room is! I feel like I'm in a dream, a "Jelitoonaa" dream!" Sentira exclaimed again, even more excitedly than the first time she spoke.

Perianne did not answer. She stared around the modern

virtually equipped room in a different kind of amazement. Perianne was amazed that this was where all the wealth that Psychiatry had earned had gone into.

In the R-v- Caulfied 2054 case, billions of pounds of compensation was paid to voice-hearing (and people who could see visions) charities, support groups, organisations, researchers, psychologists, etc... and the government were allocated millions of pounds to set up benefits and academic places of study for people who had these abilities. One of the government-funded projects was to invest in research to develop education specifically suited to advance the management and talents of people who heard voices or/and saw visions. The government's vision was to integrate more effectively people with these abilities into society. They aimed to progress their development to the highest standard to enable them to work and live productive and full lives. Fully productive lives free from stigma and discrimination. However, along with successes there were many failures with the implementation of support for HVSV people. Professor Willemina Zantend had invented and designed the plan for the Maromsaesc University in 2065, to correct the widespread government failures, and ensure that the vision of developing the abilities of HVSV people could truly become a reality for all.

"Should we sit down?" Sentira asked Perianne excitedly.

"I don't know." Perianne replied truthfully. To her surprise, she was starting to sweat a little.

I'm just tired. It's been a long day. Perianne reassured herself in her mind.

Ten minutes passed by, and the two women stood waiting by the virtual door of the Professor Willemina Zantend's office, where they had entered just over ten minutes prior. Perianne took in a few slow deep breaths to relax herself, the way she had always done when she was tense. Sentira was too preoccupied with the wonder of the office of the Professor to pay too much attention to Perianne. She walked forward, feeling as if in some kind of beautiful dream, towards the back of the one of the cream-coloured virtual sofa's and duly sat down on it.

"I'm waiting here." Sentira said to herself, knowing that Rhyle, Gina, Olamide and Louis were with her listening and watching everything. Her intuition was accurate as Rhyle immediately responded to her by speaking near her left ear.

"I'm waiting here too." a child's voice belonging to Rhyle said.

"Watching her." an elderly voice of Olamide said.

"Where is she?" a teenage voice belonging to Gina said by Sentira's right ear.

Perianne breathed in and out a few more long slow deep breaths, before joining Sentira and sitting down next to her on a separate cream virtual sofa. She felt relieved that she wasn't hearing any voices at the moment, as she wondered if they would potentially distract her from her perfect acting in front of the Professor.

Suddenly, to the right of the large, cream-coloured executive virtual desk in the centre of the spacious modern room, Professor Zantend appeared out of seemingly nowhere. She stood there smiling confidently, in a light red blouse, brown knee length skirt, black tights and flat brown shoes. Her black hair pulled into a neat bun at the back of her head with a single curly strand left out at either side of her face.

"Welcome to my office Perianne Saint and Sentira Cagney. Kindly accept my sincere apologies for running late. I assumed that you would both appreciate the inspiration of the voice-hearer stories in this room." Professor Zantend said smiling.

Perianne and Sentira glanced at each other curiously. They had both felt too intimidated by the magnificence of the virtual office of the Professor, to interact with the virtual images of the famous voice hearers and people who saw visions that were in various places in the room. Sentira replied before Perianne.

"We weren't sure if we should just wander around without your permission Professor." Sentira replied truthfully, standing up from her virtual sofa.

Perianne nodded in agreement and smiled what she hoped with all her heart, was a genuine honest and happy smile at the brilliant yet "crazy" Professor.

"Good afternoon Professor Zantend." Perianne stood up from her virtual sofa also and greeted the Professor by smiling warmly.

"Good afternoon Professor Zantend." Sentira said happily soon after Perianne started to speak. It sounded like the two of them were speaking in unison and the Professor grinned in amusement.

Professor Zantend sat down on her dark red virtual sofa at the front of her virtual executive desk and began to explain to the two students why they had been called to speak to her. The Professor described how the newspapers had already been spreading misinformation about the malfunction of the virtual lift at the student Learning block at Maromsaesc. She did not want them to continue to report lengthy false misinformation, possibly affecting the reputation of the first Maromsaesc University in Britain. The Professor requested their help in challenging the newspapers untrue version of events.

"I would like both of you to write a statement of your true version of events to be sent to me by email tomorrow morning. The news media must know the truth of what happened with the accident regarding the virtual lift, and the two of you are the best people to clarify this." Professor Zantend stated seriously and clearly, but with a calmness that put both the women at ease.

"Professor Zantend, I can email my statement this evening." Sentira replied enthusiastically.

"I can email my statement within the next hour, Professor." Perianne said assertively.

"Good. I apologise to both of you that you were involved in the accident with one of our virtual lifts today here at Maromsaesc. I can assure the both of you that this has never happened before and a full investigation will be undertook to find out how this could have occurred." the Professor said kindly to both of the women.

"Now, onto other matters," the Professor continued on. "The tutors in Term 1 have informed me that the two of you are doing excellent in your studies here at Maromsaesc." Professor Zantend beamed at them. "I am very proud of your individual joint achievements. Keep up the good work! Remember our HVSV ancestors are watching and the voices you hear are watching too."

Perianne quickly snapped out of her short-lived pride at being singled out by the brilliant Professor when the last sentence spoken rang alarm bells in her mind.

...our HVSV ancestors are watching... Perianne repeated in her mind while simultaneously smiling as genuinely as she could at the Professor. *My ancestors are Dedrick all the way back.*

As the two women thanked the Professor and got up to leave the office of Professor Zantend, the Professor spoke again.

"Please interact with the virtual images of voice-hearers and people who see visions and listen to their stories before returning to your Halls of Residence!" the Professor shouted enthusiastically after them. She then animatedly started to speak to voices around her in the air to her left and right sides of her.

Perianne glanced behind her and quickly took in the sight of the gifted Professor talking openly to her voices.

Her voices made her discredit Psychiatry. Perianne mused, filling in the gap of her own question about why Professor Zantend had invented Maromsaesc University. *I wonder what her voices say to her.* Perianne continued to think to herself as she waited for the virtual exit doors to open for her and Sentira.

Professor Zantend is insane. This will never happen to me. Perianne thought. She cleverly made up an excuse not to interact with the virtual images of famous voice-hearers and people who saw visions (in the corridor) by telling Sentira that she wanted to go somewhere quiet and work on her written statement. As Perianne walked away from Sentira, her mind raced faster than ever before with more new devious ways to sabotage Maromsaesc University forever.

ESSENTIAL POWER

Perianne emailed her statement about the true version of events surrounding the virtual lift malfunction that same evening, just as she had promised Professor Zantend. Sentira emailed her statement the next day in the morning, choosing to take her time so she could select her wording carefully. After all, this statement was going to be reviewed by the Head of Maromsaesc University, by the brilliant Professor Willemina Zantend herself. It was also going to be used by all the major News channels to clarify the truth to the world. The reputation of Maromsaesc University mattered to Sentira as much as it did to the Professor so therefore Sentira deliberated over how best to describe the events that occurred in the virtual lift.

Perianne didn't care about the reputation of the Maromsaesc University in the world, unless of course it was a terrible negative reputation. It was unfortunate that Perianne had unwittingly found herself in a position where she had to tell the truth about what happened in the virtual lift. She had to tell the truth so as not to blow her cover as Perianne Saint. Perianne Saint was the perfect Year 1 Maromsaesc student. Aridaperianne Dedrick dreamt each night of the best and fastest ways to destroy Maromsaesc University.

Today, Perianne had come up with yet another plan devised to sabotage Maromsaesc. She had dreamt of it vividly last night while sleeping in her misty grey double bed in her room at number 25 Jay Halls. She had been inspired by the breakdown of the virtual lift and all the negative news press it attracted, partially damaging the public's view of student safety at Maromsaesc. Until the Professor had compelled her and Sentira to write their true statement of events, the newspapers wrong information and inaccurate reporting could have done permanent damage to the outside's world's opinion of Maromsaesc.

What would the news channels and the newspapers say if there was a serious incident at Maromsaesc with no witnesses to report the true version of events? Perianne plotted in her mind. *The public would be left with no choice but to make up their own mind, come to their own conclusions and fill in the gaps.* Perianne grinned mischievously.

Perianne sat down in a mostly virtually furbished modern classroom waiting along with the other Team 3 students for Mr Winchester to start the class. Shaman studies was about to begin. Some of the other students were gossiping excitedly about the latest Maromsaesc news headlines and the statements that were written by Sentira and Perianne.

"Year 1 students speak their truth about the virtual lift accident at Maromsaesc University!" one of the Team 3 students exclaimed staring at their virtual mobile while reading the wording out loud.

"Gifted voice hearing students open up about Maromsaesc virtual lift disaster!" another Team 3 student read out, nearby where Perianne was seated.

Keeping up her undercover character, Perianne smiled at the man reading near her.

"That's you, isn't it? Gifted voice hearer." a man who Perianne did not know well in Team 3 asked her. He had ginger curly hair, black-rimmed glasses and pale skin. He also wore a dark blue t-shirt and grey tracksuit bottoms with black trainers.

"What does it say under the statement?" Perianne questioned him back.

The man with ginger curly hair looked down again at the news article he was reading on his virtual mobile.

"Sentira Cagney." the man with ginger curly hair read innocently.

"No, look at the other statement." Perianne said a little faster than she intended. She regained her composure again just as quick.

"Where,...oh yeah, Perianne Saint. That's you, right?" the

man replied. "I'm happy you both did this. Thank you. I don't get why the news channels are so quick to assume the worst about what we do here."

Perianne shrugged her shoulders resignedly.

"I don't know either." she cleverly lied to the Team 3 student.

"I'm Harvey." Harvey said smiling at her.

Before Perianne could continue chatting with Harvey, the tutor of Shaman Studies, Mr Simon Winchester began speaking loudly at the front of the classroom.

"Team 3 students! Welcome to your first Shaman Studies class here at Maromsaesc University for your Term 2 studies!" exclaimed Mr Winchester loudly to the Team 3 students.

The Team 3 students fell silent almost immediately.

"Good." Mr Winchester smiled satisfactorily, before sitting down behind his virtual desk at the front of the room. "Applerishin virtual security says that you are all present." Mr Winchester confirmed in a much lower tone, looking around the modern virtual classroom at each of the students briefly before proceeding.

The large virtual screen brightly lit up behind Mr Winchester's virtual desk. On the virtual screen these words appeared in a light green colour that sparkled, illuminating the letters to make them stand out more.

Shaman Studies.
Term 2. 2071
Team 3
Tutor: Mr Simon Winchester

Then, Mr Winchester (a white man with dyed blond hair in a low cut style) wearing dark brown trousers and a white shirt with the sleeves pulled up, started to lecture the Team 3 students. The lecture was entitled Shamanism and how it relates to hearing voices and seeing visions. The lecture lasted for the remainder of the class so therefore the students didn't get any free time to talk further to each other. There were however, some conversations with voices that could be heard but these were quietly spoken and very few in number.

After the lecture completed, the Team 3 students went away in groups of friends or by themselves to study or whatever they wanted to do before dinner at 6pm. Perianne, Annchi, Advik, Brandi, Sentira and Noah were standing around chatting for over an hour about their recent lecture. They stood together in a group talking enthusiastically standing near the indoor park area located on the ground floor. Perianne felt irritated. Not only had the news channels amended their stories about the virtual lift accident with new more positive stories, but also it was day 2 of Term 2. Perianne hadn't succeeded in her mission yet and subsequently brimmed with impatient anger. She miserably recalled one of the newer recent news stories in her mind: -

Amazing OBR/Human OBR staff response at Maromsaesc University saves two talented students!

Perianne couldn't waste any more time at this "mad" University so she spoke to the group.

"Hey everyone, I'm going to go back to Jay Halls to do some revision. I missed some of the Voices for healing class." Perianne said to the group half truthfully. To her surprise, no one paid much attention to her. It was like that hadn't even heard her speak.

Annchi, Advik, Sentira, Brandi and Noah were too busy discussing the concept of Shamanism in relation to hearing voices and seeing visions. They sounded so full of enthusiasm and hope that Perianne thought she was going to be sick any second. She quickly walked away from the group thinking that no one would notice.

However, Sentira noticed that Perianne had walked off from the group by herself. Sentira also noticed that Perianne didn't sound as genuinely happy about the Shamanism debate they were having as the others in the group did. In fact, if she trusted her intuitive feelings, it seemed that Perianne walked away like as if she didn't want to be there. Sentira quickly dismissed thoughts of Perianne from her mind. She was here for her second term at Maromsaesc. Her studies were of paramount importance. She retained a memory of all the things that she felt were strange about Perianne Saint in her mind and continued to happily discuss Shamanism with her classmates.

Perianne grew angrier and angrier with each step as she walked away from her classmates and made her way through the snow-ridden virtual pathways, past other Year 1 students and tutors. As the snow fell heavily all around her, Perianne blinked away the watery residue the snow left on top of her eyelashes.

This is taking too long! she thought to herself. *It's time to force Maromsaesc to shut down literally.*

Perianne soon reached her Halls of Residence at Jay Halls. Her face and clothes wet from the snowstorm, she waited for Applerishin virtual security to scan her for confirmation of her identity. It had been snowing all day but now the snow was coming down heavier and faster.

Perianne entered Jay Halls calmly and even managed to say a few casual words to some of the Year 1 students chatting to each other on the ground floor. Keeping up her composed appearance, Perianne entered the predominantly old-fashioned lift made of traditional materials and spoke to the sensor at the right hand side of the lift. The lift sensor was one of the few signs that this lift at Jay Halls was operating in the year 2071. Perianne could not use a virtual lift as some of them were closed at Jay Halls due to the ongoing investigation.

"Room 25." Perianne said to the sensor, which detected her voice even though she was standing in the centre of the lift and had spoken quietly.

As the lift started to move upwards, Perianne's mind flashbacked to the times she used one of these "ancient" lifts to go up to the top floor of the high-rise flats where she often lived with Aunty Dr Joan Dedrick. If it weren't for gifts from other members of the Dedrick family, she would have grown up struggling even more than she had already. Perianne had grown up struggling emotionally without her real mother and had to go to great lengths to hide the fact that she was part of the disgraced Dedrick Psychiatry family. None of her family took photos of her growing up and she could not post anything online out of fear of her being targeted by "anti-psychiatry gangs". There was certainly no chance of her mixing with anyone who wasn't in her family. Social skills were taught to her at home along with brilliant academic home schooling. Uncle Dr Robert Dedrick had taught her advanced social acting skills, during her training for her undercover purpose to destroy Maromsaesc University.

Home schooled in secrecy around the world by various family members, Perianne (aka Aridaperianne Dedrick) never felt settled anywhere. The place she liked the best was whenever she stayed with Aunty Dr Joan Dedrick. However, she hated that her brilliant Psychiatrist Aunty was now forced to live in hiding like the rest of her family.

Although curious, Perianne didn't question her Aunties or Uncles as to how they could still afford the most expensive luxurious items while living in poverty and in run down apartments. She knew (from listening to conversations by older Dedrick family members) that her family were in millions of pounds in debt. Therefore, she learned to just accept any gifts and money without telling anyone outside the family about it or asking too many questions. Now that she was much older, Perianne resigned herself to the possibility that some Dedrick family members were receiving these gifts through ways that they did not want to speak about.

It was a mystery. Albeit, a cleverly disguised mystery, that was hidden from the world. In the eyes of the world, the once rich and famous Dedrick Psychiatry family were now residing in poverty-stricken neighbourhoods in very poor accommodation with no hope of ever being employed again. Some Dedrick family members had undergone plastic surgery, changed their names and moved country to try and find employment elsewhere. However, even they lived very secretive lives, fearful that one day their past links with Psychiatry may be discovered. The majority of the Dedrick family members were too prideful to change their family name and lived like Aunty Dr Joan Dedrick, poor on the outside, keeping up a rich (shut off from society) lifestyle on the inside.

If only my mother were still alive. Perianne thought angrily to herself going into the unisex toilets and opening the door to an old-fashioned designed disabled toilet. The virtual toilets were currently out of use. Besides, the disabled toilet gave Perianne enough room for what she planned to do next.

"The flowers and science would not go together forever and what will happen afterwards?" a young male voice said loudly by Perianne's left ear.

"Science always prevails and the flowers do not need watering until spring returns." an elderly woman's voice mumbled more softly also by Perianne's left ear.

Perianne rolled her eyes, ignoring the voices speaking around her while using the toilet quickly before washing her hands and drying them. Then, she pressed her thumb print on the screen of her OBR Applerishin virtual mobile. Immediately, an OBR took the place where her virtual mobile had previously been. Perianne was in full control of its behaviour and actions. This special function being one of the unique features of OBR Applerishin virtual mobiles. She had pre-programmed the OBR to hack into the Maromsaesc University's main power computer systems to force a complete shutdown of all power at the University. Perianne handed the OBR a new virtual laptop from her shoulder bag. She watched amused as the OBR took the virtual laptop silently and sat down on the floor getting straight to work.

Perianne resisted the urge to giggle (her previous anger dissipating) as she watched the OBR silently work on the virtual laptop to complete the task she had pre-programmed it to do. It was the perfect plan and there would be no possibility of tracing back the laptop's activity to her, as the OBR would delete all memory and contents on it after finishing it's task. In effect, the new virtual laptop would return to being brand new again and it would seem that the earlier virtual laptop never existed. Perianne smiled a huge grin, wiped off some of the snow away from her winter jacket and sat down herself on the shut lid of the toilet seat.

Ten minutes passed by and all seemed to be going well until more voices started to speak loudly around Perianne's ears, distracting her from her triumphant pleasure in the moment.

"Buy my flowers, all different flowers, daffodils, roses, tulips, orchids, daisies, lilies.." a female child's voice said loudly around Perianne's left ear.

Perianne did not wait for the conversation to continue and spoke firmly and confidently to the air around her left side.

"Don't speak to me. I'm busy." Perianne stated self-assuredly to the space on her left side.

The voice she heard did not speak again for another ten minutes. After ten minutes the same voices spoke again, this time around Perianne's right ear.

"Red roses, daffodils, tulips, white orchids, lillies... These are the..." a female child's voice tried to continue to speak around Perianne's right ear.

Once again, Perianne cut sharply through the voice's communication by telling them not to speak to her.

I can tell these voices to stop and they will. Why do they keep coming back? Why can't they stay away for good? Perianne grumbled to herself in her mind. She stared hopefully at the OBR still swiping left and right on the new virtual laptop and touching different parts of its virtual screen and pressing some virtual keys. Perianne gradually felt better again. Soon, Maromsaesc would lose all power and the starkly obvious, dangerous safety issues at the new University (for voice hearers and people who see visions) will make front page, leading headline world news.

Another thirty-five minutes went by, and then suddenly everywhere went pitch black in colour. The OBR converted back into Perianne's virtual mobile and she quickly spoke to it, ordering it to turn on the torchlight function. A bright glow emanated from all directions of her virtual mobile, lighting up the huge grin on Perianne's face along with it.

*****

In the Student Cafeteria, most of the Year 1 students began to panic. Darkness was all around them and nobody knew what was going on. Also, crashing sounds ensued as the human OBR staff and the OBR staff fell (one by one) noisily down to the ground. Some had been carrying virtual trays filled with food and drink which exacerbated the noise. Students screamed and shouted amongst the panicked atmosphere.

Sentira quickly guessed what had happened.

"It's a power cut! Everyone turn on your virtual mobile flashlights!" Sentira said in a commanding tone. "Flashlight on!" Sentira said to her virtual mobile laying on the now dark virtual table in front of her.

"F**ks sake! Look at all the OBR's!" one of the student's sitting near Sentira exclaimed, after his virtual mobile had shone light over the area around him.

The human OBR staff and the OBR staff were now either in numerous heaps or solely laying individually on the floor, some with trays of food and drink spillage around them. One of the students forgot that the human OBR's were not alive and rushed to a fallen robot to give it CPR.

"It's a robot, Jack!" a female Year 1 student yelled at him.

"Oh yeah!" Jack said shaking his head at the female human OBR laying "lifeless" on the floor near him. "They look so real." Jack said walking back to his dark virtual seat using his virtual mobile torchlight to guide the way.

All the students discussed loudly with each other, confused as to what was going on. Some were talking to their voices and visions loudly also. The food and drink on the virtual tables were temporarily left there, forgotten in the midst of the panic. Sentira intuitively knew that soon the students would get bored and start to wander around the university buildings in an attempt to find out what was wrong. So, she decided to take control. Sentira worried that a student could get injured wandering around the darkened virtual buildings in the snow and ice with all the power gone. There would be no human OBR staff or OBR staff available to help, thereby placing her and her classmates even more at risk.

What would happen if they couldn't get access into another building with all the Applerishin virtual security not working? They could freeze in the snow. Sentira shuddered at the thought.

"Listen everyone, we should all stay in here until one of the teachers comes to tell us what's going on." Sentira shouted to be heard over the noisy chatter of the Year 1 students in the Cafeteria. The students ignored her, so she stood up on the virtual table in front of her for added emphasis, waving her arms in the air to get attention. Again, Sentira repeated her earlier sentence. Thankfully, a student noticed her this time, stood on top of his virtual table also and spoke up in agreement.

"Yeah, she's right. It's snowing outside. We won't get into the Halls if this is a power cut! Applerishin VS won't work, remember?" the Year 1 student shouted out from the other side of the student Cafeteria.

"It'll get cold in here too with the power shut down." another Year 1 student shouted out.

"And this is why we should all stay in the Cafeteria until someone comes to get us." Sentira said loudly so that all the Year 1 students in the room could hear her.

"Is everyone ok with this?" Sentira asked, trying not to sound so authoritative this time.

"Makes sense. I didn't bring my coat and it's freezing outside." Cahya replied shouting over at Sentira. Cahya settled back on her virtual chair and resumed eating her jacket potatoes and tuna with peas dinner.

"Ok, I'll do it." another Year 1 student reluctantly agreed.

"What choice do we have?" shouted a Year 1 student resignedly.

"I'm going to sit here and eat. Cahya, pass me the barbecue

sauce." a giggling Lisa said seemingly no longer affected by the unfolding drama around her.

"But, what about the OBR's? Do we just leave them there?" Jack asked the students near him.

"How is there already a second malfunction in only two days?" Annchi shouted at Sentira.

Sentira shook her head. She didn't know the answer to that either.

"Ha! Wait till my parents hear about this latest f*** up!" Tom exclaimed triumphantly to the students sitting near him at his dark virtual table.

"This is soooo un-Jelitoonaa." a Year 1 student said to the air around her left side.

And so the conversation went on amongst the Year 1 Maromsaesc students for the next thirty minutes. Wisely, not one student attempted to try to leave the Student Cafeteria through any of the emergency exits. The students remained seated at their unilluminated virtual tables, eating, drinking, talking to each other, their voices and their visions.

Sentira too, had returned to sitting down at her dark virtual table. She carried on eating while talking animatedly with the students around her about what could have possibly gone wrong with the power supply at Maromsaesc. There wasn't anyone who was educated in VT 2060 and all the explanations were guesses. The safety features in VT 2060 included that in the event of a power cut, the physical element of VT 2060 which enabled virtual items, virtual buildings, virtual equipment to be physically held, touched, etc.. would remain intact for a period of a year until power had been fully restored. This ensured that VT 2060 virtual buildings could not just drop to the floor (like the OBR staff did) potentially causing unimaginable loss of life.

"If the safety feature has worked today? What went wrong yesterday?" inquired a Year 1 student joining in with her discussion on VT 2060.

"I don't know." Sentira replied drinking the remainder of

her Hot Chocolate.

All of a sudden, Professor Zantend, Mr Simon Winchester and Mr Ben Kroon (a mixed black and Chinese elderly man who had taught the Confidence & Self-esteem class in Term 1) ran hurriedly into the Student Cafeteria through the fire exit. Their coats, clothing and hair soaked with the heavy snow still falling relentlessly outside. The fire exit through which they had been able to gain access to the Student Cafeteria, was located on the opposite side to where the virtual security entrance doors were.

Professor Zantend's face expressed genuine worry and concern as she and the other tutors looked anxiously around the room at the Year 1 students, seated on their unlit virtual seats at dark virtual tables. Then, taking a quick deep breath in, the Professor addressed the Year 1 students in her familiar assertive and confident tone.

"Year 1 students! Can I have everyone's attention, please!" Professor Zantend shouted loudly so that everyone would listen. "I, and the rest of the staff here at Maromsaesc University apologise for this unexpected and unprecedented shortage of power that has occurred. We can assure you that this has never happened before at any Maromsaec University worldwide and we have VT 2060 professionals working to restore power to our University as we speak. Mr. Kroon and Mr Winchester will do roll calls for the 8 Teams, please answer with the reply "present" to let us know that you are present. Once again, I and the staff at Maromsaesc deeply apologise for this unprecedented power loss and can assure you that we have the best VT 2060 engineers and technicians working right now to resolve this issue." the Professor rubbed something from her eyes and sat down on one of the dark virtual seats next to a Year 1 student.

"Ok, listen up for your names being called!" Mr Winchester stated loudly. "Team 1, Anton Calsy…"

"Present!" replied a Year 1 student in Team 1 called Anton.

Mr Winchester continued to call out all the names in every team up to and including students in Team 4. From Team 5 onwards, Mr Kroon took over from Mr Winchester and called out the names of every student in Team 5 to Team 8. When he had finished, he joined Mr Winchester and spoke to the Professor who was sitting down patiently waiting to hear if all the students were accounted for. Professor Zantend had listened and learned that 3 of her Maromsaesc Year 1 students were missing. They were Perianne Saint, Jodie Byerson and Matt Simeon.

"Does anyone know where Perianne, Jodie and Matt went to after their final class today?" Mr Kroon asked the students in the Cafeteria.

Some of the students started to talk to one another, querying where their missing classmates could be. Different answers were given from classmates of Jodie Byerson and Matt Simeon, as to where they went to after class. Concerning the mystery of Perianne Saint's whereabouts however, at least 5 of the Team 3 students agreed that Perianne was probably back at Jay Halls. This was where a few students overheard her saying she was going to, after the Shaman Studies class. No one could get through to the missing students via their virtual mobiles. The harsh snowstorm weather outside was interfering with the student's virtual signals. Using her virtual mobile with her left hand and fingers while brushing off more remnants of snow from her bright blue winter coat using her right hand, Professor Zantend stood up from her unlit virtual seat and addressed the Year 1 students again.

"We are going to search the Maromsaesc buildings and grounds until Perianne, Jodie and Matt are found safe and well." Professor Zantend asserted in a confident tone. "I have sent messages to all the human staff at Maromsaesc to begin the search immediately. Pelargonium fire OBR's are on their way to help with the search also but they are experiencing some delays due to the snowstorm." the Professsor glanced back down inquisitively at her virtual mobile before speaking again. "We aren't sure precisely when power will be restored, however the VT 2060 professionals can confirm that it should be within one hour maximum."

Applause and enthusiastic shouts rang out around the Student Cafeteria. Professsor Zantend waited for the students to be quiet again and then carried on talking.

"Please be patient and look out for each other while we resolve the issue. Thank you everyone!" the Professor finished and smiled gently at the students. Then, as if in an afterthought, the Professor spoke again.

"It shows exemplary courage and intelligence for all of you to have had the insight to remain inside the Student Cafeteria. Most of you are accounted for, which could have been a very different story if any of you had decided to wander around the unilluminated virtual pathways during a power cut. Well done! Maromsaesc has the smartest students in the country!" the Professsor smiled happily at the Year 1 students.

"It was Sentira's idea!" Annchi said loud enough for everyone to hear her.

Other students spoke up in agreement after Annchi initially did, confirming that it was Sentira who had taken charge and suggested that everyone stay in the Cafeteria until the teachers came to find them. Sentira lowered her head down, feeling unexpectedly shy from all the praise and attention by her fellow Year 1 classmates. Mr Kroon talked with Mr Winchester and then walked over to Sentira.

"Would you like to help with the search for Perianne, Jodie and Matt in an emergency snow hover vehicle?" Mr Kroon asked Sentira. "You don't have too…but, I see you have full protective gear with you." Mr Kroon joked light-heartedly at Sentira's combination of a thick winter jacket with a woolly hood, winter gloves (laying on the dark virtual table), winter boots, backpack and a thermal balaclava face mask also on the dark virtual table.

Sentira heard Rhyle's child voice say the words: -

"Go, stop being lazy." spoken by her right ear and next heard Gina say the words: -

"Someone needs your help." spoken by her left ear.

Sentira giggled and nodded her head at Mr Kroon.

"It's no problem. I would be happy to help look for the other students." Sentira replied enthusiastically, zipping up her winter jacket, putting on her thick brown gloves and taking her thermal balaclava face mask with her. She assumed the emergency snow hover vehicle would be heated inside so she wouldn't have to wear her balaclava just yet.

"You can return back into the Cafeteria through the fire exit at anytime. Is this ok?" Mr Kroon asked Sentira again, as they both walked towards the fire exit of the Student Cafeteria.

"This is fine." Sentira replied confidently, imitating the assertive tone of Professor Zantend.

"I've sent a message to you including the photo images of the missing students. Keep looking out of the window and I will operate the ES hover vehicle to ensure that we can manoeuvre through the snowstorm safely. Ok?" instructed Mr Kroon. He used his right hand to press on the sensor by the fire exit, to allow him and Sentira to go outside into the chilly snowstorm.

Once outside the Student Cafeteria they each got into their respective seats in one of the waiting ES hover vehicles, covered with snow on the dark virtual pathway. Professor Zantend and Mr Winchester stayed with the Year 1 students in the Student Cafeteria. The emergency safety feature of the heating had worked and the Cafeteria remained at a warm temperature, helping the Year 1 students feel more comfortable with the unwelcome virtual power outage. The students began to talk to each other and their voices and visions while Professor Zantend and Mr Winchester made phone calls on their virtual mobiles.

The OBR firemen were late arriving at Maromsaesc University. The snowstorm had badly affected so many households and organisations in Pelargonium, that their fire service was overwhelmed. The Pelargonium police were also overwhelmed with the number of emergency calls they were receiving in the midst of the snowstorm. The emergency ambulance crews also had some delays. Consequently, Maromsaesc University had been separated from outside additional help, with only the human staff, on-site VT 2060 professionals and the resilience of its students relied upon to remedy the unexpected situation.

Sentira looked searchingly through the ES hover vehicle window at the snow covered Maromsaesc buildings. The hover screen wipers removed snow from her view every few seconds. The winds had died down since the beginning of the snowstorm and the ES hover vehicle hovered high above snowy built up areas, and moved forward low and slow in other areas. Currently at ten minutes into their search for the missing students, the ES hover vehicle moved slowly through areas that didn't have as much snow because of being sheltered in some way. Peering through the window again, Sentira glanced quickly at the image of the missing students on her virtual phone. She swiped past Perianne's image. She knew what Perianne Saint looked like.

Perianne's fine. I know she is. She's too smart to let a power cut frighten her. Sentira mused to herself, swiping right on her virtual mobile to the images of Jodie Byerson and Matt Simeon.

"Jodie looks very young…like a 12 year old child" Sentira said to Mr Kroon who was jointly operating the ES hover vehicle using his left hand, while also looking out of the front and side windows to see if he could see the missing students.

"She is the youngest student at Maromsaesc. She started Term 1 at age 15." Mr Kroon said quietly.

"Oh dear. We have to find her first." Sentira replied concerned.

"We have to…" Mr Kroon started to say in response to Sentira when classical music suddenly rang out inside the ES hover vehicle.

"Answer call." Mr Kroon quickly said in the direction of the small virtual control screen in between him and Sentira.

"This is Ekon of VT Tech 2060. I'm the VT engineer. We've found one of your students. Her name is Perianne Saint…sitting down outside Room 25 Jay Halls as you suggested she could be. She is fine, drinking coffee, using her V. mobile. I have informed the Professor." Ekon's voice echoed around the internal space of the ES hover vehicle.

"Thank you Ekon. Keep her there. The weather is too bad for her to come outside to be with the other students in the Cafeteria." Mr Kroon said decisively.

"Ok. We will." replied Ekon.

"How long until everything is back up and running?" Mr Kroon asked.

"I can't really say precisely...20 minutes?" Ekon answered and the phone connection cut off.

Suddenly, Sentira heard a piercing scream from the air around her left ear. Alarmed by it's desperate intensity, she instinctively spoke to Mr Kroon with absolute certainty.

"Did you hear that scream? Stop the ES, there's someone down there!" Sentira exclaimed pleadingly, forgetting that only she had heard the scream and Mr Kroon showed no sign whatsoever of having heard it.

RESCUE AND REVENGE

Mr Kroon heeded the words that Sentira had spoken. He could hear the honesty and determination in her voice, so he questioned her on the precise whereabouts she believed the scream had come from.

"Down near the frozen lake, on that hilly area covered with snow, over there!" Sentira said with such strong certainty that it even startled her somewhat.

Mr Kroon utilised the virtual screen located in the front middle of the ES hover vehicle to navigate them down a hilly area near the Maromsaesc lake, exactly how Sentira had directed. It wasn't very long before they could see the top silver-coloured part of a student hover vehicle, nearly completely covered by white snow from the heavy snowstorm. Although the snow continued to persistently fall down fast and relentless around them, the winds in contrast had lessened to a brisk breeze since Mr Kroon and Sentira had exited the student cafeteria. The lower winds made it easier for the ES hover vehicle to hover near the marooned student hover vehicle.

Mr Kroon activated the emergency rescue feature of the ES hover vehicle. Rays of powerful VT 2060 light were emitted from the left side of the ES Hover vehicle. These rays of light aimed towards the area around which the top part of the silver student hover vehicle showed through. The VT 2060 rays of light were specialised features of the ES hover vehicle and were able to cut through snow in a very fast and safe way, gently and efficiently moving snow out of the way. The VT 2060 was considered to be so safe that if there were any living beings detected in the path of their snow removal, the VT 2060 light rays would automatically shut down.

Sentira and Mr Kroon peered through the windows of the

ES hover vehicle, through gaps in the intermittently appearing hover screen wipers. The VT 2060 light rays were working at high speed. Within a few minutes the snow had been cleared from around the previously trapped student hover vehicle. It was clear that there was a student inside. It was clear, because the person inside had activated an emergency silver glow colour to alert people to her/his presence. The student hover vehicles were usually silver in colour, but in an emergency the silver colour glowed and changed to a brighter silver hue.

"The power is off. The person has activated the emergency alert system." Mr Kroon confirmed to Sentira, who had already ascertained correctly what had happened. "I'm going to land and get this person out into the ES."

The ES hover vehicle landed smoothly on the hilly area near the Maromsaesc lake and Mr Kroon quickly got out of the vehicle with a sheltered hover mat, thermal blanket, Hot chocolate flask and first aid kit. He briefly struggled to open the door to the student hover vehicle. All the snow had gone temporarily, yet the VT 2060 light rays had not done anything to the freezing ice in some parts of the vehicle. The door lock was jammed and would not open.

Mr Kroon peered through the window and recognised Jodie Byerson huddled in the corner on a seat. She screamed when she heard the knocking of Mr Kroon at the window on the opposite side to where she was. Her eyes opened wide as she turned her small-framed body around in surprise. Jodie was wearing full winter clothing and appeared frightened but physically ok. Jodie could see one of her class tutors attempting to open the door of the vehicle she was trapped in. She watched anxiously as the snow fell fast and furious around him.

"Hurry up!" Jodie shrieked at him, still huddled in a corner on her seat and shivering despite her warm winter attire.

Mr Kroon reached in his coat pocket and used a piece of emergency equipment that Sentira had never seen before. He aimed a long thin object as small as a pen at the door handle area, which proceeded to emit a light blue ray that burned through the jammed lock of the student hover vehicle. Shortly afterwards, the door opened and moved to the side allowing Jodie to be able to exit the hover vehicle.

"I'm Mr Kroon. Are you ok? Can you reach out to this hover mat and get on it or do you need me to come and get you?" Mr Kroon said hurriedly. The thick snow was beginning to build up again around his boots and at the base of the broken, non-operational student hover vehicle.

Jodie didn't answer but moved quickly out from her seat and onto the sheltered hover mat with her thermal blanket and Hot chocolate flask. The sheltered hover mat moved Jodie Byerson (by pre-programming) into the back seat area of the ES hover vehicle. The door opened automatically to allow Jodie to enter with the transparent shelter of the hover mat protecting her from the snowy weather. Mr Kroon followed behind and reached around to his side of the ES hover vehicle to return to his seat at the front.

A virtual screen fitted to the left side of the sheltered hover mat, enabled Mr Kroon to communicate with Jodie and explain what had happened. He started to inform her about the unexpected power cut and that this is what had caused her student hover vehicle to break down suddenly. Then, a classical ring tone interrupted Mr Kroon's conversation with Jodie.

"Excuse me Jodie, I have to take this call." Mr Kroon said to Jodie via the virtual control screen in between him and Sentira.

"Answer call." Mr Kroon confirmed.

Promptly, the classical ring tone stopped playing and the voice of Ekon, the VT 2060 engineer, could be heard.

"Hello, this is Ekon again. Matt Simeon has been found about…er… 5 minutes ago." Ekon hesitated and another person's voice could be heard quietly saying something to him in the background. "And…" Ekon continued. "… all VT 2060 here at Maromsaesc University is up and running again. Total power is restored."

"Great news Ekon! Where is Matt now?" asked Mr Kroon.

"He's gone to his room at Goldfinch Hall." replied Ekon.

"Everything is back to normal, except... me and the others can't understand why your human OBR staff and OBR's collapsed during the power cut... and now have returned to work since the power has resumed. They aren't connected to VT 2060."

"Could be a programming error? I will address this with the Professor. I'm not sure why. It's very odd." said Mr Kroon while selecting an option on the virtual screen at the front of the vehicle. The option selected was to enable the ES hover vehicle to hover back to the student cafeteria fire exit to rejoin the Professor, Mr Winchester and the other Year 1 students.

The Maromsaesc University buildings returned back to all their original splendour and the eclectic mix of virtual colours and transparent building materials radiated brightly everywhere. The virtual pathways shined colourfully once again and it was simpler for Mr Kroon to navigate his way to the student cafeteria regardless of the snowy weather. On their way to the student cafeteria, the ES hover vehicle passed by some OBR Fire response staff who had recently arrived on the scene. They were busy clearing snow from the virtual door entrances of the Maromsaesc buildings. When the ES hover vehicle finally arrived at the fire exit, Jodie had turned off the shelter function of her sheltered hover mat as she felt warm enough to come out from under it. Parking the ES hover vehicle next to the other ES hover vehicles, Mr Kroon turned to speak to Jodie.

"Do you want to rejoin the rest of your Team or do you want to go back to your Halls of Residence to rest?" Mr Kroon kindly asked.

"I want to go back to my Halls, please." Jodie replied. She still appeared a little shaken by the events that had happened to her.

During the journey back to the student cafeteria, she had tearfully explained how she thought she could quickly get into one of the student hover vehicles and go to see the frozen Maromsaesc lake in order to take "selfies" (photos of herself) next to it. She believed that she could hide from the snow under the forestry hilly area on one side of the lake, which she assumed would not have too much snow. She nervously told Mr Kroon that she was shocked over how badly mistaken she was.

Jodie continued to explain that firstly the snow was falling down much heavier than she realised. Secondly, she had been in such a rush to get into a student hover vehicle (before OBR staff saw her) that she had accidently dropped her virtual mobile somewhere in between her final class and the virtual entrance to the student cafeteria. So, she could not take any "selfies" anyway. Jodie further described how instead of eating dinner with the rest of the Year 1 students, she had gotten into a student hover vehicle. At the Maromsaesc lake, a sudden blustering wind had pushed her student hover vehicle down a hilly slope where the power had cut off leaving her stranded inside a broken vehicle.

Jodie explained that the emergency light had come on (the silvery glow colour that Sentira and Mr Kroon had seen) but the emergency heating function had stopped working after 30 minutes. The only thing she had done right, Jodie concluded to Mr Kroon, was to wear thick layers of warm winter clothing. Her winter wear had helped to keep her warm after the heating completely stopped, right up until the time of her rescue. Jodie added that shortly before her rescue, she had been screaming loudly, terrified that the snow had completely covered her student hover vehicle. She thought she would be buried alive...

"I think that's the right decision. You should rest. You can use the emergency student room service to bring a hot dinner to your room number. The Professor will transport you to your Halls in her ES vehicle with Mr Winchester." Mr Kroon answered Jodie whose eyebrows raised up at the mention of the Professor. "Don't worry, she will be too overjoyed that you and the other missing students are safe and well to reprimand you. Ok?" Mr Kroon said reassuringly.

At that precise moment, Professor Zantend came out of the student cafeteria fire exit, (with Mr Winchester) and Jodie's sheltered hover mat rose up and out of Mr Kroon's ES hover vehicle. Jodie's sheltered hover mat guided itself into the equally spacious backseat area of the Professor's ES hover vehicle.

Sentira and Mr Kroon also exited their ES hover vehicle and moved as swiftly as they could from the short distance where the ES was parked, through the heavy snowfall into the student cafeteria. Most of the Year 1 students were gone to other parts of the University, now that virtual power had been restored.

"Thank you for helping with the search for the missing students, Sentira. You made a big difference in Jodie's rescue. If you had not somehow heard her scream, I wouldn't have decided to venture down near the lake." Mr Kroon admitted to her.

"That's ok. I'm happy that we found her and she was alive!" Sentira said truthfully.

Mr Kroon selected Hot chocolate on one of the virtual screens on a student virtual table. An OBR quickly served him his order nearby as if it had been anticipating that the people who entered the cafeteria would make this selection. Mr Kroon looked at the OBR with undisguised amusement.

"That was the fastest turnaround I've seen for a Hot Chocolate order!" he laughed at the OBR. He started to talk with the OBR that had served him and seemed to have forgotten Sentira was there.

Sentira quickly ordered a Hot chocolate and waved "bye" to Mr Kroon, who was now distracted in conversation with a few of the Maromsaesc OBR staff. Sentira wanted to go and see her friends to talk about the drama-filled evening's events, not hang around the teacher all night. She left the student cafeteria through the now fully operational virtual doors.

Outside the student cafeteria, even more OBR and human OBR fire staff were clearing snow away from virtual footpaths and building's entrances and exits. The snow was beginning to slow down finally, and Sentira made her way safely to Jay Halls of Residence. She entered a virtual lift and shook some of the snow from her winter coat.

"Room 10" Sentira instructed the virtual lift which understood her command via the virtual sensor. The virtual lift went up to room 10 without any issues. Sentira felt relieved. The memories of what had happened with the virtual lift at the Student Learning block and the virtual technology power cut today, were beginning to make her second guess how safe she and her classmates were.

No! Sentira changed the direction of her worrisome thoughts in her mind, halting the spread of it's fearful roots. *The VT 2060 professionals have resolved whatever caused the power cut at Maromsaesc. I am safe here.*

With that reassurance, Sentira walked a short way along the corridor and waited for Applerishin virtual security to scan her before entering Room 10, which she shared with Brandi Ropen. Brandi was laying down on her tummy upon her misty grey double bed with her elbows bent, her face propped upwards, resting her freckled chin on her closed hands. She was quiet as she watched the News report about the virtual power cut that had only just occurred that night at Maromsaesc University. She didn't acknowledge that Sentira had walked into the room, even though she must have been alerted to her presence by the virtual security in the room.

Sentira undressed from her winter clothing and took off her winter boots. It had been a long day and she knew Brandi would talk when she was ready. Sentira walked into the large silver and pink bathroom (beautifully designed using a mix of virtual and old-fashioned materials) and stepped into the warm pink-coloured shower. She softly cleansed her skin with the herbal body scrub provided free to all Maromsaesc students, and listened appreciatively to the voices of Rhyle, Gina, Olamide and Louis talk around her. She felt happy that they were around her to talk with, especially since Brandi didn't appear to be in a talkative mood.

"Very clever Sentira!" said an elderly Rhyle's voice around Sentira's left ear.

"We did it!" said the teenage voice of Olamide around Sentira's right ear.

"Thanks Rhyle. Thanks Olamide" Sentira replied vocally to her regular voices.

"There were three people missing and the three people were found. This is good news." the child's voice of Louis said, coming from somewhere in front of Sentira's face.

"There were two people missing and two were found." Gina's adult voice said from behind Sentira's soapy back in the shower.

Sentira smiled to herself. Her voices could be funny at times so she didn't think much about the error in the number of people missing that Gina had made. She continued to bathe and rinse off the soapy residue from her dark brown skin. Finally, she splashed water on her face again before reaching for the sensor in front of her to turn off the shower, with water half blurring her eyes. The shower duly switched itself off and Sentira waited for the virtual shower door to disappear, before reaching for her pink towel on the towel rack near the shower.

Brandi came running into the bathroom, lifted the toilet seat lid with a loud bang and sat heavily down on the toilet. At the same time that she landed, a fast peeing noise could be heard loudly echoing around the spacious bathroom. Sentira dried her skin gently with her pink towel. She heard Brandi mumble to herself before leaving the bathroom but couldn't understand what she had said. Sentira got dressed into light red silk pyjamas (a Christmas gift from Nanny Lisha) and slipped on a pair of cream-coloured slippers. She came out of the bathroom, threw herself down on her misty grey double bed and got under the grey duvet covers. She felt relieved that she could finally rest but still tiredly scrolled on her virtual mobile for 10 minutes before falling asleep.

In Room 25 Jay Halls, Perianne had also been scrolling on her virtual mobile but she felt far from tired or sleepy like Sentira and Brandi did. Perianne felt a self-imposed mixture of firstly elation, over how well she had implemented her plan to cause a total power cut at Maromsaesc, and secondly an unwelcome impatient irritation. The impatient irritation was because of the news headlines that she watched and read on the News channels. Different news channels broadcasted (viewed via the virtual screens) stories of what had happened at Maromsaesc University that evening and not all of them pleased Perianne…

> **Breaking News: Virtual power cut at England's first Voice Hearing University causes total chaos!**
> **Breaking News: Maromsaesc Virtual Disaster!**
> **Breaking News: Is Maromsaesc University safe for voice hearers and people who see visions?**

These news headlines brought on the feeling of triumph and elation in Perianne. While others…

> **Breaking News: Gifted Maromsaesc student finds missing student using her voice-hearing ability!**
> **Breaking News: Voices guide talented Maromsaesc student to save the life of a missing student!**
> **Breaking News: VT 2060 professionals restore power to Maromsaesc University! "New advanced safety features mean that the chances of another power cut is less than 5%." states Mr Ekon S (a VT 2060 professional) at the scene at Maromsaesc University.**

…other News stories brought on a strong sense of irritation and impatience within herself. Her purpose was to destroy the reputation and value of Maromsaesc University permanently, not give "mad" students opportunities to excel and receive worldwide praise.

Sentira is gifted! Since when! Perianne thought angrily to herself when she had first heard the Breaking News story involving Sentira, Mr Kroon and Jodie. Her mind raced fast thinking over all the other plans she had to ruin Maromsaesc. She thought about Annchi, her roommate and "friend".

Currently a virtual sound border divided Room 25 into two separate parts. Annchi had given permission for Advik to enter Room 25 so that he could stay overnight with her. Perianne didn't want to listen to whatever they had planned to do. She didn't want to see it either, and had ensured that the lighting of the virtual sound border was set to dark. Annchi and Advik were officially a couple now, confirmed by the status changes on Advik's social media pages. Perianne hoped that Annchi would become pregnant. She could easily picture the news channels headlines in her mind's eye.

> **Teenage pregnancy at Maromsaesc forces teenage voice hearer to drop out of her degree program!**
> **Maromsaesc student teenage pregnancy scandal!**
> **Pregnant student irresponsible for conceiving during the first year at Maromsaesc!**

Perianne had heard Annchi say that she didn't believe in birth control and if she met anyone she would use a condom.

This should be easy then. I just have to put a few pinprick holes in the condoms she uses. Perianne deviously thought to herself. A sudden desperation to get on with a new plan towards her purpose came over her, as her elation over her "successful" implementation of the virtual power cut dwindled.

I could somehow put cannabis cigarettes on Advik at the same time the Pelargonium Police do their "Drug raids". I could control a pre-programmed OBR from my virtual mobile to start a fire somewhere in the University buildings. I could hack into the End of Term Tests on a new laptop to fail all the year 1 students and later destroy the laptop. I could cause another total power cut. I can spread rumours about the tutors indirectly of course. I can... Perianne's mind raced full of ideas to ruin Maromsaesc University forever and the more she thought about her underhand schemes, the better she felt. However her initial elation had gone, dampened by the News Channels later reports that all was now well at Maromsaesc. The reports stated that VT 2060 professionals along with a gifted voice-hearer student had "saved the day." Livid inside, Perianne began to hear voices talking around her.

"...ending the sequence of events, we find that the realistic and most probable..." a teenage male voice said around Perianne's left ear.

"...following on from my hypothesis the synthesis theory cannot be relative to the sequence and is therefore deemed invalid..." an elderly female voice said from somewhere around the front of Perianne's face.

"...time and action will be the fortune tellers of the future. There is no room for complacency. Action must come before time if progression can be made at speed..." another elderly male voice whispered clearly from behind Perianne.

"Stop talking!" Perianne said confidently and firmly.

The voices stopped talking.

Perianne looked down at her virtual mobile phone on the misty grey duvet next to her. There were at least 3 missed calls from Mama Lucy aka Aunty Dr Joan. Perianne felt her body tense up. She didn't want to talk (albeit in an undercover way) about what had went right and wrong with the "power cut plan" to ruin Maromsaesc. She was trying her best in a totally "insane abnormal" environment. She needed time to think of what next to do. Perianne decided to message a response instead and told Mama Lucy that she could not talk at the moment, as she was about to start a new plan towards discrediting Maromsaesc. Mama Lucy texted back within minutes a simple "ok."

Perianne got out of bed and went to use the bathroom, with the noise of the News channel blaring in the background reminding her of her success and failures that night. Perianne closed the bathroom door with a slam. She used the toilet, washed her hands and brushed her teeth while staring at the reflection of Perianne Saint in the mirror. Her arms still tense, she moved to the right side of the sink and leaned on the pink surface ledge where the toiletries were under the mirror. She straightened her arms, lowering her head so that her chin was nearly below her shoulders and continued to gaze curiously in the mirror. She cocked her head to the left and then to the right a number of times, and finally moved her head in such a way that it could be inferred (by an onlooker) that she was perhaps drawing a big circle with her nose. Perianne repeated the last action ten times before blinking in disbelief at her appearance and shaking her head as she lifted her face upwards, her eyes still looking forward.

Where is Aridaperianne Dedrick below all this plastic surgery? Perianne asked herself angrily in her mind.

"oo ki akh siue khd dids dids ooo ki ahk sssss" an errie voice said loudly around Perianne's left ear.

Perianne couldn't tell if it was human or not and before she could tell it to stop, it had stopped abruptly. Frustrated, she pushed up and back from the pink surface ledge, dramatically flinging her arms into the air to express her frustration with both herself and Maromsaesc University. All at once, many of the body scrubs and hand creams that had been standing upright on the pink surface ledge, toppled over without her touching them. Perianne smiled amused at the now messy disrupted bathroom toiletries items, and wished it were that easy to topple Maromsaesc University.

Coming out of the bathroom wearing a short orange silk nightdress and mini yellow silk night robe, Perianne next got under her misty grey duvet covers and rested her head on her pillow. Her long, wavy ginger-red hair spread out over her misty grey pillow because she hadn't bothered to tie it back or wrap it that night. She stared up at the ceiling and thought about all the injustices that the Dedrick Psychiatry family had faced and were continuing to unfairly encounter. Immediately, Perianne felt her body tense up again. Just then, a young female voice spoke venomously by her right ear.

"Ook ki hss opo lsll lsoo ass deei iodi ceniii sss ook" the female sounding voice said.

Perianne was just about to command the venomous sounding voice to "stop" when it suddenly fell silent all around her.

I'm the boss. I'm good at controlling these things. Perianne mused.

Unbeknownst to Perianne, on the other side of the darkened virtual sound border, while Annchi and Advik were in bed together, the condom they were using had split silently. It was at precisely the same moment the last voice had spoken around Perianne's right ear.

HEALING SPARKS

As time passes with every moment, the weeks soon went by at Maromsaesc University. Before very long, the Year 1 students were almost a month and a half into Term 2 of their academic degree studies and already some students were busy revising for the End of Term 2 tests. Sentira and Perianne included, albeit for very different reasons. Perianne had to ensure her continued presence at Maromsaesc, just in case she did not complete her purpose by the end of Term 3. She hated to think about that possibility but nevertheless she knew she had to prepare for it. Sentira, on the other hand wanted to excel at her Maromsaesc studies for other reasons. She wanted to find a purpose for the voices she heard and have enough control over them for her to be able to work in a field suited to her abilities. She also wanted to make Nanny Lisha proud of her and felt a responsibility to succeed due to the traumatic history of voice hearers like her in the past. Therefore, when it came to studying, both women took it very seriously.

In the evenings, Perianne would read through her virtual textbooks and over the weekend she would complete assignments that had only been received a few days prior. Sentira did the same. Oftentimes, the two women would pass by each other in the student virtual library or raise their hands at the same time during class, both consistently giving an answer the teacher approved or admired.

Sentira had been treated as a type of heroine by the news media, after the virtual lift accident and the unexplained power cut at Maromsaesc University. The news media had spent the following 6 weeks up until the present day, discussing and debating the potential gifts of voice hearers and people who could see visions. The accident with the virtual lift and the power cut incident had been resolved and the news media were apparently bored with that story. If the virtual lift had not been fixed and the power cut had occurred for a longer period, the news media may have had success with continued headlines about it. It soon became clear to those in charge of what stories to report, that the general public were more interested in the gifts and abilities of the students at Maromsaesc University.

The story of the Year 1 student Sentira Cagney, who had heard a voice scream loudly around her that directly led to the discovery and rescue of Jodie Byerson, fascinated people everywhere. The news media wanted to keep up this public interest and every day articles about the potential uses of hearing voices and seeing visions were printed and/or reported about in the news. This was also due to similar occurrences happening to other students at the four other Maromsaesc Universities in other parts of the world.

Year 1 students in Germany and New York for example, were also showing exceptional skills due to their voice hearing and vision abilities. The Shaman Studies classes and the Psychic Development classes were the most topical classes with 80 % of Year 1 students showing some skills in these subjects. Sentira felt happy that one of her voices had shown some kind of psychic insight and even happier that she could consider becoming a psychic detective after her degree training. However, she was still unsure about some of the random loud voices that she couldn't control as quickly. This uncertainty only fuelled Sentira to study more fervently than her other classmates. Only Perianne Saint equalled Sentira's dedication to her work out of the entire class of Team 3 students.

The pressure for the Year 1 students to succeed at one of the 5 Maromsaesc Universities worldwide, was beginning to be felt more intensely since the news media had begun to praise their potential talents and gifts. Some students felt they needed to get everything perfectly correct during their class psychic and shaman studies exercises. Unfortunately when they occasionally did not, it sometimes was not as well handled by the majority as mistakes made in class during Term 1.

"You changed the ball behind with your hands!" a nervous Year 1 student exclaimed loudly, causing the tutor Mrs Michelle Lear and the other Team 3 students to stare over at the two people in the middle of the classroom.

The person who had exclaimed out loud was a tall thin white man with a shaven head.

"No, you got it wrong. Try again." a shorter slim-build white man with blond hair replied encouragingly.

"I've had it with this! F*** it!" said the taller man and he grabbed his black jacket and stormed out of the classroom.

An OBR quickly followed behind him out of the virtual exit.

"Julian!" the shorter man shouted after him. "So who will I finish this with?"

"Eddie, come over here and stop shouting. He's gone now." Bataar said to Eddie.

"Yeah but I'll have to start from the beginning again so all my progress will be lost." Eddie grumbled.

"It's not an exam, so don't worry about it." Bataar replied nonchalantly.

"Don't you care about your work?" Eddie retorted back at him.

Sensing and understanding Eddie's anxiety, Bataar half-smiled at Eddie and didn't say anything.

"The exams will be worse." said Lisa, standing next to Bataar. She held two different coloured tennis balls behind her back, in the middle of the quick psychic exercise, which Mrs Lear had allocated to Team 3 at the start of the day's lesson.

"Do you think they will be? Cause I'm trying my best to find a use for my voices. If I'm not psychic or a shaman then what am I?" Eddie said, a clear panic rising up in his voice during the last sentence.

"You could be a healer." Sentira interrupted Bataar before he could respond. She had overheard the conversation from a few metres behind them. "Or you could have spiritual gifts, sports talents, creative talents, voice-communication skills, Mediumship ability, be a teacher, a businessman, a sportsman, an artist, entrepreneur...you can be anything you want to be. A psychic or a shaman are not the only career paths for people like us. We have to all be patient and see what happens at the end of Year 3, ok?"

"And...once we have our Degree qualification in the Professional Development for people who hear voices, we can take our training anywhere and be successful!" Perianne chimed in enthusiastically. She was determined not to let Sentira outshine her perfect act as an ambitious and popular Maromsaesc University student.

"Sentira and Perianne are right." Mrs Lear (the Psychic Development tutor) confirmed. "Everything will be fine as long as you stick out your studies up to the end of Year 3. I, and the rest of the tutors here at Maromsaesc are looking for you to understand the ideas we teach, even more so than you excelling in any one particular area. Your understanding and application of ideas will eventually lead to you finding areas where you can utilise your voice hearing abilities, just give it time." Mrs Lear finished saying to the Team 3 students, who had also been quietly listening to the conversations between Eddie, Bataar, Lisa, Sentira and Perianne.

"Do you want me to go and look for Julian?" Perianne offered seemingly innocently to Mrs Lear.

"Did you not see the OBR that left the classroom after Julian? Mrs Lear said to Perianne.

A hastily smothered giggle escaped from Sentira's mouth, which she quickly turned into a cough. Before Perianne could reply, Mrs Lear continued talking ignoring Sentira's coughing noises in the background.

"We have a new university policy in Term 2 that OBR Maromsaesc staff will support students who accept their help if they are having difficulties during class. The OBR will approach Julian and inform him of his options, and I will follow up from the feedback sent immediately back from the OBR." explained Mrs Lear in a self-assured manner.

"Great idea!" Perianne replied enthusiastically, remaining

perfectly in the character of Perianne Saint, while also simultaneously despising Mrs Lear and everyone around her in her thoughts as Aridaperianne Dedrick.

Later that same Thursday, during the Voices for Healing class, Perianne felt familiar anger rising up within her. The Voices for Healing classroom was one of the most expensively furbished classrooms in the University and reminded her of the financial loss experienced by her family and psychiatry as a profession. She determinedly fixed her focus back to the class by rehearsing some of the phrases she had learned from the tutor, Mr Juniper.

"I am love. I am a healer. Healing energy surrounds me. Talk to me. I am listening. I am ready to help heal myself and others. This is my intention." Perianne practiced repeating some of the key phrases, which were taught to all the students by Mr Juniper.

These key phrases were to help attract healing voices to the voice-hearer according to the virtual Voices for Healing textbook. There was no requirement to meditate first. The virtual textbook directions (for this particular exercise) were simply for the student to practice speaking or thinking these words. Aridaperianne considered the entire virtual textbook an absurdity. Perianne, on the other hand, was fascinated by the virtual Voices for Healing textbook and over-excited about each new concept. She practiced the words again, while seated on her virtual sofa behind a virtual table showing intermittent images of clouds floating over a light blue sky scene. Her virtual textbook open in front of her, held securely in her left hand, Perianne privately hoped that the tutor would notice her concentration and focus.

"I am love. I am a healer. Healing energy surrounds me. Talk to me. I am listening. I am ready to help heal myself and others." Perianne said slowly and with confidence. To Periane's surprise, at that very moment voices did start to chatter around her.

"Heart attack, it hurt…the worst, extreme pain and then it

was over." an adult male voice said around Perianne's right ear.

"Ashtma, I couldn't breathe. My pump...where is it? The children. I have to pick up my daughter. She'll be wondering where I am. I...can't...breathe." an elderly female voice said loudly around the front of Perianne's face.

"Head pain. Neck pain. Back pain. Dead." a male child's voice chanted sadly around Perianne's left ear.

Perianne resisted the strong temptation to tell the voices to shut up. She wasn't here to help voices talk to her more. They were not her friends. And, she was certainly not their healer. Nevertheless, she pressed the call sensor with her left thumb, to get the tutor Mr Juniper to come over to her virtual table.

Maybe I'll get points towards my final grade if I tell the tutor about what I've just heard. Keep me at Maromsaesc longer to kill it for good! Perianne thought to herself. She was highly irritated at hearing voices, but did not show any sign of her irritation in her facial expression that could in anyway be interpreted by another person or human OBR/OBR. Or so she believed...

Mr Juniper approached Perianne's virtual table, five minutes after he had assisted a student seated in front of Perianne with her difficulty understanding the key phrases. All the while, Perianne continued hearing random voices, male and female of all ages speaking about various causes of death around her.

"The voices around me are telling me about heart attacks, asthma, head injuries, neck.." Perianne said to the tutor as he finally arrived to sit next to her on her virtual sofa.

Mr Juniper interrupted her and spoke in a loud voice to get the rest of Team 3's attention.

"Everyone! Can I have your attention?" Mr Juniper asserted loudly. "Can you all stop what you're doing and come over to Perianne's virtual table now, please! Thank you."

The Team 3 students stopped the class exercises they were working on and huddled around Perianne's virtual table, in anticipation at what could possibly be about to happen. Some of the students continued talking to their voices around them, as they waited for other students to come over.

"Ok, everyone quieten down. Perianne. Can you tell the rest of the class what you've just described to me?" Mr Juniper asked calmly, still seated next to Perianne on her virtual sofa with serene imagery of clouds and blue sky passing by underneath them, due to VT 2060.

"I practiced the key phrases from chapter 5, exercise 2, just as we were instructed. I said the words..." Perianne started to say, reaching for her virtual textbook that she had put back down on the virtual table to place in front of her for dramatic effect.

"The key phrases to communicate with voices that may require healing, include the usage of such phrases including...I am love, I am a healer. Healing energy surrounds me. Talk to me. I am listening. I am ready to help heal myself and others." Perianne pasued and looked around at the Team 3 students attentively listening to her every word, before proceeding.

"Then I heard unknown voices speak around me mentioning illnesses, diseases, health conditions, which I assume..." she glanced at the tutor Mr Juniper. "...I assume need healing. They talked of heart attacks, asthma, head injuries, neck pain, backache,.." Perianne described clearly, mustering as much enthusiasm (learned during her acting training with Dr Robert Dedrick) as she could.

At that precise moment, Mr Juniper's assertive voice cut into Perianne's speech.

"Perianne has attracted voices to her of spirits of the dead that are in need of afterlife healing." Mr Juniper explained to the Team 3 students listening around him and to Perianne. "She has healing ability and can help those spirits by healing them from deaths that have been so traumatic they are still wandering around the earth as lost souls."

Perianne tried to keep a serious, curious expression on her face, but inside as Aridaperianne Dedrick, she wanted to scream and laugh simultaneously.

I will not be helping lost souls to heal! I'll only do what is re-

quired to pass enough tests/exams to keep me a student in Maromsaesc. Perianne angrily thought. Sighing inwardly, she listened to Mr Juniper go into a very detailed explanation of how she could utilise her healing ability in relation to voices that she attracted.

Mr Juniper described how she could communicate with the lost souls to find out how best she could help to heal them from the trauma they have carried on past death. In addition, Mr Juniper explained that if she could not help, then she should direct them to another voice-hearer who was also a healer, or send them to the light.

I'll send them over to Sentira so they can harass her. Perianne mused to herself, smiling outwardly at Mr Juniper as he continued with his lengthy, in depth description on how to use healing ability with hearing voices.

"…so, Perianne…" Mr Juniper addressed Perianne directly, loud enough for the entire class to hear. "…you can communicate with the voices you attract after using the key phrases in anyway. You may choose perhaps, to utilise the skills you have learned in Term 1's Voice Communication classes. Find out what help the lost souls need, help them best you can or direct them elsewhere to another healer or to the light. Got it?"

"I understand Mr Juniper and I'll try. Thank you." Perianne said to Mr Juniper, picking up her virtual Voices for Healing textbook again and pretending to be studying it very carefully. She hoped that Mr Juniper didn't prolong the conversation. She could already feel a fiery rage building up within her over the suggestion that she would have to communicate more with the voices around her. Perianne preferred ignoring them or commanding them to stop.

This "mad" university needs to burn down to the ground! Perianne angrily thought in the privacy of her mind. She pondered how she could do this as fast as possible. Suddenly, vivid flashing imagery of fires raging from every corner of Maromsaesc University appeared instantly in her mind. Then, Perianne felt calm again.

The Team 3 students started to move away from Perianne's virtual table and back to their own colourfully designed virtual sofas and virtual tables. Most of them, similar to Perianne, returned to reading their virtual textbooks at Chapter 8 suggested by Mr Juniper. Chapter 8 of the virtual Voices for Healing textbook, explained the various ways to heal lost souls as a voice-hearer. The virtual Voices for Healing texbook included how to heal people as a voice hearer too, by intelligent communication with guiding healer voices. This chapter (Chapter 13), would not be taught until a few weeks time.

Sentira flicked through the pages of the virtual Voices for Healing textbook and skim read through some of the paragraphs of upcoming chapters. She looked forward to when she could try to use her voices to heal other people, provided she could communicate intelligently with any healing energy around her. Sentira was sure that she could communicate both effectively and intelligently. She had a strong desire to succeed and knew how to apply the knowledge learned resourcefully and brilliantly, achieving mostly A grades in every class exercise or test. Yet, there were many uncertainties and questions remaining unanswered with the voices she could hear around her.

Why do they speak at random? Why can't I control the volume and length of time some of the voices speak? Why were people like me persecuted so badly in the past? What career will I choose when I get my degree and what happens if my voices stop speaking around me permanently? Will I lose my job? Sentira considered these questions in her mind, while looking through her virtual Voices for Healing textbook.

Voice hearing (in Sentira's opinion) was experienced so randomly and unexpectedly in many different ways, they were very hard to fit into one category. Her regular voices, which Sentira immediately recognised around her, were the only voices that had some kind of familiarity since childhood. No matter what age range they spoke to her in, Sentira knew who they were and usually felt comfortable hearing them chatter around her. Usually.

As if on cue, somehow triggered by Sentira thinking about them, her regular voices began to talk around her.

"When do we go to see the Professor again? I need to speak with her." said Rhyle's adult voice around Sentira's left ear.

"There are too many virtual gadgets in this room." said Gina's elderly voice.

"Find somewhere else to sit, Gina." Olamide's adult voice said loudly around the front of Sentira'a face.

"Be careful." Louis's child voice said calmly, by Sentira's left ear.

"Be careful." Olamide's child voice said loudly, in front of Sentira's face.

"Be careful." Gina's adult voice said quietly, by Sentira's left ear.

Sentira paid attention when she heard the words that Louis's child voice had spoken. She immediately thought of Perianne and the warnings she had heard in Term 1, which she believed related to something seriously wrong with her classmate, Perianne Saint. Sentira had been so consumed with her Term 2 studies that she did not think much about the warnings she had received to "be careful" around Perianne or to watch Brandi. Now once again, here were the familiar "be careful" words back again, being spoken at different volumes around her. Sentira decided to use her tranquil mind to communicate with them, which she had learned during meditation class in Term 1 of her first year degree.

Sentira placed her virtual Voices for Healing, textbook on her virtual table, directly in front of her. She took ten slow deep breaths in and out to relax her mind. All the while, her regular voices continued repeatedly saying the words "be careful" near her at different sound volumes. Eventually, (after 5 minutes) the slow deep breathing relaxed Sentira and she felt calm. It was then that she used her tranquil mind to observe her voices without judgement or attachment for the following 10 minutes. Her regular voices gradually quietened down and soon stopped completely. At the same time as Sentira's regular voices had stopped talking around her, Mr Juniper announced loudly to the class that their individual study time was over. He began lecturing on the contents of Chapter 7 and Sentira stopped using her tranquil mind and listened carefully to every word that Mr Juniper said.

*****

Later that night, Sentira lay awake in her misty grey double bed peering up at the ceiling thinking. The night turned into the early hours of the next day and at 2am she still couldn't fall asleep, no matter what she tried. Sentira had made a cup of herbal tea, watched a movie, read a book, meditated and wrote her thoughts down in her virtual journal. Nothing worked. There were no voices speaking around her, so it was not her voices (regular or unknown) that were keeping her awake.

Sentira looked over at Brandi who was fast asleep and snoring gently. Sentira half-smiled to herself. At least Brandi was able to get some sleep tonight. It didn't seem like she was going to get any.

Feeling oddly very alert, Sentira got out of bed and put on her yellow tracksuit, white trainers and black jacket. She pulled her long, twist out styled black afro hair into a loose ponytail using a light blue scrunchie, that had previously been on her left wrist. She used the bathroom, picked up her virtual phone near her grey pillow, and left Room 10 Jay Halls to go for a walk outside. It was permitted for Year 1 students to leave their halls of residence at anytime. They were not however, allowed to leave the Maromsaesc University grounds unless it was half term, the end of their studies, an emergency, or they had permission from a member of staff for a valid reason.

Recently, the weather had been unusually warm for late February during the daytime but currently it felt chilly with cool breezes. Sentira exited Jay Halls of Residence and walked along virtual pathways to reach the new Maromsaesc gardens, that had recently finished it's building works in late January 2071. The Maromsaesc gardens were beautiful, and another stunning visual asset to the wonder of the Maromsaesc University virtual buildings themselves. With the virtual pathways lighting up Sentira's path through the gardens, she took her time to stand and stare at the spring flowers that had bloomed early due to the warm weather. There were lovely spring flowers such as golden-yellow daffodils and tulips of nearly every colour of the rainbow. There were purple, white, yellow and pink hyacinths organised in oval shaped areas and heart shaped areas in another part of the Maromsaesc Gardens which Sentira viewed in awe at it's beauty.

Sentira was not alone in her decision to have a night walk through the Maromsaesc Gardens, there were also other Maromsaesc Year 1 students wandering around. Some of the students were walking along the virtual footpaths (similar to Sentira) admiring the beauty of the spring flowers. Despite the dark night sky, the daffodils, tulips and hyacinths were lit up attractively by virtual lighting of different colours at different angles. Other students sat down near the flowers talking to each other or/and talking to their voices or visions. Sentira smiled at a few of the Team 3 students she recognised but did not join any one group of students, preferring to be by herself.

Sentira approached an area of the Maromsaesc gardens that had oak trees and sweet chestnut trees. Still feeling wide awake, she sat down under one of the oak trees, propping her back up against the thick stalk of the tree comfortably. She then took out her virtual mobile from the side pocket of her black jacket. She began to read studiously through her notes (saved on a Term 2 study app) on the home screen of her virtual mobile. Occasionally, Sentira glanced up when she heard students walk past her talking to each other or their voices or visions. She smiled happily to herself. Her dream of attending a University where nearly everyone experienced similar voices as she did had come true. She was here, a first year Maromsaesc student and had already identified that some of her voices had psychic uses. Sentira outstretched her arms lazily above her head and let out a satisfied yawn. While reading, her eyes closed momentarily a number of times. Startled, she opened them again wide when it happened on the 20th time.

The long walk must have worked. I'm feeling sleepy. Sentira mused to herself, getting up to begin the long walk back through the Maromsaesc gardens along the virtual pathways to Jay Halls.

She had just reached the exit of the gardens (after walking dreamily for 20 minutes) when all of a sudden a loud fire bell sound rang out from all directions. The fire bell noise came from virtual speakers that were inside the Maromsaesc buildings, and also from virtual speakers outside in the Maromsaesc university grounds. Sentira stopped dead in her tracks, her heart skipping a beat. Quickly recovering from her tired shock-induced hesitation, she started to run through the virtual pathways breathing fast, towards the front entrance of the University grounds. Other Maromsaesc students were also running ahead of her to convene at the allocated safe location.

Amongst the Year 1 students rushing out of the University buildings, there were also tutors and support staff consisting of human OBR and OBR's. The number of human OBR's and OBR support staff had increased since the first day of Year 1 Maromsaesc studies. Presently, there were now over 200 robot support staff at the University. The human OBR's and the OBR's came out of the University buildings in a very distinct way than the panicked racing way the students and tutors exited the University. The human OBR's and the OBR's were clearly much more calmer, self-assured and certain about what they had to do and where they had to go. They walked (not ran) to the allocated meet up area, swiftly, calmly and confidently.

Whereas most of the Year 1 students appeared worried, feeling justifiably unsure about what was happening. They were rightly unsure about the safety of themselves and their friends. The human OBR's and the OBR support staff were pre-programmed to behave the way they did. Whoever had designed this feature of the robots, had cleverly chosen not to try and imitate human panic and anxiety in the event of an emergency evacuation. The only other person who had the same level of calm and ease about the latest unfolding drama at Maromsaesc was Perianne Saint. On the outside however, Perianne imitated the exact same worry and panic that she heard in the other students around her, using her immaculate acting skills.

Professor Wilemina Zantend, the Year 1 students, tutors and support staff soon convened near the entrance gates of Maromsaesc University within 25 minutes. There were a large number of student hover vehicles orderly lined up near where the students had gathered in lines, anxiously waiting for their tutors to tell them more about the fire.

The student hover vehicles could be used in an emergency as long as there would be no risk to the person using the vehicle or other people during the travel journey. Therefore, many Year 1 students had intelligently opted to travel via the student hover vehicles that were located outside every University building and in some university corridors. This greatly reduced their walking time and made their arrival at the allocated meet up area more swift. Physically disabled Maromsasec students had hover chairs and hover scooters, which were just as efficient and fast moving as the student hover vehicles. Although, every physically disabled student could choose to use a student hover vehicle if they so desired, as there were adjustments that were automatically made to accommodate any disability. It was usually more convenient and readily available for disabled students however, to use their own personal hover chairs or hover scooters especially in an emergency.

Mr Juniper, dressed only in thin cotton grey pyjamas with black outlines around pocket areas and wearing brown slippers, had his arms folded tightly across his chest. He shivered on and off in front of the Team 3 students (who had formed a line in front of him) visibly appearing to be much colder than those students who had quickly remembered to bring a jacket with them. Luckily, an OBR nearby brought Mr Juniper a luminous green thermal blanket, which Mr Juniper gratefully accepted. The OBR placed the green thermal jacket over Mr. Juniper's shoulders and the jacket reached down to his ankles. Other people who had also rushed out of the University buildings in light sleepwear were too given luminous green thermal blankets, quickly distributed to them by the OBR support staff.

All the other teams of Year 1 students had formed lines in front of their tutors, facing towards the virtual entrance gates of Maromsaesc University. Next, Mr Juniper began to call out the names of the 25 students in Team 3, one by one. Everyone was present. Then, Professor Zantend stood at the front centre of the eight student lines and addressed everyone. Her voice amplified by virtual speakers.

"Maromsaesc Year 1 students." said the brilliant Professor assertively, calm and controlled. "It is a false alarm! No fire has been detected anywhere at Maromsaesc University. You are all safe. Everyone has been accounted for. Due to tonight's unnecessary fire alarm incident, morning classes are cancelled and you can choose whether or not to attend your Sports class before we expect full attendance at your afternoon lessons. I apologise for the disruption to your sleeping hours and can assure that a full investigation will be undertaken to find out who caused the fire alarms to activate or why the fire alarms activated tonight without a fire. You are dismissed and can return to your Halls of Residence." finished Professor Zantend with a hint of tiredness in her voice while speaking the last sentence.

You will never never guess, nutty professor. Perianne thought to herself in sweet satisfaction, joining Annchi, Advik and Cahya to walk back with them towards Jay Halls chatting animatedly about the night's events.

TENSE MOMENTS

It was fast approaching the final week of Term 2 and Perianne was still happily revelling in the chaos she had instigated up to the near close of Spring Term at Maromsaesc University. The news media had heard of the story of the fire alarm error at the University (which occurred around 4 weeks ago) and had dramatised it greatly. There were reports (albeit erroneous) of students forced to leave their halls of residence in the middle of the night, wearing nothing but their underwear due to the false fire alarm evacuation. There had been numerous other news reports which questioned the safety at Maromsaesc University, and frequently repeated past stories about other dangerous incidents that had occurred since day 1 of the first year studies.

The recent incidents, such as the virtual lift accident and the power cut, were grouped together with the reporting of the false fire alarm evacuation. Also mentioned, was the Term 1 incident of the dangerous OBR barbecue that had badly burnt the arm of Year 1 student, Kaden Sallow. The "drug raid" by the Pelargonium Police in the middle of the night, also was one of the frequently repeated stories that appeared often on news channels. Overall, a significantly large number of distorted exaggerated information was being spread about Maromsaesc University that it soon led to the safety of Maromsaesc University to be debated worldwide. Even though a random story about a gifted student benefiting from education at Maromsaesc University would occasionally appear, these were few and much shorter in length than the amount of negative press Maromsaesc received.

Initially, the Professor had refused to comment since the first false fire alarm incident was reported with numerous errors by the News media. But then, followed the older worrisome stories from the past being repeated daily with multiple errors and inaccuracies. There were many occasions when news reporters would group together outside the virtual entrance gates of Maromsaesc, demanding her view on their latest reports. Eventually, to pacify the relentless negative media frenzy, Professor Zantend agreed to give an interview to the Pelargonium News Channel in relation to the negative news reports about safety at Maromsaesc University circulating worldwide. This interview only halted the negative press for a few days before newer stories about safety at Maromsaesc (focusing this time on the human OBR's and OBR's) were erroneously reported as a serious safety concern at Maromsaesc.

Professor Zantend declined to participate in another requested interview, and assertively reminded the news media by e-mail to refer to her recent interview with the Pelargonium News Channel. During that interview, she had confirmed (with correct evidence) that Maromsaesc met the highest quality safety standards and that she would in future no longer give interviews when the news reports were so horrendously untrue. At the end of the interview the Professor had firmly stated that she had a University to lead, and therefore could not waste any more time on dealing with the news media.

Sentira felt confused by the media reports. It was obvious to her that some of the news reports were dangerously inaccurate, yet the world news channels kept on spreading fake news. Sentira remembered how Maromsaesc students had been celebrated after she had helped find missing student Jodie Byerson, using a previously unknown psychic voice ability. She recalled how (for a short period of time) students at Maromsaesc Universities worldwide had made news headlines about the discovery of psychic and shamism abiliites in 70% of all Year 1 students.

Surely the previous articles about talented students shows the importance and value of education at a University for voice-hearers and people who see visions, such as Maromsaesc University. Sentira thought to herself. She sat alone on a virtual chair in the student library skim reading through the latest depressing story of safety concerns at Maromsaesc University. This particular article focused on the negative aspects of the human OBR's and the OBR's and questioned if it was safe to use robots in numerous supervisory and responsible roles with young people at Maromsaesc. In disgust, Sentira turned her face away from the A3 sized virtual screen which was securely propped up on the virtual table she was using. She stood up and placed her yellow shoulder bag over her shoulders, walking quickly out of the student library with tears in her eyes.

Sentira allowed the tears to fall freely from her eyes inside one of the cubicles of the student unisex toilets, located in the corridor outside the student library virtual entrance. She didn't like how emotional she had become after reading the negative news story about Maromsaesc and did not want anyone to see her crying. This was not how her beautiful dreams about her first year at Maromsaesc played out when she was asleep and sometimes during the daytime. There were none of the negative dramas that the news channels insisted on replaying daily about the safety issues at Maromsaesc. In Sentira's mind and dreams, Maromsaesc was the perfect heaven-sent university for people like her. People who had the ability to hear voices and see visions.

Come on Sentira! You can do this! Sentira gently reminded herself in her thoughts. *I'm still achieving everything I've dreamed for in my Year 1 course. It's a Jelitoonaa University! I'm an A grade student. I could be a Psychic detective when I get my degree. There are no real safety concerns at Maromsaesc. It's all been exaggerated by the trouble-making media.*

"Well, how early can I get an abortion?...I missed my period twice...Yes, he put on a condom...no, I haven't been pregnant before...do you really need to ask all these questions! I just want a date and time I can get rid of this baby." Annchi's voice rang out loud and clear in the unisex student toilets.

The smell of cannabis smoke began to permeate the air. Annchi had forgotten to turn on one of the virtual smokers-extraction fans. Smoking cannabis, even medical cannabis, was illegal inside public spaces unless you used an available virtual smokers-extraction fan.

"Annchi?" Sentira said out loud from inside her toilet cubicle.

Annchi turned around and ran back out of the unisex student toilets. Sentira came out of her cubicle, rinsed her hands quickly and went outside to see if Annchi was still around. She saw her friend leave the student library building and walk briskly through the virtual pathways.

It was a sunny spring Sunday and there were no formal classes held that day. End of Term 2 tests had been taken in some classes since last week. There were only a few more to go before the students found out what their results were for Term 2. Sentira wondered if she should leave Annchi alone and go back to her room and study. She decided to take a break and continued to follow Annchi for a little while longer. She was just about to give up casually trying to catch up with her, when she noticed Annchi was headed towards the Maromsaesc lake. Perianne, Advik and Noah could be seen sitting on virtual mats on top of a grassy hilly area nearby. Annchi's pace had quickened to a run at the top of one of the hills and she moved fast down and up some hilly ground before reaching her group of friends. Advik stood up smiling to greet her, his face full of happy expectation.

"Annchi, I've been waiting for you to..." Advik began to say happily.

Annchi ran straight up to Advik and pushed him firmly in his chest, causing Advik to stumble backwards. He quickly regained himself and moved in closer to his girlfriend Annchi, his happiness instantly changed to worry and confusion.

"What was that for?" Advik said surprised, putting his arms around Annchi protectively.

Annchi fought to get out of his embrace as Advik tried to keep his arms around her, constantly asking her what was wrong.

Perianne and Noah were quietly looking on while eating

cod fish, curry noodles and stir fry vegetables that they had purchased from the student cafeteria earlier. Sentira came over to join them, sharing in their food and pretended that she wasn't watching Annchi and Advik. But, everyone knew something was going on with the usually deeply in love couple by the way they were acting. Annchi kept releasing herself from Advik's hug and Advik kept trying to pull her back into his arms again. It was like a push and pull relationship game was happening between them.

"You can order some more noodles for me Sentira. I was about to eat the rest of those." Noah said to Sentira.

Perianne grinned at Noah. She was not in a relationship with Noah but they did share a kiss sometimes when it suited Perianne for one of her schemes towards her purpose. Noah didn't seem to mind that Perianne didn't want a relationship and enjoyed meeting up with her. Annchi and Advik were always with them whenever they met up which also didn't bother Noah. He was just happy to be around Perianne and get close to her sometimes. They had never had sex, but Noah knew it was just a matter of time. In Perianne's mind however, there would never be a real relationship between her and Noah and definitely no sex. She sometimes wondered what her Aunty Dr Joan Dedrick would diagnose Noah as. With all Perianne's academic medical and psychiatry training, Noah didn't easily fit into any one diagnosis.

Mixed/unspecified psychosis? Perianne mused to herself while drinking from her water bottle.

Sentira ordered some more cod fish, curry noodles and stir fry vegetables for herself and Noah via the student cafeteria app on her virtual mobile. She felt hungry and wanted her own plate of food rather than to keep eating from Noah's plate. Annchi and Advik were now talking in loud voices at each other, while the group sitting on their virtual mats had no choice but to overhear everything that was being said.

"What?" Advik shouted. "You're not killing my child!" Advik said grabbing hold of both of Annchi's arms and looking deep into her eyes.

"Our child! And my choice!" Annchi retorted, her eyes flashing determinedly.

"Are you listening to what you've just said. Our child. It's our child, Annchi, OUR CHILD!" Advik shouted back at Annchi before managing to get hold of her in an embrace again.

Annchi fought away from him before he caught hold of her again. This time, Annchi buried her head in his chest and started sobbing uncontrollably.

"Yes. Advik wins." Noah said satisfactorily.

Perianne rolled her eyes at Noah.

"Advik is crazy about Annchi. He'd do anything for her." Noah said to Perianne and Sentira.

"I can see that. Did you count how many times Annchi pushed him away and with force." Sentira observed, but Noah was in a conversation with the voices around him and did not reply back.

Perianne pretended not to hear Sentira, picked up her virtual Psychic Development textbook and began to read it. Her face hidden behind her virtual textbook, Perianne grinned again.

Annchi is pregnant and I didn't even have to set it up! That's her Maromsaesc degree gone and I can see the headlines now... Teenage pregnancy at Maromsaesc forces student to drop out. Perianne thought gleefully to herself.

Sentira watched Annchi and Advik hugging each other near the edge of the Maromsaesc lake. Then, all of a sudden Advik's voice rang out urgently from near the lake.

"Annchi, wake up!" Advik could be heard saying repeatedly to Annchi who was now hanging lifelessly in his arms not moving or responding.

"Noah, Perianne! Annchi's unconscious. What's happening!" Advik shouted over at the group sitting on the virtual mats.

Perianne got to the couple first. Advik had laid Annchi down gently on the grassy area at the base of a small hill near the edge of the Maromsaesc lake. Perianne quickly put her medical training into practice.

"Are you ok?" Perianne asked Annchi loudly, checking her pulse and looking for signs that Annchi was still breathing. Perianne then went on to check there wasn't anything obstructing Annchi's airway by looking into her mouth and watching the rise and fall of Annchi's chest.

"She's breathing but she's unconscious. Call emergency medical OBR's!" Perianne directed Advik.

Advik called the Maromsaesc medical OBR's using his virtual mobile that had been inside his black jeans pocket. When he finished he stood back from the scene of his girlfriend laying lifeless on the grass with his friends by her side. Medical human OBR's quickly attended the scene and took Annchi away into a Medical hover ambulance to travel to Pelargonium Hospital. As if regaining his senses, Advik approached the medical OBR's as the hover ambulance virtual door was about to close.

"I have to go with her. I'm her boyfriend." said Advik to a medical OBR who stood staring at him with unemotional robot eyes.

"She can have one person with her. Ok. What is your name?" inquired the medical OBR as the virtual door on the hover ambulance opened up again.

"Advik Chandran." Advik replied, getting into the back of the hover ambulance and standing next to the virtual hover stretcher Annchi was laying on. He didn't acknowledge any of the group he left behind. The virtrual doors closed on the hover ambulance and both Annchi and Advik were transported to Pelargonium Hospital.

Perianne, Noah and Sentira exchanged bemused glances at each other.

"He's in shock." Noah said, finding an excuse for his friend's last minute decision to join Annchi in the hover ambulance.

"That's good you know first aid Perianne. Did Annchi have a seizure?" Sentira asked Perianne, curious about Annchi's sudden unconsciousness.

"I'm not sure. I know she has a medical condition that she doesn't like to talk about." Perianne shrugged. She felt a brief pang of empathy for the first time about a Maromsaesc student, which surprised her. Feeling very embarrassed about the sudden strong emotion, Perianne quickly ignored it and replaced it with images of her deceased mother and other members of the Dedrick family.

"Why don't we go to Pelargonium Hospital by hover bus or hover cab? I'm sure the Professor won't mind us supporting Annchi. It's the weekend and the next test is on wednesday." Perianne said to Noah and Sentira.

Sentira felt instantly suspicious about what Perianne's real intentions were, but outwardly she said "I'm coming too, to see if Annchi is alright."

"Go Sen...ir...aah" Rhyle's child voice said around Sentira's left ear.

"I'm in." Noah said to Perianne. "Keep quiet when I'm in the hospital." Noah said to something only he could hear behind him.

"Alright. I've sent the request through. Does anyone need to get anything from Jay Halls before we go?" Perianne asked.

Noah and Sentira both shook their head.

"Then let's head to the front entrance now. The Professor can't prevent us leaving as this is on medical grounds in support of a fellow student." Perianne said knowledgeably.

Maybe my regular voices get some things wrong or they are relevant within a certain time frame. Perianne seems genuinely concerned about Annchi. Sentira mused to herself.

Sentira, Perianne and Noah walked away from the Maromsaesc lake over the hilly ground and along virtual pathways, in order to get to the front virtual entrance gates of the University. At the front virtual entrance gates, Perianne touched the screen of her virtual mobile on a sensor at the left hand side of the virtual gates. On Perianne's virtual mobile was displayed a temporary code sent by a teacher, which allowed the three students to exit the university grounds. The virtual entrance gates gradually came apart and the three students walked out of Maromsaesc, turned to their left and waited near the hover bench at the hover cab stop.

The hover bench bent and then adjusted to Noah sitting down on it. There were three other people on the hover bench who grumbled as Noah sat down and the hover bench wobbled to adjust to the newcomer. Noah ignored them and started to speak to the voices he could hear around him. An elderly man stood up from the hover bench and watched in amusement as Noah sat talking to the air to his right and left. Then he began laughing at Noah. He laughed so much he seemed to be hysterical. The other two middle aged women on the hover bench had virtual earphones in and pretended not to notice the old man laughing at the teenager at the hover stop.

Noah ignored the old man too and continued to talk to his voices around him. Sentira was busy telling Nanny Lisha on her virtual mobile that she was on her way to Pelargonium Hospital with her friends to see Annchi, and also ignored the elderly man.

Perianne finished tapping in her I.D. number, destination and password into the old-fashioned keypad on the wall behind the hover bench and stared at the old man laughing. A terrifying image came to her mind of her cousins laughing at her in exactly the same way, but instead of Noah sitting on the Hover bench, she imagined it was her. Her emotions conflicted, she sharply turned away from staring at the old man and directed her gaze to looking up and down the road to see if she could see the hover cab approaching. She looked down both ends of the road as a hover cab could turn up from either direction. Perianne did not look at Noah, Sentira, the laughing old man or anyone else around her until the hover cab arrived. When the hover cab arrived, she called out quickly to her friends and said "Come on Noah, Sentira, let's go!"

A large acute hospital, Pelargonium Hospital was the main hospital for the people of Pelargonium. There were also other hospitals in Pelargonium, which were smaller and had other medical specialities. Applerishin virtual security scanned the trio before they entered the hospital grounds. This was for the hospital staff to keep a record of who was on their premises at all times.

As they entered Pelargonium hospital grounds, Perianne led Sentira and Noah confidently past other people and hospital staff to enter the main hospital building. Once inside, she quickly approached the reception desk and talked to the receptionist, inquiring about her recently admitted friend Annchi Kang. The receptionist seemed very busy, phone dial tones were ringing around him and there were multiple huge stacks of virtual papers on his desk. In addition, he was one of only three people at the reception desk. A young man in his early 30's, the receptionist seemed slightly taken aback by the authoritative tone of Perianne's voice, and promptly called an OBR to direct the trio to the Adult ICU.

The OBR (a member of the Pelargonium hospital staff) was by Perianne's side within minutes. The hospital OBR led the trio away from the main reception desk and a short walk over to one of the virtual lifts. The hospital OBR said "Level 3, ICU." The virtual lift swiftly got to Level 3. Perianne, Sentira and Noah walked out of the virtual lift, and followed the Hospital OBR again. It took them to the part of the ICU ward where Annchi could be seen from behind a virtual transparent panel.

Annchi's short black hair was damply matted to her face and she looked scarily drained of all energy. She appeared as if in a deep sickly sleep on her hospital bed. The clothes she had previously wore, had been changed by the Pelargonium hospital staff into a hospital gown. Annchi had all the vital medical equipment surrounding her. A virtual monitor for heart rate, blood pressure, body temperature and breathing, a feeding tube and a catheter for her to pass urine. The hospital OBR told the trio that they should wait outside the room until the doctor came out to speak with them.

The only three other people in the hospital room at this

time, were Advik and two doctors. Advik was seated on a virtual chair close to Annchi's hospital bed. He could be clearly seen leaning in towards Annchi closely, lovingly wiping away sweat from her forehead with a white tissue. He gripped and held on tightly to Annchi's hand, lowered his head and seemed to be praying for her. Occasionally tilting his head up to face the ceiling and back down again to look at Annchi in a heartfelt way. His face full of worry and concern, Advik said some more unheard words glancing up and then down again. Annchi did not respond to whatever words Advik had said. So, Advik let go of Annchi's hand and pushed back in his virtual chair visibly frustrated and stressed. He then got out his virtual mobile and called his Dad.

Meanwhile, the doctors around Annchi got on with checking her vital signs and discussed between themselves in hushed tones, what could possibly have been the trigger for her coma. Advik had on his earphones and talked loudly to his Dad on his virtual mobile, while still leaning back on his virtual chair. The two doctors believed that he wasn't paying any attention to them and spoke freely about their patient Annchi Kang.

"I cannot recall treating any patient that doesn't have no known diagnosis for their repeated comas." said one of the doctors, a slim young man of Indian origin in his mid 30's.

"Ah Dr.Ray, you're still a newbie. Haven't been around long enough." replied the other doctor, a black female in her 60's who continued to observe Annchi's sweaty sleeping body on the hospital bed in front of them.

"You stated that she has a known history of these types of coma since..." Dr Ray checked through virtual papers on a virtual clipboard. "...since birth, and there has not been a doctor in the world who could find anything in her body which would cause her unconsciousness, correct?"

"Correct." the female doctor answered.

"So if all conceivable tests, scans and medical investigations have been exhausted...then we really don't know what we are dealing with or how to treat it, Dr Wolfester. Am I right?" replied Dr Ray.

Dr Wolfester confidently turned to address her medical colleague face to face.

"No, but she is a very resilient young woman and each time she has fallen into one of these comas she eventually awakens from them." said Dr Wolfester with certainty.

Dr Ray flicked through some more virtual pages on his virtual clipboard containing copies of Annchi's medical record with a puzzled expression on his face.

"She's a student at that new school for voice-hearers and people who see visions." Dr Ray read from the virtual papers. "You know that it was only just over 16 years ago, a woman like this may have been given the (presently disused) diagnosis of psychosis. Dr Wolfester, could there potentially be a link between lack of treatment for the psychosis and her unexplained comas?"

"Or…perhaps a link between the high levels of anti-psychotic drugs in both parents at the time of conception and in the mother during pregnancy? We don't know what is the cause Dr Ray and now there is a new life to consider also. A fetus showed up in the ultrasound results. She's two months and 13 days pregnant." Dr Wolfester said calmly.

"Yes I am aware of that, thank you Dr Wolfester. Ok, so there isn't much else we can do but wait. Her parents are trying to arrange a flight back to the UK, they said it could be up to 3 days. She has her boyfriend…" Dr Ray said glancing at Advik, who still continued to talk loudly with his Dad on his virtual mobile. However, his head was down and he had resumed holding Annchi's hand again.

"Also a hospital OBR has notified me that other close friends of hers are waiting outside the room to visit." Dr Ray continued.

"Well, we should let them see her. Hopefully, the sounds of her friends speaking will bring her out of her latest coma faster." replied Dr Wolfester noncommittally.

Dr Ray nodded in agreement at Dr Wolfester and together they left Annchi's hospital room, leaving Advik and Annchi alone. They quickly introduced themselves and spoke briefly to the waiting trio, updating them on Annchi's coma condition. However, both doctors were extra careful not to disclose too much of Annchi's confidential medical history. Perianne, Sentira and Noah were told that Annchi was in a coma, a cause was yet to be found but there was a good chance she could come out of it at anytime. The long-term mystery surrounding the unknown cause of her comas and the frequency in which they occurred were not disclosed to the waiting Maromsaesc students.

Upon entering the hospital room where Annchi lay seemingly lifeless on a hospital bed, Advik sprang to his feet defensively glaring at all three of the new visitors.

"Advik. It's only us. How is she?" Sentira said reassuringly. She could see that Advik was very distressed and anxious over what had happened to Annchi. Especially since Annchi was pregnant and they had fought just before she went into a coma.

Advik slumped back down in his virtual chair and said "She... she... won't wake up." with his face contorted in pain.

Noah went up to him and put his hand on his shoulder.

"You did everything you could to help her Advik. It's going to be Jelitoonaa. She'll be awake soo..." Noah started to say optimistically hoping to reassure his friend but Advik shook Noah's hand off his left shoulder.

"How is this Jelitoonaa Noah?! How! How the f*** is my girlfriend and my first unborn child anything to do with Jelitoonaa?" Advik interrupted Noah, rising to his feet again and shoving Noah back towards the door.

Noah had not been expecting Advik to push him back towards the door and was caught off guard. It took him a few moments to process what had just happened and then he pushed Advik back in self-defence.

Advik raised his left fist and punched Noah in the face in

a temper. This punch confirmed to Noah that his friend was indeed attacking him. Noah blocked his face from any more blows and managed to punch Advik back. The two Maromsaesc students fell to the hospital floor still fighting with each other as Sentira and Perianne yelled at them to stop fighting. With all the noise and commotion going on in the hospital room, Annchi did not so much as blink an eye.

Soon two security OBR's entered Annchi's room and easily separated Advik and Noah from fighting on the hospital room floor. Human OBR's and OBR's were usually more physically stronger than the average human being, so it didn't take long for the robots to get the upper hand between the fighting men.

There were virtual cameras installed all over public buildings in 2071 and the Pelargonium hospital had a very high number installed. The virtual camera in Annchi's hospital room was monitored by hospital security 24/7 and had displayed clearly the two men fighting. Subsequently, security personnel had reacted immediately by sending robots to control the situation.

"Get off me. You're breaking my arm!" Advik shouted at the security OBR who had it's right hand gripped tightly around Advik's left upper arm, pulling him up on his feet to take him of Annchi's hospital room. Three more security OBR's entered the hospital room in order to assist the first two robots with the removal of the fighting men from Annchi's hospital room.

Separated from scuffling with Advik, Noah, did not resist the security OBR's leading him outside the hospital room. He quietly went with them. He knew from past experience that anything they both said to the robots would be relatively useless. Most security OBR's were similar to Police OBR's. Both were pre-programmed to do their job irrespective of what spoken words from the person being restrained/arrested said to them in their defence. This is why OBR's were only used when security or police were certain that the person/persons being arrested/restrained were the correct people they wanted. Security human OBR's and Police human OBR's were used when there was a need to communicate with the person concerned before any action could be ordered.

Advik however, continued on in vain to try and fight with the security OBR's but the security OBR's were far too strong for him. Unfortunately for Advik, four of the security OBR's surrounded him and led him outside Annchi's room swiftly. A security OBR had held onto both of Advik's upper arms, another security OBR walked in front of him and a security OBR walked steadily behind him.

Sentira and Perianne glanced at each other. Both women were surprised at the unexpected fighting between their friends and intimidated by the way the security OBR's had overpowered the fighting students roughly.

"Have you ever seen robots do that before?" asked Sentira to Perianne. She sat down on the empty virtual chair that Advik left behind, to look at Annchi on the hospital bed.

"No…, oh yeah I have. I saw the Pelargonium police OBR stare down Annchi in a frightening way during their first "Drug raid" of Maromsaesc." Perianne recalled truthfully, while moving a virtual chair from the side of the room closer to Annchi's bedside.

"Be careful." Rhyle's adult voice said loudly around Sentira's left ear.

Sentira ignored the voice that had spoken loudly around her left ear. She was worried about Annchi and whether she would wake up or not. Sometimes her voices could be easy to decipher and sometimes annoyingly difficult to understand.

"Be careful" could refer to literally anything. Sentira mused to herself uninterestedly, as she dismissed Rhyle's voice again that spoke loudly around her a second time. Sentira found her tranquil mind (as taught by Miss Garrison) and communicated to Rhyle that she felt very upset about Annchi. She further communicated to Rhyle that he would have to be more specific over what she had to "be careful" about. Then, she returned back to observing Annchi and began to talk to her comatose friend.

"Annchi it's Sentira. You have to wake up. I miss you…we all miss you. Annchi…can you hear me. It's Sentira, Annchi." Sentira spoke softly by Annchi's left ear.

"Annchi, everyone wants you to wake up. We love you Annchi. We're staying right here until you tell us to leave." Perianne said to Annchi from the opposite side of Annchi's hospital bed.

Sentira half-smiled encouragingly at Perianne and continued talking to Annchi to get her to wake up out of her coma.

I'm so good at this, I'm nearly fooling myself. Perianne thought deviously in her mind, returning an encouraging half-smile back to Sentira.

TERM 2 ENDS

Advik and Noah were given a firm warning by the OBR security team at Pelargonium Hospital, and then allowed back in to see Annchi again separately. Both students had bruises on their faces above their left eyes, where they had somehow landed their punches in the exact same area of each other. When they took it in turns to visit Annchi, she remained unconscious in her deep coma. Perianne and Sentira had been talking to her continually since the men had left them, but nothing worked to wake Annchi up. Advik and Noah tried to talk to her also, during their separate visiting times. It was nearly midnight, when the four Maromsaesc students left Pelargonium Hospital to return to the University. Advik refused to leave Annchi's side at first, however when he saw two security OBR's waiting to see if everyone left the hospital by midnight, he changed his mind quickly and followed the other students to walk towards the hospital exit.

The next day, the news media had once again managed to get hold of this most recent drama that had unravelled at Maromsaesc University regarding the Year 1 students. Worldwide news channels reported different versions of yesterday's events. Some of the following headlines and breaking news included: -

Breaking News: Teenage pregnancy scandal at Maromsaesc!
Voice hearing Maromsaesc student falls into mysterious unexplained coma!
Maromsaesc students fight over pregnant classmate at local hospital!
Did Maromsaesc student's voices put her into weird coma?
Fights, teenage pregnancy, a seriously ill student in a coma... read the latest stories about Maromsaesc University!

It took a week before the Professor had to reluctantly again intervene in the frenzy of inaccurate misleading half-true stories that the news media were spreading about the recent events at Maromsaesc. Professsor Zantend refused another interview with the news press. Instead, she sent the written statements of Perianne, Sentira, Noah and Advik to all the news media in order for them to amend their exaggerated reports immediately. The real way, in which the events occurred, had to be reported truthfully and fairly. The best people to do this, were those who were actually present at the time of the events, and/or those who knew Annchi Kang personally e.g. her family.

Within hours of the true statements of events being received by the news media, the stories reported about Maromsaesc were cleverly altered. The news reports changed in such a way, that even though more understandable and socially acceptable versions were given by each student, there still left wide open the possibility of many unanswered questions. Many more potentially sinister questions…

Eventually, the final results came in for the Creativity class of Term 2 for the Year 1 Maromsaesc students. Their hard work had paid off. Everyone received A grades and many received A* grades. Brandi Ropen was one of those who received an A* and she happily showed off her winning Maromsaesc sports tracksuits designs for virtual camera crews. The tracksuit designs had been anonymously entered into a Maromsaesc competition for sportswear design, and Brandi had won first place! The virtual camera crew were present for one day only, filming the Year 1's student's receiving their End of Term 2 results.

The news media highlighted the story of Brandi Ropen's success at Creativity class at Maromsaesc. Her unique design consisted of yellow mixed material and virtual tracksuits with a distinctive virtual letter "M" in orange print on the right-hand corner of the top, jumper and bottoms. The virtual letter "M" could move forward virtually while speaking the words "Maromsaesc Future" in the pre-recorded voice of Professor Zantend. The Professor loved Brandi's design and made the decision that from Term 3 onwards, all Maromsaesc students would be given their clothing size of the new Maromsaesc tracksuit for free to be word during Sports class. In addition, Brandi's Maromsaesc tracksuit design was purchased by the other 5 Maromsaesc Universities in different parts of the world.

Later that day at Pelargonium Hospital, Annchi's strange coma condition remained the same. Her parents, Advik along with Noah (who had both resumed speaking to each other again), Perianne, Sentira and other students who knew Annchi, visited her regularly. Some of the students chose to stay on campus during half term so as to be close by to visit Annchi daily. Most of them hoping that one day, she would wake up just as suddenly as she had fallen asleep. Sadly, by the close of Term 2 at Maromsaesc University, this never happened.

Annchi (in her comatose state) and her unborn baby, were numbed to everything going on around them.

COMMENCE SUMMER

And so ended the Spring Term at Maromsaesc University. The very first University in England for the Professional Development of people who hear voices and/or see visions.

Next, commenced the final term for the Year 1 Degree programme, after most of the students had returned from their two-week holiday break.

Then began the start of the Summer Term, Term 3…

FRENEMY PLOTS

Seated at the front of the newly virtually furbished lecture hall on virtual seating, sat Perianne, Noah, Craig, Brandi and Sentira. In the previous days "Welcome speech" by Professor Willemina Zantend, she had mentioned proudly that refurbishment of 10 lecture halls at the University were now completed. Four Year 1 teams were able to be seated in each lecture hall at a time. The Team 3 students were in a virtual lecture hall with 75 other Year 1 students and it was a very noisy scene before the tutor Miss Garrison entered into it.

"Ok everyone, quieten down!" Miss Garrison said to the students firmly in her gentle tone.

Some of the Year 1 students (seated at the front) stopped talking to each other and their voices when they saw Miss Garrison enter the lecture hall. Most of the students however, were unable to hear Miss Garrison's softly spoken order from the middle and back sections of the large lecture hall and continued talking loudly.

Miss Garrison walked over to her virtual podium at the front centre of the lecture hall, pressed a sensor using her handprint to activated it and repeated her earlier words.

"Good morning Year 1 students! This is your tutor Miss Garrison speaking!" Miss Garrison asserted clearly. Her voice echoed loudly around the lecture hall due to the extra sound amplification of her voice by virtual speakers situated in various places. Finally, all of the Year 1 students took notice of the young Indian woman in her 20's with long black hair in a ponytail on the top of her head. Her expression serene and calm, yet also determined and confident.

"Applerishin virtual security states that everyone is present except from three people who are currently unwell." Miss Garrison said. "Did everyone have a Jelitoonaa Spring break?"

Some of the students replied out loud "Yeah we did!" and

"Jelitoonaa!" "Yes!" "I did!".

Miss Garrison smiled widely. "Good, because this final term at Maromsaesc is going to be your most toughest yet."

Some of the Year 1 students groaned out loud. Miss Garrison's facial expression returned back to serene again.

"I know that if you all commit to your studies as Professor Willemina Zantend said to you yesterday, there is no reason why any of you won't succeed." Miss Garrison said confidently from behind the podium.

A large virtual screen showed her standing and speaking at the podium for part of the middle rows and back rows to see. A recording of all lectures was also available on the university website after the lecture finished.

"Can we repeat Year 1 if we do fail though, Miss Garrison?" called out a Year 1 student seated in the front row.

"Yes. In the rare event that any person does not achieve the standard required to pass Year 1 studies, then yes, a student will be allowed to restart the Year again. However, judging from your expected grades and overall student performance so far, there is little chance that any student will fail this course." Miss Garrison said reassuringly, directing her answer at the Year 1 female student who had asked it.

"Right, the second set of business I have to attend to before I begin my lecture on Spiritual voices is the new timetable. There have been a few changes and OBR's are going to hand out the amended summer timetable for Term 3. Don't worry, there are no changes to the classes/lectures, it's tutor changes that have caused the need for amendment." explained Miss Garrison.

The virtual door opened and four OBR's walked in carrying virtual timetables for the 100 students in the lecture hall. The four OBR's added to the two human OBR's (one at the front and one at the back of the lecture hall) who were present in every class/lecture hall since mid-Term 2 to assist the tutor in any way requested.

The presence of the human OBR's supervising in every class

had deterred Tom Puffint from releasing control of his angry outbursts and even he seemed more settled at the start of the new summer Term. Although, there was also another reason why Tom was settled more in classes at Maromsaesc. Tom had found a way to release his frustration about the classes by writing articles giving his opinions about life as a Maromsaesc student to the Pelargonium News Group. The Pelargonium News Group paid Tom well for every regular article written about student life at Maromsaesc, and told Tom that they would not print any of his stories until the end of the three academic years. This way, Tom could achieve his professional degree before any reaction to his articles affected his career prospects. Tom had agreed to their terms and listened more to what was said in each class in order to critique it later to the Pelargonium News Group.

"I've also put a copy on the virtual screens in this lecture hall." Miss Garrison said.

The long yellow virtual curtains opened up slowly from behind her, to reveal another large virtual screen displaying the amended summer timetable, which included many new lectures and classes. New classes and lectures such as Inspirational voice hearers, Voices teacher training, Mediumship, Business & marketing and Spiritual voices. Miss Garrison waited five minutes before addressing the Year 1 students again.

"Has everyone received a virtual copy of the amended timetable?" Miss Garrison's soft voice rang out around the lecture hall via the virtual speakers.

The Year 1 students either nodded their heads, shouted out "yes" "yeah", or waved their virtual timetable in front of them indicating that they indeed had the timetable in their possession.

"Great! Let's get started then. My lecture today is an introduction to Spiritual voices, including how interpreting voices in this way has proved beneficial for people who hear voices throughout history. Defining voices as spiritual has enabled voice hearers to not only make sense of the voices they hear around them, but also to interpret meaning, significance and purpose as to why they occur. Spirituality itself is a concept that is forever evolving. For example, people may call themselves spiritual with no connection to any one particular religion. A person may refer to themselves as spiritual with a connection to a religion or even multiple religions. It varies. The individual has a right to define spirituality in the way that suits that person's belief system. Most spiritual persons do believe there is a higher spiritual being or energy that is more powerful beyond human comprehension and OBR comprehension." Miss Garrison smiled and looked over at one of the OBR's standing by the virtual exit of the lecture hall.

Some of the students laughed at Miss Garrison's joke, others didn't. Perianne didn't feel like laughing at all but she kept her usual grin at the ready, in order to keep up her perfect act as a happy and dedicated Maromsaesc student.

Miss Garrison smiled again at her student audience of 100 before continuing to lecture. Behind her, on the virtual screen and on the virtual screen for part of the middle and back rows, displayed visual images related to Spiritual voices. There were images that represented some of the religions, such as a cross for Christianity and a Buddha for Bhuddism, etc... There was also a planetary system to represent the universe, images of people meditating sitting in nature, people praying in different worship buildings and also alone or in groups. Many other images related to spirituality were displayed throughout Miss Garrison's lecture, which lasted for 1 hour and 40 minutes.
After Miss Garrison's lecture, Perianne felt her familiar anger rising up within her again.

The classes in Term 1 & 2 were stupid enough. How can I endure hours and hours of these insane lectures every week! Perianne thought to herself feeling very irritated, but outwardly joining in with her friend's group discussion about the recent lecture on spiritual voices.

"So interesting! The topic of spirituality. It's similar to how

I imagine the Mediumship lecture will be. Talking to Spirits. Spirituality. Same thing!" Perianne said, laughing at her own joke while her friends smiled back at her.

Together they exited the lecture hall and made their way via student hover vehicles, to the student cafeteria to eat lunch. The lecture halls were on the opposite end of the University grounds and students could use the readily available student hover vehicles if they needed to travel quickly to another area of Maromsaesc.

Although Brandi was part of the group of Team 3 students that were seated next to each other in the student cafeteria, she was noticeably quieter than her classmates after ordering her food and drink. Sentira, Perianne, Craig and Noah could all tell that something was off with Brandi. She had ended Term 2 on a high, overly excited about her new Maromsaesc tracksuit designs which not only had earned her hundreds of thousands of pounds but had established her name as a fashion designer worldwide. Sentira assumed that it was because she still had to complete her Maromsaesc studies before she could open her own fashion store, and this was why she was quiet. Perianne assumed that whatever voices were talking around Brandi were depressive and she probably could do with some type of anti-psychotic medication. Noah assumed Brandi just did not want to talk much right now.

Craig was sweating and nervous, assuming that his worse nightmares had come true. He looked at the shape of Brandi's tummy, felt his heart skip a beat and then race fast in his chest. Brandi had put on a lot of weight and her tummy protruded more with the extra weight than any other part of her. Craig couldn't stop his heart from racing and got up from the student cafeteria virtual table, explaining briefly to the others that he was going to use the toilet.

Sentira hungrily bit into her cod fish and devoured it, along with her vegetable noodles and large salad. Perianne also had a good appetite, eating and chatting to her classmates between mouthfuls of food. Brandi had hardly touched any of the food on her plate, which only consisted of a salad and fruit.

"Not hungry Brandi?" Noah asked Brandi light-heartedly, before taking a sip of his coffee.

As if remembering her friends were around her for the first time since entering the cafeteria, Brandi spoke to Noah.

"I'm on this new healthy eating thing I saw online. Today's menu is salad for lunch with unlimited fruit." Brandi replied sounding bored.

"So where's your unlimited fruit then?" Noah teased. To his surprise, Brandi answered him sharply.

"They couldn't fit on the plate. Why do you care?" Brandi replied, her eyes blazing with fury.

"Alright, easy Brandi. It's just a friendly question." Noah said taken aback at Brandi's unexpected irritated reaction. He stopped talking to Brandi and made a point of talking with his voices around him instead.

Brandi anxiously moved the cucumbers, lettuce, peppers around her plate with a fork a number of times, before standing up and walking away from her classmates without any explanation. She exited the student cafeteria and didn't meet up with her friends again until Sports class.

During Sports class, Perianne had decided that something was definitely up with Brandi and she wanted to take advantage of it, towards her ultimate goal of sabotaging Maromsaesc University forever. Brandi Ropen (so obvious to Perianne and others in Team 3) wasn't her usual bubbly self. She hadn't joined in with none of the excited chatter about the new lectures for the summer Term and was exercising in one corner of the Games court by herself on a pink virtual yoga mat. Perianne told one of her teammates playing basketball with her, that she was taking a break. A human OBR supervising the game took Perianne's place, while another OBR (who had been waiting patiently on the sidelines) stood up to help supervise the students.

Perianne began to hear voices speak around her loudly.

"Construction of each building takes around 10 months to

a year. I cannot get the workers to do it in any less time, I'm afraid." an elderly male voice said loudly around the left side of Perianne's face.

"4 months or there is no deal." another unfamiliar voice said around Perianne's right ear.

"Are you out of your mind?" a different young female voice said from around Perianne's left ear.

"Any more name calling and I won't do the job at all. I mean, like ever." the elderly male voice that had spoken first said loudly around the front of Perianne's face.

"Ok, ok, ok, ok, ok, ok, OK!" said a female voice in a high pitched tone next to Perianne's left ear.

Perianne spoke to the voices around her in her mind. The voices speaking around her quietened down before stopping completely.

They've stopped because I ordered them to. There's no tranquil mind. It's my brain that controls them. Maromsaesc is a farce! And...most of the students need medication and therapy! Perianne thought angrily to herself. She took out her yellow virtual yoga mat and a bottle of water from her green and yellow virtual sports bag, which she had left in the seating area earlier. She drank the whole bottle of water and refilled it with water from a nearby virtual student water dispenser. Next, she carried her yellow virtual mat and newly refilled water bottle with her to make her way to the area of the Games Court where Brandi was. She found Brandi trying to stretch her hands to her feet unsuccessfully, on her pink virtual yoga mat. Instead of laughing at her (a reaction that Aridaperianne would do to every Maromsaesc student), Perianne Saint looked at Brandi with kindness and compassion.

"I've come to join you so you can teach me Yoga!" Perianne exclaimed happily to Brandi.

Brandi turned her freckled face with her dyed blonde curly hair of varied lengths, to look at Perianne. She wore her yellow mixed-virtual Maromsaesc tracksuit bottoms and top as the other Year 1 students were required to wear also. Each

Year 1 student wore their choice of combination of the now mandatory university sports gear at Sports class. Her other Maromsaesc Sportswear designs would be coming out in a few weeks time. It would include mixed-virtual yellow Maromsaesc Sports shorts, skirts, crop tops, leggings, vests, socks and trainers. All the new Maromsaesc Sportswear had the unique virtual feature of the orange letter M, which when touched would rise out of the clothing and say the words "Maromsaesc Future." in the voice of Professor Willemina Zantend.

"Is that what you think I'm doing?" Brandi replied to Perianne's comment and laughed for the first time that day.

Perianne laughed with her.

Good. Keep laughing with me Brandi. You'll be easier to fool. Perianne deviously thought to herself, placing her yellow virtual yoga mat on the floor next to Brandi on her right hand side. She was about to continue talking to Brandi, when Sentira's voice was heard behind her.

"Hey Brandi, Perianne!" Sentira said happily, placing a green virtual yoga mat on the left side of Brandi's pink mat.

Perianne frowned inwardly. Even though, both herself and Sentira were friendly to each other, she felt wariness around her that she was unsure of. Unbeknownst to Perianne, Sentira felt the same wariness around Perianne most of the time, but she was so happy to be at Maromsaesc and focused on her studies that she often ignored it.

Keeping within her character as Perianne Saint, Perianne said, "The more the merrier! We're just missing the boys and Annchi now." She lazily stretched both her arms over her head of wavy ginger red hair, which messily lay around her face untamed by any hair bands, whilst casually laying on her back with both legs in the air.

Brandi smiled at Sentira and glanced over at Perianne.

"What's that pose Perianne?" Brandi teased her friend.

"The Perianne pose!" Perianne giggled, and placed both legs back down with a thud on her virtual yoga mat.

Sentira and Brandi laughed with Perianne.

She sounds so fake at times, it's funny. Sentira mused to herself. Her regular voices started to talk around her and Sentira tuned in to what they were saying. Simultaneously at the same time choosing to tune out the conversation between Brandi and Perianne, that had also just started up around her. Sentira knew some yoga poses, so practiced them while listening to Rhyle, Gina, Olamide and Louis speak in voices of varying ages.

"Sen...ir...aa!" a toddler's voice of Gina babbled loudly around Sentira's left ear.

"Sen...ir...aa!" a toddler's voice of Olamide babbled loudly around Sentira's right ear.

"Yes I'm here." Sentira answered them quietly.

"There is danger here. We want you to be very careful." said a teenage Olamide's voice around the front of Sentira's face.

Sentira's ears perked up, suddenly very alert. She instinctively glanced over at Perianne, who was now talking animatedly with Brandi and making her laugh by performing exaggerated yoga poses. In turn, Brandi was trying to copy Perianne's funny poses but would fall over most of the time laughing at herself and her friend.

"It's Perianne Saint, isn't it?" Sentira asked her regular voices of Gina and Olamide, using her tranquil mind as taught in Term 1 by Miss Garrison. She did not want Perianne to hear what she was saying to them.

"We're warning you Sentira, we are here to protect you." said Louis's elderly voice around Sentira's left ear.

"Be careful whenever you are around her. All will be revealed in time. Trust us and trust yourself." said Rhyle's teenage male voice loudly around Sentira's right ear. Rhyle's teenage voice was so loud, it caused Sentira to quickly look nervously at her friends wondering if they had heard it too. Luckily, her friends showed no sign of having heard the extra loud teenage voice speak from around her left ear.

When Sentira heard the extra loud voice spoken around her right ear, she knew that she had to pay attention to the words being said by Rhyle. The sound volume was similar to the noise that came out of the virtual speakers in the lecture hall this morning. Her hearing ability never seemed to be affected by the louder voices she heard close to her ears sometimes, which was a mystery to Sentira. It is common knowledge that loud noises may cause hearing loss but Sentira had never experienced hearing loss at anytime so far in her life, regardless of the extra loud voices she heard at random times by her ears.

I need to know more details if it's this serious! Rhyle, Gina, Olamide and Louis! Do you hear me? Sentira insisted of her regular voices using her tranquil mind to communicate with them. Her regular voices fell silent and Sentira sighed out loud.

Perianne heard her and commented.

"What's up Sentira? Can't keep up!" Perianne said humourously, as she did another yoga pose on her yellow virtual mat.

Brandi giggled.

The yoga pose that Perianne did was a complex pose called the Tripod headstand with Lotus legs. This appeared similar to a headstand but with her legs in the air forming a crossed legs position (Lotus legs). Not to be outdone, Sentira manoeuvred her body into a different complex yoga pose called a Handstand Scorpion. She stood on her hands, lifted her body up into a handstand, arched her back to bend her legs backwards, finally touching the back of her head with the soles of her feet. Brandi gasped at the two students highly complex Yoga poses, which were performed to perfection at either side of her.

"Wow! Jelitoonaa!" Brandi exclaimed.

Sentira came down and out of her Handstand Scorpion and Perianne did the same from her Tripod headstand with Lotus legs after her.

"I'm not going to try those moves until I lose this extra weight first." Brandi said, laying on her back with both legs in the air.

"Jelitoonaa, Brandi. I will teach you when you're ready." Periannne said.

"We can both teach you." Sentira said.

"Ok, Jelitoonaa. It's not a competition." Brandi laughed and began to talk to her voices in the air around her, ignoring the other two students.

"Where did you learn that pose, Sentira?" Perianne asked curiously.

"I could ask you the same, Perianne." Sentira responded sweetly while copying Brandi by relaxing on her back with both her legs in the air.

"The internet. It's called a Tripod headstand with Lotus legs." Perianne replied sounding bored.

"Same. Mine is a Handstand Scorpion." Sentira said, lowering her legs back onto her green virtual mat before raising them again.

Perianne picked up her bottle of water and drank half of it down in one go. She didn't really want to talk to Sentira. Despite Brandi's laughter and seemingly happy demeanour, Perianne knew something was bothering her as Brandi's smile quickly dissapeared after she finished laughing. It was as if Brandi was putting on a laugh which worked for a while before a glimpse of her real sadness crept to the surface. Perianne noticed Brandi's glum expression again and decided to ask her about it.

"Brandi, are you ok?" Perianne asked, in a (pretend) innocent, concerned voice full of compassion.

"Ye-ah." Brandi replied. "Why?"

"Well..." Perianne began to say, but was interrupted by Brandi's unexpected tearful sobs.

"Brandi, oh no! What's wrong? Don't cry." Sentira got up from her virtual mat at the same time as Perianne did to comfort their friend by hugging her one after the other.

"You can tell us what's wrong Brandi. We're your friends." Perianne said kindly.

"I wish Annchi was here so I could have a smoke." Brandi said to Perianne forgetting that Sentira was there.

Sentira could not recall whether or not Brandi had told her that she smoked some of Annchi's medical cannabis with her, whenever she felt stressed. However, Sentira was unbothered if Brandi smoked or not. She just didn't want it done around her unless the person used the virtual smokers extraction fan. Sentira firmly held the belief that smoking was linked to cancer and no one could change her mind.

"Annchi will wake up soon one day…it's going to take time but…one day she'll be back." Perianne said and managed to get some tears to fall from her eyes too, like she had been trained to do by Uncle Dr Robert Dedrick. All she had to do was to think of something very sad and the tears would form in her eyes soon enough, her Uncle had taught her. Perianne thought about how her mother had killed herself after Psychiatry was abolished and tears came quickly to both eyes. She allowed herself to cry along with Brandi, but she was really crying over the painful, tragic loss of her mother and growing up without her.

Sentira talked to Brandi and tried to console her too. Sentira did not cry. There wasn't any need to. Annchi was receiving excellent care at Pelargonium Hospital and she would wake up eventually. Sentira truly believed in her heart that this would happen, so she did not worry as much as it appeared Brandi and Perianne were.

After the crying had finished, Perianne didn't try to persist and ask Brandi why she started crying in the first place. Brandi resumed talking to her voices around her and doing basic stretches and simple yoga poses on her pink virtual mat. Sentira could see that Brandi wanted to be left alone, so she concentrated on practicing more complex yoga poses on her green virtual mat. Perianne had recalled so many unhappy memories of growing up without her mother, the unfairness, the injustice and the upset, that it was steadily turning into anger. Soon, Perianne no longer felt the sad emotion to make her cry, but an enraged emotion that provoked her to take action.

My mother died because of these voice hearing people just so this mad university could be built with the money stolen from Psychiatry! Perianne thought ragefully, pretending to meditate on her yellow virtual yoga mat, sitting in the lotus position. In her mind's eye she envisioned what her life could have been like if her mother were still with her and the R -v- Caulfied case had been won by Caulfied Psychiatry World Medical Centre. She saw herself, her mother and the entire Dedrick family happy, rich and successful, practicing Psychiatry and effectively treating mental illnesses with psychotic features.

People who hallucinate require medication and care, unless they can control what they hear or see. The Maromsaesc University is doomed to fail. Eventually, other symptoms of these mad students untreated illnesses, will come to the surface and…and the world will beg Psychiatry to return. But, by then…by then…it will be too late… Perianne thought to herself in frustration.

Voices began to talk around Perianne, who was still sitting with her eyes closed in the lotus position, appearing as if she were in a deep meditation.

"…and so I said to him…there aren't any left, and get this… he said, well if you say there aren't any, there aren't any!" a male adult voice said close to Perianne's left ear.

Perianne grimaced.

"Don't think I won't tell him next time. I've had enough of him wasting all the supplies and then claiming there isn't any left! What kind of travesty is this?" a female voice said loudly around Perianne's right ear.

Perianne rolled her eyes from under her closed eyelids.

"Yeah, but…you try and tell him and see if you don't get the same reaction that I get." the first male adult voice said in front of Perianne's face.

"Stop talking!" Perianne said loudly to the air in front of her. Her eyes flew open, surprised at her own intensity and immediately regretting it, knowing that Brandi and Sentira heard her. She thought they might notice the anger in her voice and they did.

"Wow, Perianne! What did they say to you?" Brandi exclaimed, re-adjusting her position after being jolted out from her Cobra yoga pose upon hearing Perianne shout out loudly with intense anger.

Sentira narrowed her eyes, moved out safely from her side plank yoga posture and turned to her opposite side to face towards Perianne's direction.

Aridaperianne Dedrick's mind raced over how to give an acceptable answer from Perianne Saint. So, expertly regaining her character swiftly as Perianne, she took a few slow long deep breaths while formulating the correct response to say to her friends. After a short period of tension filled silence, she replied to Brandi in her familiar happy voice of keen Maromsaesc A grade student, Miss Perianne Saint.

"I had to be very firm with that voice," Perianne lied with the ease of a professional actress. "It was giving me direct orders to do things I didn't want to do."

"What things?" Brandi and Sentira both asked at the same time.

Perianne thought fast.

"Oh, you know, just things that wouldn't be Jelitoonaa." Perianne replied convincingly.

"I know what she means." Brandi said picking up for her friend and turning to explain to Sentira. "You know when you sometimes hear a random voice that says something scary for whatever reason like "death", "hit yourself" or "beat her" or "kill yourself" or "die", they're just examples. Well, often those types of voices p*** you off so much, you can get instantly angry at it."

"No...I can't remember hearing anything said around me like that. Not even by my random voices." answered Sentira.

"Really?" Brandi looked at Sentira surprised.

"Really?" Perianne joined in with Brandi who had just explained away her loud outburst with her kind wisdom.

"Well, maybe so far I haven't heard anything like that. Sometimes I do hear my regular voices of Rhyle, Louis, Olamide and Gina play fighting each other in their child voices, but I know it's not directed at me to do anything they say." answered Sentira truthfully.

Brandi and Perianne exchanged knowing glances.

Good. Brandi is on my side and Sentira looks strange. Ha ha. Perianne mused to herself.

"Perianne, whatever the voice said must have made you very angry. I've never heard you shout at your voices so loud before." Sentira said innocently to Perianne.

Perianne felt a strong instant irritation at Sentira's question.

Why is Sentira carrying it on? Brandi has already explained that she knows why I got annoyed. Perianne thought to herself. She felt a strong urge to say something to Sentira as Aridaperianne Dedrick, but she had to use all her acting skills to hold herself back. Inside, once again Perianne was fuming.

"The voice simply startled me, that's all Sentira." Perianne said smiling widely at her two friends as an elderly female voice spoke words around her right ear.

"Ook sse gd dia didi sss oood dose ghla fhssss." said the unknown elderly female voice near Perianne.

All of a sudden a basketball flew over Sentira's head, just at the moment when she had bent down to look at a new notification on her virtual mobile. The basketball hit the mixed wooden and virtual fence behind them making a clanging noise. Then the basketball rebounded back over Sentira's head to the student who had initially kicked it.

Hearing the noise behind her of the basketball rebounding off the mixed wooden and virtual fence, Sentira lifted her head safely at the right time, seeing the basketball fly forward in front of her towards one of the Team 3 students.

"Sorry!" one of the Team 3 students said. It was a short woman who was with two men, each holding basketballs.

"It's alright! It didn't hit me. Lucky, I bent down to look at my phone!" Sentira laughed, and the other students laughed with her. Brandi included.

Perianne pretended not to notice what had just happened by staring at her virtual mobile with her virtual sound devices on.

I wish the ball had hit her in the head. Breaking News! Student death at Maromsaesc University forces immediate closure for the foreseeable future! Perianne wickedly imagined the possible news headlines to herself, as she used every ounce of strength she could muster to calm the powerful fury she felt within.

CONTROL ISSUES

"After reading through chapter 4 of your Voices Teacher Training virtual textbook, Perianne, can you tell the rest of the class what you would say to a student who asked you Question 9." Miss Gower asked Perianne expectantly. Miss Gower's long natural blonde hair styled in two thin plaits on either side of her face, wearing a cream body top, brown trousers with low black heels. Around her neck, was adorned a single gold necklace which had the single initial M designed in a virtual sparkly silver design. Miss Gower had chosen a Team 3 student at random and her eyes had somehow rested on Perianne Saint, sitting next to Noah in the middle row.

Perianne hadn't anticipated that Miss Gower would single her out over 24 other students. She thought fast to give the perfect reply but hesitated. This was because inwardly she felt conflicted as to how she should answer. Perianne peered down at her virtual textbook for Voices Teacher Training and re-read Question 9 again.

Question 9: What advice would you give a person about how to control when voices spoke around them?

Perianne wanted to say that without medication there was no hope that a person could control when they heard voices speak around them. Only very smart people like herself did not require medication as her voices were controllable. However, the longer Perianne attended Maromsaesc University, the more she realised that there were some others who seemed to be able to control the voices they heard, surprisingly similar to her. This perplexed Perianne at times, whenever she thought about it.

Previously, before attending Maromsaesc, she had believed that she was unique and different, with the rare ability to be able to control her voices through her high intelligence. She was not mentally ill, her family loved her and she had studied to far beyond academic expectations at every age she undertook exams, gaining consistently high grades. Perianne excelled in every exam, every written assignment, every dissertation, every academic test. She never spoke to her family about the voices she had heard since she was child. She grew up with a mixed combination of hatred for the voice hearing community that had brought down her family's world famous Dedrick Psychiatry Practices, and also pride in herself over the way she could control her voices. Perianne originally thought that her superior control over her voices were what distinctively separated her from *them, those "mad" people who hallucinate.* Miss Gower's question had triggered off her confusion again and Perianne's mind raced.

Could it be that there are others like me? Intelligent enough to be able to control their voices. No! I've been in this mad University far too long! This will be my final term. Maromsaesc will be ruined and Psychiatry will return. Perianne finally dismissed any doubts in her mind, remembered the cruel pain and serious financial loss her family had suffered, and prepared to give a perfect A grade answer to Miss Gower.

"Perianne, do you need more time?" Miss Gower asked Perianne kindly, while the rest of the Team 3 class waited patiently.

"The advice I would give a person about how to control when voices speak around them would be for that person to keep a Voices diary about the time, date, their emotions and the circumstances when the voices talk, to see if a pattern can be identified. If it can, then the person should try to adapt to personal acceptance of these patterns in ways which can easily fit in with his/her lifestyle. If a pattern cannot be identified, then that person should attend a specialized University such as Maromsaesc University to receive development & professional voice hearing training. Professional development will help the person find suitable ways to understand, utilize, control and/or accept their voices, so the person can continue to live well, healthy and have a productive work/life balance." Perianne carefully explained her answer to Question 9 clearly and confidently.

The rest of the Team 3 students clapped and some grinned at Perianne. Perianne felt like she wanted to be sick and resisted the urge to run out of the classroom. After the clapping had quietened down, Miss Gower spoke again.

"Excellent answer Perianne! Jelit...Jelitoonaaaaa!" Miss Gower replied enthusiastically, while some of the Team 3 students laughed at her usage of their popular word Jelitoonaa (a word which could mean anything that was very good or cool). The Voices Teacher Training tutor spoke too formally most of the time for her "Jelitoonaa" to sound authentic. Miss Gower immediately realised the reason why some of the students had laughed after she had finished her sentence with "Jelitoonaa".

"I don't imitate you all very well, do I?" Miss Gower smiled at the Team 3 students, who all either shook their heads or remained silent like Perianne did.

"Ok, I won't say that again." Miss Gower said quietly to herself. She flicked through the virtual Voices Teacher Training textbook in her hand and pointed her finger at one of the pages.

"Your homework for week 3 is to answer questions 10, 11, 12, 13 and 14 with a minimum of two A4 pages for each answer. Does anyone have any questions?" Miss Gower addressed the Team 3 students assertively. She waited to see if anyone would query her homework but nobody did.

"Good. Class dismissed. See you all...with your homework on Thursday morning. Very well done today Team 3! Great start!" finished Miss Gower with enthusiasm.

Week 3! Why am I still here? Perianne thought to herself, as she faked a smile at Miss Gower and the other Maromsaesc students near her. She had wanted to implement some of her sabotage Maromsaesc ideas sooner this term, but found herself putting all her effort into concentrating on the new summer term studies.

Along with long lecture sessions and more difficult classes, increased homework was set about each lecture after every class. Perianne had to focus very intensely, and it was not because she was not smart enough to handle the academic study. It was because of the internal conflict of her true self, Aridaperianne Dedrick's views, frequently opposing the perfect "A" grade answers expected of Perianne Saint. It was of the utmost importance for her to keep up her act of Perianne Saint, so as to ensure she remained a student long enough to ruin the reputation of Maromsaesc forever, forcing it's permanent closure worldwide. Perianne had to blend in. She had to excel consistently as a student of Maromsaesc University to avoid any suspicion and to guarantee her continued place on the professional degree course.

Time to end this mad University today. I can't take this place much longer. Perianne grumbled to herself in her mind. She packed away her virtual textbook in her new red shoulder bag with virtual gold sparkles all over it. Noah was waiting for her outside the Voices Teacher Training classroom, when she exited it.

"Perianne, are you coming to the Maromsaesc Gardens to study before dinner? Some of the other Team 3 students are going to be there." Noah asked Perianne softly, with a hopeful look on his face.

"No, Noah, can't make it today. I'm busy back at Jay Halls doing something." Perianne replied to Noah's question.

"Oh, ok." Noah said, looking deflated.

Noah had assumed that Perianne would have been happy to meet up with him and others in the Maromsaesc Gardens. It wasn't a date, there would be other people there. Noah noticed that Perianne had been coming up with excuses not to meet up with him, since Annchi had fallen into a coma. Before that tragic event occurred, Perianne had met up with him, Advik, Annchi and some of the other Maromsaesc students more often to just hang out or/and study. He had gotten close with Perianne often, but she always stopped short of going all the way with him. Noah couldn't understand why their friendship was not progressing any further and now it seemed even less likely he would get as far with her as Advik had with Annchi.

Perianne smiled at Noah and said "Another time, Noah. I'm really busy."

Then, before Noah could say anything else, Perianne walked briskly past him along the student corridor and into a virtual lift which had it's virtual doors open. The virtual doors on the virtual lift closed just a second before Noah's face appeared at the front of them. He had wanted to say one more thing to Perianne before she left, but didn't reach her in time. Perianne pretended not to see him and allowed the virtual lift doors to close, without pressing on the sensor to reopen them for Noah again.

Alone in the virtual lift, Perianne rolled her eyes.

Back at Jay Halls, Perianne waited for Applerishin virtual security to scan her before gaining entry into number 25. After confirming her identity, the virtual doors disappeared and she walked inside her room. She glanced over at the empty side of the room where Annchi had previously slept on the misty grey double bed.

Every bed will be like hers soon Perianne thought to herself. *Empty. There will be no students at Maromsaesc to fill them ever again. Psychiatry will return and they will all be diagnosed.*

Her final thought brought a genuine smile of relief to Perianne's face. She sat down on her own student misty grey double bed and started up her virtual mobile which was attached to her wrist in it's original square shape.

"Applerishin virtual mobile open." said Perianne to the small purple square shape on her right wrist.

The small purple square shape sprang up into a virtual mobile phone and a ray of light purple scanned Perianne from her head to her toes, to confirm that she was the owner of her virtual mobile.

"Welcome Perianne Saint. How can I assist?" asked Perianne's virtual mobile, positioned on top of her blue jeans that she had on.

Perianne ignored the robotic sounding voice that came out

from her virtual mobile and picked it up to begin swiping on the screen to find the website she required for what she was about to do next.

Perianne opened up the Pelargonium Police Anonymous Reporting website confidently, but then hesitated before pressing out her message on the screen. She weighed up the risks of her being found out as the Anonymous reporter and the benefits of the trouble she could cause for Maromsaesc by her actions.

Even though they state they keep all reports confidential, this is not enough assurance. I can't mess up my reputation at Maromsaesc now. Not when I've come so far in fooling everybody. Perianne considered in her mind.

She searched the Internet for the privacy laws regarding the Pelargonium Police Anonymous Reporting website and quickly found the answer she was looking for. Perianne learned that if there was any leak of anonymous information from the Pelargonium Police Anonymous Reporting website, not only could it not be used in Court, but financial compensation of up to £250,000 would be awarded to the person who initially sent the anonymous information. Perianne concluded in her mind that if ever anyone found out that it was her sending the anonymous report, she could play it off utilising her brilliant acting skills. Perianne could see it now, in her minds eye. She envisioned herself standing in front of one of the podiums in a lecture hall full of news reporters, teachers, students, OBR's and the Professor. She saw herself dressed in her yellow Maromsaesc student tracksuit, wiping tears from her eyes with her left hand before bravely saying the following words with convincing integrity, truthfulness and passion.

"…I hadn't been sleeping well for months because of all the worry I had that there could be illegal drugs being taken at my university. Maromsaesc University. The university I love and am extremely proud to be a student of. I worried constantly that this would affect the reputation of Maromsaesc on the world stage. I felt I had no choice but to encourage the Pelargonium Police to check up on us more often for our own safety. I am not ashamed of what I did. I did it to protect the well-being of myself and other students around me and…I know, in fact, I am absolutely certain that everyone will appreciate that I stepped up to do so."

Perianne smiled to herself. Once again, her planning was perfect. Unfortunately, it oftentimes depended on other factors for it's success, which Perianne knew were the main reasons why her ideas had not completely destroyed Maromsaesc so far. She formulated her anonymous tip off for the Pelargonium Police and then sent her message with no name given within minutes. Perianne swiped away from the website and spoke to her virtual mobile.

"Call Mama Lucy." Perianne instructed her virtual mobile.

"Calling Mama Lucy, mother." replied her virtual mobile.

Perianne winced at hearing the word mother and wished with all her heart that it was her real mother she was about to speak to. Of course she loved Aunty Dr Joan Dedrick, but it wasn't the same as having her real mother around her. She had been told that she was very similar to her mother, Arida Dedrick, in her appearance, intelligence and beauty.

If only I could have seen her before she died, maybe I could have stopped her…somehow…helped her… Perianne thought sadly to herself. However, she soon felt happy again as she heard the voice of Aunty Dr Joan Dedrick speak through her virtual earphones.

"Mama Lucy speaking. Perianne is that you?" Aunty Dr Joan Dedrick asked suspiciously.

"Yes Mama Lucy. It's me! I miss you so much!" Perianne said to her Aunty.

"I miss you too. How are you and your studies at Maromsaesc?" Aunty Dr Joan Dedrick replied.

"I'm happy I've made progress today towards my *goals*. Another step forward for what I hope to achieve here at Maromsaesc Mama, so yes all is Jelitoonaa!" said Perianne happily keeping up her act as Perianne Saint.

Mama Lucy (aka Aunty Dr Joan Dedrick) easily read between the lines, realising instantly that her smart niece was actually referring to her *goals* to ruin Maromsaesc University for good.

"Very well done Perianne! The whole family are proud of you and are sure you will achieve all the *goals* you desire sooner than you imagine!" Aunty Dr Joan Dedrick said optimistically to her niece.

"I'm trying Mama Lucy. I look forward to the day I've succeeded and can leave Maromsaaesc with all my qualifications and awards." Perianne said hopefully.

The qualifications and awards Perianne spoke of were not any that she could potentially gain at Maromsaesc, but those in which she had already achieved in her home schooling. She greatly anticipated the day she could use her academic studies in medicine and Psychiatry to diagnose and heal people. One day, Perianne hoped to open up her own Psychiatry medical centres and hospitals in the future, just like her family (the Dedrick family) had done for generations past.

Aunty Dr Joan Dedrick started to cough loudly and very rough sounding. Perianne felt instantly afraid. She didn't need any medical training to know that her aunty sounded very ill. She tried to speak to Aunty Dr Joan Dedrick during brief gaps in between listening to her coughing fit, but realised that the coughing was getting more distant. Aunty Dr Joan Dedrick had dropped her virtual mobile and Perianne soon heard her hurried footsteps moving further and further away. Then, Perianne could faintly hear the sound of her aunty vomiting at a distance.

No! Aunty!...No, this can't be happening. Aunty? Aunty? Where are you? Drink some water! Mama? Aunty? Perianne's mind spinned around in panic.

Perianne couldn't lose her aunty aswell. Something felt very wrong. Usually, (as per her medical and acting training) she knew how to keep a calm professional composure when around a person who had any medical problem. To her surprise however, Perianne felt like her mind, her heart and her breathing were all racing very fast. She quickly reached for the bottle of water next to her misty grey double bed. She anxiously took numerous sips to try to calm herself down, while also making a determined effort to slow her breathing. All the while, she could still hear her beloved aunty vomiting violently somewhere away from her virtual mobile.

Suddenly, a distant thud noise was heard in the background and all the vomiting sounds coming from some distance away, ceased to be heard.

"No! Au...Mama! Mum!" Perianne shouted at her virtual mobile. She hung up the call and checked her app which showed video images of all the rooms in the secret location where Aunty Dr Joan Dedrick resided. She soon saw a clear video image of Aunty Dr Joan Dedrick laying in a pool of vomit with her face pale, her breathing raspy and shallow, collapsed at the entrance to the bathroom door.

Perianne rang her uncle Dr Robert Dedrick and told him what happened. She was careful to describe Aunty Dr Joan Dedrick as Mama Lucy. Uncle Dr Robert Dedrick (referred to by Perianne as Uncle) told her that he would get some of the family doctors who lived in that area to go to help his sister immediately.

"Don't worry. We have the best medical doctors in the family." Uncle Dr Robert Dedrick reassured his niece kindly. "From the video you've sent me, it looks like she's still breathing. We all need you to keep going now more than ever Perianne. Continue your *studies!*" Dr Robert finished and hung up his virtual mobile.

Sitting still in stunned silence, Perianne stared into space and thought of all the different ways she could sabotage Maromsaesc forever.

Meanwhile, near the Maromsaesc lake, Sentira, Noah, Craig, Brandi and Advik were relaxing separately on virtual mats in the warm afternoon summer sunshine. Other Year 1 students were also doing the same, so the recreation ground was very busy.

"They need to build a Maromsaesc beach next." Sentira said lazily to Brandi, as she turned her head to face her friend on the yellow virtual mat next to her.

"I know. This is Jelitoonaa, but a beach...that would be Jelitoonaa x a million!" Brandi replied shading her eyes from the sun, while reaching for her sunshades attached to the neckline of her Maromsaesc tracksuit top.

"It's a shame Annchi is missing this lovely weather. I still can't believe how one minute she was here and the next she's asleep in a coma." Sentira said sorrowfully remembering what had happened to their friend.

"She'll wake up. It's just a matter of time." Brandi said calmly. "It's Advik I'm worried about. Do you see how much weight he's lost?"

"No, I didn't notice." Sentira replied.

"Well, see for yourself. He's over there." Brandi suggested and turned her head to look in the opposite direction from where she was laying down.

"Yeah...actually, he does look slimmer than usual. Do you think he's grieving?" Sentira asked Brandi.

"Of course he is, but you know men... they don't like to show it." Brandi replied confidently.

Sentira was about to say something else, when the loud noise of virtual helicopters approaching could be heard coming from above, nearby the Maromsaesc lake. They could also be seen and heard flying high above other areas of the university grounds. Sentira sat up straight to look up at the sky, as did many of the other students, curious to see what was going on.

"They're virtual Police helicopters!" a Year 1 student exclaimed out loud, as most of the students rose to their feet to watch the dramatic noisy commotion in the sky above Maromsaesc University.

"It's another one of those Drug Raids!" exclaimed another Year 1 student loudly.

"This is sooo un-Jelitoonaa." Brandi said, gathering up her

virtual textbook, fruit and bottled water and replacing them in her yellow and blue shoulder bag.

"Well, they did say that they were going to surprise us with the timing of the next Drug Raid, so I guess this is it." replied Sentira thoughtfully, but Brandi had already got up from her yellow virtual mat and had begun to walk briskly away from the Maromsaesc lake.

"Brandi, where are you going?" Sentira called out after her friend.

"I haven't got time for their s***, I need the toilet!" Brandi yelled back at Sentira while continuing to walk fast away from where she had been previously.

"Ok! Be careful! They're probably already in the buildings!" Sentira responded back to Brandi feeling concerned. There was already too much sadness about Annchi still remaining asleep in a coma, Sentira did not want any of her other friends at Maromsaesc to have any more unfortunate events happen to them.

Noah, Craig and Advik were grouped together talking about the Police helicopters in the skies above Maromsaesc, when Noah called out to Sentira.

"Sentira, where's Perianne?" Noah asked with a worried expression on his face.

"She went back to her room, I think." Sentira replied.

"I'm going to go and…" Noah started to speak, but stopped abruptly staring at the sight of a line of twenty OBR Police walking towards the Year 1 students in a horizontal line.

Along with the noise of the virtual Police helicopters (above the sixty Year 1 students who were in the recreation ground at the time) the presence of the OBR Police was formidable and alarming. Noah stood still rooted to the spot he was standing on. Some of the other students sat back down on their virtual mats, waiting for the OBR Police to come to them. They knew that an unannounced Pelargonium police raid was going to happen one day, so even though the scenes around them were intimidating, the students were not as shocked as they had been during the first unforeseen Drug Raid. Besides, it had been explained to all the students that the Drug Raids were for their own safety and protection.

"I hope they don't find anything." Craig said to Noah.

"Why would they?" Noah replied, regaining his confidence and sitting back down on his virtual mat.

The horizontal line of twenty Pelargonium OBR Police reached the Year 1 students around the Maromsaesc lake in the recreation ground. One of the OBR Police stepped forward out of the horizontal line and spoke in a female human voice.

"As you are aware, we are the Pelargonium OBR Police and we are present at Maromsaesc University today to conduct a full drug search of the premises. We would like your full co-operation to do so. Please form separate vertical lines and come forward to be scan searched by an OBR. We will be using new Applerishin advanced virtual search technology. Leave your belongings on the floor so that OBR's can scan search them. Before being scan searched, you will be asked if you have or know any person who has been using illegal drugs at Maromsaesc. After you have been scan searched, please return back to your original place until we have completed our work. Thank you."

The sixty Year 1 students heard and understood what they had to do, duly forming varied lines of 4, 5 or 10 students depending on who they were standing/sitting near to at the time. Sentira formed a vertical line of 4 students consisting of Noah, Craig and Advik. Advik stood at the front.

The virtual Police helicopters were still flying noisily above Maromsaesc University and the students looked up often to watch them. The OBR Police did not so much as glance upwards at the virtual Police helicopters but were focused completely on the job in hand. They quickly began to scan search the students one by one. Advik was one of the first students to be scan searched.

"Do you or do you know anyone who has been using illegal drugs on the Maromsaesc University grounds?" inquired a Police OBR.

"No, I do not." Advik replied confidently without hesitation.

Suddenly, a ray of pale blue light came out of the Police OBR's eyes and scan searched Advik from the top of his head to the base of his feet and back up again, five times.

"Your scan search is complete. No illegal drugs have been found on your person at this time. Please return to your original place." said the OBR Policewoman, standing at 7 foot tall in front of Advik.

Advik turned around to begin to walk back past the queues of students to return to his virtual mat near the Maromsaesc lake. Noah decided to ask him a question as he walked by.

"What did ..." Noah began to say, but was sharply cut off by the loud voice of the 7 foot tall OBR Policewoman who had just scan searched his friend.

"Silence!" the OBR Policewoman shouted, her tone sounding much more menacing than earlier on.

Noah turned away from Advik and faced forward, uncertain of what could happen if he tried to speak to Advik a second time.

No sooner than Advik had sat down, an OBR Policewoman came over to his grey virtual mat and scan searched his blue rucksack at the edge of his mat. Just as before, a pale blue light ray came out of the OBR's eyes and scanned Advik's blue rucksack five times.

"Are you the owner of this bag?" the OBR Policewoman asked Advik, as he sat staring up at the 7 foot tall OBR now towering above him.

"Ye...yeah I am." Advik replied uneasily.

"Is your name Mr Advik Chandran?" the OBR Policewoman inquired further.

"Ye...yes." Advik answered.

"Mr Advik Chandran, you are under arrest for being in possession of the Class B illegal drug cannabis. You do not have to say anything, but it may harm your defence..." the OBR Policewoman bent down to the level Advik was seated at and swiftly moved his arms behind his back.

"Oww! You're hurting me! It's not mine! It's my girlfriend's. She's sick!" Advik shouted at the OBR Policewoman.

Many of the Year 1 students turned their heads to look towards the Maromsaesc lake, to see what was happening and find out who was shouting.

The OBR Policewoman ignored Advik's shouting, proceeded to connect a pair of virtual silver handcuffs on his wrists and pulled him up onto his feet. Another OBR Policeman joined her and held onto Advik's left arm, while the OBR Policewoman held onto his right.

"You do not have to say anything, but it may harm your defence if you do not mention when questioned something which you later rely on in court. Anything you do say may be given in evidence." the OBR Policewoman finished saying to Advik, walking him away from his virtual mat and blue rucksack and towards another area of the Maromsaesc Recreation Ground.

Sentira looked back at Advik in shock, as did the rest of the Year 1 students. She couldn't hear what had been said to Advik. She only heard Advik's shouts that he was innocent and it wasn't his.

Oh no, Advik! What did they find? Sentira wondered to herself, scared for her friend.

"Face forward, silence!" the OBR Police said in unison at the front of each line of students.

The sound of a Police virtual helicopter landing nearby in the recreation ground could be heard noisily in the background to the right of Sentira and the other Year 1 students. It was Sentira's turn to be scan searched so she apprehensively stood forward. The 7 foot tall OBR Policewoman's eyes met Sentira's eyes.

There's nothing to fear Sentira reassured herself in her mind. *They are programmed to behave like this. They can only attack if they see something they've been programmed to confront.*

However, Sentira made sure to keep her body as still as she

possibly could, avoiding even the slightest glance to her left or right, while standing in front of the impressive yet intimidating tall robot. She listened carefully to the words spoken by the OBR Policewoman before replying with her answer in as clear and an assertive voice, as she could muster.

"No, I do not." Sentira replied confidently and truthfully.

Suddenly, (similar to before with other Year 1 students), a ray of pale blue light came out of the Policewoman's OBR eyes and scan searched Sentira from the top of her head to the base of her feet, then back up again. This process was repeated a total of five times, but the OBR Policewoman held her pale blue light ray directly on Sentira's open eyes for a few seconds longer than anywhere else. The pale blue light ray did not physically hurt Sentira or any of the students during their searches, although Sentira did find herself blinking twice at the extra few seconds the pale blue light ray was held over her eyes. Finally, the scan search was over and Sentira looked at the programmed Police robot in front of her curiously to see what it would say to her next. She did not feel unsafe as she knew she did not have anything illegal on her. Sentira wouldn't do anything to jeopardize her place at Maromsaesc University. She even considered that there was a possibility that she could become a Police Psychic Detective one day, after she achieved her first class degree in the Professional Development of people who hear voices and see visions in just over two years time.

Come on. You didn't find anything. I need to see if Advik is all right. Sentira thought to herself, gradually feeling impatient as the Policewoman OBR stood looking at her without speaking.

Sentira narrowed her dark brown eyes at the Policewoman OBR curiously. Although she knew that the Police OBR's were programmed to do their job and not treat humans unfairly, there was always that small chance that the programming of any OBR could be faulty or malfunction.

Fortunately for Sentira, the OBR Policewoman began to speak in a robotic voice. The OBR's could speak in a variety of different voices, dependent on its individual programming.

"Your scan search is complete. No illegal drugs have been found on your person at this time. Please return to your original place." said the OBR Policewoman finally to Sentira, expressing no emotion in it's voice.

Sentira turned around and breathed a sigh of relief. She heard the sound of a Police virtual helicopter take off again from nearby, on another part of the Maromsaesc recreation ground. She intuitively knew that Advik had been taken away in that virtual helicopter from the direction in which she last saw Advik being led by the two OBR Police. When Sentira reached her virtual mat, she reached for her virtual mobile inside her blue jeans pocket to call Nanny Lisha. On her virtual mobile, Sentira described to Nanny Lisha all that had happened with the most recent Pelargonium Police raid. She could hear the worry in her grandmother's voice and shook her head.

This can't be happening. Maromsaesc will not turn into a nightmare. Sentira determinedly thought to herself in her mind. She mused about everything going on in her mind, while only half-listening to Nanny Lisha's passionate voice agreeing with her that the interference by the Pelargonium Police was uncalled for and unnecessary.

All this unwanted drama was potentially demoralising.

AIR OF MYSTERY

The next day in the student cafeteria, all the Year 1 students could talk about was yesterday's Pelargonium Police drug raid. Noah sat at a virtual table with Perianne, Craig, Brandi and Sentira discussing different versions of what had happened.

"It's Jelitoonaa that I changed the location of the meet up after the Voice Teacher Training class. Darren told me that at the Maromsaesc Gardens, the OBR Police trampled all over the flowers and shouted at them all the time they were conducting their scan search." Noah said to the group sitting around him, but loud enough for students seated five or six seats away to hear.

Craig smiled and said, "I don't think that's true."

"It is true! Look at the News, read for yourself online." Noah insisted.

"And we all know the News channels tell the truth." Craig laughed, taking a bite out of his ham, lettuce and tomato sandwich.

"Ok, so don't believe me but listen to this… Breaking News: Pelargonium OBR Police ruin Maromsaesc Gardens by disorganised, unplanned Drug Raid…It's all here on Pelargonium News channel's website. Read it!" Noah insisted again, ignoring his food and staring mostly at his virtual mobile.

Perianne took a few sips of her coffee and decided that this would be a good time to join in the conversation. Craig looked down at his virtual mobile in one hand and ate his ham sandwich in the other. Sentira watched the large virtual screen playing the News in front of her and moved the peas around on her plate with a fork. Brandi too sat watching the News on the large virtual screen, while occasionally eating from the chicken salad meal in front of her.

"There's so many stories in the News, they can't all be untrue Craig." Perianne said matter of factly.

Noah smiled at Perianne and then began talking to his voices in the air around his right hand side.

Perianne continued to speak about various News channels reports, pointing out that there were definitely some parts reported about the PP drug raid which actually did occur. Sentira listened to the way Perianne read all of the News headlines and felt an urge to interrupt in defence of Advik and Maromsaesc University, but instead continued to eat her food and gaze thoughtfully at the News on the virtual screen.

Only time will tell if the Police believe Advik's version. Sentira thought to herself, watching the Police video clip of when they arrested Advik for possession of cannabis, play out on the News programme. Sentira blocked out the noise of Perianne's voice near her and focused her complete attention on the words of the reporter on the virtual screen.

"...Maromsaesc Year 1 student Advik Chandran, claims that the bag of cannabis found in his rucksack does not in fact belong to him, but to the seriously unwell student Annchi Kang. Annchi Kang is currently very ill in a coma suffering from an unknown medical condition. Police will not be able to interview Miss Kang until she wakes up from her comatose state. Miss Kang (also a Team 3 student) has a legal right to possess medical cannabis for a rare medical condition she has had since birth. It is another unexpected blow to a list of unfortunate events that have occurred at Maromsaesc University since it's opening in Septembe 2070. Professor Zantend has again refused to comment. This is Tina Parsons, reporting for the World News Channel 2071. Now, over to Kevin for..." the News reporter stated clearly from the virtual screen in the student cafeteria.

Sentira felt embarrassed. She was embarrassed not only for herself but for Advik, all the Year 1 students with similar abilities to her and for Maromsaesc University as a whole.

How did it get to this? Sentira mused to herself in disbelief. Just then, she heard laughter coming from Perianne and Noah laughed with her. Next, Sentira heard the familiar voices of Rhyle and Gina talking around her.

"Sen..ir..a" Rhyle's toddler voice said around Sentira's left ear.

"Don't frighten her Rhyle? Grow up." Gina's teenage voice said around Sentira's right ear.

"How old are you Gina?" Rhyle's elderly voice said from around the front of Sentira's face.

"Older than you obviously!" Gina's elderly voice said again from around the front of Sentira's face.

Sentira relaxed as she heard her regular voices chatter around her, turning away from the worrying news broadcasts on the virtual screen. She continued to eat her Barbecue beef steak meal and listened to the words of Louis and Olamide who were now talking around her right ear.

"They took too long to build this place." Olamide's adult voice said.

"I know." Louis's elderly voice replied.

"We'll have to move soon." Olamide's teenage voice said.

"Anywhere else will be the same." Louis answered.

"Moving her will take even longer." Rhyle's teenage voice said, joining in the conversation.

"She'll be frightened." Gina's elderly voice said, also speaking up.

"Ye..ahhh rii..ghtt." Rhyle's toddler voice answered.

Sentira giggled to herself. She knew from experience that her regular voices could be talking about anything. Their words did not always relate to her or something going on around her. Sometimes, she could sense when a conversation was not directed at her and other times it was more difficult to decipher, especially with the voices that spoke at random.

*****

A month went by at Maromsaesc University. Advik had returned to his Year 1 studies after one night and a day in police custody. His statement (recorded by Pelargonium Police) explaining his version of events and innocence of any wrong doing, awaited confirmation from Annchi. Sadly, Annchi could not confirm anything as she was still unconscious in a coma. Therefore, the Police informed each student by message on their virtual mobiles that the drug raids would continue for their own safety and protection.

Sentira deleted the message from the Pelargonium Police on her virtual mobile, within seconds after she had skim read it. She didn't want to hear anymore negative news about Maromsaesc University. She had enough work to do in her final term of Year 1, as she sat waiting for the Spiritual Voices tutor to arrive. Just at that moment, Miss Garrison walked into the Spiritual Voices lecture hall and took her place behind the virtual podium. There were one hundred Year 1 students in the hall, a mix of Teams 1, 2, 3 & 4.

"Good morning Year 1. Applerishin virtual security says that you are all present, except Annchi Kang." Miss Garrison said, the virtual speakers around the hall amplifying her voice greatly. "Has anyone been to seen her recently, these past few weeks perhaps, at the Pelargonium hospital?" Miss Garrison asked looking up at the students in front of her.

Around 30 students put up their hands.

"She's the same." Advik (who was seated in the front row) said loud enough for Miss Garrison who was some distance away to hear him. He stood up and spoke again "But, the doctors think that she could wake up anytime so we shouldn't give up hope. Annchi is a fighter. I know her...I know she'll get through this." Advik said with certainty, his passionate emotions for Annchi heard easily in his voice.

Sentira glanced over at him from a few seats away.

Don't cry Advik. Annchi will come back. Sentira thought optimistically to herself.

However, a few of Annchi's other friends in different teams were allowing their tears to flow freely. Two students even burst into sobs and left the lecture hall with a supervising OBR following after them.

What is happening to everyone? Sentira thought as she

watched the concerned expression on Miss Garrison's face as the two students walked out of the lecture hall.

The atmosphere in the lecture hall appeared even more moody and tense, when Miss Garrison changed the subject to that week's homework assignment.

"Did everyone manage to write their essay to answer the question entitled "How Spiritual voices can help to provide meaning and purpose for a voice hearer?" Miss Garrison inquired.

There were loud groans from some of the Year 1 students. However, the majority of the students put up their hands to indicate that they had completed the homework set.

Miss Garrison decided to address those students who had groaned loudly about her homework question.

"Listen to me. I understand that it's more difficult to concentrate right now because of everything going on. The constant daily News reports about Maromsaesc can be disheartening, but you must not let it affect your studies for your Professional degree qualification. All of you are more than capable of achieving A grades for this final term of your Year 1 course. May I also take this opportunity to remind you, that the student counselling services are available 24 hours each day, if anyone would like to talk over their concerns with a trained OBR." Miss Garrison explained kindly.

There were some giggles heard from the Year 1 students. It sounded funny to them that they were expected to go and tell their problems to a programmed robot with set answers and oftentimes barely realistic emotions. Miss Garrison understood their humour and smiled.

"I am always hear to listen too but I just can't stay awake for 24 hours like the OBR's can." Miss Garrison grinned at the students.

The atmosphere in the lecture hall lightened and Miss Garrison began her lecture about spiritual voices throughout history. Soon the two students who had run out of the hall crying, returned within ten minutes, quietly resuming their places and opening their virtual notebooks. The supervising OBR who had followed the two students outside returned also.

"...Saint Joan of Arc, Indian prophetess Gaidinliu, Sikh founder Guru Nanak and Moses. Moses (story found in the Christian Bible) is known as having heard angelic and divine voices naming him as a prophet. Sikh..." Miss Garrison lectured confidently on the day's topic.

Perianne had to use every ounce of her acting training to not walk out of the lecture hall herself, just as the two crying students had done earlier. Her instincts were telling her to do just that, but her mind bluntly refused to give up her act or her purpose.

None of these spiritual voices can ever be proven. Some of these people were just crazy. Perianne thought to herself in her mind. Then, as if provoked to speak, voices spoke around her left ear.

"The timing of our departure will be delayed, please remain seated while the organisers resolve the..." an unknown young female voice said around Perianne's left ear.

Perianne quickly mouthed the word "stop" silently to the air around her left hand side. The female voice stopped talking. Perianne lifted up her virtual textbook to cover her mouth and permitted herself to grin.

Yes! I'm still different. I have more control. Perianne observed satisfactorily, reading through the spiritual voices chapter and listening to Miss Garrison's lengthy and tedious (according to Perianne) lecture.

The complete opposite to Perianne was Sentira. Sentira was fascinated by Miss Garrison's lecture on spiritual voices throughout history. She listened attentively and became so engrossed in hearing what Miss Garrison had to say, she forgot about the negative news media stories. She wrote notes in her virtual notebook during the lecture and when the lecture finished, started talking excitedly to Brandi about what they had been taught.

"I knew that these voices were more of a blessing than a curse." Sentira said happily to Brandi, standing up to pack away her virtual notebook and virtual pen in her shoulder bag.

"Well, some can be I guess." Brandi replied smiling back at her.

The Year 1 students gradually exited the lecture hall in their friendship groups or alone. Some went to go and eat lunch at the student cafeteria, while others went elsewhere for their hour break before Sports class.

Why is everyone so happy? Don't they realise this will be their final term at Maromsaesc? Perianne thought to herself while smiling widely and nodding her head in agreement at all the positive praise for Miss Garrison's "Jelitoonaa" lecture.

"Let's all go order lunch by the lake." Noah suggested to the Team 3 group consisting of himself, Perianne, Brandi, Sentira, Craig and Advik. They had all been talking in the corridor outside the lecture hall and time was moving on. Before long, Noah recognised that they would soon have to go over to the Sports block and he wanted to see if he could get a chance to talk to Perianne alone.

The small group made their way outside of the Student Learning Block for Lectures, using a virtual lift to get back down to the ground floor, so they could exit the building. Once outside they walked on virtual pathways to get to the Maromsaesc Recreation Ground where the Maromsaesc lake was situated. The temperature that day in Pelargonium was 30 degrees of bright sunshine with not a single cloud in the light blue sky. Most of the Year 1 students (who were already at the Maromsaesc lake) were lounging about standing or sitting on the hilly ground nearby or on virtual mats enjoying the hot weather.

Brandi, Sentira, Craig and Advik stood nearby the Maromsaesc lake chatting and looking over at the visual beauty of the shimmering blue lake. Perianne sat down on a blue virtual mat that was already laid out for the Year 1 students to use in the recreation ground. Noah sat down next to her.

"Get your own mat Noah!" Perianne laughed playfully with Noah.

Noah, you will never be my boyfriend. Perianne thought

smugly in her mind. She faked a wide smile as Noah sat closer to her before happily pushing him over onto another virtual mat next to hers. Noah laughed while Perianne pushed him, feeling happy to be touched by her even if it almost felt like a shove.

"Woah, easy on my back!" Noah said, rolling his body around to face Perianne again. "Have you ordered any food yet? Do you want me to get you something?"

"I've ordered." Perianne replied. "But… you can get me 3 bottles of water, 2 are for me to take to Sports class."

"Done my Queen." Noah smiled at Perianne before bending his head down to place his order on his student cafeteria app on his virtual mobile.

"Jelitoonaa, thank you Noah." answered Perianne self-assuredly.

"Perianne, do…" Noah started to say, but was cut short by Brandi's voice speaking beside him.

"Noah, did you get me the chips you ate off my plate yesterday?" Brandi said in an amused voice coming from above Noah who was laying on his tummy, his head facing Perianne's direction.

Noah moved his body around to laying on his back and looked up at Brandi towering over him wearing a short sleeved cream mid-thigh length summer dress, with virtual roses appearing on and off in different places all over.

Noah felt embarrassed that Brandi had interrupted what he was about to ask Perianne and responded sharply "You don't need anymore chips!"

Brandi instantly kicked Noah on his leg. Noah defensively stood up and spoke to her face to face, still feeling upset that his plan to have a serious talk with Perianne had been sidetracked.

"You don't need anymore chips, Brandi!" Noah said direct to Brandi's face.

"And you don't need to keep begging Perianne to go out with you." Brandi retorted grinning at Perianne who was watching them both while seated in the lotus position on her virtual mat.

Noah stared at Brandi, his face turning red. Then he grabbed his black rucksack, which had been placed on the grass near his virtual mat and stormed off, walking fast away from both Brandi and Perianne.

Brandi sat down on the virtual mat next to Perianne and they exchanged knowing looks.

"Mission accomplished." Brandi said, positioning her body so she could lay on her side facing Perianne.

Perianne smiled at her, but in her mind she was thinking…

My mission will only be accomplished when Maromsaesc is destroyed for good.

Sentira, Craig and Advik came over to join the women and sat down on virtual mats nearby, facing in the direction of the Maromsaesc lake.

"Where's Noah gone to?" Craig asked Perianne.

Craig knew that his friend had a big on and off crush on Perianne, and from the start of this week it was apparently on again. Some weeks he listened to Noah talk about how much he wanted to "get with" Perianne, and other weeks he heard his friend talking about how he wasn't that into her anymore. Craig thought Noah was mixed up and didn't really know what he wanted.

"I don't know." Brandi said. "He'll be back soon probably."

Brandi raised both her arms over her head and stretched them, a loud yawn released from her mouth. She suddenly felt both her eyelids drooping and brought both her hands to her eyes to rub them. Then she fell asleep, right there on her virtual mat, snoring loudly.

"Poor Brandi." Sentira said, watching her friend's loud snores gradually becoming more softer and gentler before she finally remained asleep silently.

"We can't leave her sleeping in this hot sun. I'm going to call a medical OBR to take her back to Jay Halls." Craig offered quickly. He reached in his black shorts pocket and activated the

Maromsaesc emergency call OBR app which would bring medical assistance to Brandi.

"Good idea. So sad... this falling asleep thing she does before hearing voices. I'm glad I don't have to fall asleep before mine speak around me." Advik said, accepting a green virtual tray (containing a Chicken Salsa meal with a lemonade drink) from an OBR who had knelt down on his virtual mat beside him.

"It isn't her fault, she can't help it." Craig replied.

Within minutes, he watched as two medical OBR's swiftly approached where they were seated and carried Brandi away on a virtual stretcher into a medical hover vehicle. The medical OBR staff at Maromsaesc knew about Brandi's random sleeping episodes, so they did not stop to ask for any extra details about what had happened from any of the students. They efficiently transported Brandi's sleeping body via medical hover vehicle to Jay Halls where a medical OBR duly put her into her bed. A medical OBR stood in Room 10 Jay Halls watching over Brandi and monitoring her vital signs as she slept.

"Reminds me," said Advik in between chewing mouthfuls of his Chicken Salsa. "Does anyone want to come with me to visit Annchi after Mediumship class?"

"Yeah I'll come." Sentira answered calmly receiving a virtual plate of Turkey Pasta with stir-fry veg and fruit from an OBR. Two other OBR's also brought Craig and Perianne their cafeteria app lunch orders.

"Me too." Perianne said, twirling her spaghetti round her fork as if trying to decide whether she should eat it or not.

"Craig?" Advik asked his friend who hadn't given his answer yet.

"Nah, I think I'll leave my visit to tomorrow." Craig replied. He didn't tell Advik that he was more worried about Brandi than Annchi right now. He had to remain at the university in case she needed help. Maybe (he secretly hoped) she might call him to come to her room at Jay Halls to look after her.

"Alright, so just us three." Advik replied, glancing across at

Perianne and Sentira.

Perianne half-smiled in return, which she hoped expressed her bravery and hope for Annchi's speedy recovery. Sentira on the other hand, smiled at Advik optimistic that today could be the day Annchi woke up as they visited her. Sentira began to hear voices speak around her while she ate and drank, voices that she did not recognise.

"What's happening? Why isn't this working?" a new female adult voice said around Sentira's left ear.

"I can't…this heat is too much, i…" another female adult voice said around Sentira's right ear.

"I'm sweating and I stink bad." a male deep adult voice said from behind Sentira.

"Something's wrong with this…" another male adult voice said coming from the air in front of Sentira.

Then Sentira clearly heard the sound of water falling fast like rain, slowing down gradually until no water could be heard falling after 30 seconds. High above her, there was not a cloud to be seen in the light blue sky. In fact on this day at Maromsaesc University in Pelargonium, it happened to be the hottest day for their location so far on record in 2071. Sentira dismissed the new voices she heard as just one of those "random things" and relaxed in the sun laying on her back reading her Spiritual Voices virtual textbook. Sometimes, resting the virtual textbook down on her tummy, to reach for another forkful of her Turkey Pasta. Hearing new voices randomly or sounds that no-one else heard did not bother Sentira. Although this time and ever since her first Psychic Development class in Term 2, she tried not to forget any new words, sentences or sounds just in case they had some future or past psychic significance.

Perianne activated the virtual UV shade umbrella on her virtual mat, by pressing her hand print on a sensor on the top right hand corner of her mat. She set the brightness to dark by using her finger and sliding across to the right on a section of the umbrella, similar to what someone would do when swiping right on their virtual mobile. Perianne did not only want to get some shade from the strong heat of the sun however, but also to hide what she read on her virtual mobile. Perianne re-read recent negative news headlines about Maromsaesc University and felt uplifted.

Not long before Psychiatry will be up and running again! Perianne thought to herself proudly. She was just about to read the latest negative news report from this morning, when her virtual mobile rang. Quickly activating her virtual sound device and answering the call, she spoke confidently "Hello, who's calling?"

"Perianne, this is your Uncle. It's about Mama Lucy. She's back in hospital for more tests as she fainted again a few hours ago." said Uncle Dr Robert Dedrick quickly, as if he was in a hurry to get off the phone.

"Wait Uncle, what do you mean? You said she was getting better and it was only low sugar that made her pass out." replied Perianne quietly so that the other Team 3 students couldn't hear what she had said.

"Listen to me don't you worry, just continue with the plan to achieve greatness at Maromsaesc." Uncle Dr Robert said with the faintest hint of sarcasm that only Perianne understood clearly.

"I will. Bye Uncle." Perianne said and hung up the phone, realising that her Uncle would not disclose much else to her until he knew for certain why Aunty Dr Joan Dedrick was very ill.

Just continue with the plan, to… Perianne began to plot in her mind when she felt a shiver pass through her body, despite the hot weather. All of a sudden, the perfect plan came to her mind.

Perianne deactivated the virtual UV umbrella around her by pressing her handprint on the sensor on the right hand corner of her virtual mat.

"Sentira! I've got really bad period tummy cramps, can you tell the Sports OBR's that I won't be able to train today?" Perianne said to Sentira adding slight annoyance and frustration to her voice.

"Yeah, ok." Sentira replied.

Perianne half smiled bravely at her and said, "Let Advik know too if I'm not better by this afternoon."

"Ok." Sentira said, shading her eyes from the sun to look at Perianne.

This is new. When has Perianne ever complained about period cramps before? Sentira thought to herself with a slightly amused feeling that she didn't understand fully. She watched Perianne walk away from the Maromsaesc lake and over the hilly grounds before she could not see her anymore in the distance. Then, she carried on eating her lunch while reading her virtual Spiritual Voices textbook totally interested and enthralled by every page.

Perianne walked through the virtual pathways to get to Jay Halls. After Applerishin Security had scanned her to confirm her identity, she entered Jay Halls and used the virtual lift to go up to Room 25. When the virtual lifts doors opened, Perianne stepped outside and quickly went into the unisex toilets. Inside the unisex toilets, Perianne got into a cubicle and sat on the toilet seat with the lid down. She took out a brand new virtual laptop from her shoulder bag. Then, she cleverly activated the OBR feature on her virtual mobile, grinning widely to herself. She sat on the closed toilet lid seat and watched in satisfaction as the OBR appeared and got to work on her new virtual laptop, just as she had pre-programmed it to do.

Wait till the News channels hear about the latest disturbing drama that unfolds at...at...at Maromsaesc School for the Mad. Perianne deviously thought to herself.

Perianne watched the OBR's robotic fingers swiftly move fast on the virtual keyboard of her new virtual laptop. She viewed the OBR with respect and awe as she saw it's brilliant expertise at undertaking the task it had been instructed to do. Perianne's admiration for the OBR increased as she joyfully witnessed it opening up the private and confidential security operations of Maromsaesc University. She observed that the OBR did so with probably just as much simple ease as whoever had originally designed the security operations.

Either the person who designed the Maromsaesc security systems was extremely bad at it...or my virtual mobile OBR is a genius! Perianne mused to herself, becoming more excited as every minute went by.

Perianne had pre-programmed the OBR (after completion of it's task) to delete everything on the virtual laptop which could possibly lead an investigator to successfully trace back where the laptop had originated from. Even though the new virtual laptop had never been registered in Perianne's name or anyone in the Dedrick family, Perianne didn't take any chances whatsoever of being caught. The virtual laptop had not been bought from any retailer but built by one of her family members. Every conceivable potential way of her being discovered as the instigator of damaging incidents at Maromsaesc, had been very carefully considered and planned ahead for.

Twenty minutes passed and Perianne heard other students enter and leave the toilet cubicles from either side of her. No one seemed to notice anything strange or untoward happening in her cubicle. The students who entered the unisex toilet, quickly used the toilets and left again. Perianne sighed silently to herself in relief. She didn't need another problem to worry about with an over-confident, nosy, crazed Maromsaesc student questioning her over why she was in her toilet cubicle so long.

It took a further ten minutes before the OBR stepped back from Perianne's new virtual laptop and reduced it's size before disappearing back into Perianne's virtual mobile. Perianne replaced her virtual laptop and virtual mobile in her shoulder bag, before opening her cubicle door to exit the unisex toilets. She walked a short distance to Room 25, waited for Applerishin virtual security to scan her before entering her room, then threw herself down on her bed in a fit of hysterical giggles.

Meanwhile, Sentira, Noah, Craig and Advik were at Sports class playing a basketball game in the middle of the relentless heat and sizzling Friday sunshine. They were all on the same basketball team playing against some other Year 1 students from Team 2. Their team chose the name "Heat Divers" and were currently in the lead by 10 points, while the other team named "Cherry Rollercoasters" were losing. Suddenly, Sentira began to hear many loud voices (both male and female) coming from around her ears and also some distance in front of her. They were so loud, Sentira decided she should leave the basketball game to sit down somewhere and focus all her attention on communicating with them.

"Hey Advik, I'm taking a break. I'll call Lisa to take my place." Sentira shouted over at Advik.

"Jelitoonaa." Advik said, sounding distracted as he jumped high to catch the basketball, which had just been thrown at him by a team player.

Sentira ran away from the noise of the basketball court and onto the seating area where she saw Lisa sitting down drinking a bottle of water. Upon seeing Sentira, Lisa intuitively jumped up toppling over her open bottle of water and ran to take her place on the "Heat Divers" team. For Sentira, the loud male and female voices continued to speak around her. She listened carefully, while pouring water from the nearby virtual water dispenser into a small virtual cup.

"Not safe, it's not safe here. We need you. Listen to us." a female adult voice said from around Sentira's left ear.

"You'll frighten her." said another female voice loudly around Sentira's right ear.

"Unsafe. Listen. You…will…frighten her." said an unknown elderly male voice from in front of Sentira's face.

"If it's me you are referring to. It's Jelitoonaa. I'm not scared. If it's not, then can you keep the noise down I can hear you and I'm busy playing basketball!" Sentira spoke to the air around her, first to her left side, the front of her and then her right side in a confident tone. She didn't raise her voice as she knew that whatever was speaking around her, could hear her even if she spoke as quietly as via her tranquil mind for instance.

There was a brief pause of about 60 seconds whereby no loud voices spoke around Sentira, but afterwards they resumed again saying similar words and sentences as before. Sentira got up again to refill her small virtual cup with water. She pressed the sensor with her thumb so her thumbprint could activate the water to come out of the virtual dispenser machine. However, this time no water was dispensed. Sentira pressed again harder this time with her thumb to ensure her thumbprint was read by the sensor properly. Still no water was dispensed and at that same moment, the loud unknown male and female voices previously heard, mysteriously and abruptly ceased to talk around her.

STUDENTS V OBR'S

An OBR supervising the basketball game spoke in a robotic voice that was as loud as the virtual speakers in the lecture hall.

"All Year 1 students in the Games Courts must return immediately to the student gym block and report to a supervising OBR."

What's happening now? Sentira wondered, as she got up to walk towards the student gym block, with many other Year 1 students following some distance behind her and others already ahead of her. As she slowly approached the gym block, she waited for Applerishin virtual security to scan her before entering inside. When she got inside, she could hear the shouts of students arguing with the supervising sports OBR's.

"I have to get out of here soon, it's too hot." exclaimed a male Year 1 student.

"There's no water at all…well, yes, that's what we've told you all the time." a female Year 1 student shouted.

"I have a few bottles of ice water in my bag. Here, have these." a male student yelled back.

"Please remain calm, there are emergency water bottles and nutrition bars available with a limit of four per student. There has been an unknown security error and you are all to remain here until further instructions are given. Thank you." a supervising sports OBR said in a volume as loud as those amplified by virtual speakers.

Sentira walked up to the closest OBR to her and waited again to be scanned, to confirm this time that she had made the OBR aware of her presence.

"I'm sweating in here!" a male student said angrily to the OBR, at it's right side.

"I need a shower to cool off. This is so un-Jelitoonaa" another male student shouted at other OBR's standing nearby.

"Why is there always some drama in this school!" a female student whined to herself in frustration, her Maromsaesc sports dress dripping with sweat.

"Yeah, but this is what they do when there's a security breach...they keep everyone in one place until they work out what's gone wrong." another female student said to a male student that Sentira could see was still trying to persuade an OBR to allow him to go outside. She spoke to the woman talking with him.

"What's going on? Is it another power cut?" Sentira asked her, glancing behind her briefly and observing that nearly all of the students on the Games Court were now back in the student gym block reception area. Like her, they were heading towards the student changing area to collect their belongings.

The female student with brown skin and a short afro snorted before replying "What does it look like?", then she turned away from Sentira to speak to the air in front of her, obviously hearing words/sentences that others were not. Sentira shrugged her shoulders at the woman and directed her next question at the man with her.

"So, when did this all start?" Sentira asked him.

The male student with freckled pale skin and tousled curly brown hair, dressed in Maromsaesc yellow shorts and a white Maromsaesc vest top rolled his eyes at Sentira.

"I don't know." he responded, staring at the woman next to him who was now talking excitedly to her voices in the air around her. "She was telling me but now she's distracted. I was playing football with her... and some others before I heard the OBR calling everyone inside. Now, I'm here...I need a shower cause I'm sweating...the OBR's say we can't use them!" the male student answered, only looking at Sentira during his final sentence.

"From what I'm hearing there seems to be some sort of security breach affecting the water supply and the air conditioning." Sentira said to the male student with the curly brown hair reassuringly. "Don't worry. They have to sort it out soon.

There's too many of us in here for there not to be no water for much longer and…all the windows are open so we can sit over by them and get some air."

"But, do you see how there are OBR's standing by all the windows." the male student replied.

Sentira looked around her at all the open windows in reception and near the changing rooms. The man was correct. There were OBR's at every single open window and at the main entrance and all the fire exits. Sentira took a quick fast breath in. It was quite an intimidating sight to see robots standing guard around the mixture of Teams 1, 2, 3, and 4 students in the building. It all appeared very formal and highly serious. Sentira blinked her eyes a number of times to prevent any tears from forming in front of the other Year 1 student.

"It'll be sorted out. I have faith in the technicians and engineers at Maromsaesc." Sentira replied with what she hoped was confident optimism, but her voice cracked a bit as she said the word Maromsaesc.

The male student smirked at Sentira, before walking off with the female student who had stopped talking to her voices at that precise moment.

Sentira turned around to look for someone she knew from her team to talk with. Unable to see anyone through the crowds, Sentira continued to walk towards her cubicle in the student changing areas to collect her water bottles and textbooks she had left there earlier. She could still hear the voices of disgruntled Year 1 students all around her shouting at the OBR's and complaining about the showers not working and the lack of air conditioning. Over the top of the student's distressed voices, Sentira also heard the OBR's virtual speaker type booming voices echoing every few minutes around the gym block continuously repeating these sentences: -

"Please remain calm, there are emergency water bottles and nutrition bars available with a limit of four per student. There has been an unknown security error and you are all to remain here until further instructions are given. Thank you."

Sentira watched OBR's distributing water bottles and nutrition bars to students and directing them to seating near windows in the reception, also around the gyms and changing room areas. Sentira collected her textbooks and water bottles from her cubicle in the student changing room area cautiously. She hoped there would not be another virtual power cut like there had been in the previous term at Maromsaesc University. Hurriedly dismissing those anxious thoughts from her mind, she managed to push her textbooks and water bottles into her already 3/4 full shoulder bag. She wanted to go back into the reception area and sit by one of the larger windows to try and cool down like the majority of students were beginning to do.

On her way back to the gym block reception area, Sentira could see that some virtual fans had been set up in various places. Feeling relieved and grateful, she sat down near a virtual fan and took out a bottle of water from her shoulder bag. Sentira took three large gulps of water and blinked her eyes in disbelief as she looked around the reception area and saw a number of Year 1 students arguing heatedly with the OBR's. She observed them unhappily for the next 30 minutes feeling hot weak and tired herself. Then, Sentira lowered her head momentarily after taking several further gulps of water. When she raised her head again both her eyelids blinked rapidly.

What has happened to the University I love? Sentira began to think sadly to herself, but then her worried thoughts stopped abruptly, her eyelids returned to normal and she felt a strong sense of calm and peace. Her regular voices of Rhyle, Gina, Olamide and Louis started to talk around her ears, face and behind her.

"These fans were brought in too late." Ryle's adult voice said around Sentira's left ear.

"What do you expect!" Olamide's teenage voice said around Sentira's right ear.

"Ro..bot...fa...an....go.ood." Gina's toddler voice said around Sentira's back.

"They can try to be human...It'll never work." Louis's elderly voice said from somewhere around the front of Sentira's face.

Sentira closed her eyes while listening to the comforting and familiar voices talk around her about what was happening in her current environment. She took a few slow deep breaths in and out to prepare to communicate with her regular voices using her tranquil mind. Miss Garrison had informed her that after the completion of her three year degree course, she would be able to access her tranquil mind more easily. Oftentimes, Sentira would access her tranquil mind after deep breathing for a few minutes. However, there had been some occasions whereupon she found herself instantly engaging with her voices using just her tranquil mind. No deep breathing techniques or words were needed.

"Sen...ira...i..." Rhyle's toddler voices babbled near to Sentira's left ear.

"We can hear you." Rhyle's elderly voice said around Sentira's right ear.

"No." Gina's toddler voice said loudly around Sentira's left ear.

"Have courage. Maromsaesc will not fall." Louis's elderly voice said around the front of Sentira's face.

"Heee......rigg.....htt..." Louis's toddler voice babbled near Sentira's left ear.

"Only one person to be careful with Sentira." Gina's adult voice said around the front of Sentira's face.

"We've warned you." Gina's elderly voice said around the front of Sentira's face.

Suddenly, Sentira's regular voices ceased speaking around her and the peaceful feeling she experienced when they were around left her. Adrenaline raced through Sentira's body again, just like she had felt when playing on the basketball court in the hot sun just under an hour ago.

I can't just sit here. I have to help. Sentira thought to herself optimistically. Her confidence renewed, she jumped to her feet startling somewhat the other students sitting near her.

The students near Sentira glanced around nervously wondering if they had missed something new happening in the midst of the water shortage chaos. Their faces expressed relief as they saw Sentira smile reassuringly at them before walking away towards the entrance of the reception area. Noah passed by her on her way and commented saying "Sentira has a plan! I know that look". He laughed along with Advik and Craig. Sentira ignored them and continued on to speak to the head OBR who (although still a robot) was coloured in a distinctive gold colour to indicate clearly, that he was of a higher rank than the regular silver OBR's. As Sentira grew nearer to the head OBR, the gold colour glowed brighter for some reason that Sentira did not know about. Sentira chose to ignore it and continue on with an idea that she had just thought of.

"Hi, my name is Sentira Cagney. I'm a Team 3 Year 1 student here at Maromsaesc. I think I know a way that we can cool people off without waiting for the water supply to be switched back on." Sentira said to the head OBR keeping up her optimism.

The head OBR lowered it's head slightly to look at Sentira and within seconds a pale white light had been emitted from it's eyes to scan Sentira from the top of her head to the base of her feet.

"Hello Miss Sentira Cagney. What idea are you trying to suggest?" replied the head OBR in a human adult male voice.

Some of the nearby Year 1 students watched the conversation Sentira was having with the head OBR with wonder and curiosity.

"The emergency fire water sprinklers, are they connected to the main water supply? Because...if it isn't then all we have to do is activate the smoke alarms water sprinklers, to get water to sprinkle all over the students to stop them burning up." Sentira explained confidently. "It's too hot in here for them, even with the windows open and the virtual fans." Sentira added, feeling hopeful that the head OBR would implement her idea. She peered up at the head OBR with her brown eyes open wide in anticipation waiting for it to respond to her, with either a yes or a no.

"Thank you Miss Sentira Cagney. I will inform all OBR's to activate the smoke alarms water sprinkler systems." said the head OBR, now speaking in a female adult voice.

Sentira smiled satisfactorily at the head OBR.

"Oh and by the way Miss Cagney, the emergency fire water sprinklers are not connected to the main water supply." said the head OBR quickly.

Sentira was sure she heard a hint of happiness in the pre-programmed female voice from the head robot in charge of the other OBR's. She returned back to her seat near an open window in the gym block reception area and waited.

Next, she saw a sight she had never witnessed before. OBR's from all directions she could see, began to swiftly climb different areas of the walls of the gym block to reach the smoke alarms on the ceiling. Then a booming loud robotic voice rang out around the entire gym block which was heard by all the students, saying the following words: -

"All students are to leave their belongings and any items they do not wish to get wet to the left side of the gym block entrance and then go to the right side of the reception area or in the gym changing room area. We will be activating the emergency fire water sprinklers in five minutes. Any student who does not want to get wet in front of other students, kindly make your way to a changing room cubicle where you can have privacy. Dry towels will be distributed to all, after the water sprinklers are turned off. If anyone has any questions, please talk to a supervising OBR. Thank you."

The message by the OBR's was repeated every 30 seconds and the Year 1 students rushed to get their shoulder bags, virtual mobiles, sports bags and other precious items over to the left side of the gym block entrance. Sentira included. She placed her virtual mobile inside her shoulder bag and took out another bottle of water to take with her to the right side of the reception area, where many students had already gathered.

The arguments that were previously heard between the OBR's and some of the Year 1 students ceased while everyone waited expectantly for what was to happen next.

The OBR's could be seen above the students on the ceilings in various areas of the gym block, working with the wiring of the smoke alarms. The students continued to wait expectantly, most sweating profusely and drinking from near empty water bottles. Ten minutes flew by and the OBR's were still on the ceilings in the gym block attending to the numerous smoke alarms. The smoke alarms above the area designated for the student belongings were left untouched.

Come on! Come on Maromsaesc! Sentira thought to herself, as she looked up towards the ceiling to watch the OBR's at work with the smoke alarms. She wiped sweat from her face, neck and arms using the back of her Maromsaesc yellow hoodie and continued to wait.

A dark green and blue virtual screen formed around the student's belongings near the left side of the gym block front entrance, to protect water from reaching them. Fascinated, the students looked on in awe, temporarily forgetting the discomfort they were in due to the new and dramatic scenes unfolding around them. The highly unusual (never been seen before) sight of OBR's easily scaling the walls and walking upside down on the ceilings were a feature of robots that not many people were aware of was possible.

Suddenly, fast clear cold sparkling water sprinkled down powerfully from small holes that had now appeared all over the ceilings in every room in the gym block. The Year 1 students excitedly revelled in the water that was now flowing down on them freely, squealing with joy and splashing about with each other. It felt like a miracle had occurred to them and some even knelt down on the floor lowering their heads, hands clasped together as if praying to thank a higher power or the God that some students believed in.

"Yes! Jelitoonaa!" other students exclaimed around the gym block.

"Finally! What took them so long?" another student shouted while dancing in the streams of water sprinkling down on him.

"So, I'll have my shower right here. I kept my shower gel with me." a male student said to another female student near him.

"Ewwww! Keep your clothes on or go into one of the cubicles please!" the female student with long blonde hair responded in a firm tone to the man, before moving away from her classmate.

The male student narrowed his eyes and frowned at her, but duly did as he was told by walking away to go into one of the cubicles to use his shower gel. Sentira laughed along with the female student. She felt relieved to see that most of the Maromsaesc students had cooled down and were happy again. She also felt very proud that she had been a part of the solution. She grinned at everyone near her and saw Noah, Craig, Advik and Brandi at a distance away from her wave and grin back.

Meanwhile in Room 25 Jay Halls, Perianne had heard similar instructions from a loud booming OBR robotic voice to everyone present at Jay Halls. Nearly exactly the same instructions as other Year 1 students in the gym block were given, Perianne was ordered to remain where she was until the security breach had been resolved. She was also given the instructions about the emergency fire water sprinklers. The slight difference in the Halls of Residence included that the student had to wait for an OBR to come into their room to activate the water sprinklers via the smoke alarms. Also, the students in the Halls of Residence were advised to go into the shower as only the emergency fire water sprinkler in the bathroom would be activated. This was so as to prevent damage and disruption to the students bedrooms from the water, which could have soaked all the bed sheets, personal belongings, carpets, etc...

Perianne had chosen to take a shower at the same time the OBR finished activating the emergency fire water sprinklers and waited for the OBR to install a virtual screen around the outside of the bathroom door to prevent water from escaping. Perianne was instructed to go inside the bathroom and the water sprinkler would turn on within five minutes. There were two minutes remaining of her waiting time and Perianne stood in the shower sweating and naked waiting for the water sprinklers to turn on. At that moment, she half-regretted her latest idea to ruin Maromsaesc. She had rashly figured wrongly, that she would be safe from the ensuing chaos from her devious plan if she were safe in her room. She hadn't foreseen how hot her shared room would get or anticipated that the air conditioning would also turn off, along with the main water supply. Perianne had sat by her window, using water from water bottles to splash her wrists, neck and face every ten minutes, while waiting with growing irritation for the OBR's to allow her to leave her room.

Earlier, she had peeked outside her room to see if she could devise a way to get past the supervising OBR's without any trouble. Unfortunately even with her brilliant mind, she could not think of a quick way to override the authority of the robots without attracting unwanted attention to herself. Back in her room, Perianne had sighed heavily before sitting on her bed near an open window only to observe that there was another supervising OBR standing below it outside. She actually felt relieved when after 40 minutes or so, the second OBR message had echoed around the building, stating the temporary solution of activating the emergency fire water sprinklers.

Back to the present moment, the water sprinkler finally switched on and Perianne enjoyed the feel of the cooling cold water stream all around her, refreshing her overheated hair and hot body. Cooling down with every splash of water that hit her athletic body, Perianne let herself smile at the most recent problems she had initiated for Maromsaesc University.

Wait until the News channels hear about this! Aunty would be so proud of me! Perianne thought to herself happily, but then she remembered how ill Aunty Dr Joan Dedrick had been in the past few months.

A dismayed frown replaced the wide grin on Perianne's face as she remembered how she had heard her Aunty collapse to the ground while on a phone call to her. She recalled how Uncle Dr Robert had told her not to worry and that the very best (Dedrick family) doctors would be looking after her Aunty. Uncle Dr Robert had reminded her that she need only focus on her mission to destroy Maromsaesc University and that Aunty Dr Joan would encourage her to do the same.

"Psychiatry must make a comeback." Uncle Dr Robert had told Perianne during her preparatory acting training to become an undercover student at Maromsaesc University. He had confidently asserted, that once Maromsaesc University was a worldwide disastrous failure, then society would have no other option but to seek help from professional qualified Psychiatrists like the Dedrick Psychiatry family.

As Perianne continued to bathe in the cooling fast streams of cold water from the water sprinklers on the ceiling of her bathroom, voices unknown to her began to speak around her. Perianne was just about to command them to stop talking around her when she thought she had heard her name spoken by an elderly female voice. Perianne stopped washing her skin under the water sprinklers with her organic body scrub, stood dead still and listened. She was certain she had just heard her name being called. Not her fake student name of Perianne Saint but her real name Aridaperianne Dedrick. Curious as to why her real name was mentioned, Perianne did not order her voices to stop talking around her as quickly as she usually did, but instead she resumed washing her skin and listened suspiciously.

"Bone structure biology and the factors which influence bone cells. The knowledge displayed in exemplar 1.2 cannot be distinguishable enough to make a valid diagnosis." an unknown elderly female voice said around the front of Perianne's face.

Perianne grimaced before turning her head to face in another direction. However, she still did not resort to telling the voices around her to stop talking.

"Ageing can be another factor in the hierarchical structure of the bone. All of which are built up from mineralized collagen cells. Please see exemplar 2.9." said another female adult voice again around the front of Perianne's face.

Perianne rolled her eyes and turned to face yet another direction while she was standing in the shower with the water sprinklers on the ceiling, spraying strong streams of cold water downwards at her.

"Adaptive, autonomous structure development should mimic the ability of the bone's biology so as seen clearly in exemplar 4.8. The human skeleton design can also be mimicked by the design of the OBR's. The skeleton of..." an unknown male elderly voice said in the air around the front of Perianne's face.

"Stop!" Perianne yelled to the air in front of her.

The unknown voice that was currently speaking at the front of Perianne's face immediately fell silent. Perianne's cheeks grew a darker pink as she had surprised even herself with the intensity behind her word "Stop!". She couldn't take listening to the voices speak around her any longer. She had listened for a few minutes, this was enough.

Wait. I would never have been curious about why a voice said my name before. Perianne mused to herself, pouring out some shampoo into her left hand to rub gently in her long wavy ginger-red hair. *I hate this place!*

Perianne lathered her hair from the roots onto the ends using both hands. Then, the water sprinklers cold water cleansed away all the shampoo residue naturally without her touching her hair again with her hands. She peered down at the shower drain, her head lowered. Perianne was exhausted.

*****

The next morning, Perianne felt like herself again.

Maybe it was the heat yesterday that made me overreact and feel bad. Perianne silently convinced herself in her thoughts.

She stretched both arms lazily above her head and let out a big satisfied yawn. Regardless of how her mood had fluctuated about yesterday's events, today was a new day and according to the news reports, she had succeeded in her plan. There were more negative news Reports about yesterday's security breach than positive stories of Maromsaesc. The news media generally overlooked the fact that eventually the emergency fire water sprinklers had generated as much water for the students as the main water supply would have. They generally overlooked that it was a student's clever idea to initiate the water sprinklers, often overlooked the skills of the OBR's in implementing the idea and focused nearly entirely on the uncertain future of Maromsesc University. News headlines led with articles entitled: -

Water shortage chaos hits troubled Voice Hearing/ Visionaries University!
Another dangerous security breach at top Voice Hearing/Visionary University!
Maromsaesc fails again to keep teenage students safe!
Safety at Maromsaesc under serious review!
Maromsaesc University: What went wrong!
Student saves the day! Why did Maromsaesc staff not consider the water sprinklers in the first place?
Two hundred students trapped in hot University for hours with no water! We demand answers from the Professor at Maromsaesc! Sign the petition!

Perianne laughed loudly. She would gladly sign the petition if it wouldn't jeopardise her undercover purpose at Maromsaesc University. Instead, she forwarded the link from a World News channel to all her undercover contacts on her virtual mobile who were either part of the Dedrick family or allies to Psychiatry's return. She was in the middle of doing this, when she saw an audio message from Advik flash up on her phone's virtual screen. In his audio message Advik could be heard saying the following words: -

"Annchi has opened her eyes…well, briefly! The doctors say

those closest to her should see her immediately to help her to wake up fully. I've got permission from the Professor for 6 of us to go to Pelargonium Hospital. Noah, Craig, Sentira. Brandi are all coming too. Are you coming? Annchi would like to see you. Be quick though Perianne, we're meeting at the front entrance gates in 30 minutes." Advik said excitedly in his audio message sent to Perianne's virtual phone.

Perianne raised her blonde eyebrows and tilted her head to the side causing her long wavy ginger red hair to cascade prettily to the left side of her, softly creasing when touching down on her misty grey bedsheets. Perianne appeared deep in thought for a while before standing up on her feet to go to the bathroom, in order to get ready to meet up with the others to visit Annchi. She hadn't had time to eat breakfast but knew she could pick up something to eat at the Pelargonium Hospital café.

She deliberately desired to go to see Annchi with the others for one main reason. Her main reason was to see if she could pick up new ideas to formulate skilful plans for other forms of trouble she could potentially cause, for the crazed unsuspecting and naïve students of Maromsaesc. Annchi, (just like every other Year 1 student) was simply a pawn in the game of defeating Maromsaesc University forever.

It took Perianne 20 minutes to get dressed and another 10 minutes to come out of the Jay Halls building, walking through virtual pathways to reach the front entrance of the university. She passed Miss Gower on her way and the blonde-haired teacher of the Voices Teacher Training class pleasantly complimented Perianne on her recent homework assignment.

"Perianne, excellent...Jelitonnaa homework assignment! Very impressed! You will make a great teacher of voice hearers one day." said Miss Gower knowingly as she walked past Perianne on one of the virtual pathways.

"Thank you Miss Gower!" Perianne replied back loudly over her shoulder walking fast. She had wanted to ignore Miss Gower but she believed that would have been too obvious, so all she could instantly think of was to accept the compliment.

Upon reaching the front entrance of Maromsaesc University, Perianne greeted the waiting five students happily. Together they waited for Applerishin virtual security to scan Advik's permission code on his virtual phone before allowing them all to exit the university grounds. Outside the university, the small group waited for a hover cab to take them to Pelargonium Hospital.

At Pelargonium Hospital, a hospital staff OBR met them at reception to take them up to Annchi's hospital room. The doctor had instructed the OBR to bring them straight up to Annchi's room when they arrived, as Annchi currently had her eyes half closed. The doctor feared that she might shut them again at any moment and return fully to her comatose state.

Advik was the first to enter Annchi's room. He entered noisily and speaking louder than anyone else who came in behind him. The other students knew how much Advik loved Annchi so they held back from trying to talk to her until Advik had finished.

"Annchi you are my heart, you are my soul, you are my one love! Wake up Annchi! We miss you.! We need you." Advik exclaimed, his voice breaking with emotion during the last sentence. He wiped a tear from his right eye and spoke again more softly "Annchi it's Advik…I'm here. So are all your closest friends." Advik smiled up at the other students bravely. "Wake up. I've got so much to tell you about what you've missed at Maromsaesc. There's so many new ideas and information to be learnt about the voices we hear. I can teach you. I'll help you catch up Annchi. You're smart. The smartest girl I know. Wake up please, wake up, wake up…Annchi…Annchi."

Brandi, Noah, Craig, Sentira and Perianne all watched Annchi for any sign or reaction that she had heard the words that Advik said around her. Standing or sitting around Annchi's hospital bed, all eyes were on Annchi.

"Keep going Advik. She can hear you." Brandi said encouragingly.

"Wake up Annchi…We need you…Maromsaesc needs you." Advik said hopefully.

Suddenly, Annchi's eyes both flew open wide and she said the words "Maromsaesc. Advik. I'm here."

AWAKENINGS

"Yes! Annchi, can you hear me?" Advik said excitedly, smiling and gazing adoringly at his girlfriend laying still on her hospital bed.

Annchi shut her eyes again and Advik's smile dropped.

"Ha ha Advik! Of course I can hear you. I love you." Annchi replied in an upbeat voice, her eyes still closed shut.

"Annchi, I love you too beautiful. Open your eyes if you can hear me." Advik requested gently, leaning his face close to Annchi's and speaking into her ear.

Both of Annchi's eyes flew wide open again. Advik grinned at Annchi and Annchi half-smiled back. Advik hugged her and the other students one by one came over to Annchi's hospital bed to hug her and say that they were happy she had returned back with them.

"We missed you so much Annchi!" Sentira exclaimed happily.

"Maromsaesc has not been the same without you." Perianne enthused.

"Did you dream in the coma Annchi? I mean...what was it like in there?" Noah said bemused.

Advik gave him a quick nudge in his ribs.

"Ow!" Noah yelped, jumping back dramatically.

Annchi, Advik, Perianne, Brandi and Sentira all laughed as Noah exaggerated how badly hurt he was by the nudge he had just received from Advik.

"Advik! You don't know your own strength." Annchi said, turning away from watching Noah's comedy routine to look at Advik, who was now holding her hand tightly.

"Yeah I do, that's why you love me." Advik said winking at Annchi.

Annchi smiled again and her cheeks glowed a warmer pink. Advik reached over to kiss Annchi on the forehead.

Annchi blushed again.

"Hey stop it! We're still in the same room." Noah joked good naturedly.

Annchi and Advik acted like they had not even heard him and continued gazing lovingly at each other smiling.

"Has anyone told the doctor that she's awake?" Brandi asked, turning to Craig who was standing behind her. "I think someone…" Brandi choked on her words.

Craig looked at her with a worried expression.

"Brandi you look pale, are you alright?" Craig said moving closer to her.

Craig was just about to touch Brandi's arm when Brandi ran past him with both hands covering over her mouth. Craig ran after her, following her outside of Annchi's hospital room and down along the busy corridor into the unisex toilets. Brandi did not even glance behind her to see who the footsteps belonged to. Craig quickly hid inside one of the men's toilet cubicles, while listening to Brandi vomiting in one of the female cubicles nearby. His heart racing fast, he tried hard to control the anxiety building up within him but he couldn't. He felt sweat dripping down the sides of his face and his palms were clammy too. He tried to slow his breathing by taking slow deep breaths in and out.

However, Craig's emotions were too intense for him to comprehend and in frustration he banged his upper arm onto the side of the toilet cubicle's virtual wall, on the opposite side to where Brandi was still being sick in her cubicle.

"What! Oh God!" Brandi exclaimed and vomited again.

Craig wiped the sweat away from his forehead with his right sleeve and dried both his sweaty hands on his dark grey jeans, leaving a stain mark.

"S***!" Craig mumbled to himself nervously and hesitated before cautiously opening his toilet cubicle door.

"Aaargh!" Brandi screamed out loudly from inside her toilet cubicle. "Aaargh! Aaarrr….Aaaaarrrrrr!"

"Brandi!" Craig shouted out from outside Brandi's locked

cubicle door.

Brandi opened her cubicle door and looked at Craig with her face expressing astonishment and wonder, then she said "You're not going to believe this! I can feel something kicking and moving about in my tummy! I...I... come here feel this."

Craig reluctantly allowed Brandi to place his hand on her large tummy area, just as nurses rushed through the unisex toilet doors to find out where all the screaming was coming from. With his hand shaking uncontrollably, Craig felt what could only be interpreted as a strong kick, precisely where his hand was resting on Brandi's tummy. Craig took a few small steps backwards in shock and fell to the floor with a loud thud.

DREAM OR REALITY

"Craig!" Brandi exclaimed.

Two nurses promptly bent down by Craig's fallen body on the floor of the unisex toilet, checking his pulse while also tilting his head back to look and feel if he was still breathing.

"He's unconscious. What is his name? Did I hear you say Craig?" one of the nurses asked Brandi.

"His...Craig." Brandi stumbled out the words feeling shaky herself.

"Was it you that screamed out a couple of times or him?" another nurse asked kindly, standing by Brandi's side.

"I...it...I don't...there's something kicking me in my tummy...it...it's moving. Here feel it!" Brandi said to the nurse quickly grabbing the nurse's hand which was closest to her and placing on the same area that Craig's hand had originally been.

"Ooooh yes I felt that!" the nurse, a tall woman with long ginger hair and distinctive high cheekbones exclaimed in agreement with Brandi. "I don't want to alarm you but I am 99% sure that you have a baby kicking away in there."

"But this is the thing nurse...I haven't had sex! So it's not possible!" Brandi laughed nervously. "Nurse, it's not possible is it? I mean...could something else grow inside me that could move and kick similar to a baby perhaps?" Brandi opened her eyes wide in disbelief that she could be carrying a baby.

The tall nurse smiled at Brandi, then gently said to her, "Come with me to the Ultrasound Department and we'll be able to confirm what's growing inside of you. It's not far, just a short walk away."

"Well...al...all right it's ...it...we... only way to find out right?!" Brandi managed to stumble out a reply even though her voice wobbled with excitement and confusion. "But what about Craig? Is he going to be all right?"

Craig was still laying on the unisex toilet floor unconscious with two nurses about to lift him onto a hover stretcher to take him out of the toilet. Craig appeared to be asleep, just like Annchi had been when she was in a coma.

"I feel so sorry for him." Brandi continued to say, as the tall nurse led her out of the unisex toilet behind Craig's hover stretcher.

"Is he your boyfriend?" inquired the tall nurse curiously, while walking outside of the Intensive Care Unit and into the building next to it, which was the Radiology Department.

They both waited for Applerishin virtual security to allow them access, then Brandi replied to the nurse's question.

"No. I don't have a boyfriend." Brandi replied.

"Ok." the tall nurse answered dismissively, with a hint of disappointment in her tone.

"Well, here we are. If you take a seat over there by the window and a radiologist will be out shortly to perform your scan. Did you come here with anyone else?" the nurse asked.

"Yes, five other students who I study at Maromsaesc University with." Brandi answered. She continued to hold both her hands protectively over her tummy area, in order to feel the odd movements and kicks that still persisted.

"Oh, I know that one! Maromsaesc University! The university for voice-hearers and people who see visions. I've read all the News stories and heard all about it." the tall nurse said, before leaving Brandi alone in the waiting room outside the ultrasound room.

Brandi kept her left hand on her tummy and used her right hand to initiate recording a voice message to the student group she had travelled to Pelargonium Hospital with.

"Hey everyone, it's Brandi. You're not going to believe this! I'm outside an ultrasound room over in the Radiology Department." Brandi paused and laughed. "I vomited in one of the toilets and felt this weird kicking and moving in my tummy and guess what…well… to cut a long story short the nurse thinks I could be pregnant! No, I said to her. I haven't had a boyfriend or sex for over a year." Brandi laughed nervously again, before ending the voice recording. She sent it to the student group chat, which consisted of Sentira, Perianne, Noah, Craig, Advik and Annchi. Suddenly, she remembered what had happened to Craig and started to record another voice message.

"Craig, I nearly forgot! He passed out after feeling something kick in my tummy area, when I asked him to feel it for himself. He went into some kind of trance... I don't know what's wrong with him. Two nurses had to take him away on a hover stretcher. Please find out how he is and let him know that I'm sorry I couldn't stay with him but...there...there's something very weird happening." Brandi explained and then ended her voice message by sending it to everyone in her student group chat.

Brandi began to listen to voices speaking around her about the virtual mat in the waiting area. The voices (both male and female) were talking about the design of the virtual mats including the colour patterns and the choice of location of them in the waiting room. Brandi half-listened to them and replaced both her hands over her tummy area. She wondered if it could be true that she was pregnant, but how could this be possible? Could she have been carrying a baby for over a year since her last relationship ended, before starting Maromsaesc? It didn't make any sense.

Brandi decided not to say anything to her parents until after she had the results of the ultrasound scan. It wasn't worth worrying about them anyway, Brandi figured. She could always have an abortion or give the babies up for adoption. Absolutely nothing, was going to ruin her fashion career. Since her Maromsaesc tracksuits and sports wear designs had proved very popular, Brandi felt more at home at Maromsaesc now than ever before. She had less random voice hearing experiences in her sleep too. When she did have some voice hearing experiences in her sleep however, she had learned that it helped to sometimes talk about it with other classmates or a teacher. As Annchi wasn't around lately, she hadn't been smoking much cannabis either. Brandi was changing and proud that she had contributed her fashion designs to the university, which she was beginning to feel more and more happy to be a part of. She was also ecstatic that she had made a very high income from her designs too.

"Brandi Ropen?" a petite sonographer with short black hair and light brown skin called out into the waiting room.

Brandi stood up to follow the sonographer into the Ultrasound room. Both hands still protectively over her tummy area and her virtual mobile secured safely in her left blue jeans pocket.

"Hello Brandi, my name is Kadence and I will be performing your ultrasound today. Can you lie on your back and pull your t-shirt up so I can put gel on your tummy. This gel is used to ensure there is good contact between our ultrasound machine and your skin. The virtual screen to your right will show what images we receive from your scan. Ok?" said Kadence, while waiting for Brandi to lie down so she could move a handheld device called a transducer over Brandi's tummy area.

Brandi giggled at the feel of not only the strange movements and kicking she was experiencing inside of her, but the craziness of the situation she found herself in. It didn't have any logic to it. She wondered for a couple of seconds if she was lost in one of her random voice hearing dreams, totally unaware that it was all in fact, just a dream.

"Congratulations you're expecting twins!" the sonographer said cheerfully.

Brandi turned her head sharply to look at the screen, her bottom lip dropping down in amazement. When she saw the images of twin fetuses on the virtual screen, Brandi gasped and was speechless. Thinking that this whole crazy scenario could not possibly be real, Brandi shut her eyes tightly as if she were asleep.

"I would estimate by the size of them…you are about 20 – 24 weeks pregnant." Kadence said while moving the transducer over the length of Brandi's tummy again.

Brandi's eyes flew open immediately upon hearing the

word "pregnant". She quickly closed them back again and squeezed her eyes tightly shut for the second time.

"Is everything all right?" Kadence the sonographer asked Brandi with concern.

Brandi kept her eyes tightly closed until Kadence repeated the same question.

"No." Brandi whispered in reply. "No, this isn't real. None of this is real."

FUTURE UNSEEN

Brandi appeared deep in thought as she sat at a virtual desk in the Spiritual Voices lecture hall, with a virtual pen in her right hand and a virtual answer book in front of her. This past month and a half at Maromsaesc had been like none she could ever have possibly imagined she would experience at anytime in her life. The world news media had reported many inaccurate stories about her mystery pregnancy and how it may have occurred. After weeks of having to reassure her bewildered and confused parents that all the articles were false, Brandi eventually (very reluctantly) resorted to writing a written statement. Brandi's written statement about her true version of events was distributed to the news media worldwide. However, her statement only calmed the waters for a few days before new conspiracy theories about her twin pregnancy once again hit the headlines. Some of the news headlines included: -

Twin pregnancy at Maromsaesc! Voice hearing teenager claims she doesn't know the father!

Teenage pregnancy hits Maromsaesc! We answer your questions about the safety of the students.

Why is there so much controversy at Maromsaesc? Our reporter investigates...

Parents of Maromsaesc pregnant student demand answers from Professor Zantend!

Professor Zantend refuses to comment on latest Maromsaesc scandal!

The Maromsaesc University failure. Sign our petition to request the DfE undertakes a thorough critical review of Maromsaesc.

Brandi's friends had supported her along with Professor Zantend and all the teaching staff at Maromsaesc. Even the OBR's would approach her and ask her if there was anything they could help her with. Brandi had decided almost immediately, after the day she had found out that she was carrying twins, that she would be giving both of them up for adoption. If it weren't for the news media somehow getting hold of her story, she wouldn't have told her parents anything. As it happened (unfortunately for Brandi) the news media had reported on her mysterious twin pregnancy the very next day after Brandi had just found out herself. This had pushed Brandi into having a very awkward video call with both her parents.

Initially, Brandi's father was very angry and judgemental about what he perceived as the "lack of protection of students and the poor standards of safety" at Maromsaesc. He even suggested that it could have been when Brandi was in one of her deep voice hearing sleeps, when a rape had occurred without his daughter's knowledge. Brandi had shaken her head and laughed nervously. She knew her Dad had no filter whatsoever with his words, and would just say the first thing he thought of. Brandi's mother had told her father to "stop scaring our daughter" and said that "the truth would be revealed in time". Brandi's mother was more sensitive to her daughter's emotions and although it perplexed her as to how her daughter insisted she had not had a relationship, she decided it was best not to question her daughter too much.

Today was the final day at Maromsaesc for the Year 1 students and the truth had still not been revealed as to who could be the father of Brandi's unborn twins. A DNA test was to be taken after the twins were born, but the doctors could only find a match from men who volunteered to participate in the search for the father. So, if the father did not participate in the DNA test search, then it was highly likely that the father would never be found.

All Brandi had desperately wanted to find out about, was if her parents would still buy her a fashion store after she successfully completed her degree course. Her parents gave her their full support and reassured Brandi that nothing had changed. She was still their daughter and they believed her and loved her. They also respected her decision to give up the twins for adoption after birth, agreeing with her that it was her body and her choice. Brandi thought her parents had been real "Jelitoonaa" but she wondered if they would still say the same thing after the twins were born. There were often conditions to her parents agreement with events in Brandi's life. Just like their condition that she had to attend the Maromsaesc University and gain her Degree in Professional Development for voice hearers and people who see visions, before they bought her a fashion store.

Brandi directed her thoughts back to the present moment and easily wrote down detailed answers on her Spiritual Voices virtual answer book. The answers came easily to Brandi as she had spent long hours reading through her Spiritual Voices virtual textbook to help her understand her mysterious twin pregnancy. Her mother was keen on spirituality and she had recommended that she pay close attention over how to interpret spiritual messages, in case she could one day find meaning in what she was going through. Brandi had explored praying to different higher powers and had been surprised to hear new voices (both male and female) speak around her, that often called her name and said the words "don't be scared." "change.". Of course, Brandi did not know who the voices were referring to but with encouraging advice from Miss Garrison and her mother combined, she felt happy to continue to research spirituality and spiritual voices with great interest. She hoped that one day she would find meaning as to why she was mysteriously impregnated with twins without having sex.

Forty minutes passed and an OBR announced that there were five minutes remaining for the Spiritual Voices End of Term 3 test. Brandi had completed her virtual answer book twenty minutes ago, but was not allowed to leave the Lecture Hall until the test time had run out or she had to use the toilet. Soon, the final five minutes ended and an OBR announced over virtual speakers in the lecture hall, that the students should stop writing as the Spiritual Voices test had now ended.

There were no more classes or tests left on the final friday, the last day of Term 3 at Maromsaesc University. The rest of the day was for the students to pack their belongings in suitcases to travel to their respective homes for the summer and say their goodbyes. Most chose to relax on the university grounds after they had finished packing. Some students lay down on virtual mats near the Maromsaesc lake, some ate and drank in the student cafeteria, others walked around the Maromsaesc Gardens, some played sports in the Games Courts and others read virtual books in the library. There were even some Maromsaec students who were having fun travelling around the virtual pathways on student hover vehicles. The atmosphere was light and joyful mostly everywhere the eyes could see. Except, if anyone could see beyond the physical eyes of each student, they would see that one student was actually not joyful at all, but extremely angry and unhappy.

Perianne walked through the Maromsaesc Gardens with the friends she had made at the university to blend in with her fake identity as a keen, ambitious voice hearing student. She believed that she was hiding her deep resentment for all of them perfectly. She smiled widely at Annchi, laughed with Noah, talked about the End of Term tests with Sentira and empathised with Brandi's bemusement at her twin pregnancy. Craig and Advik were chatting to each other behind her.

However inwardly, Perianne felt great disappointment, anger and irritation over the fact that Maromsaesc University was still open at the end of it's first year. She swiftly calculated her present and future options. Cleverly analysing in her mind whether or not Year 2 studies would still go ahead, despite the chaos she had helped to instigate. Perianne concluded that it was still very much possible that Maromsaesc could close before Year 2. Everything is subject to change at anytime.

Perianne further considered Maromsaesc to be in a significantly weaker position than at it's opening in September 2070. The scandals and dramas that had been exaggerated or directly caused by Perianne's clever sabotage skills, had already seriously affected the credibility and reputation of Maromsaesc

University. The news media had not reported on any positive stories about the first professional university for people who heard voices or saw visions for months.

Wait till the End of Term 3 test results come out. I'm sure most of these mad people will fail. Perianne grumbled to herself, smiling and laughing with Annchi at the same time.

Annchi, completely unaware of the thoughts going through her friend's mind, smiled back and hugged Perianne tightly.

"Oh Perianne, I'm going to miss you!" Annchi said enthusiastically, still tightly hugging Perianne.

Perianne embraced her back and said, "I'll miss you more!"

Their group had reached an area of the Maromsaesc Gardens which had purple, white, yellow and pink hyacinths organised in oval and heart shapes in the brown soil with nature inspired hover benches in different places. Elder trees and Blackthorn trees bordered around the outskirts of this beautiful part of the university gardens. The students who were in the garden were dressed in summer clothes. Some pulling along suitcases and carrying virtual bags on their way out of the gardens to go to the front entrance to leave Maromsaesc, until their return for Year 2 dependant on passing the End of Term 3 tests.

Craig watched some of the students walk past him on their way towards the exit of the Maromsaesc Gardens and wanted to go with them. He didn't know how long he could stay around Brandi and pretend that he didn't know anything about her twin pregnancy. He wasn't sure why he had agreed to come along to this final meet up with his friends in the Maromsaesc Gardens and was beginning to realise that it was a bad idea.

Brandi sat down heavily on a nature inspired hover bench displaying beach and sea waves images. Craig ran to catch up with her and sat down next to her on the hover bench. He opened his mouth to say something but no words came out. Brandi looked at him expectantly waiting for him to speak, because that is what he appeared to be about to do. Craig closed his mouth, looked forward and turned to face Brandi again with his mouth open as if he wanted to say something. Brandi began to feel unnerved and shuffled her body away from Craig on the hover bench.

Craig blushed a dark pink colour and looked away. Sentira sat down in between Brandi and Craig and started talking to Brandi about how beautiful the flower arrangements were in their oval and heart designs. Brandi chatted back enthusiastically with Sentira leaving Craig alone with his unspoken thoughts. Advik had caught up with Annchi and they sat on a different hover bench together with Perianne and Noah also sitting on the same bench. Advik and Annchi had their suitcases with them and planned to leave the Maromsaesc Gardens together shortly after their group meet up.

Craig felt very conflicted in his mind over whether he should tell Brandi the truth or not. He did not want to ruin his future career, whatever that may be. He couldn't afford to pay to raise a baby, let alone two babies. He had heard a rumour that Brandi was going to give the babies up for adoption, which heightened his confusion. The thought of never knowing what had happened to his two babies and them never knowing that he was their Dad troubled and disturbed Craig. He tried to work out which scenario was worse and concluded that all the scenarios were bad. What happened if Brandi thought that he had raped her? What would the news media say if they heard that a rape had happened at Maromsaesc?

Craig had excelled in all his academic studies so far at Maromsaesc, and felt very proud to be a part of history in the making for the progression of people who heard voices and saw visions in modern day society. He didn't want there to be anymore negative stories about the University that had given him hope, purpose and ideas for careers whereby he could utilise his abilities. Every negative news story in the media had secretly depressed him, but he had only studied harder to counteract his hidden fear that one day Maromsaesc may close for good. He knew that if the news media ever found out that he was the father of Brandi's mystery twin pregnancy, the headlines and news reports would be merciless and unrelenting. He was not a rapist, Brandi had consented to sex with him, but would the news media believe his story? He could picture the news headlines in his mind and it terrified him: -

Rapist voice hearing student admits he is the father!
Maromsaesc student is expelled after serious
rape accusations!
University for Voice Hearers under investigation by
Pelargonium Police amongst rape allegations.
Can Maromsaesc survive this latest criminal scandal?

Craig gulped and switched his focus onto watching a squirrel in front of him jumping around with another squirrel in between the purple and white hyacinths on the heart shaped garden design nearby him. Voices began to speak around Craig and he soon felt relaxed by joining in conversation with them. Obviously these voices that only Craig could hear were familiar to him and friendly so therefore Craig began to appear more at ease, even smiling at times to the air around his left and right side.

There were many other Year 1 students talking to their voices in the air around them as far as Craig's eyes could see. He felt an instant sense of pride that he had completed the first year of his degree course and that all the students around him experienced similar abilities as he did. There had never been a university like it. Craig watched Perianne and Noah talking with their voices in the air around them. Both were sitting on a hover bench on the other side of the heart shaped, colourful hyacinth design. Craig suddenly remembered that some of his friends had been with him the night that he had spent with Brandi. He wondered why none of them had tried to talk to him about the possibility of him being the father. Annchi and Advik were too in love to think straight, Craig concluded to himself, but then why hadn't Perianne or Noah guessed that Brandi was carrying his babies. Craig resumed the conversation he was having with the voices he heard by his right ear and smiled feeling somewhat relieved. It was easier for him to not have that conversation with any of them anyway, he figured. It would just make things even more complicated.

Unbeknownst to Craig, Perianne and Noah were actually just starting to talk about him, having finished their brief conversations with the voices in the air around them. Perianne had put on a perfectly crafted acting display in front of Noah. She appeared to be having a friendly conversation with the voices she heard around her so as to keep up belief in her character as a genuine Maromsaesc Student. Noah had stopped talking to his voices so she stopped talking to hers, faced Noah and spoke to him.

"When do you think we should talk to Craig about that night we all got drunk in Brandi's room?" Perianne asked Noah with her face full of concern and worry.

"I don't know." Noah replied. "I honestly don't know."

"He looks so down." Perianne added.

"No, he doesn't. I saw him laughing with one of his voices just a minute ago." Noah answered confidently.

Perianne resisted the urge to say something short and sharp to Noah. Instead, she took a deep breath in and out in front of him before speaking again.

"I think he manages to hide it sometimes. Has he spoke to you about that night?" Perianne persisted.

"No. Nothing. He talks about his classes or..." Noah said, rubbing his right thumb and forefinger on his chin thoughtfully.

"Come on Noah. I'm sure he's said something to you." Perianne said feigning disbelief.

Noah laughed at the expression of surprise on Perianne's face.

"We're not a couple you know, we don't tell each other everything. Unlike me and you." Noah said winking at Perianne.

Once again, Perianne resisted the urge to tell Noah what

she really thought about him and all the other voice hearing, visionary students at this mad University. She composed herself again by taking in another long, slow deep breath in and out.

Noah watched Perianne curiously. "You're really getting upset about this whole Brandi thing, aren't you?" Noah asked, softening his voice a little.

"Well, I think Brandi has a right to know who the Dad is. It's not fair on her or Craig. Did you hear that she's going to give the babies up for adoption after giving birth? Craig doesn't have any chance of knowing his children then." Perianne said emotionally, with her best brave concerned expression showing realistically on her face. "It'll be hard to talk to Craig, but it will be harder if one day both of them hate us for not trying to intervene so that the truth about the real father comes out."

"Don't forget our part in this story Perianne." Noah responded sounding defensive. "We all left her drunk alone with Craig. If we tell her this, she'll hate us earlier than whenever the truth comes out."

Glad you remember Noah. Yes, you are partly to blame. You Annchi, Advik, Craig... We were all there. And...if your story gets me in trouble, then I will tell my own adaptation. Perianne thought smugly to herself.

"I don't know Noah. It's very hard for me to see my friend like this. Tell you what, I'll think about it over the next few weeks and work out what we can do. Don't worry." Perianne replied.

"I'm not worried. You are." Noah answered and resumed talking to his voices in front of him.

Perianne felt like snickering but she controlled it and pretended to talk to her voices around her, even though they were not speaking at this time. She replaced her worried look with a happier expression, which Noah noticed and smiled back at her.

Noah, if this university for the insane does not close this summer...you will be part of my first plan to sabotage Maromsaesc in

Year 2. Perianne thought angrily to herself. Outwardly, Perianne blended in remarkably and looked like most of the other Year 1 students in the Maromsaesc Gardens, happy contented and relaxed.

Sentira held her right hand on top of Brandi's tummy and felt one of the twins kick twice.

"Awww yes, I definitely felt a kick, two of them." Sentira confirmed to Brandi.

Brandi smiled down at her tummy before responding to Sentira. "You know I'm giving them both up for adoption right?"

Sentira nodded her head. She didn't think that Brandi should give away her babies but it was not her choice to make. There was a high chance that the twin babies she was carrying would have voice hearing or visionary abilities like Brandi had. Sentira remembered how Brandi struggled sometimes with her random voice-hearing sleep episodes and recalled the stress her friend had been under whenever they occurred. So, Sentira chose to remain silent and not give her opinion.

"It's your decision Brandi. You know what's best for you and your body." Sentira said, pointing out the squirrel that had jumped out of the heart design of hyacinths to land close by Brandi's trainers.

"Hey squirrel, here have some of these." Brandi threw a handful of peanuts (from a pack she had been eating) in the squirrel's direction, accidentally hitting it on the head a few times. The squirrel retreated back each time it got hit but eventually managed to scoop up four peanuts and scuttle back in between the purple and pink hyacinths.

"Yes it is. I'm not messing up my fashion career to raise children that I did not plan for." Brandi said self-assuredly.

"I totally understand." Sentira answered.

There was quiet between the two women for a few minutes before Sentira spoke again.

"Do you want any of us to come with you to the hospital when you give birth for support?" Sentira asked.

"Of course you can all come!" Brandi replied happily. "They probably will only let two people in the actual delivery room though. That's a good idea, thanks!"

"You're not in this by yourself. We're all here for you. We love you." Sentira said emotionally and hugged Brandi.

Brandi hugged her friend back.

"Wow, it's been both Jelitoonaa and stressful this first year, don't you think?" Brandi said nonchalantly.

"More Jelitoonaa than stressful for me." Sentira answered.

"Not everyone has things come easy to them like you Sentira." Brandi replied standing up and putting both hands on her back. "My back is hurting so bad."

"Is someone coming to pick you up from the University? I think the sooner you get home and rest, the back ache will go away or at least easier to deal with." Sentira suggested.

"You're right." Brandi said sitting back down on the hover bench that they shared with Craig. "I'm going to call my Dad and tell him to come and get me sooner." Brandi activated her virtual mobile and began speaking to her dad.

Sentira had planned to go back to Jay Halls after saying goodbye to her friends, to collect her suitcase and virtual bags before travelling by hover cab home to Chero Coast. She felt a mixture of emotions about Year 1 coming to an end. It had been the best year of her entire life so far and she felt "Jelitoonaa" and excited to have completed Year 1 at Maromsaesc University. Yet, she also felt tired of the news media mainly negative reports about Maromsaesc and disappointed that she was not able to control the louder voices she heard. Unexpected loud voices still spoke at anytime around Sentira and would often ignore her requests for quiet, irrespective of any technique she had learned to communicate with them.

It's only the end of the first year. Sentira reminded herself. *In Year 2, I will study even harder and there will be new and more advanced classes at Maromsaesc.*

Sentira's regular voices started to speak in the air around her ears and in front of her face. Sentira smiled as she recognised the familiar voices of Rhyle, Gina, Olamide and Louis speaking around her at different ages.

"It's finished!" Olamide's adult voice said from somewhere around Sentira's right ear.

"No, it's not!" Gina's elderly voice said around Sentira's left ear.

"We've had so much fun and will return next year!" Louis's elderly voice said around the front of Sentira's face.

"It…noo…..ov…..er." Rhyle's toddler voice said also from around the front of Sentira's face.

"If you're referring to Year 1 at Maromsaesc… Rhyle, Gina, Olamdie and Louis, it is finished. Year 1 is over. Year 2 is coming in September 2071!" Sentira talked back with her voices, smiling at the air around her in three different directions.

"Down here!" Rhyle's adult voice said loudly.

There was laughter heard from all of Sentira's regular voices. Sentira laughed with them.

If only all the voices I heard could be as approachable as my regular voices normally are. Sentira wondered to herself.

"Depends." Rhyle's teenage voice said softly around Sentira's right ear.

"Depends on what we have to say and if we choose to listen to you or not." Gina's teenage voice said gently around Sentira's left ear.

"You're not in control." Louis's elderly voice said in front of Sentira's face.

"Weeee…..ar….ar.." Olamide's toddler voice said also in front of Sentira's face.

Sentira was not surprised by the way in which her regular voices had answered the thoughts she had, and not surprised that her voices could read her thoughts as well. This was why she needed a professional university like the Maromsaesc University. She desired to find more ways to control her voices especially when she wanted them to be silent, as in class for example. There had to be a way. She remembered the times when she was younger and her regular voices had teased and make jokes around her. She knew not everything they said was factual and she secretly hoped that they were wrong about her never being able to have full control of her abilities, if they were in fact... referring to her.

I know you can hear my thoughts too. Let everyone who is listening to me know that I have the highest respect and faith in Maromsaesc. I am certain that one day during my studies I will find a way to permanently control the volume, time and content of what I can hear around me. Of this I am sure. Sentira thought assertively to herself.

There was a still silence for a few minutes around Sentira, as her regular voices suddenly stopped talking. Brandi was no longer sitting next to Sentira but had walked over to Perianne's hover bench with Craig standing next to her.

"I didn't mean for you all to go." Sentira exclaimed regretfully at the air around her left and right side.

There was no reply from Rhyle, Gina, Olamide and Louis. Sentira sighed and got up to sit on the grass in front of Perianne's hover bench where Annchi and Advik were now sitting down too.

"My Dad's picking me up in an hour." Brandi told the group, shading her eyes from the hot glare of the sun.

"I'm leaving at that time too by hover cab." Perianne said.

Best day so far! Perianne mused to herself.

"When are you leaving Sentira?" Craig asked Sentira looking down at her sitting on the grass.

"Probably a few hours. Hover cab." Sentira replied in a dreamy tone.

"You don't want to leave do you, Sentira?" Craig said intuitively.

The rest of the group laughed. Sentira smiled at all of them one by one.

"You're right. I don't want to leave. I wish we all could stay here over summer and the classes would never end!" Sentira said enthusiastically.

The others in the group laughed more and Sentira felt herself blushing. She couldn't help feeling extremely passionate about education at Maromsaesc. She knew she was very privileged to have been born at a time when these opportunities were available for her to make use of. Others unfortunately, those that were in Nanny Lisha's generation and generations going back hundreds of years had not been so lucky. Times had changed and Sentira was determined to try her best to learn how to manage and utilise her voices. Not only for herself, but to honour all the voice hearing and visionary people in the past who did not get to experience the same professional training that she was receiving at Maromsaesc. Maromsasec in Sentira's mind was a dream come true for all voice hearing people and people who could see visions.

This woman is pathetic! Perianne thought to herself. *She will be my first patient at my new Psychiatry clinic after Maromsaesc is discontinued.*

"Noah and Craig are getting a hover cab and Annchi is coming home with me." Advik said hugging Annchi again. "I'm so happy you're back beautiful."

No, actually everyone here in this group will be joint first patients at my new Psychiatry clinic. Perianne angrily thought to herself. She heard voices beginning to talk around her, quietly at first and then gradually getting louder.

"Stop." Perianne commanded the voices talking around her ears, in front of her face and behind her back.

The voices stopped talking.

Sentira looked at Perianne with interest.

"Do your voices stop every time you order them to?" Sentira asked Perianne curiously.

"Yes they do." Perianne replied, happy that she could do something that most of the other students could not.

This is why I'm different! Perianne thought to herself smugly.

"Oh, ok. Could you teach me?" Sentira asked. "Not now. In Year 2."

"I'll try!" Perianne answered enthusiastically, remaining

perfectly in her character as Perianne Saint, a keen and friendly voice hearing Maromsaesc Student.

"Thanks Perianne." Sentira said with a smile.

My voices were mistaken. She's really nice and just like the rest of us. Sentira thought to herself.

"Be careful." Olamide's elderly voice said around Sentira's left ear.

"Sh…eee..nooo….noootttt." Gina's toddler voice said in the air at the front of Sentira's face.

Perianne smiled widely at Sentira feeling happy that she had her fooled like everyone else, but Sentira did not smile back. She was shocked that Olamide and Gina were again seeming to warn her about Perianne, when she personally did not have any hard facts of any wrong doing by Miss Saint. In fact, Perianne Saint could help her control her voices the way she claimed she was able to.

Sentira found a quiet place in her mind and accessed her tranquil mind, the way that Miss Garrison had taught her to during meditation class. Once in her tranquil mind, she asked any voices around her to reveal the meaning of the words "be careful" that she heard on different occasions since she had been accepted at Maromsaesc University.

"We cannot tell you." Gina's adult voice said around Sentira's left ear.

"It's not your time to know." Olamide's teenage voice said around Sentira's right ear.

"Be careful." Rhyle's elderly voice said around the front of Sentira's face.

Sentira turned away from Perianne and started up a conversation with Annchi and Advik.

Perianne sensed that Sentira had turned her back on her and felt angrier.

Can she see me? Perianne wondered to herself. It wasn't the first time Sentira had reacted that way around her. *Who cares. I'm having a long break from this mad house and hopefully Maromsaesc will close this summer so I'll never see any of you ever again!*

"Ooo ki s s dhdh dhdh gei eiii shh ial p ook" a loud female voice said at the back of Perianne.

The female voice was so loud, that Perianne turned her head sharply and moved her body to face whatever was behind her.

Then, just as suddenly as the loud female voice had spoke, it stopped speaking.

Perianne turned her body back around to face the direction she had been in previously.

"Year 2 is going to be Jelitoonaa! Year 2 will…" Sentira's voice faded away mid-sentence with both arms still in the air exuberantly.

She had been interrupted by the noisy obtrusive sound of Pelargonium police virtual helicopters, which could be heard from high above the Maromsaesc Gardens.

Year 2 is going to be Jelitoonaa. Perianne deviously thought to herself, as the Maromsaesc students looked up into the sky at the sight of many virtual helicopters circling above them.

Printed in Great Britain
by Amazon